WANTING

The simple touch of Cale's work-roughened hand sent fresh tears to Miranda's eyes. She blinked them away, feeling fragile, as if the warm mountain breeze streaming through the open window could shatter her into a thousand pieces and then scatter them like dandelion fluff.

"I don't want to feel weak," she whispered.

She wanted to lie down. She wanted to curl into a ball and go to sleep. She gazed into Cale's eyes. She wanted . . .

She wanted. As she took a tentative step closer, she heard the air whoosh out of Cale's lungs. His gaze strayed to her mouth. And he sucked in a ragged breath. His hand fell away from the side of her face, but he made no move to set her away from him.

"You're stronger than you realize, Miranda. And you still have time."

"Time?"

"Time to turn away, time to tell me no."

Another step brought her within inches of him. "I was trying to give *you* time to tell *me* no."

Then, as if they both knew they were out of time, out of diversions, out of reasons to resist, he lowered his face to hers. His lips touched hers so gently, so sweetly, she very nearly cried out. . . .

<u>BOOK YOUR PLACE ON OUR WEBSITE</u>
<u>AND MAKE THE</u>
<u>READING CONNECTION!</u>

We've created a customized website just for our very special readers, where you can get the inside scoop on everything that's going on with Zebra, Pinnacle and Kensington books.

When you come online, you'll have the exciting opportunity to:

- View covers of upcoming books
- Read sample chapters
- Learn about our future publishing schedule (listed by publication month *and author*)
- Find out when your favorite authors will be visiting a city near you
- Search for and order backlist books from our online catalog
- Check out author bios and background information
- Send e-mail to your favorite authors
- Meet the Kensington staff online
- Join us in weekly chats with authors, readers and other guests
- Get writing guidelines
- AND MUCH MORE!

Visit our website at
http://www.zebrabooks.com

THE COTTAGE

SANDRA STEFFEN

ZEBRA BOOKS
KENSINGTON PUBLISHING CORP.

http://www.zebrabooks.com

To friendship.
Some are formed in childhood and span a lifetime.
Other friends walk through a short period of our lives,
touching us, then moving on. All are heartfelt, and true
blessings.

A special thanks to Mary Nelson, who so graciously gave me
my first book about natural healing. And to Linda Thelen,
for her "listening ear," her prayers, and her advice.

CHAPTER ONE

"Looks like you have company again, Miranda."

Miranda Sinclair nodded without looking up from her task, her hoe never missing a stroke in the rich organic garden soil. Although she hadn't actually seen the boy Ruby McCoy had referred to as company, half an hour ago Miranda had glimpsed a spot of white, probably his T-shirt, through a gap in the new spring foliage a little to the right of the mountain road.

The evening was quiet except for the rhythmic scrape of her hoe, the hum of a lone honeybee, and the occasional chirping of several pairs of sparrows that had roosted in a sourwood tree on the other side of the gate. The boy hadn't moved in so long, Miranda had begun to wonder if he'd gone.

"Think he's a tourist?"

"It's possible, I suppose." Miranda glanced across her well-tended patch of yard.

"Why would a tourist hide?" Ruby asked from her perch on the back step of Miranda's cozy little cottage in the northeastern hills of Georgia.

"It's hard to say, but he probably has his reasons."

"He was here yesterday too."

"And the day before."

Ruby tut-tutted. "I suppose he could be one of the kids from the high school. After all, it's that time of the year again, the time of rebirth and spring fever."

A horrendous squawking and flapping broke the evening quiet. The sparrows took to the air, beaks open in protest to the disruption. Ruby shook her head at the feathers floating to the ground. "Sounds like he could use a few lessons about staying quiet and surviving in the hill country. I ran into Hattie Arrowood coming out of the grocery store yesterday. She was complaining that half the kids in her ninth-grade English class don't give two hoots about word usage, tense, or punctuation. But you and I both know that every one of them could creep through these hills undetected. Wherever your visitor is from, it isn't the Blue Ridge Mountains."

Resting her hands along the top of the hoe's handle, Miranda lifted her face into the breeze. "You're probably right, Ruby, but then, you usually are."

There was a new note of pleasure in Ruby's voice as she said, "I heard somebody bought the old Donovan place. If your visitor is just a curious new kid who's heard the legend, he'll grow bored watching you. After all, you look like an ordinary woman wearing ordinary clothes tending an ordinary garden."

Miranda smiled at that. When Ruby failed to get the argument she was after, she sputtered to herself, which sent warm affection through Miranda. "I suspect we'll know soon enough whether he's a local boy, a tourist, or even a runaway, Ruby."

"How will we know?"

Returning to her task, Miranda said, "I left a stack of sandwiches and a thermos of milk on top of the mailbox. Tourists and local kids wouldn't pay it much attention."

Ruby's scowl suited her harsh, angular face, but she rose to her feet with an agility that was at odds with the streaks of gray in her hair and her daily insistence that she wasn't as young as she used to be. "Guess it's your prerogative if you want to feed somebody who's spying on you. He'd better have someplace safe to crawl back to is all I can say, because the storm that's been hugging those mountains is gonna circle back this way, and when it does, it isn't gonna be pretty."

Miranda looked out across the mountain. The sky had been clear half an hour ago. Now it seemed to be pressing down on the rooftops and chimneys of the houses in Dawsons Hollow. Farther west, gray clouds were banding together, churning and roiling like thick smoke. Shivers ran up her arms. A storm was brewing all right, the kind of storm that left its mark on the earth in broken limbs, swollen creeks, and other, more subtle ways.

Ruby broke into her reverie. "If it's all the same to you, I'd like to stay at your place until it's over."

Miranda lowered her hoe to the ground. On the one hand, she wondered how she'd ever been so lucky to find a friend like Ruby McCoy. On the other hand, she wondered how long they would both continue to pretend that *Ruby* was the one who was terrified of storms.

"I don't like the looks of this one," Ruby declared, already hurrying along the curving path that led to her place a stone's throw away. "I'll be back as soon as I batten down the hatches at home."

The first clap of thunder shook the entire mountain. "You hear that?" Ruby asked from the edge of Miranda's yard.

Miranda listened intently. She could feel the storm's electricity, could sense a kind of inevitability mixed with danger, but she didn't hear anything unusual. "What is it?"

"An airplane. Unless I'm mistaken, some blasted fool is heading right for these mountains and that storm."

Miranda scanned the horizon but saw no sign of an airplane of any kind. "I don't hear anything, but I guess you're the one who can hear a fly sneeze. Isn't that right, Ruby? Ruby?"

When she lowered her gaze, the path was empty.

Thunder rumbled again, closer, more menacing than before.

Miranda ran to the gate that led to the mountain road. An empty plate sat on top of the mailbox, all that was left of the sandwiches and milk she'd set out an hour earlier. Feeling warm despite the cool drops of rain wetting her arms, she almost smiled. At least the boy wouldn't go hungry.

She hurried into her cottage. Heart racing, she latched the windows, then waited by the door for Ruby to return. Five minutes later her friend slipped inside, rain-soaked but none the worse for wear. Panting, Ruby leaned against the wall just as thunder rumbled a third time. "I got here just in time."

With the next clap of thunder, the storm ran out of patience. Shards of lightning stabbed the treetops. Miranda peered through the deluge of water. Already branches had broken, falling heavily to the rain-drenched ground.

The lights went off without so much as a flicker. Ruby tried the phone.

"Dead?" Miranda asked.

At Ruby's nod, Miranda went in search of candles and matches. Rain pelted the roof, lightning snaked across the sky, and the very air they breathed seemed to rumble.

"Now did you hear it?" Ruby asked from the center of the storm-darkened room.

A low drone, similar to far-off thunder, drew Miranda's eyebrows down. She nodded, and Ruby pushed her graying hair away from her face. "I can't imagine any reason good enough to fly an airplane in this weather. Only a fool would even attempt it."

Miranda held a match to the wick of a scented candle, but she didn't reply, because she knew, perhaps better than anyone, that what some called foolishness, others called courage.

"You're a fool!" Caleb Wilder shouted at himself over the engine noise and the storm.

One second, lightning ripped the center out of the sky.

The next second, static drained out of the radio like the blood out of Cale's face.

He'd lost radio contact. Without it, he was completely alone. He knew the mountains were nearby, closing in on him on all sides, but he couldn't see a damn thing except clouds and rain.

Uttering a cry that was half curse, half prayer, he cut through the clouds, leveling off beneath them. The old Cessna's windshield wipers sliced a path through the onslaught of water, allowing him an intermittent glimpse of what was directly in front of him. He was soaring above a valley that was surrounded by mountains and covered with trees. Lightning snaked across the horizon, raising the hair on the back of his head. He craned his neck, but all he could see were more trees, more mountains.

He banked. Still more trees. But wait. He blinked, waited for the windshield wipers to give him another glimpse, and banked again. There in the distance was a field, around two hundred yards long, maybe fifty yards wide, and undoubtedly far from level. Landing in it would be risky. Hell, it would be suicide. The way he saw it, he had two choices. Take a chance that he could land the plane in that narrow clearing or let the lightning and the mountain get him.

He gritted his teeth, swiped the sweat away from his eyes, and gripped the control with everything he had. This was it. The moment he and earth came to terms about life. If lightning hit him, he would crash and burn. The same thing would happen if he overshot the meadow. Easing the pressure on the control, he tried not to think about putting Danny through the ordeal of having his father identified through dental records.

Danny.

He headed down, his landing gear a hairbreadth above the tops of the trees. Gripping the control with all his might, he vowed that for Danny's sake he would ride in on the rudder if he had to.

The plane met the ground hard and bounced twice, the single-engine Cessna Cardinal shaking so hard, Cale half expected the entire structure to disintegrate all around him. Anything not tied down clattered and clanked. The bottle of Chianti his best friend had shoved into his hands moments before he'd taken off bounced and rolled across the floor. Sam Kennedy believed in rituals. Cale didn't believe in much anymore.

The wings shook and the fuselage shimmied, the wheels plodding across a meadow strewn with rocks and logs and crater-sized holes. To his right was an outcropping of rocks, to his left, a steep incline. Straight ahead, woods loomed, closer, closer. He used every trick he knew to slow the plane down. Still, the plane lurched toward the trees. Thirty-five feet. Twenty feet. Fifteen. Ten.

He tried to shut his eyes but couldn't.

Wood splintered. Metal creaked and bent. He jerked forward, the sound his head made as it came into contact with the control panel echoing in his ears. A strange numbness settled over him. He tried to get up, but he was too tired, too groggy to move. Calm now, he closed his eyes and waited for the explosion.

Cale came to with a jerk. He winced and realized he wasn't dead.

It took a lot of doing, but he pried his eyes open, turned his head, and winced again. It was dark. The thunder and lightning had stopped, but the wind was still strong, pelting the plane with a wall of driving rain. He took a deep breath and then another. His head hurt like a son of a bitch; a couple of ribs weren't much better. In the darkness it was hard to tell if there was anything wrong with the rest of him. His fingers shook as he lifted them to his head. Feeling the stickiness of his own blood, he tested the rest of his limbs.

I'm alive, Danny, he thought. *Danny, I'm alive.*

Relief surged through Cale. Now, where the hell was he?

Standing shakily, he felt for the latch. He tried it twice. Twice the door didn't budge. He slammed his shoulder against it and groaned out loud. The door creaked open far enough to allow him to crawl through. Half sliding, half falling, he made it to the ground. It required everything he had to keep from blacking out again. With both hands braced on his thighs, he took a steadying breath and waited for his legs to stop shaking enough to support his weight.

Testing his strength, he took one step. He was alive. It had been a while since he'd been glad about that. Grinding his teeth against the pain shooting through his head and ribs, Caleb Wilder swore that if that kid whom he loved more than life itself put him through anything like this ever again, he was going to tan his stubborn hide.

By the time Cale found the path through the trees, he'd lost all concept of time. His teeth chattered, his clothes chafed, but still the cold rain came down. He had no idea where the path led, no knowledge of the area, no intuition to rely on. All he had was luck, not necessarily the good kind, the will to survive, and a deep-seated need to find his son.

He navigated the path, his mind strangely blank, all his energy and attention trained on walking. He fell twice and stumbled a third time, somehow managing to keep from sprawling face first in the mud.

His luck couldn't have been all bad, because a few more steps brought him to the edge of the woods and into a clearing. He stood, shivering, squinting against the rain, his sights set on the flicker of candlelight in the window of a small white house in the distance. Like a man in a trance, he followed that flickering light to a soggy, weathered porch.

"Hold it right there, mister."

The beam of a battery-powered flashlight brought him out of his trance. He jerked backward so fast, stars flashed in his eyes. When his vision cleared, he was able to make out the outline of a gaunt woman peering down the barrel of a shotgun.

Cale blinked. "Don't shoot."

"Give me one good reason why I shouldn't."

He'd heard stories of mountain people who lived in cabins with no electricity or running water, who planted their corn by signs of the moon and shot first and asked questions later. But he'd assumed that was all they were. Stories. Now he wasn't sure.

Keeping his voice as steady as possible, he said, "I won't come any closer."

"You got that right. Who are you?"

"Caleb Wilder. My friends . . . call me Cale."

She moved the gun up and down as if to run him off her land. "I'm not your friend, and I don't know any Wilders. That makes you a stranger, and I don't take kindly to strangers."

Cale tried to think. It had taken all his energy to make it this far. He didn't know what he would do if he had to search for another house. "All I need . . . is a dry place to spend the night . . . a barn or a shed . . . I'll clear out at first light."

The gun moved again. "What are you doing here?"

"I'm looking for my son. . . . He's fourteen . . . and his name is Danny. . . . Have you seen him?"

The woman lowered the light but not the gun. "What makes you think I would know anything about your son?"

Even in his groggy state, Cale thought that was a strange question, but since he was in no position to point that out, he took a moment to study the woman's gray hair, her thin, hawkish nose, and gaunt face.

"Well?" she prodded.

"You look like . . . the kind of capable person . . . who knows a great deal . . . about a lot of things."

Very slowly, she lowered the gun.

"Ruby, what are you doing?"

He turned his head so fast, his vision blurred all over again. The porch pitched in one direction, the ground beneath his feet shifting in the other.

"You have another visitor, Miranda."

Ruby? Miranda? Another visitor? Cale's knees gave out

before he could voice any of those questions out loud. Clutching the handrail, he looked from one woman to the other. The single beam of the high-powered flashlight cast shadows onto the siding behind both women. The one named Ruby was probably in her late fifties and looked haggard. The other woman was a vision in comparison, with her long brown hair and white robe. She was a good twenty-five years younger, and yet her eyes looked as old as time. Cale knew, because the eyes staring back at him in the mirror these past eighteen months had held a similar look.

Both women gasped. Cale figured they must have noticed the gash on his head.

"Hurry, Ruby," Miranda said, the hint of a faint Southern lilt in her voice. "Help me get him inside, where it's warm."

Doing everything in his power to stave off the darkness that was closing in on him, he whispered, "Have to find Danny . . . this storm . . . my plane . . ."

Cale felt himself being drawn up the steps and across the threshold. "So you're the fool who was flying in the thunderstorm," Ruby declared.

"It wasn't . . . raining . . . when I left . . . Columbus."

A soft trill of laughter drew his gaze to the woman on his right. His breath caught in his throat, and he didn't want to look away. But his head was spinning, and darkness was closing in. His eyelids dropped over his eyes, and blackness swarmed around him.

He was lowered to the edge of something soft. Feminine hands, at least four of them, pulled and tugged at his wet clothes. And then a mattress reached up and cradled his back, and blankets that smelled of home covered him. That soft Southern voice carried to his ears again but from a great distance. "That gash is going to need stitches. Ruby, bring me my first aid kit."

"It's late, Miranda, and stitching him up will take time. Why not just heal him? He's asleep. He'll never know."

"My first aid kit, Ruby."

Cale tried to make sense of the conversation, but his mind was too hazy for reasoning, his thoughts disjointed and unclear. Feeling weightless in a blessedly warm, blessedly dry room, he gave in to injury, weakness, and exhaustion and drifted into a dreamless sleep.

Who's there? Who is it? No. Nooooo.

From someplace far away, Cale heard a whimper. He felt his eyelids flutter. Someone was crying. Ellie? The whimper came again, louder this time.

He opened his eyes to complete darkness and the searing knowledge that it couldn't be Ellie, because Ellie was dead. He stared at the ceiling. If Ellie wasn't crying, who was?

Where was he?

He turned his head, the slight movement setting off an explosion in his skull. Now he remembered. He'd hit his head and screwed up a couple of ribs when he'd landed his plane. He wondered if he was dreaming or delirious or both, and had almost dismissed the sound as unreal, when it came a third time.

"No. Please. Nooooo."

It was a plea, so soulful and sorrowful, it knotted his insides. He rolled out of bed slowly, then stood in indecision. He remembered being led into a room and being helped into bed, but his eyes had been closed, and he had no recollection of the layout of the room. He could make out the outline of a window. Everything else was pitch black. Goose bumps prickled his flesh. Looking down at the darkness of his own body, he realized he was naked. He rotated his shoulders carefully, expecting pain to shoot through him where his hand rested over his ribs. Strangely, there was little pain there. His head was another matter.

Cursing the fuzziness in his mind, he felt his way to the door. He'd opened it only a few inches, when Ruby's voice carried to his ears. "It's a dream, Miranda. Just a dream. The thunderstorm's over now. You're safe. There, see?"

A door farther down the hall was ajar, the glow of candlelight dancing and flickering, turning the darkness in the hall into a hazy gray.

"I'm fine now, Ruby. You're right, the thunderstorm's over. You can go back to bed now."

The two exchanged more conversation, but their words were too hushed for Cale to hear. Leaving the door ajar, he made his way back to bed and crawled between the sheets.

There was no rain hitting his window. The storm had either blown itself out or it had moved on. It had been a mother of a storm, no doubt about that. Cale knew people who were afraid of storms. It seemed like only yesterday when Danny used to crawl into bed with him and Ellie whenever he was awakened by thunder and lightning, his warm little body tucked close and safe between them. The memory sent a yearning through Cale, an ache that hurt worse than his bruised head.

One of the teachers he worked with in Columbus had a fear of spiders that bordered on a phobia. Alice had screamed like a banshee the last time she'd discovered a terrifying though harmless gray spider in her desk drawer. It hadn't been half as gut wrenching as Miranda's whimpers had been tonight.

What was this woman with the lilting Southern accent and the soft touch really afraid of? Before he could complete another waking thought, sleep claimed him once again.

CHAPTER TWO

Cale awoke in a room bright with sunshine. It didn't do much for his headache, but if felt good where it fell across his arms and shoulders. Squinting, he studied a pattern on the opposite wall. It was a shadow as intricate as a spiderweb and was the result of the sun shining through some sort of woven decoration hanging in the window. A memory pulled at him, but the more he tried to concentrate on it, the more vague the notion became.

He was in the process of pushing himself to a sitting position, when a knock sounded on the door and Ruby bustled in, shaking her head and clicking her tongue. "Miranda left strict instructions that you're to lie flat."

Cale sat up the rest of the way, which set off a brand-new series of tongue clickings from Ruby. She was beside him suddenly, placing a steadying hand on his shoulder. "Give me a second to prop up your pillows."

He swung his feet over the side of the bed. "Which way to the bathroom?"

It took her a few seconds to answer. When she did, it was grudgingly. "First door on the right. Do you need any help?"

"Not since I was four." He stood, the blanket falling from

his body. He thought he heard a mild gasp, but he didn't stick around to make sure.

Most of his memories of the previous night were vague, but he recalled more than two hands helping him out of his clothes, which meant that this woman had already seen him naked. Therefore, the sight of him in the raw couldn't have come as a surprise.

He let himself into the small bathroom. Closing the door, he was mildly surprised to find his clothes, freshly laundered and neatly folded beside a towel, a washcloth, and a bar of soap. It was almost as if Ruby hadn't expected him to spend any more time in bed than was absolutely necessary.

He used the facilities, then turned, flattening his palms on either side of an old porcelain sink. Leaning heavily on his hands, he studied his reflection. He looked like hell, bleary-eyed and pasty-skinned. A bandage covered the gash on his forehead but not the outer edges of the bruise that had formed overnight. Bright red scratches crisscrossed his face and arms, a dark, nasty-looking bruise marring the skin low on his chest. He touched the bruise with the pads of two fingers. The flesh was tender but not terribly sore. He didn't get it. Last night, he'd been certain those ribs were broken.

A memory hovered slightly beyond his consciousness. He had a vague recollection of someone touching him with hands far softer than his, and he was almost certain he'd looked into eyes the color of amber. Hoping a shower would help clear his head, he turned on the taps. He stepped beneath the warm spray, being careful to keep the bandage on his forehead dry.

The shower worked wonders, and although he wasn't quite a new man when he left the bathroom, he felt a lot more like his old self. Dressed in his own clothes, he followed the scent of strong coffee. He found Ruby in a kitchen at the back of the cottage.

Removing his watch, which had stopped at seven past eight the previous night, he strode as far as the doorway. "What time is it?"

She glanced sideways at him, answering while she stirred something in a big pot on the stove. "Twenty after ten."

Damn. The morning was almost over, and he hadn't even begun to search for Danny.

He took a few tentative steps into the room. "What happened last night?"

Ruby motioned for him to have a seat at a table beneath a row of windows where a place was set, steam rising from what appeared to be a bowl of oatmeal. She wore a flowered housedress, the kind that buttoned down the front and hung straight from a pair of bony shoulders. Going back to the stove, she said, "You landed your plane during a raging storm and hit your head."

His gaze fell to the white-knuckled grip she had on the spoon. That wasn't what he'd meant, and he'd bet his airplane that she knew it. "I mean later," he said quietly. "I heard someone moaning and crying."

Ruby stopped the stirring momentarily. When she took it up again, her movements were slower and more precise. "You hit your head very, very hard. Have a seat."

So, this was how it was going to be, Cale thought. Ruby didn't want to talk about Miranda's nightmare. Since it was no skin off his nose, he strode to the table and pulled out a chair.

Normally, he was a bacon-and-eggs man, but he swore nothing had ever smelled better than this. He sank into the chair, reached for his spoon, and took his first mouthful. "My wife was always trying to get me to eat this stuff."

"You're married?" Ruby asked.

The question caught him off guard and drove reality home. "I was."

"Divorced?"

He shook his head, a memory washing over him. *Your eating habits are going to be the death of you, Caleb Wilder.*

Cale took another spoonful of the oatmeal in front of him, remembering how often Ellie used to tell him that. He'd finally given in and had his cholesterol checked even though he swore it wouldn't be necessary for years and years. He would never forget how smug he'd felt when he'd relayed his incredibly low levels to Ellie. She'd punched him playfully, and he'd grabbed her and kissed her and proceeded to show her how healthy and energetic he was. She didn't complain about his eating habits after that. He continued to eat his high-cholesterol food and she continued to eat her low-fat ones. In the end, her alfalfa and vegetables hadn't kept her out of the path of an eighteen-wheeler that had swerved to miss a van full of people.

Suddenly, the oatmeal tasted bland. He sniffed the air and said, "Do you mind if I help myself to a cup of that coffee?"

"No coffee for you. It'll make your headache worse." Ruby pushed a ceramic teapot toward him.

Removing the lid, he peered at the murky liquid inside. "What is this?"

"Gizzards and chickens' feet. An old family recipe."

Ruby poured the liquid into a ceramic mug, then strode back to the stove. "I'm kidding. It's white willow bark tea. Nature's aspirin. It's a pain reliever as well as a fever-reducing anti-inflammatory agent. It'll help with that headache."

"What makes you think I have a headache?" Eyeing her knowing expression, he turned his head very carefully. When even that movement increased the pain in his skull, he lifted the cup to his lips and took a sip.

"Well?"

He shrugged, but he took another sip.

"I added a little peppermint. Miranda's against stacking her herbs, but like I always tell her, what good are all her natural remedies if a person can't gag them down?"

Cale stored the information, if that's what it was, finished his oatmeal and tea, and rose to his feet. "Where is Miranda this morning?"

"She isn't here."

He glanced around, his movements as sharp as Ruby's tone had been. "I noticed. Where is she?"

"Why do you want to know?"

He paused. Why? "I want to thank her."

"What for?"

Cale hadn't expected the third degree. "For stitching up my forehead and for allowing me to spend the night here. Why else?"

"Oh." Ruby glanced at the front of his shirt, then went back to stirring whatever was bubbling in the big pot. "It's always nice to be appreciated. She's at her clinic. Just follow this road west. It's not much more than a stone's throw away, although you can't see it now that the leaves are back on the trees. You head on over there if you think you're up to it. Tell Miranda I'll be along in a few minutes."

Cale looked out the window in the direction Ruby was pointing, his gaze catching on the woven decoration hanging in the top pane. A similar one hung in the room where he'd slept. Turning around, he glanced into the next room. Another was in the window there.

"What are those?" he asked.

"They're called dream-catchers. The Cherokee Indians who used to live in these mountains believed nightmares couldn't get through a window as long as there was a dream-catcher in it."

"They didn't work last night."

Ruby McCoy tapped the wooden spoon against the top of the pan. Then, in a deliberate movement, she met his gaze. "You must have hit your head harder than you thought."

He held her dark-eyed gaze for several seconds. She was about as good at lying as the white willow bark tea was at tasting good. Maybe both served a purpose. His headache *was* better. For all he cared, Ruby could lie all she wanted. He had problems of his own.

Touching the tender area on his forehead, he said, "I'm looking for my son. Have you seen a strange boy around here?"

"What do you mean by strange? What's wrong with him?"

Cale's temper flared. "Nothing's wrong with him. He just isn't from around here. Have you seen a boy you've never seen before?"

"Miranda and I might have seen a boy hiding in the bushes.

Since it was Miranda's yard he was watchin', I guess it's up to her to choose to tell you what she saw."

Or to choose not to hung in the air between them.

Cale turned, slowly making his way to the door. He'd been up for only an hour and already he felt tired to the bone. "Thanks for your help, Ruby."

"You're welcome, but I've gotta tell you, it was a toss-up. Shoot you or help you."

He smiled in spite of himself.

Ruby followed him to the door, where she said, "You're not so bad for a stranger. Turns out I'm glad I didn't shoot you. If you'd like, I could run over to my place and get you a buzzard's feather. Rheumatiz is likely to set in now that you've injured yourself. Only two things I know of that'll ward it off is drinking water dipped out of an open stream before sunrise on Ash Wednesday, and wearing a buzzard's feather. Since Ash Wednesday is over with, that buzzard's feather is your only hope."

He continued down the porch steps. "Maybe another time."

She made that clicking sound with her tongue again, then disappeared inside the cottage. Cale followed a curving path to a white gate. He walked through and stood looking back at the quaint little cottage. It was the first of May, and already flowers were blooming throughout the yard. The sun gleamed white on the siding on the house, delineating the dream-catchers in every window.

Dream-catchers, white willow bark tea, and buzzards' feathers. The mountain folklore came as a bit of a surprise but not the mountain's beauty. Ellie had once told him that this mountain was the first place she'd loved. And yet she'd never come back here, not once in the ten years they were married.

Why?

Cale wasn't surprised that Danny had come here. It was only natural for a boy to want to visit the place his mother had loved the most. Since his intelligence bordered on genius, it was also natural that he would want to understand why she'd never returned, and why she'd spoken of it moments before she'd died.

Danny had come here to understand his mother. Cale had come here to understand his son.

First, he had to find him.

He shoved a hand through his hair, wincing because he'd forgotten about the gash. It was almost noon, and time was wasting.

The village of Dawsons Hollow wasn't much more than four corners in the middle of nowhere. There was a grocery store on one corner, a one-pump gas station on another, a diner/gift shop on a third. Cale read the sign in the gift shop window on his way by. QUILTS. ANTIQUES. VIDEOS TO RENT — 3 MOVIES, 3 DAYS, $3.00. A big square building that must have once been a livery stable sat across the street on the fourth corner. All the buildings except the livery stable were made of brick. The street was paved with tar, not cement. There were no curbs, no sidewalks, no stop signs. There *was* a "SLOW, children playing" sign, an American flag flying high on a telephone pole, and wooden buckets filled with newly planted flowers on every corner.

A few cars, mostly older models, were parked in front of the Bootlegger, which Cale assumed was a bar. Two more vehicles sat a little farther down the street. One was five years old, the other was more like twenty. The older one had mismatched doors and cardboard in one window. It reminded Cale of his first automobile.

He walked past an open lot and nodded at a couple of old-timers who were whittling and shooting the breeze on a bench in front of a barbershop. They returned his nod, their eyes sharply assessing, their curiosity obviously aroused.

He knew the clinic the instant he saw it. It had little to do with the fact that it was the last building before the blacktop ended and the street turned residential. It just seemed like the type of building a woman like Miranda would choose to set up her medical practice in. The structure looked like an old log cabin, complete with a stone chimney and a quaint front porch, flower boxes spilling with pink and yellow flowers. The sign over the steps read "Morningstar Medical Clinic. M. Sinclair, Nurse Practitioner." Another sign, this one over the door, read "Georgia, the state of Wisdom, Justice, and Moderation."

Cale opened the door and strode inside. He'd been in enough pediatricians' offices in his day to take the crying baby and squealing kids in stride. He gave the two little boys who were quibbling over a toy a wide berth and took a seat. It wasn't long before a woman emerged, a whimpering baby on her hip, another on the way, and two young children trailing behind, a thumb in the toddler's mouth. Cale thought the woman was far too young to look so tired and worn out.

"Jeremiah, Joshua, stop that this instant."

The boys paid her no mind.

"I had it first."

"Did not."

"Did so."

"I mean it. Stop that right now."

"Le'go. It's mine!"

"No. It's mine!"

"Boys!"

The children's voices were insistent, the mother's was shrill. As a teacher and a father, Cale knew the routine. There wasn't much he could do except sit back and wait for things to get louder and hell to break loose. Before anybody had a chance to say another word, Miranda stepped into the room. Going down to her knees, she spoke calmly and softly. "If it's all right with your mother, you two can take this truck home with you."

Jeremiah and Joshua suddenly turned shy.

Miranda smiled up at the young pregnant woman before glancing at Cale. Her smile changed in the most subtle of ways, but it didn't fade. Something shifted inside Cale, rising up like longing, scaring the hell out of him.

To his relief, Miranda turned her attention back to the little boys. She reached into the toy box, pulling out another truck and two storybooks. "I'll tell you what," she said, that soft Southern lilt working wonders with the sniffling children. "I want you two to play with these, but you have to be nice. You enjoy them, and when your mother comes back for her appointment next week, you bring these back."

She handed each of them a tissue, motioning with her head that she expected them to use them. When each child raised the tissue to his nose, she continued. "If your mother tells me you've been courteous and nice to each other, I'll let you take another toy home next time."

The boys accepted the used toys as if they were holy.

"Can you say thank-you?" their mother asked.

The children mumbled something that might have passed for thanks. Cale couldn't help noticing how relieved the mother looked. He couldn't help noticing that she paid Miranda with some sort of smoked game either.

The room seemed very quiet after the woman and her children left. Ellie used to say that Cale could have struck up a conversation with the man in the moon himself. And yet, standing in the cozy waiting area in a small town in the Blue Ridge Mountains, he couldn't think of a thing to say.

Miranda went to an appointment book, pointed, and made that humming sound doctors and nurses were notorious for. She seemed like a real medical professional even if she didn't look like one in her long, gathered skirt and pale yellow blouse.

"So you're a nurse practitioner," he said quietly.

She hummed an answer again and glanced up at him so quickly, he didn't have time to look away. "Your color is much better this morning," she said.

His hand automatically went to the bandage on his fore-head. "Thanks to you, and to Ruby's white willow bark tea."

Their eyes met. She smiled. And Cale swallowed hard.

He noticed she had the foil-wrapped package the young mother had given to her in one hand. Turning toward the next room, she said, "The examination rooms are this way."

He followed her as far as the first doorway before he came to his senses. "I didn't come here for an examination."

"You didn't?" she asked, closing a small refrigerator where other foil packages were stacked.

Cale glanced around. The clinic was nothing like he'd expected. Neither was the woman who ran it. It was obvious that Miranda Sinclair wasn't from these mountains. It was also obvious that it had taken money, not smoked game, to pay for the high-tech, state-of-the-art medical equipment lining the examination rooms.

"I came to thank you."

"You're welcome."

Her simple, immediate acceptance rendered him speechless all over again. Clearing his throat, he said, "We weren't properly introduced last night." He held out his hand. "I'm Caleb—Cale—"

"Wilder," she finished for him. "You told me last night."

She placed her hand in his, and that yearning filled him again, making him ache. He wondered what else he'd told her last night when he'd been too delirious to know better. That she was beautiful? He felt a stab of guilt just thinking it. On the heels of his guilty conscience, he realized it wasn't quite accurate anyway. She wasn't beautiful exactly. Her hair was brown and long and tied away from her face. Her skin was smooth but lacked any trace of makeup. Her lips were full, her nose a little too narrow at the bridge. And her eyes were brown. No, not brown, amber. Only the rings around the outside were brown. Beautiful.

Damn.

He broke eye contact, shuffled from one foot to the other, and felt a tug on his hand as she drew her fingers out of his grasp.

"Actually," he said, as much to break the hold she had over him as to cut through the tension filling the room, "I came for several reasons. The first was to thank you. The second was to pay you, and the third was to ask you a couple of questions. Ruby mentioned that you've seen a boy around."

Miranda's gaze dropped to Caleb Wilder's hands. It wasn't the money he was reaching for that mesmerized her but the blunt-tipped fingers and tanned skin, slightly marred by a scrape, that held her spellbound. They were strong hands, working hands, caring hands.

With the pads of her fingers she touched the edge of a particularly nasty-looking scrape, her actions as automatic to her as breathing. She supposed the sound of Cale's quickly drawn breath was natural too. Ruby probably could have heard his heart beating had she been there. Miranda could see the telltale signs in a vein pulsing on the side of his neck. She glanced up at him. "Does this hurt?"

He shook his head, the action drawing her eyes upward to the purple bruise visible along the edges of the white bandage. "That gash took seven stitches. People around here would say that was lucky."

"People around here have strange ideas about luck." He smiled, and it struck Miranda that in her youth she would have said he looked as if he'd just stepped off a steamboat from northern Italy. His hair was nearly black, his eyes a vivid dark blue, the angles and hollows that made up his face striking and strong.

The outer door opened and Ruby bustled in. Startled, they both took a backward step. They looked at each other, at the floor, at each other again. Cale recovered first. "Ruby mentioned that you saw a teenage boy last night. I think it's possible it was my son. Can you describe the boy you saw? What he was wearing, the color of his hair?"

Miranda accepted the twenty-dollar bills without thinking, because for a moment she was beyond conscious thought. It required all her concentration to form a coherent reply. "Ruby and I did see a boy. I didn't see him up close, but his hair looked quite a bit lighter than yours."

"Did he seem okay to you? Healthy, I mean? Unharmed?"

The honest worry in Cale's voice brought Miranda to her senses. Feeling Ruby's eyes on her, she assumed a business-like attitude and said, "As far as I could tell, he was fine.

He's come to the edge of my property three evenings in a row.''

''That means he must be staying nearby.''

Miranda nodded.

''Any idea where a fourteen-year-old boy who's been camping only once in his life might be living?''

Ruby was the one who answered. ''There aren't any hotels around here, but there are abandoned cabins all over the hills. He's probably staying in one of them.''

Cale's shoulders drooped. Wanting to ease his worries and disappointment, Miranda said, ''I have a feeling he'll pay me a visit again tonight. You're welcome to stop by and see for yourself that he's all right.''

Their gazes met, held, only to slide away all over again. He ran a hand through his hair and made noises about leaving. Halfway to the door he stopped suddenly and turned around. ''What time has Danny been arriving?''

Danny, Miranda thought. So that was the boy's name, if the boy who'd been watching her was the son Cale was looking for. ''Around seven. Maybe a little later.''

Cale nodded and backed up, bumping into a table in his haste to leave. Mumbling under his breath, he pulled himself together and walked stiffly out the door.

Ruby seemed unusually quiet after he'd gone. Peering out the window that faced the mountain road, she shook her head.

''What is it, Ruby?''

''Oh, I was just thinkin' that it's mighty strange that a man who has enough courage to land an airplane in a rocky field during a raging thunderstorm would spend so much time staring at the toes of his shoes instead of at you.''

Miranda strode to the window, where Cale could be seen strolling away. ''We undressed him and put him to bed last night, Ruby. He probably feels a little uncomfortable around us.''

''Trust me. Caleb Wilder isn't the type of man who minds letting a woman see him naked.''

''How do you know?''

Ruby clamped her mouth shut and made no reply.

"What exactly went on in my cottage this morning?"

Ruby's dark eyes flashed with indignation, but her lips twitched as she said, "Nothin' went on. Landsakes, girl, he's young enough to be my son. But he sure does have nice shoulders, a washboard stomach, and a fine . . . behind."

"Ruby!"

"Well, he does, and there's no sense denying the fact that you noticed those features. Among other things."

Miranda didn't deny anything, but she had to admit she was relieved when the door opened and Angus Warner rushed in on bowed legs. The sight of the blood dripping from his hand spurred her into action.

"Angus," she said, already reaching for his injured hand. "What happened?"

"I seen him!" Angus exclaimed. "The granddaddy of all panthers. Me'n Elmer both seen him sittin' on the ridge overlookin' the town. He was huge. Had a tail so long, he kept it curled around his neck. Got so scared I pert'near sliced through my own dang finger."

Miranda wrapped a clean towel around the wound and slipped an arm around Angus's stooped shoulders. So, this year it was going to be tales of the granddaddy of all panthers. Last year it was ghost stories, called haint tales by the people of the mountain.

"Okay, Angus," she said, steering Angus into an examination room. "Let's get this cut disinfected and stitched up, and you can tell me all about what you saw."

Daniel raced up the mountain. His blood rushed through his head and pounded in his chest. He paused at the crest of the hill to catch his breath and to calm himself down. Those two old men had almost seen him.

Dumb. Dumb, dumb, dumb, dumb.

Why did he have to be so uncoordinated? Last night he'd scared up a whole flock of birds. He'd wanted to be so quiet. He hadn't meant to move at all, but his arm had gone to sleep. This morning it had been his foot. He'd tried to move it carefully but had wound up sending a small rock tumbling down the hill. The two old men he'd been watching had jerked to their feet and peered up the mountain as if they were expecting to see Bigfoot himself.

Rats. Those old-timers would be watching that ridge tomorrow for sure. That meant that he wouldn't be able to sit up there, where he could look down at the town. It was his second favorite lookout on the mountain.

Breathing normally now, he listened intently. Satisfied that nobody was following him, he sank onto a grassy area near a fallen tree a dozen feet off the trail. The leaves and underbrush were so thick, he could see only a narrow patch of sky. He liked looking at the sky. He liked almost everything about these mountains.

He didn't even mind living on his own, although washing in the ice-cold stream was taking a little getting used to. He'd been afraid that first night, but by the second, he'd faced his fear. By the third night he'd slept right through all the mountain noises, the baying of dogs far away and the hoot of owls and the rustle of branches in the wind. Living up here sure beat going to school back in Columbus.

He'd studied books all his life, had taken tests and answered questions in order to obtain a high score that showed up on standardized test results and on his report card every ten weeks. What good did it do him? All it had gotten him was the nicknames Brain and Geek and other taunts that were a lot worse.

Who cared about square roots and foreign languages and the splitting of atoms? What difference did A's make?

He was fourteen. Understanding calculus didn't make him proud of himself. It made him what the kids called him. A geek. It sure as hell hadn't made him any friends. Getting good grades hadn't kept his mother alive.

It hadn't been so bad before she'd died. Hearing her laugh at the end of the day had made everything else seem less stark, less lonely. Daniel used to lie in his bed late at night, just listening to her laugh and his father talk.

Caleb Wilder wasn't his real father. Daniel had always known it. When he was younger, it hadn't mattered. The sound of that deep baritone had made him feel safe somehow, good, loved. His father, er, Cale, was a teacher, but he taught with his hands. Daniel had never had much interest in working with his own hands, but he'd secretly loved watching Cale work with his. The man could do anything, fix anything. But he hadn't been able to keep Daniel's mother alive. She'd closed her eyes and slipped away no matter how tight those big, strong hands with the calluses and the grease underneath the fingernails had held on.

They'd put her in the ground. His beautiful mother, whose hair had smelled like sunshine and whose laughter made everyone smile. And the next morning the sun had come up, and his father had gone back to work, and he'd gone back to school. Everyone told him to give it time. Time had only made it worse, until he couldn't take it anymore. He'd had to get away from the sadness in Cale's eyes and from the kids who called him Geek and from the stupid-ass teachers who thought the sun rose and set on getting the right answer. He'd figured it out. Why couldn't they?

There were no right answers.

Daniel knew it was only a matter of time before Cale came for him. He didn't care. He wasn't going back there. Ever. He was going to stay in these mountains his mother had loved and be a recluse forever.

It was strange, too, because he'd never given much thought to small mountains or small towns. He'd sure never thought about living in them. But there'd been something in her words and in her voice when she'd spoken about this place moments before she'd died. He'd gone over and over it in his head after the silence had settled in and he and Cale had started pretending that everything was going to be all right. Oh, Cale had tried to talk to him, to comfort him, to get him to talk in return. What was there to say? Nothing made sense anymore. Not facts, not things he read in books, not digits on a calculator or blips on a computer. At first, he'd lain awake every night, wondering where she'd gone.

As the weeks had turned into months, another question took on an even louder voice. Why had she waited until she was dying to talk about this place?

He didn't believe in coincidences, so the fact that his birth certificate listed this county as his place of birth, and his mother had spoken so lovingly of it, took on a significance he hadn't been able to ignore. He was his mother's son, after all.

He was someone else's son too. Someone who probably lived in these very hills. Somewhere.

Climbing to his feet, he brushed off the seat of his pants and headed back up the mountain toward the deserted cabin he'd discovered his first day here. He tried to keep quiet. He knew he had a lot to learn about the mountain and living off the land before he could be a true recluse. A recluse. Wouldn't his guidance counselor have a conniption fit about that?

A scene from an imaginary skit played through his head. In his fantasy, he was sitting in Mr. Delvecchio's office.

"Danny. You really must buckle down and give careful consideration to what you want to be when you grow up. I know what it's like to be extremely bright. Why, I graduated from high school when I was barely seventeen and finished college in three years."

Whether it was in real life or in Daniel's imagination, Mr. Delvecchio never missed an opportunity to brag.

"There are so many more career opportunities offered to you kids today. But you must buckle down. I gave you several brochures weeks ago. I assume you've studied them. Have you decided which university you want to attend? Have you, Danny?"

In this fantasy, Daniel would look across the desk and smile just as meekly as that pansy-ass wanted him to, and then he would say, "As a matter of fact I have decided what I want to do, Mr. Delvecchio. Bud. I'm going to be a recluse."

Mr. Delvecchio would gasp, steeple his lily-white fingers, and stare at him through his Coke-bottle glasses. Daniel would leave then. Just walk right out the door, smack in the middle of the jerk's annoying mannerisms and holier-than-thou speech.

Daniel was a little sorry he'd run away. Not because he cared if anybody back there thought he was a coward, least of all Delvecchio, but because he hadn't told him what he could do with his charts and graphs and test scores.

Goose bumps rose on Daniel's arms. At first he blamed them on the cool shade. He slowed, wondering if it was possible that they were the result of thinking about Bud Delvecchio. But the chill on his arms increased, climbing onto his shoulders, up his neck, into his scalp.

Something crunched beneath his shoe. He glanced down and jumped backward. He was cold now. And spooked. He'd stepped on the skeleton of some animal. He thought of his mother turning into a skeleton in her casket, and felt sick. He shuddered and veered to the right. He'd passed a fallen log, when another round of shivers climbed up his arms. He'd almost given in to the urge to run as fast as possible, when a patch of gray caught his eye.

It was an animal, tiny and alone.

Careful now, Daniel checked for more skeletons and crept closer. The closer he came, the more he felt the cold and desolation surrounding the animal. He went down on his knees and dared to reach out and gently touch its soft fur.

It was a baby raccoon, and it was so tiny, it could have fit in his hand. He tried to remember what he'd learned about raccoons. Unfortunately, there wasn't a lot about nature in the program for the gifted and talented.

It didn't matter. The raccoon was dead.

A sob lodged in Daniel's throat. He squeezed his eyes shut. He hated tears. He hated feeling so weak. He hated . . .

The creature moved beneath his hand, sending Daniel straight into the air. Oh, my God! It wasn't dead after all.

He wondered where its mother was. He knew for a fact that maternal instinct was strong—in animals as well as in humans. That meant that the mother was either dead or worse.

He paused at the notion that there could be something worse than death. He would have to think about that later.

Daniel picked up the raccoon and tucked it inside his shirt to keep it warm. Funny, he felt warmer too, as if something he hadn't felt in a long time were burgeoning deep inside him.

He didn't know what to do for the animal. Mammals drank mother's milk. He hadn't gone three steps before he remembered the thermos of milk the lady with the long brown hair and beautiful garden had left for him. Breaking into a run, he paid little attention to being quiet, all his energy trained on getting to that cabin and feeding the animal whose only chance at life lay in his hands.

Daniel left the raccoon in his shirt while he warmed the milk in a tin he placed on the coals that were left from the fire he'd banked hours before. He held the raccoon's mouth close to the milk, but the animal was either too small or too weak to lap from the plate.

Daniel didn't know what to do. He was practically a genius, for heaven's sake. Think.

He tried wetting his finger and placing it to the animal's mouth, but the raccoon didn't respond. He dipped a corner of his shirt into the warm milk. It took a little finagling to hold the tiny animal's mouth open and let the milk drip in. It was a tedious and frustrating process, but some of the milk must have made it into the raccoon's stomach, because by the second feeding, the animal was licking its lips and Daniel was pretty sure that more milk ended up in its little stomach than on its fur.

He fed the raccoon two more times, using up the last of the milk in the thermos. Making a bed out of his shirt, he placed the animal, shirt and all, in a crate he'd found in the corner.

Daniel heaved a huge sigh as he watched the baby raccoon sleep. It was alive, fed, and warm. Daniel wondered how long before it would want to eat again. Glancing outside, he noticed that the sun was so low, it shone in the grimy window on the west wall. He started to panic all over again.

He'd brought some money with him, but the grocery store closed at seven. He couldn't feed the animal without more milk.

But wait. He stared at the empty thermos, a feeling of calm settling over him. There was one place he could go to get what he needed.

He shrugged into his jean jacket. After checking the crate where the raccoon was still sleeping, he tucked the empty thermos under one arm and set off toward the mountain road.

CHAPTER THREE

It would be dark soon, Cale thought as he scanned the edge of the woods. And there had been no sign of Danny. Wishing he could see beyond the ferns, wildflowers, vines, and bushes that grew lush and thick on the other side of the gate, he said, "Do you think we missed him?"

Miranda paused in her weeding long enough to cast a sweeping glance at the horizon. With a mild shake of her head, she returned to her strange-looking plants and said, "I don't think he's been here. Do you hear the sparrows in that sourwood tree? They're chirping and gossiping about their day, about who found the most seeds and whose nest is the softest. They wouldn't be doing that if somebody was nearby."

Cale had been straining to catch a glimpse of Danny's blue jeans or T-shirt or jacket, but Miranda's statement drew his attention. Birds gossiping? He'd never heard such a thing. And yet he found himself wondering if it was possible that she could understand what the birds were saying. He shook off the notion and rose stiffly to his feet.

"I don't think he's coming. It's getting late, and I should probably be going. After last night, you must be tired."

"Yes."

That was it. No explanation, no elaboration. Just a simple, straightforward word uttered without looking up. Cale didn't mind, because it gave him the opportunity to watch her a few moments longer. He didn't know many women who could look artful and serene pulling weeds. She was fine-boned and long-limbed, the kind of woman who would look good in anything, even the faded jeans and plain white T-shirt she was wearing just then.

She glanced up as he neared, and he saw dark shadows beneath her eyes. His steps slowed. "You had a nightmare last night."

She stared so deeply into his eyes, he wondered what she saw. And then she said, yes as simply and quietly as before.

"Do you have them often?"

She shook her head and took her time removing her garden gloves. "I used to, but I don't anymore."

"Ruby said it had to do with the storm."

She held perfectly still, the breeze fluttering through her white shirt, blowing her hair behind her shoulders. When she finally spoke, her voice was so quiet, he had to strain to hear. "The storm was part of it. I think it had more to do with the fact that a man was sleeping in my house."

Cale stared into her eyes for several seconds, but he didn't ask any more questions. He didn't have to. Her nightmares had something to do with men. There weren't too many things a man could do to instill that kind of fear in a woman. The fact that some man had done it to *her* turned his stomach.

It seemed everyone had problems, sadnesses to work through, life's troubles to deal with. Casting one last hopeful look at the trees and foliage along the edges of Miranda's yard, he sighed. The sun was going, and so was the day. It was time for him to go too.

He started for the gate, saying, "It was Danny's choice to leave his warm bed and three square meals a day, but I still hate the thought of him being cold and going hungry. I keep telling myself he's very resourceful. Still, I can't help worrying. I guess there's always tomorrow."

Miranda watched Caleb Wilder walk away. Aside from Ruby, and Verdie, a dear, old granny-woman she'd known years before, Miranda hadn't talked to anyone about what had happened to her in a long, long time. It wasn't because she was ashamed. There was no shame in being overpowered and violated and left to die. She'd cowered in fear those first months, unable to eat or sleep. The therapist she'd seen later at college had asked how she'd gotten through it. Miranda wasn't sure. How did anybody get through tragedies and horrors beyond description? Was it a will to live? Or was it something far more elemental? It hadn't been easy, but she'd been determined to move on with her life. She refused to live in fear, less than what she might have been.

She hated the man who'd done it to her, but she didn't hate all men. In fact, she felt a special connection to this Cale. It was a connection she didn't understand, but a long time ago she'd learned that there were some things beyond human understanding.

She supposed she could have thanked him for not prying for details. It was as if he understood on a soul-deep level. Therefore, words weren't necessary.

"Cale?" she called to his back.

He turned, first his head, and then the rest of him.

"If the boy who came here last night is your son, he isn't going hungry."

"What do you mean?"

She motioned with her right hand. "There are two suppers on top of my mailbox. The one on the left is for you."

He strode stiffly to the white mailbox. When he turned, she saw that he had one of the clear plastic bags in one hand.

"You're feeding my son?"

She folded her arms and said, "I have to do something with all the food people give me."

Cale's smile took years off his face. His laughter took years off hers. The deep masculine sound might have been responsible for the way the sparrows had suddenly grown quiet, but intuition told her there was more to it than that.

She walked over to the mailbox. One of the bags was still there, but the thermos was gone. Catching a movement in the foliage to the right of the sourwood tree, she placed a hand on Cale's arm and quietly said, "I think there's someone here to see you."

Twenty feet away, a twig snapped. Leaves fluttered, bushes parted, and a boy stepped into her yard. The thermos she'd left for him yesterday dangled from the fingers of one hand; the full one he'd just picked up was held tightly in the other. Without saying a word, he leaned down and placed the empty thermos on the grass.

She watched his actions in silence, noting the fluid movements, the strength of youth. His eyebrows were dark and straight, his hair cropped short and sticking up as if it hadn't seen a comb in days. He was tall for fourteen, and proud. No matter what problems the family had been having lately, the boy obviously wanted her to know he wasn't a thief.

"You must be Danny," she said.

His shoulders came up, along with his chin. "My name is Daniel." He turned, meeting his father's stare head-on, his look challenging Cale to dispute his statement.

"Are you all right?" Cale asked.

It required a stretch of the imagination to call the slight movement of the boy's head a nod. Deciding it might be fortuitous to fill the silence growing taut between the two Wilders, Miranda said, "Why didn't you take the sandwiches?"

"I don't need them." The words were proud, the delivery defiant.

"And the milk?"

She thought he was studying her, gauging how much he dared or wanted to tell her. With a thrust of his chin that reminded her of Cale, he said, "The milk isn't for me."

"Who is it for?" she asked quietly.

She wasn't certain whether he paused for effect or because he was afraid to say more. Trying to put him at ease, she said, "I left it out for you, to use any way you want."

He took his time answering. "It's for an animal I found."

And he was feeding it. No wonder Cale loved this boy.

"What kind of animal?" she asked.

Once again he paused for a few moments before answering, "A baby raccoon."

Miranda smiled to herself. Aside from her and Ruby and a couple of high school girls, she didn't know anybody who would attempt to save a raccoon's life. Folks up here didn't like the creatures, blaming the animals for making their dogs bark in the night, for getting into their trash, even for drawing skunks. This boy probably had no way of knowing that. To him, the animal represented life. That was the way Miranda looked at God's creatures too.

"Are its eyes open?" she asked.

He nodded suspiciously. She supposed she didn't blame him. She was asking a lot of questions. "That's good," she said. "That means it's more than three weeks old and has a chance. How are you feeding her?"

"Her?"

"The raccoon."

"Oh. I'm . . . I soak up warm milk with my shirt and drip it into its, *his*, mouth."

She hid a smile. "I have something that might make the process a little easier. I'll be right back."

Hurrying away, she could feel two pairs of eyes on her, but she didn't look back. Her shoes thudded on her back steps. The door bounced shut behind her, a drawer squeaked as she opened it and hastily rummaged through its contents for the items she was looking for.

She returned to her garden within minutes, and found Cale and Daniel exactly as she'd left them, shoulders back, gazes locked. She had a feeling they hadn't spoken a word in her absence, and she wondered what had happened to cause such a huge chasm between them. Since Daniel looked as if he might bolt at any moment, she said, "You can borrow these if you'd like. I used them a few years ago to feed a family of orphaned rabbits."

Daniel held out his hand, accepting an eyedropper and a little bottle with a special nipple. Her fingers brushed his palm, and something went warm inside him. He glanced at her and couldn't look away.

She told him what to do, how to heat the milk, how much to feed the raccoon. He listened to every word, but he didn't answer. Not because he didn't want to, but because he couldn't. The kindness in her eyes had closed off his throat. It hurt, kindness. Tucking his hands into his pockets to hide their trembling, he quickly turned to go.

"Please," she called. "Take the sandwiches too."

Indecision slowed his steps. The next time she spoke, her voice was coming from the vicinity of her mailbox. "You're that little animal's only hope, and you're in for a long night. *He's* going to need all the nourishment and strength you can give him. In order to do that, you need nourishment and strength too. There's no shame in accepting help if it enables you to do life's most important work."

He accepted the plastic bag filled with enough sandwiches to feed him for another day, then once again started back the way he'd come.

"Danny. Daniel, wait!"

He stopped at the sound of his father's voice.

"Are you warm enough? Where are you staying? Are you really all right?"

Daniel swung around. "What difference does it make? I'm not going back to Columbus. You can't make me."

Cale wanted to argue, but he and Danny had done enough of that the first year after Ellie died to last a lifetime. The silence that had arisen between them these past six months had been even more difficult to bear. "I'd like to see where you're living, that's all. Maybe you could show me the raccoon."

For a second, Cale thought Danny was going to smile. He didn't know how badly he yearned to witness that small softening until the moment passed and the smile never came.

"I have to get back," the boy said. Without another word, he disappeared the same way he'd come.

Cale stared at the dark woods for a long time. Behind him, the garden was utterly silent. It was too early in the year for crickets, too late in the day for the buzzing of bees. "Well," he said, running a hand through his hair. "At least we're speaking again."

Miranda's low chuckle set off a round of squawking and chirping in the branches of the sourwood tree.

"That wasn't supposed to be funny," Cale said.

"I see," she answered, still smiling.

He studied her face for an extra heartbeat, his gaze lighting on the merriment in her golden-brown eyes. He was all set to return her grin, but his gaze caught on her mouth, and he couldn't seem to move. Her lips were pink and full and kissable. No. Yes. He tried to banish the thought. Still, something stirred inside him, something he hadn't felt in a long time, something he didn't want to feel now.

He swallowed, straightened, and forced himself to turn away. With a bag he hoped didn't contain possum sandwiches held loosely in one hand, he said, "I'd better hit the road."

Miranda stepped aside so he could pass. "Where will you sleep tonight?"

The breeze lifted the hair that had fallen across his forehead. Perhaps it was relief that made him seem younger, boyish almost. Or perhaps it was coming from a place inside him.

"I have a bedroll and a change of clothes in the plane." He looked away, toward the mountain road.

"He'll be back," she said softly.

Cale nodded. "I suppose you're right. He'll probably show up the next time he runs out of milk for that raccoon he's feeding."

Miranda had a feeling the boy would be back for more than food for his sick animal.

"Get some sleep tonight," Miranda said when Cale reached the gate.

He nodded. "Yeah, you too."

Rather than tell him about the decoctions and tinctures, old-fashioned words for old-fashioned remedies, which she planned to prepare before she went to bed, she tucked the empty thermos beneath her arm and started for her cottage, calling over her shoulder, "I will. Good night, Cale."

She strolled up her porch steps and walked inside. The dream-catcher hanging on the glass in the door swung back and forth. Stopping it with one finger, she traced its intricate pattern. And she thought about Verdie Cook, the woman who'd given it to her. In the days before modern medicine had made its way to the mountain, it had been Verdie Cook—Aunt Verdie to everyone in the area—who folks sent for when they were sick or about to give birth.

"Folks believe I have special healing powers," Aunt Verdie used to declare, a corncob pipe clenched tight between her teeth, a plump, work-roughened hand on each ample hip. "What I have is experience. Shoot, girl, anybody can do what I do. The brush of a finger takes away a tear, and a hug eases loneliness a piece at a time. But a smile is the most pow'rful healing tool there is, because a smile can reach deep inside a person, healing two hearts at once."

Lost in thought, Miranda strolled into the kitchen. She placed dark glass jars, a large wooden spoon, and an eyedropper on the stove near the pot containing the valerian root she'd simmered before Cale had arrived. She enjoyed this time of night, when the only sounds were the clank of a spoon, the swish of a towel, the rattle of lids on glass. Preparing herbs and natural remedies was as soothing as growing them. Aunt Verdie used to tell her that too. When Aunt Verdie's hands had grown stiff and arthritic, Miranda had helped tighten the lids on the jars. Beneath Verdie's watchful eye, Miranda had learned how to plant her herbs and tend her gardens and prepare her decoctions and tinctures. It had been a healing experience, an affirmation that life goes on. In those early months, it had given her a reason to live, but it had taken her a long time to learn how to smile.

She couldn't count the times Aunt Verdie had said, "Smile, girl. I'm not sayin' it's easy. I know you don't feel like it. Do it anyway. Every time you think of it. One of these days you'll find yerself smilin' and meanin' it."

Miranda closed her eyes at the memory. Aunt Verdie,

with her eighth-grade education, her wealth of knowledge concerning natural remedies, and her affinity for recognizing the strengths and needs in those around her, had been the wisest woman Miranda had ever known.

She thought about Cale sleeping in his airplane and his son sleeping in one of the abandoned cabins on the mountain. She didn't know what had brought them to Dawsons Hollow, but she hoped that before they left, they would both discover that they could smile again and mean it, as she had done.

Damn, the water was cold. Being careful to stay out of the center of the stream where the current was swift, Cale leaned over backward to rinse his hair, being careful to keep the bandage on his forehead dry. He straightened, sputtering. The ice-cold bath had accomplished everything he'd hoped it would accomplish. He was clean, and he wasn't thinking about sex.

He grimaced. At least he was clean.

He probably looked comical, picking up his feet as far as he could, trying not to splash more than was absolutely necessary. He didn't care how he looked. He was more concerned about getting out of that cold mountain stream.

Using a clean shirt as a towel, he dried himself off as soon as he reached the rocky bank. He pulled on briefs, a clean pair of jeans, and a dry, long-sleeved shirt. By the time he'd laced up his shoes, he was decidedly warmer. He hiked back to his plane, combing his hair with his fingers. Next, he made a number of passes over his face with his rechargeable razor.

His sleeping bag was a mess. No wonder. He'd put it through the wringer last night. Cale tried not to think about how much of the night he'd spent tossing and turning.

Shading his eyes with one hand, he peered up at the clouds. An uncomfortable night's sleep, followed by an ice-cold bath. He'd had better experiences. He glanced at his plane. And he'd had worse.

He'd checked out the damage to his Cessna as soon as

the sun had come up. One wheel was flat, one wing crinkled, a metal panel dented. The plane was a little broken up but fixable. He supposed the same could be said for him. He'd planned to fly in, find Danny, and fly the two of them home. It looked as if his son and his plane were both going to take a little convincing.

His mind wandered, and he pulled at his jeans, annoyed at the telltale snugness. Great. He'd gone a year and a half without giving sex much thought. Suddenly he couldn't seem to get it out of his mind. That wasn't quite true. His mind wasn't the problem.

He'd always had a strong sex drive, but he'd always been able to control it. When he'd needed release these past eighteen months, he'd dealt with it. He'd wanted Ellie, wanted to touch her red hair and look into her green eyes and cover her full, lush breasts with his hands. His remedy had been simple, private, and natural, and had usually taken place in the middle of the night, when he'd awakened after dreaming of her.

It wasn't Ellie he'd dreamed of last night. Last night he hadn't wanted a simple, swift remedy.

He'd spent a good share of the night telling himself he had nothing to feel guilty about. Ellie was gone. He was alive.

He'd spent another part of the night reminding himself of the reason he was on the hard ground in a cramped sleeping bag in northeastern Georgia. He was there because Danny needed him.

Cale didn't need entanglements. He told himself he didn't need sex either.

It wasn't as if Miranda Sinclair had come on to him. She'd been kind to him, nothing more. And she'd been kind to Danny. She was a nurse practitioner, for chrissake. Being kind went with the territory. It was part of her job.

His job was to reach Danny. In the process, he had to find a way to prove that they could still be a family even though Ellie was gone. Because whether Danny admitted it or not, they needed each other more now than they ever had.

No wonder he was tired this morning. When he hadn't been dreaming about sex and denying it, Cale had thought about his son. When he'd first discovered that Danny had run away, Cale had panicked. Once he'd calmed down and was able to think rationally, he'd had a feeling the boy had set off for Dawsons Hollow. After all, Ellie had spoken of these mountains moments before she'd died, and Danny was bound to be curious. His son was extremely bright. A lot of people called him gifted, although Danny hated the term. Cale had a feeling there was more to his son's decision to come here than a need to visit his mother's favorite place. Danny wanted answers. His son may not have formed a solid plan yet, but subliminally, he'd come to find the answers he needed.

He'd come to Dawsons Hollow to find his real father.

The thought turned Cale's stomach. He believed in honesty. And he honestly hoped the man had one tooth, a third-grade education, and big ears. It was a pleasant thought but not very probable, because Ellie wouldn't have taken a man like that into her bed. She'd been young. And young people were known to do foolish things. Still, she would have loved the man, whoever he was. Although he obviously hadn't turned out to be the man for her, he wouldn't have been stupid. Because Eleanora Stanoway had loved to laugh and talk and argue and discuss. Lord, what an understatement. And Cale just couldn't imagine her falling in love with someone who wasn't interested in politics and world peace and saving the rain forest.

Danny had always been interested in those things too. At fourteen, Danny thought he was grown-up. Cale knew how young fourteen was. If Danny wanted to find the man who'd sired him, Cale would help him. He would be there for his son, just as he'd always tried to be.

Danny had been two when Cale had met Ellie, three when he'd adopted him. The few times Cale had asked about Danny's biological father, Ellie had placed her hand on

Cale's cheek and smiled, saying that he was the only father who mattered. At the time, it had felt true. He'd wanted it to be true. Now Cale wished he had delved a little deeper. As it was, all he knew of the man who had fathered Danny was that he'd once lived on this mountain.

It wasn't much to go on, but at least searching for answers should keep his hands busy and his mind occupied with things other than a brown-haired woman who had kind eyes and a kissable mouth.

Stashing his gear in the cockpit, Cale set off for town.

His first stop was the diner. Once his stomach was full, he went across the street to the gas station, where he bought a map he hoped would indicate that an airstrip was nearby. Next, he crossed the street in front of Pratt's Grocery Store.

Two old men with stooped shoulders, bowed legs, and shaggy gray whiskers that gave all beards a bad name clammed up the second he set foot inside the store. The man behind the counter was in his early thirties and clean-shaven. He had jet-black hair and an assessing stare and was waiting on a woman who seemed to be hanging on his every word.

Cale ignored them, strolling down the first narrow aisle, scanning some of the dusty items on the shelves. Five minutes later he placed a container of orange juice he'd taken out of a glass-fronted cooler with a noisy motor, a loaf of bread, a jar of peanut butter, a package of cookies that would probably taste like cardboard, and a container of plastic knives, forks, and spoons on the counter.

The man behind the cash register studied the items and then Cale. "Mornin'."

Cale could feel several pairs of eyes on him, but he held the man's gaze and returned the greeting. The other man reached for the loaf of bread. "Looks like camping food."

Cale nodded.

"I'm J. R. Pratt. I operate this grocery store and two others here in Georgia. You probably noticed the big white house up on the hill there. Biggest house in the county. Three stories high. A person can see every inch of Dawsons Hollow from there. Got a Jacuzzi bathtub and a skylight right over the bed, not to mention a shiny old Cadillac that had belonged to my father, parked in the garage."

A braggart. Great.

"I flew in," Cale said, taking his wallet from his back pocket. "I'm afraid I haven't done much sight-seeing."

The two bearded men inched closer. The one on the right said, "You're the fella who crash-landed a coupla nights ago."

"I didn't crash. Exactly," Cale said.

J. R. Pratt made a point of eyeing the bandage on Cale's forehead. "Looks like you didn't *exactly* escape without a scratch either. Elmer and Angus here said they saw a stranger going into the clinic yesterday. Miranda fix you up good, did she?"

The refrigerator motor clanked off, leaving the room strangely, almost unnaturally quiet. Cale touched the bandage and nodded once. For some reason, the hair on the back of his neck prickled. He glanced around just as a heavyset woman with straight gray hair shuffled toward the front of the store. She pushed her way past the two old men and nudged the younger man out of her way behind the counter.

"I'm Ruthie Pratt. Folks up here call me the widow Pratt. No matter what my boy here tells you, I own this store."

Basically, Cale didn't give a damn who owned it. Since it seemed very important to the widow Pratt, he refrained from comment.

"You got family in these parts? Friends?" she asked, as if it was any of her business.

The two bearded men on Cale's right were still watching him openly, while the woman who'd already paid for her groceries was feigning an interest in last week's newspaper on a stand near the door.

"You might say that," Cale answered.

"Where you stayin'?" the widow Pratt asked.

Cale would have liked to be able to dismiss the question with a quick shrug and an unaffected glance at the woman's face. But Ruthie Pratt's wasn't the kind of face that allowed for easy dismissals or quick glances. She watched him closely through eyes so light, they looked a little spooky. She'd probably been pretty once, before she'd let herself go. He wondered if she'd ever been nice.

"I'm camping out by my plane until I can make other arrangements. Any of you know of a place I could rent for a week or so?"

Ruthie shook her head. One by one, the others followed her lead.

So, Cale thought, that was how it was going to be. It seemed unlikely that people who didn't welcome strangers would welcome questions about a man who might have lived here some fifteen years ago.

"You're campin', you say?" Elmer asked. "Be mighty careful. Yesterday me'n Angus seen a monster-sized panther."

The other man held up a bandaged finger as if it had some significance. "Didn't use to believe in haint tales and stories of babies bein' drug right outta their mama's arms or stolen out of the bathwater, never to be seen again. Now that me'n Elmer seen him with our own eyes, we believe. Ain't that right, Elmer?"

Elmer nodded reverently. "Been known to come after grown men and women too."

Cale looked from one whiskered man to the other. And people claimed teenagers were strange, with their tattoos, baggy clothes, and irreverent stares. At least kids back in Columbus didn't carry buzzards' feathers around in their pockets or believe in monsters that ate babies and lived in their neighborhoods.

A screech, high-pitched and ear-piercing, split the air.

"Help!"

"Quick, Elmer. Sounds like that panther's got somebody."

"Help. It's my Benjie. Somebody help me, please!"

Cale ran outside just as the scream came again. A woman was running toward him down the middle of the street, half carrying, half dragging a young boy who was screaming and writhing in pain.

"Help me!" the woman cried. "My boy got into poison. Got it in his eyes."

Cale raced to the woman. He glanced at the boy's face, swung him into his arms, and sprinted toward the clinic. The boy tore at his eyes, writhing and kicking and crying the entire time it took Cale to shoulder through the door Ruby held open.

"It's Celia Winter's boy," Ruby shouted. "What happened?"

Cale shook his head. "The mother said he got into some kind of poison."

The mother arrived, and Miranda said, "What did he get into, Celia?"

The woman was sobbing. "A homemade potion. He and Georgie mixed gasoline and lighter fluid and dish soap and dirt and I don't know what else. Said they were makin' a magic potion, in case the panther came."

Good God, Cale thought. And he got it in his eyes?

"Hurry. Lay him on the counter," Miranda commanded.

It required both Cale and Ruby to hold the boy down. Everywhere, people were yelling and crying. In the midst of it all, Miranda's movements were calm, brisk, and efficient. She turned on the faucet, crooning to the boy in a soft voice. At first he screamed louder, but the cool water must have been soothing, because he relaxed. Soothing or not, Cale doubted that the child would ever see again.

The mother was still crying, and Ruby motioned for Cale to get her out of there. Cale had a sudden flashback of another emergency room, of doctors moving briskly and barking orders. Helpless and horrified, he'd allowed an orderly to lead him into a waiting room, where he sank to his knees, numb and hollow. Looking into the young mother's eyes, he understood her fear and the way she moved automatically as he guided her from the room.

Angus and Elmer were in the waiting area, along with the injured boy's younger brother, the woman who had been hanging on J. D. Pratt's every word back in the grocery store, and a few others Cale had never seen before. They swarmed around the distraught mother, everyone talking at once.

"Donchoo worry . . ."

"Lucky for you Miranda was here . . ."

"Did you see how Benjie calmed down soon as she laid her hands on him?"

"A few seconds later mighta been too late."

"Your Benjie'll be as good as new, just you wait and see."

Cale stood by himself near the window. He understood how badly these people wanted to believe everything would be all right. But he'd seen the burns around that boy's eyes. He'd smelled the stench of gasoline and other chemicals on his skin and on his clothes. Cale felt for the boy's family, but he didn't see how that child would come out of this with his sight intact.

Since it wasn't his place to dash their hopes no matter how false they were, he nodded at the mother and left the clinic. He went across the street to the pay phone attached to the front of the grocery store, took his calling card out of his wallet, and dialed his friend's number back in Columbus. After leaving a message on Sam Kennedy's answering machine, he strode to a picnic table in front of the Tastee Treat window on the side of the diner and unfolded the map he'd bought earlier, spreading it out on the rough surface.

The adrenaline rush had left him clearheaded, his finger going to a landing strip twenty miles away. He studied the map carefully, memorizing the lay of the land. The northern part of Georgia was riddled with towns, rivers, and mountains with unusual names. There were places called Chickamauga, Hiawassee and Chattahoochee, Toccoa Falls, Tallulah Gorge and Currahee Mountain. He paused at a squiggly blue line labeled Panther Creek, wondering if it had anything to do with the legend of the baby-snatching panther old Elmer thought he saw. Cale put the map to memory, picturing the winding climb of Hawksbill Road, the curve and curl of Warwoman Road, and the juts and angles of Old Ridge Road.

No one talked to him, but everyone watched him. The

man behind the Tastee Treat window didn't even try to disguise his scrutiny behind the pretense of keeping busy. Neither did the man who ran the gas station. Cale ignored the censure.

He noticed activity in and out of the clinic from time to time. One by one, the onlookers left. So far, there had been no sign of the mother, but the injured boy's younger brother skipped past with an older woman. Ah, the innocence and naïveté of youth, Cale thought, listening to the sound of the child's chatter. There would undoubtedly be tears when reality set in.

An hour after the incident, Cale had refolded the map, retrieved the groceries he'd left at Pratt's store, bought himself a Coke, and had done everything he'd come into town to do. He'd half expected to see an ambulance pull up to the clinic. Nothing could have prepared him for the sight of little Benjie Winters leaving the building, his hand in his mother's.

How? What?

The child held a wet cloth over part of his right eye. The other eye was covered by a big white bandage. The mother rushed to Cale the second she saw him. Pumping his hand, she thanked him profusely. Cale didn't know what to say. He glanced at the boy, amazed and shaken. "Shouldn't he be in a hospital?" he finally asked.

Celia Winters was a large-boned woman with short, straight dishwater-blond hair. Her earlier tears had left tracks on her cheeks, but at the moment her heart was full of gratitude and her smile transcended her plainness. "Praise the Lord," she said. "Miranda healed my boy, she did. Benjie here has to keep quiet for a few days, but he's gonna be as good as new. That woman is amazing. Me and Charlie don't have much, but we woulda given her anything. Know what she told me?"

Cale shook his head slowly.

"She said the best way to repay her would be to make sure the gasoline and lighter fluid are locked up tight from now on. Praise the Lord, I say. And praise Miranda Sinclair."

Everything inside Cale went perfectly still. His thoughts, his heart, his breathing. The events of the past two days were staggering. But this . . .

The implications were unfathomable. Celia Winters had called Miranda a healer.

Healers, haint tales, buzzards' feathers, white willow bark tea. What the hell had he stumbled into?

Superstition. That's all it was. What else could it be?

Gradually, he became aware that he was crushing the loaf of bread in the bag beneath his arm. Easing the pressure, he touched the bruise on his chest with his free hand. A bruise where he'd been certain broken ribs had been.

A fleeting memory hovered like a balloon just out of his reach. *He's asleep, Miranda. And it's late. Why not just heal him?*

Heal him. Heal him. Heal him.

He didn't remember crossing the street or climbing the steps or striding into the clinic. He paused inside the door, his breathing ragged, his eyes straining to see in the dim interior. He turned toward a sound—and came face-to-face with Ruby McCoy.

"Where's Miranda?"

Ruby glanced at a door on her right and then returned her gaze to him. "She's resting."

"What's going on? What's wrong with her?"

Ruby's eyes narrowed and her lips thinned. "Nothing's going on. And nothing's wrong with her. It always takes a lot out of her, that's all."

"What takes a lot out of her?"

He was halfway to the door when Ruby stepped in front of him, blocking his path. "What are you doing?" she asked.

"I have to see her."

Ruby didn't budge. "I told you she's resting. I don't want her disturbed."

Ruby McCoy was on the tall side, but she was thin. Cale knew he was capable of getting past her. She knew it too. But she didn't back down.

Before either of them moved, the door opened and

Miranda stepped into the room. She stood in a wan shaft of sunlight, the yellow rays picking up streaks of gold in her light brown hair. She glanced from one to the other, then calmly said, "You wanted to see me, Cale?"

Good God, Cale thought. What had happened to her? Her clothes were wrinkled, her face looked tired, pale, and drawn, as if she'd overexerted herself and needed to rest. She was beautiful.

Cale's heart jumped as if somebody had flipped a switch. His lungs heaved, his thoughts scrambled. He was aware that Miranda was looking at him, just as he was aware that she turned to Ruby and quietly said, "You can go now."

Ruby stiffened and started to protest. Miranda silenced her with a mild shake of her head. Eyeing the two of them, the older woman backed from the room.

When the door clicked shut, Miranda raised her eyes to Cale's. "I believe I heard you tell Ruby there's something you want to ask me."

The blood drained out of Cale's face. He planted his feet, squared his shoulders. "Who are you?" he asked, his voice little more than a rasp in the quiet room. "What are you?"

CHAPTER FOUR

Miranda regarded Cale in silence. He was rugged and serious, the kind of man who would have set the hearts of the wealthy Southern belles she'd grown up with aflutter. At the moment, his scowl suited his face. His dark hair was windblown; his eyes were hooded. She suspected that he would be a formidable opponent, a trustworthy friend. Either way, he was accustomed to getting what he wanted. Right now he wanted answers. He was grappling with the convoluted twists and sharp turns his life had taken. He didn't appear to be a man who took kindly to change, and he wasn't a man who would be easy to convince.

She'd learned to live with people's curiosity a long time ago. It had been years since being watched by somebody she couldn't see had sent her, heart racing, into her cottage, where she could bolt the door and pull the shades. If that type of inquisitiveness no longer intimidated her, she wasn't about to let Caleb Wilder do it.

She was still feeling a little light-headed and had to concentrate to keep her eyes focused and open. "Who am I?" she asked as she walked farther into the room. "I thought we covered that. I'm Miranda Sinclair."

She could tell by his expression that he was neither amused nor satisfied with her answer. He didn't get angry exactly, but he watched her even more closely. Other than the rise and fall of his chest, the only things that moved were his eyes, his gaze following her hand as she pointed to a wall where her diploma hung.

"What am I?" She spread her arms wide, encompassing the entire clinic. "*I'm* a certified nurse practitioner. Tell me, what do *you* do for a living, Mr. Wilder?"

The *mister* threw Cale for a second. He recovered, but he was more cautious with the wording of his next statement. "I teach welding and woodworking and auto mechanics to high school students in Columbus."

She nodded in a way that made Cale wonder where the conversation was headed. "And are you good at what you do?"

"I like to think I am," he said quietly.

"Have you ever reached a student other teachers labeled a lost cause?"

He nodded very, very slowly, still waiting for her to make her point.

She folded her arms and shifted her weight to one foot. "Have you ever had a parent or fellow teacher question your methods?"

Her point hit its mark. Cale got the message loud and clear. She didn't appreciate having *him* question *her* methods any more than he appreciated others questioning his. She was smart; he'd give her that. But she still hadn't answered his question.

He took his time crossing the room and made a show of studying the framed documents on the wall. It was just as she'd said. She'd obtained a master's degree in nursing from the University of Georgia in Athens and was licensed in this state.

Turning slightly so that he could look at her, he said, "Celia Winters claims you healed her son."

She held his gaze. "Would you have preferred her to say I *treated* Benjie?"

"I would prefer you to answer the question."

"And what question is that?"

Cale's breathing deepened and his temper started to flare. "I saw the chemical burns around the boy's eyes. I heard his cries. How could he simply walk out of here an hour later with injuries no more serious than scratches?"

He noticed the way she straightened her back and squared her shoulders. Most people would have given in to anger and uttered something scathing. Apparently, Miranda Sinclair wasn't like most people. She strode to a large cupboard, unlocked it, and took out several glass jars. Gesturing to the sink, she said, "You saw me flush Benjie's eyes with plenty of pure, cool, cleansing water. Besides air, it's life's most important and abundant commodity. Luckily, the human eye closes in a reflex action. That's what really saved Benjie's sight. That is what you're asking, isn't it? Why he still has his vision?"

"That's it?" he asked. "That's what you want me to believe? That you treated his chemical burns with water?"

She held out three small jars. Placing the first in his outstretched hand, she said, "This is aloe. It's most women's first natural healing agent. The second jar contains eyebright. It's primarily used as an eyewash. The third contains vitamin E capsules. I generally poke a hole in one, squeeze the liquid onto my finger, and apply to a cut, rash, scrape, or burn. I applied it to your injuries a few nights ago."

"Does it heal cracked ribs too?"

She took the jars from his hand and moved to put them back on the shelf. "No topical ointment can do that."

"Then you are what people say you are? You're a healer?"

She stopped in mid-stride and held perfectly still. "Define healer."

Cale was at a loss for words. How in the hell was he supposed to define healer? The only perception he had was from movies that portrayed them as sorcerers with silver eyes and two-inch-long fingernails or as witch doctors and shamans who painted their faces and danced around a fire, shaking gourds and chanting to the spirits.

She looked at him as if she understood his dilemma. "Did you ever believe in Santa Claus or the tooth fairy?"

"You're saying this is just a myth?"

She neither nodded nor shook her head. "What about God and angels and heaven, aliens, ghosts, and reincarnation?" When he failed to reply, she said, "I generally leave people to their own beliefs, whatever they might be."

"Then you're not going to give me a straight answer."

"You strike me as a man who has to make up his own mind. But I will tell you this. A very wise woman once taught me that all women are healers, Cale. I suppose that's the bottom line, the real answer to your question: What am I? I'm a woman."

She placed a key on the desk and strode to the door.

"Where are you going?" he asked.

Her gait was even, her head held high, her tone cool as she said, "I have a few house calls to make. I have to check on Benjie and change his dressing, because no matter what you think, his injuries *are* more serious than scratches. You're welcome to look around for eye of newt and bats' wings. Please lock up when you leave."

The door closed before Cale had formed a reply.

Alone in the room, he ran his fingers across the bandage on his forehead and on through his hair. So this was how his students felt when he put them in their places.

He went to the desk and took the key in his hand. The comment about eye of newt and bats' wings aside, Miranda trusted him. That much was clear. But she still hadn't answered his question.

What was she?

She'd said she was a woman. He shook his head at the desire that seemed to have taken up residence in his body. He was aware that she was a woman, dammit. Too aware.

Did that give him the right to storm in here and demand explanations to things that didn't concern him?

"Smart, Wilder," he said to himself. "Bite the hand that feeds you." Worse, it was the same hand that fed Danny.

He supposed he had two options. Forget about it. Or make it up to her. As he strolled around the interior of the clinic, one of Ellie's favorite sayings played through his mind.

When in doubt, do nothing.

Caleb Wilder had never been very good at doing nothing.

Miranda took one hand off the steering wheel and waved at the Anderson kids, who looked up as she passed. With the sun glinting off the hood of her Explorer one second, and shade dappling the road the next, visibility was poor, forcing her to drive slowly.

The breeze streaming in her open windows felt warm and smelled faintly of the wild lilacs that bloomed beside the road. She'd told Angie Patterson she would look in on her around four. She'd stayed at the Winters' longer than she'd planned. Now she was late. No matter how late she was running, she always tried to take the time to appreciate her surroundings. Normally, it wasn't this difficult, because normally, she didn't have a man's scowl permanently ingrained in her mind.

Something moved from the shade into the sun up ahead. She gripped the steering wheel, swerved, and slid to a stop in the loose gravel. Suddenly, she wasn't simply remembering the scowl on Caleb Wilder's face. She was staring at the real thing.

"Cale," she called through the open window. "I almost didn't see you." He took a deep breath, probably in relief, but he was squinting too, making it difficult to read his expression. "Where are you headed?" she asked.

For a moment she thought he might pursue his earlier line of questioning. She felt inordinately pleased when, instead, he shoved his hands into his pockets and said, "I want to try to find the cabin where Danny's been staying."

"On foot?"

"Do you have a better idea?"

Pushing a strand of hair out of her face, she said, "I have one more stop to make before heading over to Hawksbill Road. You can ride along if you'd like. Maybe we'll come across him between here and there."

He made no answer, no move to come closer.

"If you want a ride," she said, "it might help if you got in."

He looked at the road behind him, and then at the road ahead, and finally at her. "It could be dangerous for you to give a stranger a lift."

She strummed her fingers on the steering wheel and released a breath of pent-up air. He sounded like her mother or, worse, like Ruby. "I appreciate your concern, but you don't have to worry about me. I have extensive self-defense training. Unless you have a stun gun in your pocket, you would end up much more seriously injured than I, believe me."

He pulled his hands out of pockets that were too flat to contain anything larger than loose change. "Are you telling me you're capable of throwing me across the road?"

"That would be one of the nicer things I could do to you."

She wasn't sure he believed her, so she said, "Would you like a demonstration?"

His answer had a lot in common with a snort, but at least he walked the remaining distance to the passenger side, opened the door, and climbed inside. He didn't say anything when she put the four-wheel-drive vehicle in gear, but she noticed that he placed the key on the dash that she'd given him earlier, then slid his hand over the leather interior.

"It's a lot faster than the mule I used to ride." She slipped a Mozart disc into the CD player. "And a lot less dangerous than a broom."

Cale jerked his head around to stare at her. When she smiled, he said, "I can't believe you can joke about that. You're not one to hold a grudge, are you?"

She took her eyes off the road long enough to look at

him and shake her head. "Not anymore. Too much negative energy."

They met a pickup truck that had been new in the sixties. The driver was so old and stooped over, Cale could hardly see him behind the wheel.

"That's Moot Nelson," Miranda said. "He's not supposed to be driving. He's ninety-three."

"Not everyone on this mountain lives to be ninety-three."

Miranda's expression changed in the most subtle of ways. Her lips thinned slightly, her eyebrows lowering a fraction of an inch. Cale could have kicked himself for his lack of tact. Aw, hell. Since there was no way out of it now, he said, "I took a little walk through the cemetery earlier."

"I heard."

There was a bit of a Southern lilt in her voice, but as far as he could tell, no anger. He supposed he wasn't surprised that she'd heard about his little stroll through the cemetery west of town either. Gossip seemed to travel through Dawsons Hollow faster than the speed of light.

He hadn't been sure what he'd been looking for when he'd passed through the cemetery's wrought iron gate. It wasn't as if graveyards were his favorite places to spend his time. That hadn't stopped him from reading the names and dates carved into headstones. Most of the graves dated back a long time, but some were more recent. A forty-year-old woman had died last summer, a baby boy a few years before. He wondered how the people of Dawsons Hollow, people who believed Miranda had special healing powers, explained those deaths. Cale scrubbed a hand over his face, because really, it was no business of his.

They hit a bump in the road; she steered around another. "Nice vehicle," he said, meaning it.

"My parents gave me the Explorer three years ago for my thirtieth birthday."

"My parents gave me a twenty-dollar gift certificate to Wal-Mart."

Her laughter swirled over him, right past his defenses. It made him want to forget his misgivings and laugh in return.

He hadn't felt like laughing in a long time. It was unsettling. *She* was unsettling.

He'd spent a good part of the afternoon telling himself he appreciated everything Miranda Sinclair had done for him and for Danny. What he was feeling right now was much more elemental than gratitude. It was interest, very masculine, very strong. Completely unsettling.

"Cale?"

He turned his head.

"Your parents," she said in a manner that let him know she was repeating herself. "They sound practical. Do they live in Columbus too?"

"They used to, but they retired to Florida five years ago."

"They must miss Daniel."

Cale shrugged. "Ellie and Danny were a package deal. I've never been certain who I loved first. God, you should have seen the two of them together. I adopted him when I married her. My parents never fully accepted him as mine."

"Parents can be difficult," she said.

He looked at her and was struck by how easy she was on the eyes. She'd secured her hair in some sort of intricate knot on top of her head. Several strands had escaped, only to blow wild in the breeze streaming through her open window. He'd never been good at judging a person's age, but he'd assumed she was somewhere in her late twenties. "If your thirtieth birthday was three years ago, you must be thirty-three." He almost groaned out loud. "Another surefire way to offend a woman. Notice how quick I was with the math. If I shut up now, you might not be sorry you didn't run me down."

She glanced in the rearview mirror, navigated a curve, and bounced through a rut in the road. "I'm not sorry, Cale."

She'd done it to him again. Struck him speechless with her straightforwardness and her honesty. He peered out the window, amazed at how beautiful the landscape was. It reminded him of camping trips he and his brother used to take with their parents when they'd been kids. It had been a long time since he'd been in wilderness like this. Looking at it now, he realized he'd missed more than the sights of nature. He'd missed the silences too, the stillness of a meadow covered with wildflowers, the quiet flutter of a butterfly's wings, the hush of a lake on a starry night. It made him ache. The woman sitting beside him made him yearn.

The grief counselor he'd seen with Danny would have been fascinated with his reemergence into the world of the living. Cale had felt safer feeling numb. "Are you and your parents close?" he asked, searching for something to fill the silence.

She seemed to be pondering the question. Or perhaps she was contemplating her answer. "In some ways, we're very close. Besides my mother and father, I have an older brother and a younger sister. They all love me, but they don't understand me. So you're not alone. For years my parents tried to convince me to return to Atlanta. They've never appreciated my decision to practice medicine up here when I could be doing it in the city, if I have to do it at all. I can hear the distaste in my mother's voice every Sunday when she calls. She wants to keep me safely under her control. That isn't where I want to be. Since my parents couldn't change my mind, they decided that at least they could rest assured that I wouldn't get stranded in a blinding snowstorm or stuck in knee-deep mud. Thus the four-wheel-drive vehicle."

Cale stared out the windshield. He'd heard every word she'd said, but he'd done a double take at her reference to the fact that he didn't understand her. How did she do that? She was right though. He didn't understand her, but he understood a parent's desire to keep a child, no matter how old, out of harm's way.

"I wish I could come up with a way to keep Danny safe. I'd like to hog-tie him and drag him home. Unfortunately, unless I kept him locked in his room, I'm afraid he'd only run away again."

"You and your son don't get along."

Cale noticed it wasn't a question. He shook his head,

answering anyway. "We used to. That little kid used to light up when I walked through the door. And he followed me around like a shadow. He never liked to get his hands dirty, but he'd sit up on the workbench while I changed the oil in the car or puttered around with my saws and drills and hammers. I'd work, and he'd tell me how many light-years away a star was, or how the Roman Empire fell, or how mountains formed. God, I loved listening to him. One day he stopped talking."

"Do you know why?"

Cale answered quietly. "He's mad at me."

"Does he have a good reason?"

"His mother died, and I couldn't stop it."

"How long has Ellie been gone?"

It always amazed him, what hearing something as simple as Ellie's name did to him. "A year and a half."

The words sounded empty to Cale. Eighteen months, one week, and two days didn't sound any better. Time. That's all it was. Stretches of time measured in days, weeks, months, years.

Other than Mozart's forty-first symphony playing in the background, all was quiet inside the Explorer. They'd turned a corner, and Cale noticed that Miranda no longer squinted into the sun. Rays of sunlight streamed in her side window, delineating the smooth lines and graceful curves of her profile. Her nose was narrow, her cheekbones prominent, her skin soft-looking and smooth. It was unusual to come across a woman who didn't wear makeup in this day and age. It was unusual to come across a woman who didn't utter trite condolences too.

"You're not like other women."

The vehicle slowed to a crawl. Looking neither right nor left, she said, "I'm not a freak, Cale."

There was a current in her voice like a taut rope being strummed with one finger. He'd hurt her. The fact that she'd misinterpreted his meaning didn't matter. He'd hurt her. And he was sorry.

"I know that, Miranda. No matter what else I don't understand, I know you're not some kind of freak. I also know you're beautiful.''

Her eyes widened, her surprise giving way to a slow smile. Cale's gaze caught on her mouth, and his breath caught in his throat.

She glanced back at the road, but Cale shifted closer. Closer, until he could see the shadow her lashes cast on her cheek. Closer, until he could smell her shampoo, the scent of her skin.

They were traveling at a snail's pace now, and he wanted her to stop. He wanted to kiss her. He wanted . . .

''Miranda?''

She slammed on the brakes, pitching them both forward in their seats. Cale turned his head in time to see a large black animal dart into a stand of pine trees.

At first Cale thought it might have been the panther. The idea conjured up an image of a fierce creature that was capable of tearing a grown man limb from limb. Acid churned in his stomach, because Danny was out there in that wilderness.

''What was that?''

''It was a dog,'' she answered, her voice as raspy as his. ''A big one.''

Their gazes collided, shied away, only to become trained on something in the distance. Miranda was the first to find her voice. ''That was a close one.''

What? Cale wondered. The near miss or the near kiss?

They both glanced at the road, at each other, then back at the road again. ''Well,'' she said.

''Yeah,'' he said a moment later.

She took her foot off the brake, setting the vehicle in motion once again. Resting his arm along the open window, he said, ''For a second there, when you first slammed on the brakes, I thought you were going to demonstrate a few of those self-defense tactics you mentioned. I've gotta tell you. My life passed before my eyes.''

''You don't say.''

''I'm not kidding. Would you have poked my eyes out, Miranda?''

"I guess that's for me to know and for y'all to find out."

Y'all? Something soft and warm nudged him from inside. She didn't look at him, but she smiled, and it occurred to him that she was flirting with him. He was thirty-six years old. Suddenly, he felt seventeen. He wondered how long it had been since a man had kissed her. Staring out the window, he spent far more time than was prudent imagining the taste, texture, and feel of doing just that. Of doing a hell of a lot more than that.

They drove on in silence until they came to a small house where the little boys Cale had seen in the clinic the previous day were swinging on a gate. "Jeremiah," Miranda called, cutting the engine. "Didn't anybody ever tell you it's bad luck to run around with one shoe on and the other one off?"

The boy nodded solemnly, then stood back to wait for Miranda to get her bag. "The baby's frettin', Mama's feeling poorly, and Daddy's fit to be tied. Me'n Josh comed out here to wait for you."

She closed her door and looked over her shoulder at Cale. "Are you coming in?"

He shifted in his seat, stretched his legs out in front of him, and shifted again. "I think I'll just wait out here." And he let his body return to normal and his blood return to his head, where it belonged.

"Suit yourself." With a wink befitting a woman who said "y'all," Miranda Sinclair followed the little boys into the small house.

Cale closed his gaping mouth. He didn't know if it was possible that she had healing powers. He didn't know if it was possible that *anybody* had healing powers. But she definitely had feminine wiles. And he'd bet his airplane that she knew what she'd done to him.

He counted to ten. He strummed his fingers on his thighs. He hummed the first five rounds of "One Hundred Bottles of Beer on the Wall."

His mind wandered, and he looked toward the hills where the mountain road cut a path through the trees. Danny was up there where mountain folklore and legends still flourished, and where wild dogs and God only knew what other animals roamed. Cale closed his eyes and sent up a silent plea for Danny's safety.

Daniel stood on the rotting back stoop for a moment, peering out at the mountain and the sky. He took a deep breath and grinned. His hands smelled of raccoon, his clothes of warm milk and something a lot more offensive than that. He needed a bath. Yesterday, he'd discovered the perfect place to take one.

With the shirt and jeans he'd washed in the stream tucked under one arm, he set off through the wilderness he was learning by heart. He glanced over his shoulder at the cabin. It was only four walls and a leaky roof. There was no electricity, and the only running water was the water he ran to get out of the creek. It was all he needed. Here he didn't have to deal with yesterday, with doubts or regrets. He didn't have to deal with tomorrow either, with worries or logic.

He was free here. Every day felt like an adventure.

Without conscious thought, he took a detour off the beaten path, startling a squirrel who scolded him from a branch high in a tree. "Sorry," he whispered, placing the clean clothes in the grass and getting a foothold in the wall of rocks that jutted nearly straight up.

By the time he reached the top, he was winded and even more filthy. But the view awaiting him was worth it. He shaded his eyes, squinting into the sun that was starting its slow decline in the west. An eagle soared directly in front of the sun.

Daniel huddled behind a rock, afraid to close his eyes in case he might lose sight of the beautiful majestic creature. It was a golden eagle, one of the few kinds that bred in the United States. His mother had told him that years ago.

His mother had been fascinated with so many things, but the eagle had always been her favorite bird. She'd kept an envelope containing an eagle's feathers in her top dresser drawer. Every once in a while she'd get them out and just hold them in her hand. Once he'd asked her why she'd kept them, and she'd said, "To remember."

At the time, he'd been content with her answer. Now he wished he'd asked a hundred more questions. Now he might never have his answers.

Spying a feather nearby, Daniel picked it up and smoothed it between his fingers. Far above, the eagle circled, gliding and hovering on air currents in a way that men had been dreaming of doing since the dawning of time.

Without warning, the eagle changed direction. Head pointed, wings back, he dove toward the earth. Daniel heard a screech of terror and then of pain. And then there was only silence. He turned away at the sight of the rabbit, now limp and bloody, in the eagle's talons.

Scientists called it the food chain. Daniel thought it was much more complex than that. Life and death. Beauty and pain. Happiness and sorrow. All those things were enmeshed in the same design, the threads woven so tightly, it was impossible to draw out only one without touching, sometimes dislodging, the others.

Thankful his raccoon was safe back in the cabin, he climbed down the rocky wall and headed for the pool that had formed where the stream took a sharp turn. Ten minutes later he was submerged to his waist. He splashed cool water on his face with one hand, being careful to hold the soap in the other. He'd learned the hard way that not all soap floats. It had taken five minutes and several dives to find this particular bar after making that discovery.

He washed his hair with hand soap and bathed in record time. He'd almost finished, when he was struck by how quiet the evening had become. The breeze had died down. Even the birds had stopped chirping.

He lowered his arm and peered into the bushes and wild ferns growing nearby. He had the strangest feeling he was being watched.

The evening was utterly quiet. Too quiet. He swallowed hard and glanced uneasily over his shoulder, his misgivings increasing by the second. The other side of the stream looked as still as this one. His teeth chattered, reminding him that he couldn't stay in the cold water forever.

He emerged shivering and hurriedly pulled on his clothes. He was fastening his jeans, when a sound, low and menacing, carried through the thick foliage.

He froze, his hand on the zipper. What sort of animal made that sound? So deep. So deadly.

He didn't know what to do. Should he climb a tree? Or run like hell?

God, he was so tired of being afraid. When he was little he'd been terrified of storms. To this day they made him nervous. For as long as he could remember, he'd been afraid of kids who threatened to beat him up because he was smart. He'd had it with fear—of other kids, of the dark, of things that went bump in the night. And of death.

A sense of calm settled over him. He had a pocket knife. And he had cunning and intelligence. He was young and agile, and if he had to be, fast. Steadier now, he slid his arms into his shirtsleeves and his feet into his shoes.

The growl came again. This time it was followed by a faint feminine voice. "Stay away. Get back, ya hear?"

Daniel ducked into the underbrush, his feet automatically moving in the direction the voice had come from. Twigs and leaves caught on his open shirt, scratching his naked torso. He broke into a clearing on a run. Twenty-five feet away, a large black dog had a girl cornered, her back literally flattened against an outcropping of rock. The animal inched closer, closer, teeth bared, ears back.

"Easy," Daniel whispered.

The dog's growl grew more menacing, his movements more aggressive and calculated. The girl screamed. For a second, Daniel feared the dog would lunge at her.

"It's okay," he crooned to the dog, his eyes never leaving the animal. "I'm not going to hurt you. Of course, you probably already know that. If anybody's going to do any hurting, it's going to be you. I'll bet you're just hungry, aren't you? I sure wish I had one of Miranda's sandwiches with me."

The dog eyed Daniel. His teeth were still bared, but his growl was quieter, less threatening.

"That's it," Daniel said. "You're fierce and strong. It would be beneath you to attack such a scrawny, helpless little old girl. And if you kill me, there won't be anybody to feed my raccoon. So you might as well leave us both in one piece. We wouldn't taste good anyway. You've already figured that out, haven't you?"

The dog's eyes were pink around the edges. It matched the inside of his mouth, bared each time he growled. He stared into Daniel's eyes for what seemed like forever. "That's it," Daniel said. "There's nothing undignified about choosing to walk away from an unfair fight. In fact, I've always thought it was a sure sign of intelligence. Maybe you should go steal some other dog's food. What do you think?"

The dog took a long look at Daniel. Without so much as a backward glance at the girl, he raised his head, as huffy and majestic as a spoiled king, and darted into the underbrush without making a sound.

Daniel's knees knocked, his chest heaved. Gulping in huge breaths of air, he ran to the girl. Her lips were quivering, her face was pale. She raised a shaking hand to her throat and took a quavering breath.

"How'd you do that?" she whispered. "And who're you calling scrawny?"

CHAPTER FIVE

Daniel straightened so fast, he saw stars.

The girl's eyes flashed too, but with indignation, not surprise. "I said, who are you calling scrawny?"

"I ..." He'd thought the girl was doomed. Dead. He'd thought they both were.

"I'll have you know I'm thin, fine-boned, maybe even skinny, but I'm not scrawny."

"I ... er, that is, I didn't mean anything by it," he stuttered. "I just said whatever I could think of to keep that dog calm."

"Oh. Well. Next time, do it without insulting me. Besides, y'all shouldn't talk. I haven't seen knees as knobby as yours in a coon's age."

The fog in Daniel's head disappeared like vapor. His blue jeans completely covered his knees. There was only one way she could have known whether his knees were knobby or not. He stuck his hands on his hips and glared at the girl. "You were spying on me."

"What if I was?"

He turned in the direction the dog had gone and placed two fingers to his mouth.

"What are you doing?"

"I think I'll call back that hungry dog."

"Please," she said, rushing toward him. "I won't peek again. And really, I didn't see much anyways."

"What's that supposed to mean?"

She shook her head and touched him softly, tentatively. "Everything's coming out wrong. I was a long ways away, and I really didn't see all that much. Even if I had, I have six brothers, so it wouldn't have been anything I haven't seen before. You're new around here, aren't you?"

Daniel nodded, still ticked. He didn't care if she did have six brothers and had seen all of them naked at some time or other. That didn't make it all right to see him, especially when the water had been close to freezing, and every guy knew what cold water did to a guy's, er, anatomy. She had no business spying on him.

"What are y'all doin' here?" she asked while he was still seething.

He studied her longer than was considered polite, and then he studied her a little more. Her hair was wavy, shoulder length, and nearly black. It was held away from her face with a pale yellow ribbon. Her eyes were light blue and were surrounded by thick, spiky black lashes. She wore makeup, lots of it. He wondered what kind of a person put on makeup to go hiking in the mountains. She wasn't very tall, maybe five two at the most. He glanced lower, where her shirt fell softly over two perfectly shaped mounds, the centers puckered. He felt himself beginning to blush.

"Well?" she prodded.

He swallowed. Okay. He admitted to himself that she might have been a little older than he'd thought. That didn't mean he had to admit it to her. "Well what?" he asked.

"Y'all gonna tell me what you're doing here or aren't you?"

Daniel shoved his hands into his pockets and made a show of staring out across the mountain range in the distance. "Who wants to know?"

"Why is it that men always answer questions with questions?'' she sputtered. ''I'm Willow Pratt. I live down yonder in Dawsons Hollow. Now, who're you?''

Daniel shook the hand she'd stuck in front of his face, amazed all over again at how small and slender it was. ''My name's Daniel Wilder. I'm from Ohio, but I live here now.''

''All by yourself?''

He nodded.

''How old are you?'' She studied his face, making him proud of the dark hair that was growing above his upper lip.

''I'm almost fifteen,'' he answered. ''How old are you?''

''I'm almost fifteen too. Betcha I'm older. When's your birthday?''

He glanced sideways at her. ''For a girl who just came close to being eaten by a wild dog, you ask a lot of questions.''

She wrinkled up her nose, grimacing. ''I know. I drive most people crazy. Am I driving you crazy?''

The strangest sensation came over Daniel, and he shook his head. She beamed up at him for a second, her expression turning thoughtful and assessing. ''You ran away from home, didn't you?''

''So what if I did?''

Shrugging as if it were all the same to her, she peered all around. ''You had the rest of the world to run away to. And yet you came here.''

''What's wrong with Dawsons Hollow?''

''What isn't wrong with it? It's boring. It's backward. It's so darn stifling, I want to scream. There's nothing to do in Dawsons Hollow. There's nothing to be.''

''Then what are you doing up here?'' he asked.

She glanced at her shoe and commenced to move a pebble around with her toe. ''Promise you won't get mad?''

Daniel hated making those kinds of promises, but he nodded.

''I came up here to spy on somebody.''

''You mean me.''

Her head shot up. ''I didn't plan that. Although I have to say, coming across you was a pleasant surprise.'' The little wretch had the nerve to grin. "Come on. I'll show you what I mean."

"Where are you going?"

She placed a finger to her mouth and then gestured for him to follow her. They trekked along the narrow mountain lane in silence. The path wound between trees, around boulders, climbing, leveling off, and climbing once again. Willow slowed suddenly. Veering to the right, she crept silently to a spot where a huge boulder was nearly hidden by wild ferns.

She parted the ferns with her hands, whispering, "That cottage over there is the Sprague place."

Daniel peered across the rocky slope. Other than the dark green Explorer that was parked in the driveway, the small white cottage looked a lot like every other small white house up here. The siding could have used a coat of paint, the yard a good mowing. There were a couple of cars up on blocks, a couple of dogs snoozing on the porch, wood smoke curling from a stone chimney.

"What are we looking for?" he whispered.

"Just wait. You'll see. There," she whispered, pointing. "See that girl over there? Her name's Lavender. Folks are worried about her."

Daniel studied the people who had gathered on the porch. Other than some kids who looked more like boys to him, the only females he saw weren't girls at all, but women. One of them was the woman who'd given him milk and food and the bottle for his raccoon. The other was a woman who was going to have a baby sometime soon.

"You can't tell from here, but she's real pretty. She's twenty-four, and the baby she's expecting is gonna be her seventh child."

"She's only twenty-four and she already has six kids?"

"Two came too early and died right after they were born. But this one'll still be her seventh child."

"Isn't she a little young to have so many kids?"

Willow made an exasperated sound. "You're missing the point."

"What point?" Daniel asked.

"The seventh child of the seventh child is said to have special powers. Magical powers. Lavender was her mama's seventh child. And this baby will be Lavender's."

Daniel saw the door in the little white cottage open. Two men walked outside; one of them was his father. Daniel swallowed. His adoptive father. Caleb Wilder had been good to him. And Daniel loved him. He wished it were enough. But it wasn't. Not anymore. He didn't want to have these yearnings, this unsettling need to look into the face of the man who had planted the seed that had made him. But he couldn't help it.

He thought about all the things people questioned. His mother had been fascinated with things that had no answers. She loved to talk about stars and galaxies and the rain forest and species of plants and animals scientists haven't even identified. A lot of people thought the number seven had great significance. There were seven days in a week, seven seas, seven continents, seven sacraments, seven great sins. Some people considered seven lucky, but this was the first he'd ever heard about the magic of a seventh child born to a seventh child.

"Do you believe it's true?" he asked.

Willow shrugged. "The old-timers tell stories about a granny-woman—that's what people used to call midwives— who was the seventh child of a seventh child. She died when I was little, so I don't remember her, but her name was Verdie Cook, and it's said that she had the strongest healing powers these hills have ever seen. Stronger even than Miranda's." Willow's voice faded to a whisper. "And then there's me."

Intrigued, Daniel stored the reference to Miranda and said, "What about you?"

"My father was the seventh in his family, and I'm the seventh in mine."

"And?"

She shook her head forlornly. "Far as I know, the only unusual power I have is a knack for getting into trouble and a penchant for spying on folks. Come on. It looks like

Miranda's going to be leaving in a few minutes. We have to hurry.''

Daniel wanted to ask for more information, to delve, to discuss. But Willow had disappeared through the thick foliage, and he had no choice but to follow.

He caught up with her in almost no time at all. They scurried along the same path they'd taken earlier.

"Here," Willow said, stopping at a tree with branches that hung out over the road. She whisked the ribbon from her hair and hurriedly tied it to the lowest branch in plain sight of the road.

"What are you doing?" he asked.

"Miranda says spying's the same as taking something without somebody's knowledge, you know, like stealing. I always leave her a ribbon or something else she can give to the poor kids she treats. This way, I'm not getting something for nothing."

Daniel looked both ways. He couldn't see any cars, but sounds carried a long way this time of night, and in the distance, tires crunched over the gravel mountain road. He thought about the times he'd watched Miranda from the bushes growing on the other side of her gate. He remembered the gentleness and warmth in her touch, the kindness in her eyes when she'd given him the items to use to feed his raccoon. Wishing he had something to leave her, he shoved his hands into his pockets, his fingers coming into contact with a smooth feather. He took it from his pocket and carefully poked it between the ribbon and the branch.

When he turned around, Willow was hurrying away from him. "Where are you going?" he asked.

"It's late. My brothers're going to kill me."

"Wait!" he called. "Are you coming back?"

She turned when she reached the path, and she nodded.

"When?" he asked.

"Tomorrow, or the next day. As soon as I can get away."

"But you don't know where I'm staying."

"Don't worry. I'll find you." Like a forest sprite, she twirled around and disappeared.

Being careful not to make a sound, Daniel set off in the opposite direction, where he would retrieve his discarded clothes before making his way back to the cabin up by the creek. Down near the road, a truck stopped, or was it a car? Daniel held perfectly still, listening, wishing. He didn't even know what he wished for anymore.

He heard two doors open and click shut. And then he heard a deep voice ask, "What's this?"

Daniel closed his eyes. That was his father's voice.

Miranda's voice came softer, quieter than his father's, Cale's, had been. "It's a thank-you from a young girl named Willow Pratt. She usually leaves a ribbon, but she's never left an eagle's feather before."

"Let me see that." There was a lengthy pause, and then Cale said, "I don't think the girl left the feather, Miranda."

Daniel closed his eyes, lulled by the clear, deep tones in that familiar voice. He imagined Cale peering into the woods and was struck by a yearning to race down the hill and see him. And maybe talk to him.

No. He couldn't do that. Not yet. First there were things he had to discover—about his biological father—and about himself.

"If it isn't from Willow," Miranda said, "who could it be from?"

"I think it's from Danny. He and his mother were fascinated with eagles. I'd say he's made a new friend. You said this girl's name is Willow?"

Daniel considered the notion. A friend, he thought. Yes, he'd made a friend. He'd come to the Blue Ridge Mountains. He'd found a place to stay. And he'd made a friend.

He started up the mountain, shaking his head. He should have known the first friend he made would be a smart-mouthed girl who liked to spy on people and who believed in mountain folklore and magic.

He grinned in spite of himself. He should have known.

* * *

Cale stared at the feather, then peered up where an out-cropping of rock was visible through the trees. "Danny's obviously finding his way around these hills. He's feeding a raccoon. And it looks as if he might have made a friend. I don't think he's getting ready to come home."

Miranda shook her head, but there was a faraway look in her eyes. For the second time in a matter of hours, Cale was struck by her beauty. She seemed almost ethereal in the gathering twilight. She had an essence, a glow. He didn't know where it was coming from. He knew only that it wasn't store-bought. He wondered how she did it. Where did she get her energy, her stamina? She'd made four stops since she'd picked him up. She'd listened to heartbeats, taken blood pressure, doled out bottles of her homemade medicine, prescribed exercise to one patient, bed rest to another, and prescription drugs to a third. She'd taken a four-year-old's temperature, and she'd held an old man's hand. By the end of the run, Cale had nearly convinced himself that she was just an ordinary nurse practitioner, an ordinary woman.

Watching her climb into the Explorer for the drive back down the mountain, the feather and ribbon still laced between the fingers of her right hand, that faraway look still in her eyes, he knew better. Oh, she was a nurse practitioner, but she wasn't an ordinary one. And she was certainly no ordinary woman.

He looked out the window where the road cut a path up-ward through the trees. Upward, not down. "Where are you going?" he asked.

"I heard you've been asking around for a place to stay."

"Do you know of someplace?" he asked.

She looked straight ahead. "I know of a few. Care to take a look?"

He peered at the sky outside the window on the passenger side. "It'll be dark soon."

"It isn't far. Besides, we have time. The night always deepens over this ridge first. Up here, the shadows form quickly, like spirits gathering strength. The Indians believed the shadows held great power. Night Shadow they called this place.''

Cale wondered if the slight quaver in her voice had to do with the shadows or the tale. Or did it have something to do with the way she touched that feather? God. Every time he saw her, he had more questions. And Cale was so weary of asking questions that had no answers.

She didn't drive far before she turned onto a lane that was deeply rutted and overgrown with grass and weeds. Something dark loomed up ahead. He strained to see. It looked like a cabin, its windows dark, its exterior weathered to a deep, dull gray.

There was an emptiness about the place, a kind of silence that made him lower his voice. "It's deserted."

"Yes."

"Who owns it?" he asked.

"I do."

She slid to the ground and started toward the cabin, her skirt swishing around her legs, loose tendrils of hair feathering across her cheek. "It isn't in the best condition, but it has four walls and a roof. And it's within walking distance to town. Come on. I'll show you around."

Cale assessed the cabin. Except for the electrical wire fastened high on one side of the porch, they could have stepped back in time to the previous century when people traveled by mule and made their soap, cut their own hair and planted their corn by the signs of the moon. The notion that it belonged to someone so refined, someone so cultured, someone so young, was difficult to fathom.

"This is really yours?"

She lifted the latch on the door and pushed, the old hinges creaking in protest. "It belonged to an old friend of mine, a midwife named Verdie Cook. She was an incredible woman, wise beyond her years as well as ahead of her time."

Cale followed Miranda inside. It didn't take his eyes long to adjust to the dim interior. He could see most of the cabin from where he stood. The front room was small, the floor made of rough-sawn boards, the wood old and worn smooth over the years. There was a layer of dust on every surface, a broken window on one wall, and two doorways on another.

Miranda strode through the first, leading the way into the next room, talking as she went. "For years nobody from the rest of the world ever gave these mountains much thought. They certainly never dreamed of moving here. But bit by bit, the Appalachians became more and more accessible, and people from cities as far away as New York and Philadelphia, and others as close as Charlotte and Louisville, discovered the peace and quiet and beauty. Throughout many areas in the neighboring peaks, outsiders began buying up the land. In the process, they raised the prices so high, the very people who had grown up and lived here and worked here could no longer afford to own homes. Aunt Verdie saw it happening all around her, but she didn't allow it to happen here."

"How did she stop it?" Cale asked, more intrigued with the tale than with the run-down old cabin.

They'd entered the kitchen, where an old stove sat in one corner, a marred wooden table with mismatched chairs in the other. Wiping her hands on the sides of her loose-fitting dress, she said, "In her old age, Aunt Verdie didn't have any family of her own left, but she took in people who needed nursing or tending. Some of those people didn't have any living relatives either. Before they died, they deeded their places to her. When I set up practice in Dawsons Hollow, she passed them on to me."

Cale went down on his haunches to peer inside a rustic cupboard next to the stove. In it he found a few enameled pans, a couple of chipped plates, and a metal bowl. "What do you do with the houses and property?"

"Every now and then, I sell one. But only to the people from the mountain who have a strong commitment to stay, and then only for a pittance of what I could get if I sold to outsiders. The real estate people downstate know me by name."

Cale glanced across the room. The entire area was in shadow now, the sun lower than the mountain peak silhouetted against the western sky. Miranda was standing in the doorway, a torn screen behind her, a broken window on her left. Her hair appeared darker, her eyes artful and serene.

"No wonder the people in these hills believe the sun rises and sets on you," he said quietly.

He'd spoken the words like an invocation, his voice a strong whisper, his emotions stronger still. If he'd been in church, he would have called it a prayer. Here on the mountain on the edge of the world, he called it awe.

He rose to his feet slowly, that telltale thickness in his body reminding him of things he'd tried to forget. He wondered what she would do if he strode across the splintery floor and kissed her right there in the kitchen in the cabin she was saving for a poor young couple from the hills. He hadn't kissed anybody since Ellie, hadn't wanted to or needed to. He wished he didn't want to now.

Kneading a muscle that had knotted at the back of his neck, he decided it might be best to put a little distance between them.

He checked out the rest of the cabin. There was a water stain on one wall, broken windows throughout. The house had an ancient bathroom with running water, but only cold. Somebody had wrapped wire around old-fashioned white transformers that looked like empty spools of thread. It would have to be tested for safety, but at least there was electricity. With a lot of cleaning and new glass in the windows, it would be livable.

Turning in the doorway, he said, "How much?"

Miranda finished closing a cupboard door before glancing at him. "Pardon me?"

"For me to rent it. How much for one month?"

"Oh," she said, starting to shake her head. "It isn't for rent. You need a place to stay. You can stay here."

"How much?"

"It's old," she said. "Unkempt, overgrown with vines and weeds and spiderwebs. And those are its good qualities."

"Two hundred dollars."

"Cale, it probably has mice."

"Two hundred and fifty."

She took a step toward him. "Are you crazy?"

"Three hundred. You can use the money to buy bandages for your clinic or shoes for the Sprague kids."

"They would never take the shoes or the money outright."

He felt himself starting to smile. "You'll think of something. Three hundred and fifty."

She held up one hand.

He waited, eyebrows raised expectantly.

"I would have to have new windows installed and clean the entire place up."

"I'll do it." Rather than give her a chance to put her thoughts into words, he said, "I'll have the time, Miranda. I might as well fill it."

"You're as stubborn as a mule, do y'all know that?"

The *y'all* was his undoing. Smiling with gusto now, he strode the remaining distance to her and held out his hand. "I've been told that a time or two. Do we have a deal?"

She rolled her eyes expressively, but she placed her hand in his. "Fine. You're only cheating yourself, you know."

Cale's fingers closed around hers. Damn. He'd won the argument. For his trouble, he was going to pay three hundred and fifty dollars to live in a run-down cabin with a leaky roof, rotting floors, and no hot water. There must have been something right about the deal, because he couldn't seem to stop grinning.

A few feet away, Miranda smiled too. She didn't understand what was happening to her, but she felt like singing. Actually, she felt like dancing. It had been a long time since she'd enjoyed a smooth waltz, a gentle glide around the room, her hand on some kind man's shoulder, his hand resting gently on her waist.

A whippoorwill called through the evening twilight, reminding her that this wasn't a dance floor, and there was no music. It was getting late. She opened her mouth to tell Cale so, but she looked into his eyes, and she forgot what she'd been going to say. The air was thick with humidity and the sweet scent of honeysuckle. Staring up at him, she knew there was something else in the air that was headier than the spring blossoms or evening shade.

She swallowed, and so did he. She tugged at her hand, but he held it fast, his thumb moving over her wrist. His gaze roamed her face, lighting on her mouth.

She was overcome with sweetness and with anticipation. It nudged her heart and her fantasies. "It's been a long time," she whispered, swaying closer. "Twelve years, actually."

Cale's breath gushed out of him. He told himself to back away. Instead, his hands glided to her shoulders, their bodies swaying ever closer. She was slender and pliant, at once soft and strong as only a woman could be. The bones beneath his hands felt fragile, as if the warm mountain breeze could shatter them into a hundred pieces and scatter them like dandelion fluff. Cale wanted more than fluff. He wanted to touch her, to glide his hand around her waist, to inch it slowly upward until he cupped her breast.

Desire pounded through him. He wanted to lower her to the floor and roll her underneath him. He wanted . . .

He wanted.

What the hell was he doing? He straightened suddenly. Setting her away from him, he looked out the window, at the ceiling, anywhere except at her. "It's getting late."

Miranda's heart was racing, and her face felt hot. She thought she saw a muscle move in Cale's jaw, but she couldn't be sure. In the tight space so near him, she couldn't think of a single thing to do or say. She took a backward step, chastising herself for feeling hurt at his sudden rejection. She managed to turn her back to him and busied herself with the latch on a cupboard door.

"Yes, it is getting late," she said. Hadn't she thought the same thing moments ago? "Did you want a ride back to your airplane? Or were you thinking of sleeping here tonight?"

"I would appreciate the ride, thank you." He strode past her, as stiff and formal as the words had been.

They left the cabin together and drove down the mountain in silence. Miranda had no way of knowing what he was thinking, but her thoughts darted from one thing to the next.

How many times had Ruby tried to get her to take an interest in men? How many times had she sputtered that Miranda's feminine juices had gone dry? Oh, but Ruby had been wrong.

These past few days Miranda had felt as if she were slowly coming to life. She knew nothing would come of her feelings. Caleb Wilder wasn't over his beloved Ellie. Miranda had seen over. She'd felt over. She'd lived, breathed, experienced over. And he wasn't it. She wished there were some way to tell him how rare that kind of devotion was, especially in this day and age.

"Cale," she said, coming to a stop near the meadow where he'd landed his plane.

"Miranda," he said at the same time.

They both paused, waiting for the other to speak. He opened his door and got out, the dome light flickering on and then off again, and stood outside the vehicle, where it was too dark to see his expression.

"I appreciate everything you've done for me and for Danny. And I'm sorry about"—he cleared his throat—"well, you know what I mean."

Miranda didn't allow herself so much as one small moment to wish for something that wasn't going to be. Staring straight ahead, she said, "There's nothing to be sorry for. I think your Ellie was a very lucky woman. What happened, or almost happened tonight was my doing, not yours. So you see, you have no reason to feel guilty. You haven't been unfaithful to her memory." She paused and decided against saying more. "Good night, Cale."

With the flick of her wrist, she put the shifting lever into drive. If Cale spoke, she didn't hear it over the sound of her tires churning up the loose gravel in the road.

Cale didn't move from the side of the road until Miranda's taillights had disappeared around a curve. He was completely alone. And he felt it. He also felt miserable. Raw.

Ellie? That's who Miranda thought he'd been thinking

about when he'd gathered up his last shred of restraint and resisted his desire for her? She wasn't even close.

He started down the seldom-used path, getting more agitated by the second. Miranda thought he'd pulled away because he'd turned his life into a sacrificial offering to his dead wife. He should be so saintly. Sure, he felt guilty, but that wasn't what had stopped him. He'd pulled away because he hadn't trusted himself to stop if he kissed her. She'd been raped, violated, brutalized. She'd been so traumatized, she hadn't made love in twelve years.

Twelve years. He wondered how someone so sensuous and sensual had gone so long without a lover's touch. Hell, lately the eighteen months he'd gone without sex felt like forever. He placed his hand on his forehead. The bandage felt rough beneath his palm, the cut underneath it still sore to the touch. It was nothing compared to the ache much lower.

Think about something else, goddammit.

He increased his pace, breaking into the clearing on a run. Winded, he wiped his mouth on the back of his hand. He could use a drink. He eyed his plane. Out of the blue, he remembered the bottle of Chianti Sam Kennedy had shoved into his hands moments before the takeoff from the airport in Columbus. There was no way in hell that bottle could have survived the landing. A sucker for a lost cause, Cale hurried to his plane, climbed up, and pried open the door.

He'd been in the cockpit a couple of times since he'd landed. He didn't recall seeing a bottle. He didn't recall smelling any spilled wine either. Dropping down to his knees, he flipped on a small flashlight and rummaged around. He picked through clothes that were strewn about. Cautious of broken glass, he ran his hands under the seats. He came up with a pair of socks, several tools, and a slew of discarded wrappers. He made another pass. Delving deeper, he reached all the way into the corner, where his fingers glided over smooth glass.

Well, what do ya know? He drew out a straw-encased bottle of Chianti, aged to perfection and unbroken.

Balancing on his haunches, he considered digging his Swiss Army knife out of his pocket and uncorking the bottle there and then. If it had been whiskey, he would have taken a long pull straight from the bottle. But Chianti was meant to be savored, sipped from a glass. It was meant to be shared.

He peered in the direction he'd taken the night he'd landed his plane. Although he couldn't see it, beyond the path through the woods was a gate beneath a sourwood tree where sparrows roosted and gossiped. Beyond the gate lived a beautiful woman with a lilting Southern accent, who had been nothing but kind to him.

Cale was accustomed to hard physical work, to skinned knuckles and grease under his fingernails. He'd gladly give anybody he knew the shirt off his back along with a helping hand. He was a hell of a lot more comfortable pulling somebody out of the ditch or fixing a neighbor's leaky faucet than putting his feelings into words. And there probably wasn't another man on earth who was worse than he was at saying he was sorry.

He shone the flashlight over the label. Chianti might have been made for celebrations, but suddenly, he had another use in mind.

Tucking the bottle beneath his arm for safekeeping, he climbed stiffly to the ground. There was a new sense of urgency in his steps as he headed for the path that led to the gate that led to Miranda Sinclair.

CHAPTER SIX

The first thing Miranda did when she returned to her cottage was take a brisk, invigorating shower. When she finished, she pulled on a loose-fitting cotton dress, combed out her wet hair, and tried to decide what to do next.

She came from a long line of doers. If there was one thing she'd learned at the knee of her ever-petite, elegant, and socially driven mother, it was how to stave off those bothersome melancholy moods. Charlotte Sinclair believed an active mind was the key to happiness. If she had a headache, she would lie down for twenty minutes. If she had the flu, she allowed herself twenty-five. Miranda smiled to herself as she thought about the woman behind the whirlwind. Her mother worked diligently for her charities. Luckily, Miranda's clinic happened to be at the top of the list.

Miranda was tempted to call her for the sheer pleasure of hearing her mother list everything she had to do this coming week. It would be fun to hear who her mother had convinced to chair one of her many committees, who had had a face-lift, whose husband had been caught running around with the clerk in his office, or whose children were graduating from college. She could catch up on who Gwen,

Miranda's younger sister, was dating, or what outrageous thing her older brother, Alex, had done to shock them all. The only reason she didn't pick up the phone was that her mother would know something was wrong. Not that there was anything wrong. Miranda wasn't feeling rejected. She certainly wasn't disappointed because Caleb Wilder hadn't wanted to kiss her. The man was still grieving. Besides, he was just passing through this little neck of the woods in northeastern Georgia. He had more important things to do than to kiss her. And so did she. Have more important things to do, that is, than kiss him, or anyone for that matter. She was feeling a tad blue, that's all. What she needed to do was get busy.

She had charts to update, a newsletter to read concerning some interesting findings regarding Violet, a holistic, non-drug treatment for cancer. There were always more tinctures to prepare, herbs to simmer, capsules to fill and seal.

Ruby wandered over most evenings, and would probably show up sometime soon. Miranda tuned the radio to a station that played old rock and roll, then took a big pot from the shelf, only to place it on the counter, forgotten. Barefoot, she wandered into the living room, where she lit her aromatic candles, seven in all. Candlelight was supposed to be soothing, aromatherapy even more so. She didn't feel soothed. She felt . . . what?

She strolled to the door. One finger on the light switch, she leaned a shoulder against the doorjamb, crossed her arms, and pressed her face close to the screen. A floorboard creaked. Miranda screamed.

A man jerked backward, one hand still raised as if to knock.

"God! It's all right, Miranda. It's me."

"Cale," she said shakily, straightening from the crouch she automatically assumed when threatened.

He took another backward step just as she turned the porch light on, the dim bulb illuminating his white T-shirt. His eyes were shadowed, his jaw set, a bottle of wine clutched stiffly in one arm.

"What are you doing here?"

She thought she heard him cuss under his breath, and she was sure she saw his throat convulse on a nervous swallow. "I didn't come here to scare the hell out of you, that's for sure. I came to set the record straight."

"What record?"

"I didn't withdraw because of Ellie. Up in that cabin. I did it because of you. More specifically, because of me. Oh, hell. I'm not saying this very well. I wasn't sure I could stop if I kissed you. And I didn't want to frighten you."

Miranda had heard more eloquent apologies, more effusive explanations, but she'd never heard more depth or candor in a man's voice. Cale's eyes were trained on her, a vein pulsing in his neck. He seemed as nervous as a boy on prom night. The analogy was endearing, and she smiled.

Her smile had the desired effect on him. He sighed and visibly relaxed. There was warmth in his blue eyes, and a dark, seductive gleam that reminded her of the way he'd looked at her up in that cabin an hour and a half ago. She'd misread his reasoning, misinterpreted his motivation, but she'd been right about what his expression had meant. He'd wanted her then. He wanted her now.

He didn't look very pleased about that. "I mean it, Miranda. I really am sorry I scared you."

She opened the door and slipped through, joining him on her small front porch. Closing the door very quietly, she leaned against it, both hands behind her back. "I'm not afraid, Cale."

They stared at each other, and although Miranda was the first to smile, she wasn't the only one to do so. Cale used the moment of silence that followed to try to get his thoughts in order. He swore his breath had solidified in his throat. Miranda didn't appear to have any such problem. She looked warm and womanly and completely at ease. Her hair was damp, and it occurred to him that she'd just gotten out of the shower. Unless he was mistaken, there wasn't much except soft, warm flesh beneath the thin fabric of her pale blue dress.

Cale's sigh went as deep as his frustration. He took another backward step. If he wasn't careful, he was going to back off the porch. "If you knew what I was thinking, you'd be afraid."

He wondered if she was aware of the smile that stole across her face. He wondered if she had any idea what that smile of hers was doing to him.

A late night breeze blew in, billowing the hem of her skirt, ruffling the scalloped edges of her sleeves and collar, and lifting the fine flyaway tendrils of hair that had dried. She tilted her face so she could stare up at him. Holding his gaze, she said, "I was an imp as a child. Fearless and freckled and happy. And then, suddenly, after one horrible act, I was none of those things. Nightmares will always be more terrifying, more violent, more I know what violence is. It took me a long time to be happy again. It took me even longer to face the night unafraid. I suppose the darkness will always unnerve me. But I'm not afraid of you."

Uncertain how to proceed, Cale chose his words carefully. "I didn't come here, to this mountain, for this."

"I understand."

"What do you see happening between us?"

"I think you're going to kiss me."

He shot backward and stumbled off the top step. His arms flailed in his attempt to right himself. Cale felt foolish. Miranda had the nerve to smile. She was still an imp, dammit.

"Of course," she said, her voice laced with laughter, "I could be wrong." Turning serious, she added, "No matter what you said about the reason you didn't kiss me up in the cabin in the hills, I don't think you're ready."

"You don't."

"There's ready, and then there's ready. When I went back to school after the rape, I was determined that I wasn't going to let that bastard rob me of some of life's most simple pleasures. I slept with the light on, and I made love the same way. The moral of the story is this. I kissed a boy before I was ready. I wasn't being true to him or to myself."

Cale could have done without the lecture. He started to

glower at her, but that guileless grin stole across her mouth again, and he didn't have it in him to stay angry. "Ellie's been gone for eighteen months."

"Eighteen months isn't that long, Cale."

It had been the longest eighteen months of his life. He raked a hand through his hair, shook his head, shrugged. "The vows I took said until death do us part. I took an attractive colleague of mine to dinner a few months ago. I spent the entire evening talking about Ellie. I kept my vows, and yet I still felt guilty as sin."

"There's no shame in feeling lonely. There's a good chance this will pass, given enough time."

"Please don't tell me I'll know when I'm ready."

"I wouldn't be telling you anything you don't already know now, would I?"

Her accent was as softly Southern as she was, a breathy "ah" for "I," a smooth glide over words containing *y* or *ing*. It held him immobile and caused his breathing to deepen at the same time.

She took a step toward him, glancing at the bottle clutched tightly beneath one arm. "Were you planning to drink that?"

For an instant, he could picture her as a child, fearless and freckled and happy. In many ways, her inner spirit wasn't so different now.

"As a matter of fact," he said, sighing, "I was. At the time, I planned to use it as a peace offering."

"Italian wine is my mother's favorite."

Without another word, she turned on her heel and went back into the house. Cale was left standing alone on the porch, staring at the label on the bottle in his hand. His heart rate was still unsteady, his thinking skills shaky. Evidently, ten years of marriage had wiped out whatever ability he'd ever had to behave like a normal single man.

He was acting like an idiot. He hadn't been this inept at fifteen. Calling himself every kind of fool, he followed her inside.

She waited until the door had bounced shut to say, "I'll be right back with two glasses."

Cale watched until she disappeared into the kitchen. She'd listened to Mozart during the drive up the mountain earlier. Now Billy Joel was belting out a tune from a radio in the corner. Cale had slept in this house his first night on the mountain. Tonight, he took the time to study his surroundings. Candles flickered throughout the room. The elegant-looking rug on the floor went well with the brocade sofa but not with the rustic, rough-hewn shelves and assorted homemade knickknacks throughout the room.

Bookshelves took up one entire wall, stretching from corner to corner, from ceiling to floor. They contained hundreds of books, some old, some new, some hardcovers, some paperback. Cale wandered to them. Miranda had an interesting and rather eclectic collection of reading material. There was an entire shelf of books about the Appalachian Mountains, books about quilting and cabin building and mountain folklore. There were narrow volumes about the ballet, others about great battles of the Civil War, still others about nursing and modern-day midwives. She had a book about sorcery, another about Australian legends, and others about ancient healers. The books about dreams caught his attention. He counted twelve volumes in all. Pulling one off the shelf, he leafed through.

He exchanged the book about dreams for one about mountain folklore. Opening it, he scanned one page, and then another.

A sound near the doorway drew his attention. Miranda was strolling toward him, two long-stemmed glasses in one hand, the wine and a corkscrew in the other. With a quirk of one eyebrow, he said, "Did you know that if two crows are spotted in the same tree, the first person to see them will undoubtedly take seriously ill before the month is through?"

"I seem to have heard that somewhere, yes."

He put the book back in its slot. "Have you ever treated anybody for this malady?"

"I can't say that I have." She handed him the bottle and a corkscrew.

"That's interesting," he said, twisting the tool into the center of the cork. "I wonder what happens to the second person. If the first one takes seriously ill, does the other one go bald?''

"You're a skeptic, Cale, do you know that?''

The cork came loose; Cale placed it and the corkscrew on a low table. "I'm just a man, Miranda. A simple man.''

"There's nothing about you that's simple.'' She held the glasses out so he could pour. "Not who you are, not what you are, not where you've been or where you're going.''

He took a sip, and so did she. She smiled and took another sip. "This Chianti is very good.''

"It was a gift from a friend. Sam discovered Chianti by accident one night years ago. It's a long story, but the wine has been his standby ever since. He gave Ellie and me a bottle on the day we were married.''

Cale paused. He didn't want to think about his wedding day. So he started talking again—about Sam Kennedy, and flying and landing, about teaching, and about students she couldn't possibly relate to. He talked for twenty minutes straight. And Miranda let him. He wondered if she had any idea what a rare gift listening was. On a whim, he reached out with one hand.

Startled, Miranda flinched before she could stop herself. This time they both paused. He'd intended only to smooth a strand of hair away from one side of her face. That a gesture so innocent could cause such a reaction in her brought home the fact that they were quite a pair. Only they weren't a pair. They were just two people, alone and lonely and deeply scarred.

"Do you ever talk about it, Miranda?''

Miranda skimmed her finger along the rim of her glass. The way he said her name sent a fluttering to her heart, a gentle warming, a soft mewling that caught in the hollow at the base of her neck. *It* could have referred to a lot of things. Her childhood, her practice, her garden. But he wasn't asking her about any of those things. He wanted to know about the moment in time when her life had changed, the moment everything inside her had been irrevocably altered.

Needing something to do, she opened a window and

looked out. The night was dark, quiet. Beneath the mountain stillness was a hum, not quite the sigh of the wind, not exactly the sound of insects. It was more like the thrum of a heartbeat, as if the mountain were alive.

Miranda was alive too. Oh, she'd pretty much proven that she hadn't completely conquered her occasional involuntary reactions to an unforeseen or unexpected touch. She supposed there were some traumas that people never got over completely. Cale certainly hadn't made peace with his loss. Perhaps that was why she was considering telling him about that fateful night. She rarely talked about it. In fact, few people knew of it. Tracing a finger over the dream-catcher in the window, she began to speak.

"I was coming from a friend's house. I didn't have a car then, and hers was in the shop. The air was heavy with the threat of rain. I loved my work, loved the people and the freedom. I'd attended a party Verdie had thrown for the family of a young patient who was recovering from a terrible fall. Our spirits were high, and those of us who were new were feeling as if we could do anything. It was dark when I left the party, but I wasn't the least bit afraid. I knew the way by heart. It was a path I took often. Everybody did."

She turned slowly, talking as she came to a stop an arm's length away from Cale. "There were no known ax murderers or rapists on the loose. Even when I heard footsteps behind me, I didn't get really afraid. Until I heard him whisper my name, I never knew how real fear felt. That kind of fear changes a person, you know?"

Miranda knew Cale didn't know what to say. She didn't expect him to, not really. She ran a finger around the rim of her glass again, around and around and around, staring into the dark table wine, remembering. "I started to run. He was faster. He grabbed me from behind and held me to him. Sometimes, in my nightmares, I can still hear the sound of his breathing so close to my ear."

Cale reached for her hand and held on, as if he wanted his touch to convey his concern and sadness over her ordeal. "You don't have to continue, Miranda. Not for me."

She left her hand in his and looked up at him. "It happened a long time ago. The counselor I saw later said it's good to talk about it from time to time." She paused, gathering her thoughts. When she was ready, she continued. "He wasn't brutal. At least not the way some rapists are brutal. Oh, he was vile, but he didn't torture me first or after. He didn't use a knife or a gun. His only weapon was his strength. I fought so hard against him. Later, I had to scrape his flesh from underneath my fingernails and scrub his blood from my skin."

Miranda grew silent, reliving the next part to herself. There had been blood elsewhere too, for although he hadn't sliced her neck or bound her wrists or beat her, she'd been a virgin, and he'd been a large man. "Relax," he'd whispered in her ear. "Don't cry. You're so pretty. Don't cry. I'll make you feel good, so good. I'm the best there is. You'll see." To this day she could still hear the hiss and filth in that whisper.

"I screamed," Miranda said out loud, starting to pace. "Over and over, but the storm had come, and my voice couldn't compete with the wind and the thunder and the driving rain. He was my enemy. My first and my last. I hated him. I still do. I hate what he did to me and what he took from me. I hated the smell of him, the horrible weight of him. When he was finished, that hatred roiled up inside me. And I brought my knee up hard and swift. He hit me before he doubled over. The force of his fist knocked me off my feet and sent me crashing backward through the pouring rain. My head cracked against a rock. I could see the shape of him in a flash of lightning, and I closed my eyes. I wanted my mother, my bed in Atlanta, my father's voice carrying up the open staircase. I wanted to go home. I wanted to go back in time, an hour, a day, a year. I felt like I was dying, and a deep welling sadness washed over me at the thought of the man who had done that to me watching me do something as private as taking my last breath."

"I'd like to kill every bastard who's ever done that to

another human being, and I'd like to start with the one who did it to you."

She nodded sadly. "I've dedicated my life to making people well, but I wish he were dead. Maybe death would be too good for him."

"Not the kind of death I have in mind, a slow, painful, tortured ending to the life of a man who would deserve every cruelty he got."

"I don't talk about it often, Cale. And I don't want your pity. It happened a long time ago. It's over. My physical wounds healed within weeks. The wounds violence left on my soul took years to stop festering, but they've healed too. I won't stand here and lie to you by telling you it didn't change me, but I'm stronger than I've ever been, physically and emotionally."

"Then, why?" he asked quietly. "Why has it been twelve years since you've kissed a man?"

The haunted look hadn't left her eyes, but Cale noticed there was no fear. She wet her lips, smoothed her hands down her dress, and finally looked him in the eye once again. "I don't know. I kissed boys in college. Maybe I've gotten more selective. It's not something I spend a lot of time analyzing."

It occurred to him that she was closer to him than she'd been a moment before. She wasn't the one who had moved. He reached a hand to her. This time, she didn't flinch. He brushed a strand of hair off her cheek with one finger and stared into her eyes, those amber eyes that had mesmerized him from the first moment he'd looked into them. She was barefoot. She was on the tall side of average, five six or seven, and slight of build. She was beautiful, but it wouldn't have mattered if she'd been plain. He would have been drawn to her anyway.

Candles flickered, casting a golden glow on her cheeks and hair. Her eyelashes fluttered down once but came up again, the expression in those golden-brown eyes enough to send the blood surging through him. She could have initiated a kiss, but she didn't. She was leaving that up to him.

He drew in a deep breath, inhaling the scent of wildflowers and candle wax and something that called to mind the pomander still hanging in Ellie's closet back home.

He straightened. Jaw clenched, he drew his hand from Miranda's cheek and slowly lowered it to his side.

It was a good thing Billy Joel kept singing in the background, because Cale couldn't think of a thing to say to fill the ensuing silence. He tipped back the rest of his wine, placed his glass on a low table, and finally settled for "I could use a little fresh air."

He strode out to the porch without another word. He was on the top step when Miranda's voice sounded behind him, calling his name.

She extended her hand, holding the bottle of Chianti toward him. "I think you need this more than I do."

He heaved a heavy sigh. "I'm certifiable."

"Maybe a little." She twined an arm around a post and leaned her hip against the railing.

"Don't sugar-coat it on my account."

"I'm sorry," she said, sounding as if she meant it. "I'm afraid Ruby's rubbing off on me. Really, I'm seriously concerned about that."

Cale relaxed in spite of himself. The air smelled like deep summer. He supposed that here in Georgia, May was considered summer. With one hand on his hip, the bottle of Chianti dangling from the fingers of his other hand, he looked out at the mountain. Night had a way of making a man feel smaller. There were few lights here, even fewer man-made sounds. The night was clear and quiet except for the occasional scuttle of unseen animals, the call of an owl, the buzz of insects drawn to the light.

The night seemed deeper on the mountain, the sky darker, the stars brighter. Before his eyes, one of those stars shot toward the horizon, leaving behind a trail of glitter that flickered mere moments before it disappeared.

Cale remembered the first time Danny saw a shooting star. He'd been four, and his eyes had grown as round as saucers. He'd asked a hundred questions, wanting to know everything about the sky and the heavens. The memory was a happy one, and yet it made Cale ache.

"The Indians used to call falling stars Spirit Hoppers," Miranda said. "They believed spirits rode the stars to heaven."

When he turned his head to look at her, she shrugged and said, "Just a little mountain trivia."

She was an incredible woman.

He went down to the bottom step. "Did Danny stop by your mailbox tonight?"

She nodded her head slowly. And Cale thought that at least his son had eaten today. Suddenly tired, he said, "It's beautiful up here. I can understand why you moved here."

"Tell that to my mother the next time she calls, will you?"

He glanced up at her, remembering when she'd mentioned that parents can be difficult. "Surely your mother understands why you've chosen to live up here."

"Why *have* I chosen to live up here?"

The tone of her voice set off a warning in the back of Cale's mind. "Because of what happened in Atlanta."

"It didn't happen in Atlanta, Cale."

He closed his eyes, willing her not to say what he dreaded she was going to say.

"It happened at the base of the ridge where night falls first. It happened at the place the Indians called Night Shadow."

There were a lot of things Cale didn't understand, but he understood his rage. "The bastard was from these hills? I hope he's rotting in prison."

When she didn't answer, he squeezed the long neck of the bottle in his right hand. "Tell me you went to the police."

She nodded. "My best friend, Nora, found me. She helped me up in the pouring rain. She held me, and she cried with me. She took me to Verdie Cook first, and then they took me to the emergency room downstate. I had a gash on my head and a serious concussion. The police came, a report was filed, an investigation was conducted."

"And the man? The son of a bitch who did it to you?"

She shook her head. "I never saw his face. It was dark.

And raining. The only part of him I saw with total clarity was his hands.''

"Good God. He was never caught?''

This time, she didn't have to shake her head. Her expression said it all. She let her arm fall away from the post, straightening to her full height. "The memory of what he did to me has haunted me. Sometimes, in my nightmares, I still see those hands. I lived in constant terror that first year. It happened here, and yet the fear was as great off the mountain. The only other rape reported in this area was that of a man who periodically used to beat his wife into submission and then force himself on her. The sheriff called me about it while I was finishing up my master's degree in college. Evidently, one night she'd had enough. She shot him in cold blood, and then she shot herself. It's possible it was the same man who raped me.''

Or it might have been someone else went unsaid between them. The thought turned Cale's stomach and sent unease all the way through him.

"He could be out there, watching, waiting.''

"Over the years,'' she said quietly, "I've developed a kind of sixth sense about that. I don't know how or why, but I can tell when I'm being watched. I knew your son was here before I saw him through the leaves. I don't know the man's identity, but I don't believe he's here. My skin would crawl if he were.''

Cale didn't have her sixth sense, dammit. He knew, because suddenly, the shadows seemed darker, the night blacker, the unknown more menacing.

"Cale?'' she asked.

He started nervously.

And Miranda sighed. "If you ever stop by for another visit, maybe we could talk about something more uplifting, something like nuclear warfare or the decline of family values.''

His laugh sounded more like a bark. Why wouldn't it?

His throat felt raw, his heart was heavy, and his nerves were standing on end. He'd thought he'd gone through hell when Ellie had died. Miranda had gone through her own kind of hell a dozen years ago. She'd lived through it, and she'd gone on. The least he could do was let it rest as well. "I think that sounds like a good idea. Good night, Miranda."

" 'Night. Thanks for the Chianti. And good luck finding your son. Oh, and, Cale? If you'd like to stop by the clinic in two or three days, I'll remove those stitches."

He stared into her eyes for a long time. Finally, he nodded, and she turned and walked inside. He heard the latch click firmly in place, saw the dream-catcher swish back and forth in the window.

He took the path to the sourwood tree. He opened the gate and went through, latching it behind him. The wind picked up, raising goose bumps on his flesh. Or was his sudden unease the cause of that?

The moon cast shadows everywhere. Night shadows were always more spooky. That was all it was.

He listened intently. He thought about Danny, up there somewhere, in the very hills where Miranda had been raped and left to die. It had been bad enough when he'd thought the man who'd forced himself on her had been some drug addict who hated his mother and blamed all his problems on every woman on the planet. But it had happened up here, and the man who'd done it had never been caught.

An owl hooted. Sweat broke out on Cale's upper lip. He glanced back at the little white cottage where dream-catchers hung in every window and candlelight flickered through lacy curtains. A twig snapped. Heart racing, Cale swung around.

A woman stepped onto the path. "Landsakes, boy, you're as jumpy as a cat on hot bricks."

Cale couldn't see the woman's expression in the near darkness, but he could make out the shape of her head, and he would recognize her voice anywhere. "Ruby."

He released his breath slowly. She must have noticed the

bottle of wine, because she said, "You pay Miranda a little visit?"

He stammered through an explanation about the cabin he was going to rent from her, and all the work he had to do to make it livable. He didn't know why he told her about the arrangements he planned to make to extend his leave from his teaching position back home. He mentioned his need to find his son. "Danny's my top priority. I might not be able to talk him into moving in with me, but I'm damned well going to try. At the very least, he's going to let me supply him with food and clothes. And I have to fix my plane before the two of us can fly home."

"Tonight?"

"What?" he asked.

"Do you have to do all that tonight?"

"Of course not."

"In that case, maybe you'd better get a good night's sleep, because from the sounds of things, you're going to be busy come morning."

An owl hooted again. This time it didn't unnerve him. "I'll try to do that."

She shoved the garden gate open and walked through.

"Ruby?"

She stopped beyond the shadows, the moonlight bleaching the colors from her straight housedress, turning everything to shades of silver, black, and gray.

"Do you walk in these hills after dark often?"

She studied him for a long time before asking, "Miranda told you?"

He nodded only once.

"No wonder you're jumpy. I suppose I'm more careful because of what happened to her, but yes, I often walk these woods at night. And in answer to the question you don't want to ask, no, I don't think he's here. Now, go on. Get some rest."

Cale did as Ruby said. By the time he reached the meadow where he'd landed his plane, his breathing was normal and his mind was clear. He took care of business, spread his sleeping bag out beneath his plane, and crawled inside.

"Caleb Wilder's a handsome devil, isn't he?" Ruby asked.

Standing on tiptoe, Miranda reached onto a high shelf. She found several jars containing alfalfa capsules, nine containing the black cohosh capsules she'd filled months earlier, but only one remaining jar of the blue cohosh she had prescribed for Lavender Sprague in her efforts to ensure that the young mother carried this baby to term.

"Did I mention that I ran into him out by the garden gate?"

"Seven times," Miranda said under her breath.

"Seven's lucky."

This time, Miranda didn't risk commenting, not even under her breath.

"He mentioned he'd stopped by. I saw the bottle of wine. So, what did you two talk about?"

"This and that."

Ruby tapped her foot on the kitchen floor. "You know, Miranda. If you try real hard, you might be able to work your way all the way up to vague. Do you have to do that now? What are you doing in there anyway?"

"I'm looking for the chickweed I prepared last fall."

"Chickweed. What do you want with that? No, wait. Emmaline Gillespie was in today. When I asked her why she needed to see you, she clamped her mouth so tight, I couldn't have pried the answer out of her with a crowbar. She wants a miracle cure to lose weight, don't she? If she'd keep her mouth shut that tight a little more instead of eating twenty-four hours a day, she wouldn't need chickweed."

"It isn't that easy for some people, Ruby."

"Emmaline holds her plate at chin level when she eats. I've never been sure whether she does it to save time or to keep from missing a crumb. So, did he kiss you?"

"Ruby."

"Well, did he? There was candlelight and wine, a quiet house, a warm May night. How was it?"

"Ruby," she said again.

Ruby grasped Miranda by the wrist, drawing her away from the shelves containing her homegrown remedies. "You can't blame an old woman for being curious."

"You're not old, and you know it."

"Don't try to change the subject. You like him, don't you? And he kissed you, didn't he?"

Miranda finally met her friend's inquisitive stare. Folding her arms, she shrugged. "He's staying for only a little while. He has a mission, a purpose, and when he's done, he has a life to go back to. I have a very full life too, you know. I have my patients, my practice, my family and friends. For heaven's sake, I even own real estate. There aren't enough hours in the day to do everything that needs to be done. Lavender needs that blue cohosh. My garden needs weeding. And I have to put in an appearance down in Atlanta in a few weeks. You know what my mother says. I'm the star of the fund-raiser."

Ruby had a crooked smile, and it was growing by the second.

"Why are you looking at me like that?" Miranda asked.

"Oh, I was just acknowledging the coincidence."

"What coincidence?"

"Caleb Wilder made it a point to list all the things he had to do too."

"He did?" Miranda asked before she could stop herself.

If Ruby's grin got any larger, it was going to extend past her face. "You gonna keep me in suspense all night? Did he kiss you or didn't he?"

Miranda lifted one shoulder a fraction of an inch. "No, he didn't." Ruby's smile slipped a notch, but only until Miranda added, "But he wanted to."

"Well, fan me with a brick, girl. Of course he did."

"Nothing is going to come of this, Ruby."

"That," Ruby said, rubbing her hands together, "remains to be seen."

Miranda could have argued, but she'd learned a long time ago that sometimes it was best to simply wait and see.

CHAPTER SEVEN

It was a mile-long hike from Cale's airplane to the cabin he was renting on Hawksbill Road, uphill all the way. He'd loaded his arms with nearly every worldly possession he'd brought with him from Columbus. He was about halfway when the sun cleared the mountain peak in the distance. Already, the day promised to be hot and muggy. Mosquitoes buzzed around his head and neck. With his hands full, it was next to impossible to swat the bloodthirsty little suckers.

It felt strange to be completely on his own. He still had responsibilities, but things looked different up here. Maybe it was that near-death experience, or maybe it was the change of scenery. His troubles didn't feel quite as weighty now, his life quite as pointless. He supposed it could have been time or distance or both. He knew only that after casting one last glance at his airplane in the rock-strewn meadow, he'd felt almost young and free as he set out for the place he would hang his hat for the next few weeks. Swiping at his ear with one shoulder, he wished he had a hat.

He didn't come across anybody else on foot, but two old pickup trucks passed him. Judging by the amount of time each of the drivers spent looking at him, Cale figured they would both recognize him the next time they saw him, although neither of them offered to give him a lift. People up here didn't exactly go out of their way to make a stranger feel welcome.

Cale had taken another—hopefully his last—frigid bath in the creek shortly after sunrise. If the electrical system in the cabin was adequate, he planned to install a small water heater as soon as possible. In the meantime, he could heat water on the old stove in the kitchen. He wondered if the cabin where Danny was staying had running water. While he was at it, he wondered what it would take to convince his son to move into the Hawksbill Road cabin with him.

Cale hitched the bags a little higher in each arm. Funny, he didn't remember filling them with bricks. He left the road, following the path Miranda had taken the previous night when she'd shown him the cabin. The trail rose steeply for the next hundred yards, veered to the right, then cut through a stand of pines. The minute he cleared the other side, the cabin was in plain sight.

It looked different in the light of day. Not necessarily better. The entire exterior was a dull shade of gray. The tiny porch had a nasty lean. Cale had never lived in anything so rustic, and yet he thought it was going to suit him perfectly.

He dropped his duffel bag and his bedroll on the ground near the porch steps. He was a little more careful setting the toolbox nearby. He had a cell phone, although he wasn't sure what good it would do him up here, where he was surrounded by so many tall trees. He'd packed his rechargeable razor, his toothbrush, a small bottle of shampoo, a bar of soap, and a couple of changes of clothes. Since room in his duffel bag had been at a premium, he'd left the Chianti behind, opting to bring the paper plates, cups, and plastic dinnerware he'd picked up at the local grocery store a few days before.

The last sandwich Miranda had so graciously given him the day before yesterday had been stale but edible. He'd eaten it for breakfast, perched on the wing of his plane, his feet dangling over the side, his eyes drawn to an eagle soaring far in the distance. He still had more than half of the loaf of bread, and most of the peanut butter was left, so he wouldn't starve. The meager supplies reminded him of his college days.

A mosquito buzzed close to his ear. Now that his hands were free, he nailed it with one swat, then strode inside to inspect the rest of the cabin. Besides the kitchen and living room, there were two bedrooms. One was on the main floor, the other was a loft. Both contained handmade chests, metal beds with old-fashioned bedsprings, and thin mattresses. The bed downstairs was the larger of the two, but it was still a far cry from his queen-size, pillow-top mattress set back home. Still, it had to be better than sleeping on a rock-strewn meadow underneath his plane.

He splashed his face with cold water in the tiny bathroom, then drank from his cupped hands. The bathroom had probably been added in the early fifties; the fixtures had most likely been secondhand even then. Claw-footed bathtubs were making a comeback in other parts of the country. This one looked as if it had seen better days. The toilet flushed, the sink was small and rust-stained, the mirror spotted and wavy. A quick glance in it reminded him that he needed a shave. It looked as if the cut on his forehead was healing nicely.

He was trying to decide where to begin when he made his way into the kitchen. He'd seen the ancient refrigerator, stove, and table and chairs last night. The broom, mop, and bucket containing a box of heavy-duty detergent had been added since then. He wondered who had left them.

He rolled a kink or two from his shoulders, shook a knot out of his left arm, and spent more time than he cared to admit staring into space. Thinking. Ellie used to call it his Einstein pose. It wasn't Ellie's face he was picturing. He didn't know what to think about that, let alone what to do about it, so instead of doing anything about it, he got to work.

By the time he'd swept down every cobweb and had attacked the thick layer of dirt that clung to every surface,

a cloud of dust permeated the air and forced him outside.
Circling the cabin, he decided to check out the exterior of
the structure. He doubted the siding had ever been painted.
Some areas were rotting, but most of it was still intact. He
backed up to get a look at the roof. It was constructed of
wood shakes, probably cedar, definitely old. Judging from
the water stain on the living room wall inside, it leaked. An
old open-topped washing machine sat on the back stoop,
and the remnants of a rotted clothesline that had once
stretched from the house to a nearby tree. All that was left
were two ends.

The yard was overgrown with bushes and weeds. Vines
trailed up telephone poles and trees, growing across electric
wires. It would take a machete to cut through them. Cale
didn't plan to spend his time on yard work. He wanted to
spend his time with Danny. He didn't know how he was
going to reach that boy, but he hoped a way would present
itself real soon.

For now, Cale got back to the business at hand. He discovered two sheds out back. Both were filled with junk and a
few useful items. It took a little doing to uncover a ladder.
After testing it for strength, he carried it to the back of the
cabin, where the ground was fairly level, swiped the back
of his hand across his sweaty brow, stripped off his shirt,
and climbed up. Several shingles were missing, but structur-
ally, at least, the roof was sound.

He made a trip down to the porch for his hammer and
out to the shed for a stack of thin slats of wood he could
use to patch the roof. The first time he felt his skin prickle,
he was crouched near the peak, his hammer raised to hit
the nail in his other hand. He drove the nail, swatted at a
bothersome insect, then peered into the distant hills. The
ground rose up sharply in the west and was literally covered
with wildflowers and shrubs. The mountains were green in
the distance, the sky blue.

Nothing appeared amiss, but he swore he was being
watched. Maybe Miranda wasn't the only one who had a
sixth sense when it came to this. He resumed his task, fitting

used shakes where they were needed, nailing them into place, then moving on to the next section of the roof.

It went on that way for fifteen minutes, Cale working, whoever was out there watching.

On a guise to stretch cramped muscles, he arched his back and glanced around. The sun was hot, the air heavy with humidity. There wasn't so much as a whisper of a breeze filtering down the mountain. When he noticed the leaves in the center of a wild huckleberry bush move, he knew it wasn't Mother Nature's doing.

He nailed down the last shingle, swatted at another mosquito, and nonchalantly rose to his feet. Keeping his back to whoever was watching him, he wiggled the stovepipe sticking out of the roof and called, "You might as well come out."

Silence.

"I know you're down there in that huckleberry bush."

Twigs snapped, leaves rustled, and a huffy-sounding voice called, "Do you have eyes in the back of your head, or what?"

Planting his feet near the roof's peak, Cale finally looked at the spy or the peeper or whatever a girl who watched people from a distance was called. Slight of build, she was dressed in faded jeans and a baggy T-shirt, and had dark, unruly hair. Her hands were on her hips, her chin thrust upward defiantly. She didn't look more than twelve or thirteen. He was pretty sure Miranda had mentioned that she was older than that.

"Are you Willow?"

"How did you know?"

The girl had a lot of spunk, or a lot of nerve. She'd been spying on him. He was the one who should have been huffy. But he simply said, "I teach shop class to high school kids. Having eyes in the back of my head was part of the job requirement." He slapped a hand to his neck. "Damn mosquitoes."

"You probably eat your steak practically raw."

Cale did a double take. "Pardon me?"

She sashayed a little closer. Shading her eyes with one hand, she had to tip her head way back in order to look up at him. "Only female mosquitoes bite. They eat blood. It's gross, I know, but they only do it because their babies need it. They hardly bother vegetarians like me. Didn't you know that?"

Cale shook his head.

"The Indians knew it, but white people are harder to convince." She must have noticed the look he gave her, because she had the grace to duck her head and shrug. "I read it somewhere. Honest." And then, peering around, she said, "You fixin' this place up for Miranda?"

Cale headed for the ladder. "Actually," he said when he was halfway down, "I'm fixing it up for me. I'm renting it for the time being."

He jumped the last few feet to the ground. She hung back, hugging the row of boxwoods and lilac bushes along the edge of the overgrown yard. She was keeping her distance, and yet Cale could feel her eyes on him as he lowered the ladder and carried it toward the shed.

"Noticed you didn't walk underneath that ladder," she called. "Does that mean you're superstitious?"

"I've never met a black cat I didn't like."

Most girls her age would have laughed or rolled their eyes or commented. She only stared at him. She was still watching him closely when he returned. Cale bent at his waist, rummaging through the small toolbox he'd brought from his plane. Gripping the smaller of two flat bars in one hand, he went to work digging the broken glass out of the old window casing on the back of the cabin.

"Miranda tell you who used to live here?" she asked.

He thought about the old furniture and dishes that had been left, unclaimed by relatives or neighbors, apparently unused for years. "No, but if you're going to tell me that whoever it was died a tragic and painful death and now haunts the place, don't."

"All right, I won't."

The implication hit him between the eyes. He looked over

his shoulder in time to see her lips twitch. It was all he needed to let him know he'd been had.

"Anybody ever tell you you're jumpy?"

Not before he'd come here, they hadn't.

"A lot of folks around here do, you know. Believe in ghosts, I mean. I've read books about it, but I've never seen one myself. Think I'll reserve judgment until I do."

"Do you read a lot of books?" he asked.

"When I'm not feuding with the Hatfields or running moonshine or sailing off the edge of the flat world, you mean?"

Cale's hand slipped off the crowbar, and he gouged the same knuckle he'd scraped the night he'd landed his plane.

They stared at each other, this girl with a lot of spunk but not much tact and the restless man with the Northern accent and bruised ribs and stitches in his forehead. After drawing in a deep breath, Cale said, "I meant when you're in school, out of school, whenever. Do you read a lot of books, period?"

"Oh." She glanced at the ground at her feet. When she next met his gaze, he detected an apology in her eyes. "My mouth gets me in a lot of trouble. It got washed out with soap so many times when I was little, it's a miracle I didn't blow bubbles every time I opened it. I think it stunted my growth. My mother says I'm sassy. Really, I'm just bored."

"Maybe if you didn't skip school . . ."

She made a disparaging sound. "School bores me silly."

No wonder Danny liked her, Cale thought. She sounded just like him.

The girl started toward him, only to stop abruptly. "Y'all won't tell anybody you saw me, will you?"

After swatting at another pest, Cale went back to his task. "I'm not on speaking terms with too many people around here yet, Willow."

"It's just that my brother will have a fit if he finds out I stopped to talk to you." She leaned down to tie her shoe. "I swear J.R. would keep me locked in the attic if he could. He's always telling me I have to be careful and that I shouldn't trust any man, no matter how young or old he is. He claims these hills are dangerous.''

If Willow had been looking, she would have noticed the change that came over Cale, how his shoulders tensed and his expression sharpened. But Willow wasn't looking. She'd moved on to tighten her other shoe. ''I'm sick to death of that speech. I mean, it isn't as if there are men waiting to attack me around every corner. I know these hills by heart, and they're not that dangerous. No matter what folks say, there are no panthers left in Rabun County. Nobody's even so much as seen a bear around here in years and years. Some of the kids in school believe in werewolves. Even if there was such a thing, according to the legend, they only come around when the moon is out, don't they? Which is really a silly legend, because the moon is always out. It's just sittin' up there waiting for the sun to set and its competition to fade away for another day.''

She must have noticed that Cale hadn't moved, because she looked at him and shrugged sheepishly. ''I sometimes go on and on. Guess you noticed that by now.''

''It's funny,'' Cale said, ''but you don't look like a fussy old lady.''

That won him her first grin of the day. ''Ruby says I'm old beyond my years.'' Rising to her feet, she backed up, glanced all around, and said again, ''You won't tell anybody, will you?''

When she'd asked the first time, Cale had assumed she'd been worried about truancy laws. There was more to her desire for secrecy than that. It had something to do with her brother, J. R. Pratt. Cale never would have put Willow and the man who operated the grocery store in the same family. Now that he thought about it, they had the same hair color. Remembering the brief conversation he'd had with J.R., Cale wanted to question her further. Since he preferred to do that without raising her suspicions, he had to keep her talking. ''Your secret's safe with me, Willow.'' He returned to his task, and in a conversational tone of voice said, ''I'm curious. Who really used to live in this old cabin?''

She didn't readily reply. Cale didn't mind prodding. "It couldn't have been a whole family," he said. "At least not a large one, because there are only two kitchen chairs and two bedrooms."

Again, there was only silence behind him.

"Willow?"

The utter stillness of the mountain drew him around. The sun was bright overhead, brutal in its intensity. Shading his eyes with one hand, he made a sweeping perusal of the entire area. Other than the bees buzzing from one honeysuckle blossom to the next, and those blasted mosquitoes, nothing moved. Willow was gone.

Cale stared at the quiet mountain. He and his college roommates had hiked in the Rocky Mountains the summer after their sophomore year, but this was his first trip here. The Rockies consisted of huge rock formations and vast sky and great open spaces. The Blue Ridge Mountains weren't nearly as tall or wide. They were covered in trees, closed to the world below. Anyone traveling through them wouldn't have a clue what the people of these mountains were like, their past, their present, their tragedies and triumphs.

Cale had been here only a matter of days, and yet it seemed that everyone he'd met had a story. He'd come to find Danny. He wondered how many unanswered questions he was going to uncover before he discovered the truth about his own son.

He hoped Willow would mention that she'd met Cale the next time she saw Danny. In the meantime, all Cale could do was wait. And waiting had never been his strong suit.

He retrieved his shirt from the splintery porch railing and shrugged into it before resuming his task. He was accustomed to grease under his fingernails, but it had been a long time since he'd partaken in this particular kind of manual labor. In a strange way, it felt good. He had shelter and food and water but not much in the way of creature comforts. What he had was plenty of time to think. And that was the strangest thing of all, because he'd spent the better part of the past eighteen months trying to keep so busy that he wouldn't have time to think.

He thought for the rest of the morning. He got a lot of work done in the process. By lunchtime he'd removed all the broken glass from the windows, had made another pass through the cabin with the broom, and hauled the mattresses outside for a good airing. He slathered a thick layer of peanut butter between two slices of bread and let the conversation he'd had with Willow replay through his mind. Going back to work, he thought about some of the things he wanted to tell Danny the next time their paths crossed. He even thought about the kiss he'd almost given Miranda Sinclair.

"Almost," Sam Kennedy was wont to sputter, "is a lot like close. And you and I both know that close counts only in horseshoes and hand grenades."

Cale didn't know where Sam got his pearls of wisdom, but the man had hundreds of them. On a whim, Cale retrieved his cellular phone from his duffel bag and climbed one of the old maple trees along the edge of the road. Shimmying onto a sturdy branch that had grown straight out from the others, he dialed the high school's number and Sam's extension back in Columbus. It wasn't a good connection, but between the static and Sam's voice cutting in and out, arrangements were underway for Cale to take a short leave of absence from his job. Sam asked about Danny and the flight to the Blue Ridge Mountains. After Cale had given a brief rundown of the situation with his son and his plane, Sam joked about the lengths some people went to in order to get out of going to work in the morning.

Cale was in the process of calling his friend a few choice names when the connection was broken. Next, he dialed the bank back in Columbus and had funds transferred from his savings account to his checking. Pushing a button to cut the power, he tucked the phone inside the waistband of his jeans and peered around. He had a bird's-eye view of the mountainside. A pair of crows were perched in a dead tree to the right of the road. It reminded him of the folklore he'd read in one of Miranda's books. Far in the distance, an eagle was soaring again. Either the mosquitoes were afraid of heights, or they hadn't discovered him yet. He was considering the benefits of living in trees, when he spotted a paper bag sitting on a rock a hundred yards away. He'd noticed the rock's unusual shape when he'd been repairing the roof. That paper sack hadn't been there an hour earlier.

He didn't see another living soul. He didn't feel anyone's eyes on him either. After climbing to the ground, he hurried over to take a look. A Pratt's Grocery Store logo was printed on the side of the bag; a pale yellow ribbon was tied around the top. One tug, and the ribbon came away in his hand. Reaching inside, he drew out a can of insect repellent.

Cale turned in every direction.

There was only one person who could have known he needed this, one person who would have thought of it. Willow must have circled back around when he wasn't looking, leaving the little gift where she knew he would find it, before creeping away, undetected. Willow Pratt was an unusual girl.

Something warm nudged him from inside, and he smiled.

Not everyone in Dawsons Hollow was as friendly as Willow. The people in the diner were especially antisocial. Taking a seat at a table for two, Cale ate his supper alone. The food was filling, the service adequate, the other patrons coolly aloof. He took advantage of the opportunity to hone his newly developed sixth sense. By the time he dropped some loose change on the table and paid for his meal at the counter near the door, he was pretty good at it. Of course, open stares were easy to sense.

The old man behind the counter in the bait and tackle shop that doubled as a hardware store was a little more subtle about the whole thing. When Cale had asked if there was any good fishing in the area, the old-timer had scratched his scraggly beard and stammered something about the time of the year and the depth and temperature of the water. He'd probably been using the same spiel on tourists for years.

The average Joe would have been back on the highway before he'd realized that an honest-to-goodness yes or no hadn't been forthcoming. Cale didn't blame the man. A good fishing spot was a secret worth guarding.

He was coming out of the grocery store, his eyes still adjusting to the bright evening sun, when he noticed Miranda locking her clinic for the night on the other side of the street. His steps slowed, coming to a complete stop as she cast a sweeping glance all around. He knew she'd noticed him, because she changed course and smiled, as if seeing him in town were the most natural thing in the world.

In this day and age, natural probably wasn't the way most women preferred to be described. But everything about Miranda seemed natural. The way she wore her hair, long and loose around her shoulders, the way she called hello to two little girls wearing tattered dresses and sunny smiles, the way she walked, glancing both ways before crossing the street. Her white cotton blouse and softly pleated beige slacks weren't normal nursing attire. Yet, on her, they looked as natural as could be. Her stride was long, the sway of her hips graceful, her smile artful and serene.

"Cale?"

He came to his senses, only to realize that she'd spoken his name twice, once before she'd asked him a question, and once after. "Hmm? Oh. I mean yes," he stammered. "The cabin's fine. It's really all I need. A roof over my head, a place to eat and sleep. I'll have the rent money for you in a few days. I know that sounds suspiciously like the check is in the mail, but I contacted the bank back in Columbus as well as a friend of mine. Sam's keeping an eye on my house, getting my mail, feeding the cat, that sort of thing. We go way back. We teach at the same high school. Anyway, I've transferred funds from one account to another."

When his voice finally trailed away, he found himself staring into Miranda's eyes.

"What's his name?" she asked.

Cale blinked. "Whose name? Sam Kennedy?"

"No. Your cat's."

With a shake of his head, he shifted the sack of groceries higher into his left arm and ran his right hand through his hair. "Curly."

"What happened?" Without forewarning, she took his sore fingers in her hand. She probably meant her touch to be a companionable gesture, a token of friendliness. It wasn't her fault that the merest brush of her finger on his palm sent need shooting up his arm.

He drew his hand out of hers. Turning it palm side up, he stared at the skin worn raw by his hammer. "It's been a while since I've done carpentry work."

"I see. Are you a Three Stooges fan?"

Okay. There was probably a perfectly good reason he was having a little trouble with the change in topic. Maybe it was because he was having a hard time concentrating. Maybe *that* was because all the blood seemed to have left his brain, heading for a place directly south of there. "No, why?"

"A cat named Curly?"

"He was Ellie's cat."

A car in dire need of a new muffler rumbled by. Cale glanced at the driver, a little old man who was too busy gawking to watch where he was going. And he was headed right for them.

Cale lunged backward, taking Miranda with him. Pebbles crunched beneath the bald tires before the driver slammed on his brakes, lurching to a stop exactly where Cale and Miranda had been standing.

"Ever'thing okay there, M'randa?" the man called, giving Cale the evil eye.

While Cale scowled, Miranda said, "I'm fine, Jed. Nice night for a poker game."

The old man nodded for all he was worth, grinned a little, mumbled something about feeling lucky, then drove off the sidewalk and on toward the Bootlegger. Cale was still scowling when Miranda looked at him. The more he scowled, the more her smile grew.

"Lucky? That old man almost ran you over with his car,

and yet he acted as if I were with the Russian Mafia or something. He's a menace behind that steering wheel.''

''Jed Hershey only drives once a week, and then only to the Bootlegger and back. He'll play a little poker with his friends, have his weekly smoke and shot of whiskey. He'll complain about the weather, his rheumatism, and his cards, and then he'll drive back home again. Folks know to stay off the street on Thursdays at eight o'clock and ten o'clock sharp.''

''You're kidding.''

She was still smiling.

''Dammit, it's not funny. Even if he doesn't hurt anybody else, he could hurt himself. What if he drives over the edge of a cliff?''

''Cale?''

''There are hairpin turns in these hills. I'm surprised he hasn't ended up at the bottom of a ravine.''

''Cale?''

It wasn't the soft voice so much as it was the gentle hand on his forearm that finally got through to him. He glanced at her fingers first and then at her face. Her eyebrows were arched, her lashes dark, her eyes pools of humor and appeal. She pointed down the street. ''See that brick house down the block there?''

He gave her a grudging nod.

''That's Jed's place. As y'all can see, there aren't many hairpin turns between here and there.''

She averted her eyes, but not before Cale saw her bite her lip in an unsuccessful attempt to hold in her laughter. She wasn't even laughing with him. She was laughing at him. He understood that. What he didn't understand was why he felt no anger. Hell, he was dangerously close to laughing right along with her, and Caleb Wilder hadn't felt like laughing in a long, long time.

''I'd be careful if I were you,'' she said. ''If y'all actually laugh out loud, there's a chance you'll feel human. Worse, you might even look approachable.''

She sashayed away from him. Shaking his head, Cale called, "You think you're smart, don't you?"

She turned around, still smiling.

"*I'm* not unapproachable," he said, moving slowly toward her. "It isn't my fault that the people on this mountain aren't partial to strangers."

Tucking a strand of hair behind one ear, she glanced around and lowered her voice. "People up here are cautious, that's all. They're hospitable but not wholly trusting."

"That's like saying the ocean isn't wholly dry."

Miranda grinned. She couldn't help it. She couldn't remember the last time she'd truly enjoyed herself with a man. The only other man on the planet who made her laugh like this was her brother, Alex. There was nothing brotherly about Cale. His eyes looked at least five shades darker than the sky behind him, his voice every bit as deep at the force that drove him. Still, she couldn't help laughing again. When Cale joined in, her heartbeat quickened, and a traitorous softness drew her attention to her chest, to the pit of her stomach, and very slowly to nether regions a good Southern girl simply didn't think about in broad daylight.

"By the way," he said. "Thanks for the housewarming gifts."

"The what?"

"The broom and the mop and the bucket. They were in the cabin when I got there this morning."

Just then, Ruby came bustling out of the grocery store, and Miranda said, "I didn't leave those items for you, Cale."

"Who else knows I'm renting that cabin?"

They both turned, staring as Ruby barreled past them. Miranda crossed her arms and tapped one foot. "I think somebody has a crush on you."

Ruby stopped abruptly. "I heard that. He's young enough to be my boy. Can't a person be neighborly?"

Since Cale had already exhausted that topic, he simply said, "I owe you one, Ruby."

Eyes narrowing, she looked him up and down. "You mean that?"

Cale was almost afraid to nod.

"In that case," Ruby said bossily, "you can help me carry these groceries to my place. Unless there's somethin' else you'd rather do."

Of its own volition, Cale's gaze returned to Miranda. She was walking away from him, on her way to see a patient or tend her herbs. The waitress from the diner was peering out the window. The old man in the bait and tackle shop was doing the same from his. Even the man who'd nearly run him down was eyeing Cale suspiciously.

Cale strode to Ruby. Hefting one of her grocery bags into his free arm, he said, "If these folks ever need to find work, they could apply for a position as a government spy."

Ruby gave a derisive snort. "Half of these folks could use a job that paid decent, but I doubt any of them would wanna work for a government that's spent the last hundred years alternately exploiting 'em and ignoring 'em."

They turned the corner, heading north along one of the few side streets in town. "How many people live in Dawsons Hollow, Ruby?"

"In the village limits? About eighty. There's a handful of families that still live in remote cabins, but most of the other residents live in hilltop communities we call pockets and outsiders call clusters. Early settlers built their homes close together, as many as five and ten in a pocket, anyplace the mountain leveled off enough to build a house where an egg wouldn't roll off the table." She pointed to a hill that was visible between the branches of trees. "That there's the closest pocket to town. My cousin Ruthie Pratt lives in that big house up there."

"Ruthie Pratt's your cousin?"

Ruby readjusted the sack in her arms and pulled a face. "You'd never know it by lookin' at us, but, yeah, we're first cousins. 'Course, a young doctor who wanted to set up a practice here a few years back used to like to say that everybody in Dawsons Hollow was related. Once told me that DNA testin' would never work up here on accounta everybody has the same. At the time I didn't know what it meant, but I could tell by the way he said it that it wasn't no compliment.''

A pickup truck with lifts so high it surely required a ladder to climb in and out of its cab rounded the corner. The driver and passenger, two dark-haired young men in their early twenties, gawked at Cale as they passed him, just like everyone else in town did.

Ruby waved. The driver put his foot to the metal, brake torquing all the way to the next corner. Ruby said, ''That was two of Ruthie's boys. Skeeter and Tommy Lee.''

''Willow's brothers?'' Cale asked.

Ruby made that clicking sound again with her tongue, the one she made without opening her mouth. ''Hellions, those two. Not that they're much different than the rest of 'em.''

''How many are there?''

''Six boys and Willow. She ain't exactly been a picnic to raise either. Not that Ruthie's tried real hard with any of 'em. Some folks say she comes by her laziness naturally. I think that's a pitiful excuse to let kids run wild.''

Cale and Ruby had reached a lane that led to a neat little house with pretty blue siding. ''Always wanted to get my hands on 'em,'' Ruby said. ''Maybe mother 'em a little. Ruthie wouldn't let me, of course. Said I was cursed.''

Cale came to a stop, his right foot on the first porch step, his eyes on Ruby's back. ''Cursed, how?''

She kept walking and talking even as the screen door bounced closed behind her. ''It's a long story. Bring those groceries on in here.''

Cale followed her as far as the kitchen, but he lost sight of her beyond a doorway on the far side of the room. Since he couldn't very well stand around with his arms loaded down with groceries, he placed hers on the marred countertop and turned to go.

He was heading across her porch when her voice sounded

behind him. Cale jumped, swore, and had to juggle his own sack of groceries to keep from dropping it. The woman had to be pushing sixty and she moved without making a sound.

Coming through the door, she carried what appeared to be a homemade pillow. On top of the pillow was a stack of threadbare towels and faded sheets.

Cale could have asked a hundred questions about the Pratts alone, and another hundred about the curse Ruby had mentioned. Before he could voice any of them, Ruby handed the linens to him. "I figure this is all you can carry tonight. It'll get you through for a coupla days. Your boy'll be wanting a pillow when he figures out a place with running water beats the tar out of a place without."

"You know where Danny's staying." It wasn't a question.

"What makes you say that?"

Tucking the linens beneath his left arm, Cale said, "It's like I said my first night on the mountain. You look like the kind of capable woman who knows a great deal about a lot of things."

"And you look like the kind of man who knows how to flatter a woman. Now, go on. Git off my property before I get my gun."

Since it wouldn't have been the first time this week that Cale found himself staring down the wrong side of a long barreled shotgun, he gave her a wide berth and did as she'd said.

"Mr. Wilder?" she called to his back when he'd reached the end of her driveway. "If that boy of yours doesn't look you up in the next day or two, I'll show you where he's staying."

Powerful relief surged through Cale. It reminded him that he wasn't completely alone. Not in this life, not in this situation with Danny.

"If my hands weren't full, I'd walk back up those steps and hug you."

That got a cackle out of her. "You do that and I'll get that gun for sure."

Thinking that he liked this bossy mountain woman with

the wide gray streaks in her hair and the lines in her face she didn't even bother trying to hide, Cale bid her good night and set off for his cabin on Hawksbill Road.

It was almost dark by the time he reached his place. He turned on a light, which, he was pleased to discover, worked, and hauled the mattresses inside. He was tucking in the sheets Ruby had lent him, when he noticed that his hand didn't hurt anymore. He turned it over, staring at his palm. The blisters were still evident, but they were no longer sore; the redness was nearly gone. Which was strange, because they'd hurt like a son of a bitch when he'd reached into his back pocket for his wallet in Pratt's Grocery Store.

That was just before he'd run into Miranda, and she'd taken his hand in hers. He hadn't given his blisters any thought after that. Why would he, when he'd been more aware of a different sort of ache totally unrelated to swinging a hammer?

That a simple touch could heal a wound was impossible, wasn't it? He thought about Celia Winters's boy and his own bruised ribs. And Cale didn't know. He just didn't know.

He finished making the bed, and since there was no sense broadcasting a free midnight snack to any mosquitoes that hadn't already discovered him, he turned out the light. He didn't have a radio or a television, so he hauled a cane-backed chair out to the porch and sat there while the sky geared up for its nightly production. Tipping the chair back, he balanced on the rear two legs and stared at the mountain ridges in the distance. His thoughts formed the way the night did—slowly, deeply, reverently.

He was beginning to understand why Ellie had loved this place, but he didn't understand why she hadn't come back to it. He thought about Willow Pratt and Ruby McCoy and Miranda Sinclair, about bark tea and yellow ribbons and curses that seemed as prevalent up here as the rich mountain folklore. He didn't see any shooting stars. And when he went inside the rustic though relatively clean cabin an hour later, when he crawled into the bed with the creaky bedsprings and thin mattress, and when he rubbed his eyes with the hand that ached less than it had two hours earlier, he noticed that the place deep inside him, the place some people called the heart, others the spirit, still others the soul, ached a little less too.

CHAPTER EIGHT

Birdsong.

Daniel wasn't dreaming this time. Birds really were singing. When the same sounds had so rudely awakened him his first morning here, he'd rolled over on the narrow bed, grumbling about the annoying twitter of robins and sparrows and the obnoxious caw of blue jays. Today, it was blessed, for the sound of birdsong could mean only one thing. It was morning. The long night was over.

His stomach growled so loudly, the raccoon stirred in his sleep in the box nearby. Swinging his feet over the side of the bed, Daniel sat up. He'd slept in his jeans, and it took only a moment to shrug into his shirt and slip into his shoes. After that it was just a matter of tiptoeing over the splintery boards that made up the floor and heading on out to the rotting front step.

He stood there, one hand on his sore stomach, his eyes on the mountain that was just now coming awake. Dawn. There was no one word in the entire English language to describe the color of the sky.

Night had a way of unnerving him, but morning was a gift. At least morning here.

He hadn't given morning much thought back in Ohio. In fact, before his mother died, he'd taken morning for granted. He'd taken a lot of things for granted. His mother's death had started an ache that began in his chest and stretched to a place he couldn't name.

He missed his mom. The words seemed as inadequate as calling the dawning sky blue. Last night, when he'd been trying to pass the minutes of a night that dragged into eternity, he'd tried to decide what he missed the most. A dozen things had swarmed into his head. The way she smiled, the way she laughed, the way she moved, breathed, hummed while she was fixing supper. Even the way she didn't let him railroad her. She didn't feel sorry for him either. When he complained about the kids at school, she told him to try harder or give it time or both. He thought about Willow Pratt, his newest, and strangest, friend. His mom had been right.

He smiled, and it hurt. She was always right.

He missed his mom. Saying it didn't change the fact. But it was more than he'd been able to do a few months ago. Maybe that healing his dad talked about had finally started.

He didn't miss her less up here, but at least up here he didn't have to try to pretend everything was all right. He didn't feel as if there were a time bomb waiting to explode if he didn't make a decision in ten seconds or less. He wasn't sure people were meant to spend their entire lives running around like ants, taking tests and measuring themselves by someone else's standards, trying to be something or somebody. As far as Daniel was concerned, it didn't matter whether the person was a kid trying to make good grades or an adult trying to make good money. A lot of adults who made a lot of money and a lot of kids who made good grades were awfully unhappy.

Not everyone was unhappy. His mother had been the happiest person he'd ever known. She'd made it look so easy. Ellie Wilder had the kind of calm and serenity that drew others like cool shade on a sweltering day. He'd loved being her son. Maybe that connection was what he missed the most. He'd always known Cale had adopted him. He'd felt honored that a man like Cale had wanted to give a skinny little freakish kid his name, his time, his love. In deference to the gift Cale had given him, Daniel had stored away the questions pertaining to his real father. He couldn't do that anymore. Now he needed to know how he'd come to be. He needed to learn about the part of his mother's life he knew nothing of and the man she'd never talked about—his real father.

Daniel always thought there would be time to ask about his biological father. But then, time ran out.

One second he and Cale had been hanging around the garage, talking and waiting for his mother to get home like they always did. And the next second the phone rang. And everything changed.

They'd rushed to the hospital, bursting into the emergency room on a run. She'd been taken into surgery; a lifetime passed while he and Cale waited for word about her condition. When the surgeon finally appeared, he was somber yet cautiously hopeful. She'd suffered internal injuries. The next several hours would be critical.

And then, finally, they brought her to her room. For an instant, the fear that had burrowed into Daniel's chest had eased. His mother wasn't dead. She was right there in that hospital bed with an IV in her arm and doctors all around. She was gravely injured. But she opened her eyes when he entered the room, and she smiled at him. His mother.

And he smiled in return.

Then she closed her eyes again. And the fear had come back, worse than before. During the next two hours, he and Cale were banished to the hall several times while the doctors and nurses took her vitals and assessed her condition. Each time they returned to her room, she opened her eyes and smiled at them. Daniel was no longer relieved or fooled. There was a glimmer in her eyes he'd never seen before, a secret knowledge that instilled the greatest fear he'd ever known.

The same horror Daniel was feeling had been etched in

Cale's face. They told her to rest, but she wouldn't. Her lips had been so dry, her throat convulsing each time she swallowed. It was as if she'd known that she had but a matter of minutes to say everything that was in her heart. She told them both she loved them, and she talked about the first time she held Danny when he'd been but minutes old, and how proud she'd always been of him. She spoke of the day she'd married Cale, and how much the two of them had filled her life that had once been so empty. She spoke so softly, it had been difficult to hear. Daniel and Cale had leaned close, their heads nearly touching from opposite sides of the bed, their eyes trained on her, memorizing her face, her hair, the beauty deep inside her.

She talked about people Daniel had never heard of, and places she'd rarely mentioned. Sometimes she talked out of her head. Mostly, she spoke of love, and birth and life and how she'd never been sorry.

And then she closed her eyes. Her fingers went limp in each of their hands. Daniel knew she was slipping away from them. And he begged her not to leave him. She was too weak to do more than sigh. Buzzers sounded, and doctors and nurses rushed in, barking orders.

Again, Cale and Danny were banished to the hall. The doctors and nurses worked on her for a long time, but with every passing moment, the expressions on their faces became more telling. So Danny had turned to Cale, his last hope. "You can do anything, Dad. Don't let her die."

Cale rushed through the door, but a hush had fallen over the room. The team of medical professionals shook their heads gently as they removed the emergency medical equipment and quietly left the room. Cale had wrapped his arms around Danny's mother, holding her in his big, capable hands, holding on for dear life. Later, it had taken two doctors and an orderly to gently pry him away from her.

Her injuries had been too serious, they'd said. There was nothing anybody could have done.

It didn't make sense. After that, nothing had.

They drove to the lot where her car had been taken. It

was so grotesquely misshapen, it was no wonder she hadn't survived. The man who'd been driving the semi truck that had jackknifed directly in front of her on that fateful day had called to tell them how sorry he was. Cale had spoken to the man. Danny had been beyond words by then. It turned out the truck driver hadn't been at fault. He'd been trying to miss a van full of people whose vehicle had spun out of control when a deer had leaped into the van's path. The animal had paid with her life. Sometimes, in his sleep, Daniel saw his mother and that doe standing together on a distant cloud. He couldn't talk about it though.

Cale had tried to help him, but without his mother there, they had become strangers. He and Cale had gone to see a grief counselor. It had been that counselor who'd put the idea of finding his birth father in Danny's head. Not that he'd intended to. Danny scowled. When it came to helping him sort out his feelings, the guy was about as effective as Delvecchio.

"Let's talk about your anger," he'd said.

"Who says I'm angry?" Daniel had asked before he could stop himself.

"You seem to have directed it at your father. I understand he adopted you when you were three."

Daniel had clamped his mouth shut, and no amount of prodding from someone who only thought he knew what went on in the deepest recesses of a boy's mind could get him to talk. Daniel and Cale had both come away dissatisfied and more distant than ever. Someone had sent him to the guidance counselor at school after that. That was even more useless. Then, a month ago, Mr. Delvecchio had shoved brochures from some of the most prestigious colleges in the country into his hand. Good old Bud had insisted it was time for Daniel to get over his mother's death and on with his own life.

Something had started to rage inside Daniel. Maybe that grief counselor had been right. Maybe he was angry. He wasn't even fifteen years old. Did he have to know this very minute what he was going to be doing five years from now? Ten years? Twenty?

What difference would it make? In a hundred years, hell, in fifty, nobody would remember him anyway.

When Daniel had first decided to come to Dawsons Hollow, he'd thought he was running away from something. Now he believed he'd been running *to* something all along.

To what remained to be seen. More important, to whom.

In the light of a brand-new morning, Daniel felt hopeful for the first time in eighteen long, lonely months.

He didn't want to hurt Cale. That much he knew for sure. Maybe other kids wouldn't have needed to find their real father. Maybe what they said about him was true. Maybe Daniel really was weird. Maybe his IQ made him need answers more than other people did. Once, he'd blurted out that being smart was a curse. His mom had waited a few heartbeats to say, "It can be whatever you make it, a curse or a gift. I guess it's up to you. What do you want, son?"

What he wanted was to make her proud. What he needed was answers. *See,* he thought as he set off for the stream nearby, *life really is simpler up here.*

He was learning to move quietly along the trails. Yesterday he'd come across a doe and her fawn. Even though he'd held perfectly still, the mother must have sensed him. With utmost caution, she'd nudged her baby to his feet, then bustled him into the nearby woods. The family of rabbits Daniel had seen last night when he'd been gathering berries had been just as cautious. The birds were different. As long as he made no sudden moves or loud noises, they went about their business as if he weren't there.

He reached the stream hours before he would have attempted to get up back home. Standing on the grassy bank, he ran a hand across his empty stomach. The wild berries he'd eaten for supper had made him sick as a dog, too sick to hike down to that pretty woman's mailbox. Now he had no food, and very little milk for the raccoon.

He'd been awake much of the night, writhing on the narrow wooden bed with its mattress made of straw ticking. He'd fed the raccoon around three. Shortly thereafter, the pain had subsided. Lying in that drowsy place between sleep and wakefulness, Daniel had decided that he couldn't go on this way indefinitely. He couldn't survive on wild berries, and one day soon, he was going to start looking for the man who had fathered him. He didn't exactly know how to go about doing that. But there had to be a way.

While birds twittered in trees overhead, Daniel went down on his knees and splashed his face with mountain water, then drank from his cupped hand. The blessedly cool water left a soothing trail from his lips all the way down to his empty stomach.

He'd brought two hundred dollars with him from Ohio. He'd spent thirty of it getting here. Unless he found a way to earn more, the rest was going to go fast.

Peering into the shadows in the distance, he wondered what kids around here did for money. If that girl, Willow, happened to stop by, he would ask her. Even if she didn't, it looked as if he was going to have to go into town.

He glanced down at his clothes. His pants were dirty where he'd kneeled on the ground, and his shirt had two stains, compliments of his raccoon. Most people didn't trust teenagers. Folks up here trusted strangers even less. At best, he had a slim chance that anyone would hire him. His uncle Sam always said, "If you're going to leave a lasting impression, might as well make it a good one." Since Daniel couldn't very well make a good impression smelling worse than a skunk, he peeled off his shirt, dropped it on the stream bank, and went back to the cabin for the soap and the rest of his clothes.

Cale hefted a large branch onto his pile of debris. Rubbing the crumbling bark off his hands, he returned to the pickup truck he'd discovered earlier. Hidden in the tall weeds as it had been, and covered with fallen branches and dead leaves, he'd practically overlooked it. It had been idle curiosity that had caused him to begin dragging the dead branches off the hood and out of the truck's box. At first he didn't see how it could have been anything other than junk. Upon closer inspection, it didn't look that bad. It was a late-sixties model. Underneath the dirt, it was dark blue. There was surprisingly little rust, which just went to show that they didn't make 'em like they used to. The tires were flat, of course, the upholstery torn. Rodents had chewed through its engine belts. It needed oil, spark plugs, a tune-up, probably a muffler, and who knew what else. It would have been the perfect vehicle to take into school back home. He would have enjoyed showing his auto-mechanic students how to fix it, then give them enough room and freedom to take it apart and put it back together.

He heard the sound of a car or truck in the distance. Sounds carried for long distances up here, and Cale didn't pay this one much attention until it turned off the road and pulled to a stop near his cabin. The man from the bait and tackle shop climbed out.

"May I help you?" Cale called.

"Nope." Probably in his sixties, the man went around to the back of his truck, pulled on a pair of brown jersey gloves, and slid a sheet of glass toward him.

Baffled, Cale asked, "What are you doing?"

The other man took his time answering. "M'randa ordered new glass for them windows of yours."

He went about his business without further explanation. After hauling a half dozen items from his truck, he carted them to the cabin. He wore bib overalls and a long-sleeved shirt despite the humidity and high temperature. His movements were slow but efficient, his procedure methodical.

"Are you sure you couldn't use a little help?"

"Yup."

Cale had heard of yup-and-nope talkers, but this was the first time he'd actually met one. Not that he and the other man had been properly introduced.

Another car turned onto the lane. Ruby McCoy pulled up

in a car the size of a small ocean liner. "Your boy show up yet?" she called through her open window.

Cale shook his head.

"Might as well come with me, then."

Cale glanced from the car that would ultimately take him to Danny, and the cabin where the quiet craftsman was busy working. Everything he had with him was in that cabin. In Columbus, hell, in the rest of the world, men didn't leave a stranger with free access to all his possessions.

"Better get a move on," the other man said without looking up. "Ruby McCoy ain't the kind of woman a man keeps waitin'."

Cale started toward Ruby's car, thinking that for a man who hadn't so much as introduced himself, he gave good advice. Cale only hoped he was also trustworthy.

"Would you give me a minute to grab the sack of groceries I picked up for Danny?" he asked.

"Leave 'em until next time."

Cale would have liked to argue, but since he could take the food to his son anytime once he knew where Danny was staying, he did as Ruby said.

It was a good thing, because she didn't leave Cale much time to get in, and started to back up before he'd closed his door. She looked straight ahead, both hands on the steering wheel, her grip so tight, her knuckles looked white. "Miranda said she was gonna hire Clyde Sturgis to put some windowpanes in that place."

Clyde Sturgis. So that was his name.

"Clyde's a jack-of-all-trades, and a hard worker, but not much of a talker."

Cale couldn't argue there. Just then a mouthwatering aroma wafted to his nose. Glancing at the picnic baskets resting on the backseat, he said, "You taking me on a picnic, Ruby?"

A lesser man would have been impaled by her piercing look alone. Cale felt himself smile.

"I take a meal up to Moot Nelson every Friday. Figured I might as well make enough for your boy while I was at it. Fixed my famous beef Stroganoff and whole wheat bread. Don't know if he likes vegetables, but I fixed some anyway.''

"That's nice, Ruby." And then, more quietly, "Is Moot a man's name?"

Her lips twitched a little at that. "His real name's Maurice. I wouldn't call him that if I were you. He's over ninety years old, skinny as a rail, ornery as a badger, and stubborn as a mule. He got a hearing aid once but refuses to wear it. It would be easier to talk to a stone than to him. My Harlan was Moot's last livin' relative.''

Cale stared out the window, thinking about that "was," and wondering if it had anything to do with the curse she'd mentioned last night. The old car's automatic transmission downshifted as it climbed the mountain road. The ground on the right rose steeply and fell away on the left. The road curved so much, he wouldn't have known which direction they were going if it hadn't been for the sun. They drove on in silence, Ruby clutching the steering wheel, Cale putting the route to memory. An unusual outcropping of rock marked one turn, a stump piled high with boulders another. She turned right onto a trail somebody had marked with a tin bucket stuck upside down over a rotting fence post.

It was hard to imagine Danny living up here. Even more difficult to imagine was that his son had *chosen* to live up here. "I never knew he liked the wilderness," Cale said, thinking out loud.

"Must be some mountain man in him somewheres."

Cale glanced sharply at Ruby. She was just making conversation, wasn't she? Could she know anything about Danny's—Cale swallowed hard—father? Aside from having Ellie back, there wasn't anything in the world he wanted more than to have Danny decide he didn't want or need to know who his biological father was.

Ruby's gravelly voice broke into Cale's thoughts. "This here's Hickory Gap Road. Your boy's stayin' in the old Morris place. You think yours is rustic, wait'll you see his.''

"It's a long way from town."

She nodded. "Three miles on foot if you take the shortcuts. Closer to five in a car. Seems farther on account of all these curves.''

They drove past one of those pockets of houses Ruby had mentioned, and two or three rustic cabins, before she pulled into a path that had probably once passed as a driveway. Cale climbed out of the car, peering all around. Ruby was right about the shape the place was in. It had a tin roof, a crumbling stone chimney, rotting steps, and no front door.

Eyeing the socks, underwear, shirts, and jeans hanging over the bushes nearby, Ruby said, "Looks like laundry day. Don't forget the picnic basket. I'll be back for you in an hour or so.''

She pulled away slowly as soon as Cale took the basket from the backseat. Practically staggering beneath the basket's weight, he lifted one hand and waved. Ruby didn't look back. Keeping her white-knuckled grip on the steering wheel, she continued on up the mountain and out of sight.

As the crunch of tires faded into the distance, Cale looked around and called Danny's name. There was no answer. He strode to the cabin and poked his head inside. Again, he called Danny's name. Again, there was no answer. Leaving the basket on the rotting front steps, Cale shaded his eyes with one hand and studied the mountainside. He could hear water rushing over rocks nearby and started in that direction.

He'd taken only a few steps when Danny crested the hill. They both came to a stop, Danny in a patch of sunlight, Cale in the shade of an old hickory nut tree. Cale spoke first. "Hi.''

Danny, make that Daniel, Cale reminded himself, said, "I thought I heard a car.''

"Ruby McCoy gave me a ride.''

"The woman who lives around the corner from Miranda?''

"Yeah,'' Cale answered. "That's her.''

"Oh.''

Silence.

Cale felt close to bereft. He and Danny used to talk about everything. He didn't know how such a silence had formed between them. There had to be a way to breech it. If they'd been on better terms, he would have used a joke as a way to lure a smile out of his son. Trying to remember how it felt to be fourteen, Cale turned around, and with a sweep of his hand gestured to the clothes hanging on the bushes near the cabin. "Looks like you're getting the hang of rustic living."

"I washed everything in the creek. Somehow I don't think stonewashed jeans got their name this way. Are those stitches in your forehead?"

Cale's fingers went to the cut automatically. "I got caught in a bad storm flying down here. Had to make an emergency landing in a narrow meadow. It was a bumpy ride, and I got thrown around a little. My head broke my fall."

Father and son shared a small smile, the first in a long, long time. When Danny came closer, Cale was struck by the intensity in his son's eyes. The boy was getting tall. In a year or two, he'd probably be looking him in the eye. His son was thin, proud, defiant. There was a depth to his eyes, and wisdom in them, and upon closer inspection, dark circles underneath them.

"Rough night?" Cale asked.

A few weeks ago a question like that would have produced a deafening silence or an angry litany. Today Danny glanced away, but he answered. "I think it was something I ate."

Maybe they were making progress after all. "What did you eat?"

"Wild berries."

"Eat a lot of them, did you?"

Danny grimaced, as if just thinking about it was turning him slightly green.

"Think you could eat something now?" Cale asked.

"Did you bring food?" He'd spoken fast, too fast, giving his hunger away.

"I didn't. Ruby did. Let's take a look."

Cale opened the basket's lid and removed a heavy bowl and plates, cutlery, and glasses for two. Ruby was either a saint or a genius or both. She'd fixed beef Stroganoff and crusty bread and green bean casserole. She'd packed lemonade and a gallon of milk, and a plate of butterscotch cookies too. There was a lot of food. There wasn't a doubt in Cale's mind that Danny could eat it all in one day.

"Where do you want to eat?" Cale asked.

"I usually sit out here on the steps."

The silence that settled over them as they ate wasn't hostile, but it wasn't altogether companionable either. Danny was too busy eating to notice. And eating. And eating. Cale tried not to be caught staring, but it wasn't easy. Oh, how he'd missed this boy.

When Danny had eaten his fill, they packed up the leftovers. They worked well together. They always had. Once the work was done, neither of them knew what to do or where to look. There were a hundred things Cale wanted to tell Danny. Not a single word would form.

A tiny mewling sound came from the cabin. "What's that?" Cale asked.

Danny climbed slowly to his feet. "That's the raccoon. Would you like to see him?"

Following Danny inside, Cale wondered when Danny had become so polite. He'd always been shy, but this reserve was different. It was difficult to penetrate and impossible to overlook.

The raccoon teetered up on his hind legs, so insistent and chubby and overzealous, he tipped over backward, legs flailing like a turtle stuck on his back. Cale couldn't help laughing. He couldn't help noticing that the animal quieted when Danny picked him up too. "He thinks you're his mother," Cale said. "Or his father," he amended quietly.

"No. He thinks I'm his mother." The raccoon nuzzled Danny's neck, making him chuckle the way he had when he was a little boy.

A yearning so strong it was difficult to suppress washed over Cale. He'd never been a demonstrative man. He loved his son, and he'd loved his wife. Putting it into words or actions was something else. Now he wished he were better at it, wished he knew how to reach a hand to Danny's shoulder, how to convey the depth of feeling he had for this boy.

Cale moved his hand an inch, and then another.

Danny's attention was on the raccoon as he said, "If the guys back home ever found out about this, I'd never live it down. Mr. Delvecchio would have a field day with it."

Danny turned, and the moment was lost. Sighing, Cale slid his hands into his pockets. "Bud Delvecchio gives all high school guidance counselors a bad name."

Danny looked at his, er, Cale with surprise. "You don't like Delvecchio either?"

"Nobody likes Bud Delvecchio."

"No shit?"

Cale grimaced slightly, then nodded. "Has he been giving you trouble?"

Danny glanced away. "Forget the fact that he has the personality of an eel. He thinks everybody should know what they want to be before they enter the second grade."

Cale sighed. He hadn't known. He wondered what else was bothering his son. "Is he putting pressure on you?"

"He was."

"Next time he asks you what you want to be when you grow up, tell him you've decided to be a zookeeper and see what he says."

They shared a smile of sorts before they both glanced away. Danny busied himself preparing a bottle for the raccoon. Cale mumbled something about bringing Danny's clean clothes in. They may not have been blood related, but they were both experts at dodging uncomfortable silences.

As soon as Cale went outside, Daniel sat on the edge of the bed to feed the raccoon, thinking. A zookeeper indeed. He'd had no idea they could joke about that. He doubted Mr. Delvecchio would think it was funny. He would undoubtedly sneer, insisting that Daniel wasn't working up to his potential. No matter what Delvecchio said, Daniel had given his future a great deal of thought. Grudgingly, he supposed the little weasel was right about one thing. Daniel's IQ was going to open a lot of doors for him. The question was, which door? He was good with numbers, but they held little appeal. He was the most interested in science. The solar system intrigued him. He'd toyed with the idea of becoming an astronaut. Unfortunately, even the most notorious astronauts went into space only a handful of times if they were lucky. Everything else was training and theory and numbers. Daniel wanted a more hands-on occupation. He was a fair violinist and a relatively good pianist. His teachers had shaken their heads, because although he had great finger dexterity, he didn't feel the music the way great musicians did.

He had little interest in business. Even less in law. That left medicine. He'd always been fascinated with the human body, with all its systems and cell structures and all the hundreds of things that could go wrong with it and the millions of things that went right. Early on, his fascination had probably stemmed from his mother, for she'd been a neonatal nurse at City General. The sight of blood didn't bother him, but as he'd scrubbed at the disgusting by-product of all the milk he'd fed his raccoon, he knew he would rather be a surgeon or an oncologist or a neurologist than the person changing bedpans. Not that there was anything wrong with doing that. It was just that if he was going to get his hands dirty, he would rather do it on the other end of a patient.

The raccoon finished his milk, then nuzzled Daniel's neck. It tickled, and he grinned. Maybe he would become a zookeeper after all. Or maybe he would stay up here forever.

Cale hauled the stack of clothes inside and put them on the bed. Daniel lowered the raccoon back into the box. Now that their tasks were done, an uncomfortable silence fell over them.

Cale strode to the window. Daniel hung back, closer to the old wood stove. Gathering his courage, he said, "Cale—er—Dad?"

"Hmm?"

"I came to Georgia for a reason."

After a long stretch of silence, Cale said, "I'm listening."

"I'm going to look for my biological father." There, he'd said it. It was finally out in the open. He didn't know what to expect. It didn't take a genius to read Cale's reaction. He took a deep breath, ran a hand through his hair, and slowly turned around.

Something went warm inside Daniel. He wished he knew what to say to the man who'd raised him this far. Until then, he'd thought only about his feelings, his needs. For the first time, he wondered how Cale would feel about his wish to look for his biological father. Would he understand, try to stop him?

Daniel felt the need to defend his decision. "I can't explain it, Dad, Cale, Dad. But it's something I have to do."

"I figured as much, Danny. Daniel." Cale swore under his breath. Hell, neither of them knew what to call the other anymore. "Do you know how you're going to do that?"

The boy shook his head. "Did Mom ever talk to you about him?"

Cale thought back to the conversations he and Ellie had had before he'd married her. "She didn't say much about him. We fell in love quickly. From the moment I met the two of you, it felt right, as if it was meant to be. I didn't ask many questions. I didn't care who the other man had been. You were both mine by then. That's all that mattered. I guess I always knew you would grow up and want to know. But I always thought your mother would be here to handle it."

They both fell silent, thinking about that. Finally, Daniel said, "Then she told you nothing?"

Cale searched his memories. Ellie had told him that she'd grown up in North Carolina. Her mother died when she was fifteen, and although she never knew her father, she went to live with his distant relatives. She was very lonely. She'd once told Cale that they didn't give her a lot of love, but they gave her an education, which, when all was said and done, was nothing to shake a stick at. Despite all that, she'd had a marvelous sense of humor and an incredible inner strength. During that time in her life, she spent summers in the Appalachian Mountains with an elderly aunt on her mother's side. The space for the father's name was blank on Daniel's birth certificate. Since it listed Rabun County as the place of birth, Cale had always assumed this was where she'd met Danny's father. Why else would she have had him here?

Danny was extremely bright, and in many ways older than his fourteen years. But he was still just a kid. A kid whose jaw was set, his eyes steady, his mind made up. Still, Cale had to try to warn him. "I think there was a reason your mother didn't talk about your father."

"You think he went to prison or something?"

The differences in the way a teenager's and an adult's mind worked never ceased to amaze Cale. "I doubt that. I've always wondered if perhaps he'd been married to some-one else. Your mother was lonely, and if she'd fallen in love with a married man, it would explain a lot. She was twenty-one when you were born. She once told me that six years of loneliness were wiped out the first time she held you."

The sound of an approaching car carried through the gap-ing windows and doorway. It was too early for Ruby to be back, but Cale glanced at the lane anyway. "I know you miss her, son. And I know you wouldn't reach a decision like this lightly. I'd hate to see her memory marred in any way."

"Marred?"

"People who keep secrets usually have very good reasons. What if we discover that he was married, or any number of other scenarios? It's the proverbial Pandora's box. Once we open it, there'll be no turning back."

"We?"

A car pulled into the lane, its driver laying on the horn. It was Ruby, and she wasn't alone. Cale and Danny walked out to the porch for a better look. Something was wrong. Cale had to go, but first, he said, "You're not in this alone. No matter what you call me. No matter what you want me to call you. And no matter who your biological father is, you're my son. I wouldn't have followed somebody else's kid to these mountains."

Several yards away, Ruby was getting out of the car. "Moot's taken sick. I've gotta get him to Miranda's clinic. If I drive, I'll kill him for sure."

Cale glanced from Ruby to a feeble-looking man huddled in one corner of the backseat. His eyes were shut, and he seemed to be in pain. Turning back to Danny, he said, "Come with us."

Danny shook his head.

"I know you're a bright kid. But you're only fourteen."

"My raccoon needs me."

Cale's throat convulsed on a swallow. It had always been difficult to put his feelings into words. Forcing the words past a lump the size of a fist in his throat, he looked Danny in the eye and said, "Your raccoon isn't the only one who needs you."

He saw Danny's surprise. But then the boy was shaking his head again, reminding Cale of all the times Ellie had said, "If stubbornness were blood, you two could share a kidney!"

"You coming, Cale?" Ruby called.

"Yeah." To his son, he said, "I'll be back."

And Danny said, "I figured you would be. I'll think about what you said."

"That sounds fair," which was strange, Cale thought, hurrying toward the car, because lately, little had seemed fair. He climbed behind the wheel. "What's wrong with Moot?" he asked Ruby.

"I'm old, what do ya think's wrong with me?"

While Ruby sputtered about old coots with selective hearing, Cale put the shifting lever into drive and started down the mountain. He looked back just before pulling onto the mountain road. Danny stood on the top step near the picnic basket, watching him drive away.

CHAPTER NINE

Cale steered around deep potholes, navigated sharp curves, and turned at corners marked by an old bucket, stones piled on a rotting stump, and an unusual outcropping of rocks. The squeal of tires as he rounded the final corner alerted the townsfolk, who came out of their houses and stores to investigate the commotion. Miranda must have heard his noisy approach too, because she met him at the clinic's door.

It didn't take long to get Moot out of the car, into a wheelchair, and inside the clinic. Miranda spoke quietly to Ruby, and then to Moot before wheeling him into an examination room and closing the door.

Suddenly, the atmosphere inside the Morningstar Medical Clinic was quiet. Too quiet. In the aftermath of the adrenaline rush, Cale's stomach twisted into one huge knot. He had to get out of there.

"You leavin'?"

That *had* been the plan. Planting his feet, he glanced around the sparsely furnished waiting room. Toys were scattered about, a child's storybook was still open to a colorful page, and what appeared to be a woman's lightweight sweater had been left behind on the back of one chair.

Miranda had obviously seen other patients, but right now Cale and Ruby were alone in the small outer room. If he thought Ruby's knuckles had been white during the drive down the mountain, it was nothing compared to how white they were where she gripped the arms of her chair. Obviously, she didn't like waiting rooms any better than he did. Rotating a kink from between his shoulder blades, he strode to a low table, reached for a sports magazine, and took a seat across from Ruby, as if he'd planned to stay all along.

He leafed through the magazine. Unfortunately, he didn't have much interest in a basketball player who dyed his hair a different color every week or a boxer who fought dirty. Therefore, the magazine held little appeal. Maybe talking would help.

He ran a hand through his hair. "My wife had nerves of steel when it came to waiting. Danny's like that too."

Ruby loosened her grip slightly. "How'd it go with your boy?"

Now, there was a question. "We're speaking again, if you can call it that. Your beef Stroganoff was a hit."

"Always is."

Cale settled himself more comfortably in his chair. "I gave him a lot to think about."

"Thinkin's good." She very nearly shuddered. "So long as you don't do too much of it."

He wasn't about to argue with that.

"Trouble is," she said, studying the bony knuckles in her right hand, "it's difficult to know how much is too much and how much ain't."

Cale was fairly certain he couldn't have put it better himself. He wondered if Danny was thinking about that Pandora's box he'd mentioned. While he was at it, he wondered how long it would take his son to make up his mind.

A creak on the other side of the room brought Ruby and Cale to their feet. They'd both taken three steps before the door had opened all the way. Miranda strode through, pushing a subdued Moot in a modern wheelchair.

Ruby rushed forward. "How is he?"

"He's going to be fine. His angina's acting up a little, that's all."

Moot Nelson had probably been a tall man once, but the years had shrunk his frame a decade at a time, and now he sat huddled in the chair, looking small and pale and thin. His nose stuck out from the center of his deeply lined face, and the top of his head was so freckled, it practically defied description. He had a little fuzzy tuft of hair in the front, and two more that resembled eyebrows directly over his ears. His eyes might have been blue once. Today, they were watery, the color a nondescript shade of gray.

He moved stiffly in the chair, nodded at Cale, and held out a gnarled hand. "Haven't had so much fun takin' a trip to the doctor in years. Usually have to rely on Ruby here, and she drives like a danged old woman."

"You don't have to shout!" Ruby exclaimed. "We aren't deaf. You are."

She turned to Miranda. "Don't suppose you talked this stubborn old fool into taking any medicine back up to his place with him."

There was an air of calm acceptance in the look Miranda gave her friend. "I convinced him to take a nitroglycerin tablet here, but you know Moot."

Moot sputtered, "Did she say medicine? I ain't takin' no more pills. Why, a man starts takin' pills for what ails him and before long he's takin' another pill to fix what the first pill did tryin' to fix what was wrong with him in the first place."

Cale almost followed that. Miranda glanced at him and smiled. His thoughts scrambled as if short-circuited. It was a few minutes before he followed much of anything after that.

Miranda and Ruby analyzed Moot's condition. His blood pressure was discussed, his stubborn streak mentioned. Luckily, Cale wasn't expected to participate.

"Come on, Moot," Ruby said, wrapping a stiff arm around his bony shoulders. "I'll take you home."

Surfacing, Cale said, "Do you think it's wise to take him back to a remote cabin with no electricity or amenities?"

"He always rests at my place for a coupla hours before I take him home. Besides, his cabin's more modern than my house. He's got a phone, a microwave, a dishwasher, a big-screen TV, and a satellite dish on the roof." She turned her head slowly, as if she'd just had a revelation. Raising her voice so Moot would hear, she admonished, "You've been watching girlie movies again, haven't you?"

The old man only grinned.

"Why," Ruby sputtered, "you ought to be ashamed. A man your age."

"I ain't dead. 'Sides, a man my age ought to be proud he can still . . ."

He turned to Cale. "Tell her, young fella."

Cale opened his mouth, only to clamp it shut without making a sound, all his efforts to dispel the earlier surge of awareness wasted.

"Besides," Moot said, still on the subject. "I don't know what yer all fired up about. It ain't as if watchin' the girlie channel involves exchangin' chickens."

Ruby tut-tutted and led Moot to the door. Cale noticed that the old man drew a wad of bills out of the pocket of his baggy overalls and dropped several on the desk on his way out. Not everyone on the mountain was poor. It was a strange thing to ponder at a time like this, but Cale decided it was better than thinking about the traitorous heaviness that was drawing his attention to the fly of his jeans.

The door closed. In the aftermath of Ruby's hustle and bustle and Moot's booming voice, the clinic was very quiet. Awkward, he cleared his throat. Miranda didn't seem ill at ease at all. As natural and unaffected as always, she wandered to the desk, pocketed the money Moot had left her, and jotted something in a ledger she took from a drawer.

She'd worn her hair up today, the heavy strands twisted and secured on the back of her head with a single yellow clip. Her dress was yellow too. It was one of those dresses that fit just loose enough to stir a man's interest and just tight enough to look damned attractive.

Finished with her task, she looked up at him, her expression serious and thoughtful. She smiled, and Cale's tension changed slightly.

He was a fool. Worse, he was acting seventeen. Gliding one hand into his pocket, he said, "What did Moot mean when he mentioned exchanging chickens?"

She busied herself with a stack of patient files. "The expression dates back to the early nineteen hundreds. It's one of the sillier installments of mountain folklore."

"Go on." Cale was intrigued by mountain folklore. He was intrigued by her too, but folklore was safer.

She led the way into a small room that held a large semi-cluttered desk and an entire wall of filing cabinets. Opening one, she replaced the top file, talking as she worked. "Today Georgia is the leading state in the production of poultry. Eggs and broilers are practically produced on an assembly line. It wasn't always that way. In olden days, every family had at least a few chickens. Verdie Cook used to say that even if the cow kicked over the milk bucket, there would be eggs for breakfast. Girls from these hills didn't have dowries. And back then, nobody had any money."

She gestured for Cale to have a seat on the corner of her desk. "Let's take a look at those stitches."

Once he was seated, she continued. "Chickens were the only things anybody had in plenitude. If a boy wanted to call on a girl, nine times out of ten, her father extracted a chicken from his family as a token of good faith. It worked in reverse too. When a girl married a boy, the father of the bride gave away more than his daughter."

She smoothed a lock of hair away from his brow and leaned closer, her gaze intent upon the gash on his head. "Thus, the expression, chickens were exchanged. Inadvertently, the practice kept the gene pool replenished and the flock strong."

Cale closed his eyes and held perfectly still. Her touch was soft, her fingertips just cool enough to be soothing. He'd kept his emotions locked up so tightly these past eighteen and a half months, he didn't know how yearning found its way inside his chest. It twisted and curled around him, constricting his heart, cutting off his air supply. It would have been so easy to lean ahead slightly, to turn his face into her touch.

"That cut has healed extremely well. If y'all have a minute, I'll remove these stitches."

The *y'all* was nearly his undoing. He opened his eyes and found himself looking into hers. His thoughts slowed, and he didn't move.

"Are you all right?" she asked.

He swallowed. His jeans were a good size too small, and he hadn't gained any weight. "I'm fine. If the stitches are ready to come out, go ahead."

The skirt of her dress swished as she spun around and left the room. He could hear a drawer being opened, the scrape of metal, the rattle of plastic, and finally, a cupboard door being closed. Cale put the time alone to good use, getting his hormones under control. By the time she returned with a tray of dangerous-looking instruments, he'd pulled himself together.

"You might feel a little pinch," she said.

Any pinch Cale felt was below the waist.

"I was wondering . . ." Her voice trailed away.

He opened his eyes. A big mistake. This close, he could see the brown rings around her irises, the slight tinge of color on her cheeks, the moisture on her lips. She wasn't wearing lipstick. Her mouth was pretty without it, the bottom lip fuller than the top. It was the kind of mouth a man fantasized about, the kind of mouth that—

"I'm planning to go to Toccoa tonight," she said.

He was so busy watching her pretty mouth move as she talked that he barely noticed the faint snip, the slight tug on his forehead, so busy fantasizing about how that pretty mouth of hers would feel beneath his, not to mention—

"And I wondered if you would like to go along."

His gaze flew to hers. "You mean like a date?"

There was another tug and another snip. He tried to concentrate on the slight discomfort on his brow, but he caught a movement along the edges of her lips, and he wound up wondering if she knew what she was doing to him.

"I was thinking more along the lines of a drive."

Cale sucked in a shallow breath. Her smile only broadened. Oh, she knew what she was doing to him all right. And she was enjoying it very much.

"A drive," he said, holding her gaze.

She nodded.

And he said, "I guess that depends."

She arched one perfectly shaped eyebrow. "On what?"

Something primitive took hold deep inside Cale, and something instinctive took over. He shifted on the corner of the desk, folded his arms, and tilted his head slightly. "Would it involve the exchange of chickens?"

It was Miranda's turn to shake her head, her turn to acknowledge a traitorous softness that drew her attention to her heart, among other places. "No," she said quietly. "It wouldn't involve anything as final as that."

They shared a smile. But he didn't answer. While she waited for his reply, she smoothed her fingertip along the edges of the thin line where his cut had been. His eyebrows were dark, the skin above them tan, strong, resilient, just like the rest of him. Still, he didn't reply. She'd been very straightforward about her invitation. He hadn't accepted. Telling herself she wasn't disappointed, she took a backward step. "That's healing nicely. A year from now, you'll hardly know it was ever there."

He slid his hand into his pocket, something she'd noticed he did whenever he didn't seem to know where to put them. Today, he drew it right back out again. In it was a check.

"The rent money," he said. "Unless you take Visa."

His attempt at humor nudged her from inside. He'd changed the subject and was letting her down easy. She accepted the check, and the rejection, with quiet dignity.

He was her patient. She'd had no business flirting with him in the first place. Besides, she never flirted. That was her younger sister's department. Caleb Wilder had good reasons for remaining quietly aloof. She respected him for it. It made meeting his gaze a little awkward though. Calling on her professionalism as well as the social graces she'd learned at her mother's knee, she squared her shoulders and led the way into the outer waiting area.

"What time?"

She glanced in the direction his voice had come from. His hand was on the doorknob. His eyes were on her.

"I beg your pardon?" she asked.

"What time did you want to go for that drive?"

"I thought. I mean, you . . ." The more she stammered, the broader his smile grew. "Seven?" She gave him that one word in a voice she didn't even recognize.

He was in control now, all male, all man. "I'll see you then." He was gone an instant later.

Miranda wasn't sure how many minutes passed before she moved. Something was happening to her and had been for several days. For a moment, when her hand had been touching Caleb Wilder's forehead, and her gaze had met his, she'd lost her train of thought, her purpose for being there in that room. She'd lost herself in his gaze. But she'd resurfaced, a little gangly perhaps, but she'd come back to reality. She was attracted to him. There were no two ways around that. Maybe he was attracted to her in return, maybe he wasn't. He certainly wasn't there to find love. She wasn't either, really.

It had been fun to flirt, especially when she hadn't done it in so long. It had made her feel young, no small feat for someone who felt old beyond her years most of the time. There was a perfectly good reason for that. At eighteen, she'd faced her own mortality. Years later, she'd faced her fear. She may have been robbed of her youth, but in its place she'd discovered an inner serenity and tranquillity few people possessed. It was a gift as delicate and indefinable and unexplainable as a healer's touch.

Caleb Wilder wasn't going to stay on the mountain. But

he was there now. And he'd agreed to go for a drive with her.

At seven.

She couldn't help the smile that stole across her face any more than she could help crossing her fingers. After all, seven was said to be very, very lucky.

By the time Cale reached the cabin on Hawksbill Road, his clothes fit comfortably again. The brisk hike had been good for him. His breathing was deep, his heart rate healthy. Best of all, his mind was clear. It was a good thing, because Danny was waiting for him on the porch.

The boy rose to his feet as Cale approached. "I thought about what you said."

That was fast.

Cale knew without asking which decision Danny had reached. He wouldn't be there unless he'd decided to go forward with his search.

"Did you mean it when you said you'd help me?"

Cale raked his fingers through his hair. The day was getting more complicated by the hour. "I meant it, Daniel."

"That's what I thought."

"It isn't going to be easy."

"I know. Mom didn't leave us many clues."

That too.

Planting his hands on his hips, Cale looked around. The sun glinted off the new panes of glass, and tire tracks had been left in the tall weeds, the only signs that Clyde Sturgis had been there. It reminded Cale that people didn't come and go in these hills completely undetected, and they couldn't leave without a trace. Someone had to know something about a girl named Ellie Stanoway and the baby she'd had in these hills nearly fifteen years ago.

"Did you take a look around?" he asked his son.

Danny shook his head. "I haven't been here that long."

"Come on in." Cale took him inside. The place wasn't very large, but compared to Danny's, it was a lot more modern. Seeing it through his son's eyes was like seeing it anew. Now that it had windows and it was relatively clean, it didn't look half bad.

Cale didn't say anything about the way Danny tested every light switch, but he couldn't help grinning when the boy turned on the tap in the bathroom and sighed.

Only one burner on the stove heated. The refrigerator had an old-fashioned handle that clanked when Danny opened it. A distant memory washed over Cale. Six mornings out of seven, Danny used to grunt something that passed for "Good morning," then wander over and open the refrigerator and just stand there while he woke up. It used to drive Ellie crazy. Funny, it wasn't an unhappy memory.

Cale nudged Danny aside the way Ellie used to. Together, they strolled through the back door, where a washing machine that was so old it had been designed with no lid, sat on the ground next to the stoop. Danny stared at the rope somebody had draped between two trees. "I thought about what you said. About how I'll feel when I discover the truth. About Mom, I mean. And it won't matter. She was the best. Whatever she did before I was born won't change who she was after."

A lump came and went in Cale's throat. "What about him? The man." Cale swallowed. "Your biological father?"

Danny glanced away into the distance. "I don't know how I'll feel about him. I know a lot of kids who are adopted dramatize the circumstances leading to their births and subsequent adoptions. I've wondered about him for a long time, but I haven't written a scene in my head about him. I wonder what kind of man he must have been and why he never acknowledged me as his son. Maybe he had his reasons. Maybe he was just a selfish bastard. I want to find out which it is."

Danny was still looking into the distance. He wore a clean white T-shirt and baggy jeans, typical attire for a boy his age. He was thin, wiry, and strong. And yet there had always been a fragility about him. It wasn't unmasculine. It was just there.

Cale glanced to the right of the makeshift clothesline where he'd uncovered the old pickup truck. He'd memorized Danny's birth certificate long before the adoption became final and his name had changed to Wilder. Daniel James Stanoway had been born on June 7 at two thirty-five A.M. in this county here in Georgia. Ellie had given her baby her maiden name. All these years, Cale had been glad about that, glad she hadn't given Danny another man's name. All these years, Danny had felt a burning need to know the other man's identity.

Danny's voice broke into Cale's reverie. "The fact that we don't know his last name is going to make searching more difficult." It was almost as if Danny had read his mind.

"Difficult," Cale said, striding toward the old pickup truck. "But not impossible. We're going to need a car."

"A what?"

"A vehicle. A means of transportation. You were born somewhere in these hills less than fifteen years ago. A lot of people have come and gone over the years, but somebody must remember your mother. I'll ask Miranda if records were kept, and where. We're going to have to ask some people some difficult questions." Danny made a disparaging sound, and Cale said, "I know. People up here aren't exactly what I'd call open with perfect strangers. We can start with Ruby and Miranda. I've met a couple of old-timers. We'll talk to them too. It'll go a lot faster if we don't have to try to get there on foot."

The hood of the truck creaked and clanked as Cale lifted it. Peering at the engine, Danny said, "Are you going to go to Columbus and bring our car back?"

Cale fiddled with a corroded battery cable. "I thought about doing that, but it would take a day to get there and another day to get back. This old relic's a beauty, isn't she? I'm going to need something to do. If I can find used parts, I could have this old Ford up and running in almost no time at all."

Danny stepped back in order to get a better view of the old truck. "You want to drive this?"

"If we're going to be mountain men, we might as well look it. You can help by making yourself useful."

"Useful, how?" There was more than mild suspicion in Danny's voice.

Keeping all expression off his face, Cale said, "Hand me a nine-sixteenth socket wrench, would you?"

Silence.

Cale leaned farther over the engine, but he didn't utter another word. Danny released the kind of long-suffering sigh teenagers were noted for. Metal clanked as he shuffled through the metal toolbox on the ground nearby. Slapping a socket wrench into Cale's hand much the way a nurse would slap a scalpel into a surgeon's palm, Danny said, "I know what you're doing."

Fitting the socket over a rusty nut, Cale gripped the wrench with both hands, thinking, then that makes one of us.

She was late.

Cale glanced at his watch. It was seven-fifteen. Exactly one minute later than the last time he'd checked. And Miranda hadn't arrived.

He strode out to the porch, scanned the horizon, listened intently, then turned on his heel and strode inside again. If he would have known she was going to be late, he would have heated more water—no small feat when only one burner worked—so his bath would have been more than lukewarm. If he'd known she was going to be late, he would have worked longer on the pickup truck. If he would have known she was going to be late, he wouldn't have finished getting ready forty minutes early.

He was fidgety, antsy. Hell, he was nervous. Why? This wasn't even a date. They were only going for a drive. She probably had a very good reason for forcing him to cool his heels and count the minutes.

He slid his hand into his pocket, jingled his loose change.

The next time he checked, another minute had passed. He swore under his breath.

He wasn't really irritated with Miranda. He was irritated with himself. Ruby had said it best earlier today. Thinking was good, just as long as a person didn't do too much of it. The twenty-four, make that twenty-five minutes Miranda kept him waiting had given him far too much time to think.

At seven-thirty, he circled the cabin for something to do, inspecting the new windows. At seven forty-three, it became apparent that she was more than fashionably late. He wandered out to one of the sheds and began rummaging around. The older of the two was filled with junk, but the other building contained several useful items. It required a practiced eye and a lot of digging, but Cale uncovered an old shovel, four screens, and old glass jars filled with rusty bolts and square-headed nails.

He was installing one of the rusty screens when he heard the crunch of tires on the mountain road. It was eight-ten. When the sound came closer, he strode around to the front of the cabin. He was wiping his hands on a rag that until that day had been one of his favorite shirts, when Miranda pulled to a stop in the lane, cut the engine, and climbed out of her dusty silver Explorer.

She was still wearing the yellow dress she'd had on when she'd removed his stitches. Either she'd taken the clip out of her hair or it had fallen out. Her hair was mussed and hung free around her shoulders.

His first impulse was to mention the time. But as she walked toward him, he took one look at her face, at the grim line of her lips and the dark smudges underneath her eyes, and his annoyance evaporated into thin air.

"Trouble?"

She held up a hand, took a shuddering breath, and shook her head. An instant later, her knees gave out.

CHAPTER TEN

Cale shot forward, an arm automatically going around Miranda's waist. "Easy."

He felt the shudder that went through her just as he felt the effort she put forth to stand on her own. She glanced behind her as if the terrain were responsible for her faltering footsteps. In a shaky voice, she said, "My mother is convinced I'll fall in a gopher hole one of these days."

"We wouldn't want that to happen." The ground wasn't uneven. If she'd tripped on anything, it was thin air. But if she wanted to save face, so be it.

"I'm sorry I'm late, Cale."

The quiver on her lips might have been a smile. It struck a vibrant chord inside him, making him feel big and strong and tender at the same time. He steered her toward the porch with a minimal of body contact, waiting to release the gentle hand he had on her upper arm until she'd taken a seat on the second step. He lowered himself to a spot a few feet away and studied her face feature by feature. Her eyes were hooded, her face pale. She looked exhausted and fragile. "I could use a glass of iced tea, how about you?"

Without waiting for her reply, he rose to his feet, took

the steps two at a time, and disappeared inside the house. He returned momentarily with two glasses in his hands that in years past had been jelly jars.

She took a sip as soon as he handed her the drink and wrinkled her nose before she could catch herself.

"Something wrong with your tea?"

She started guiltily. "No offense, but this colored water is not tea."

That's what Ellie used to say. *Cale, I do declare, you Northerners simply do not know how to make iced tea.*

Cale swirled the liquid in his glass. "It is not colored water. It's tea, pure, refreshing. Tea. You might not recognize it, because you Southerners prefer to drink iced tea that doubles as industrial-strength garage floor cleaner."

That won him a small smile that didn't quite reach her eyes. Still, it was an improvement over the haunted look she'd worn minutes earlier. Reaching for her glass, he said, "I'm assuming you take yours with sugar too?"

"I can drink it this way, Cale."

"Nonsense. I'll be right back."

He went back to the kitchen, where he stirred in another heaping spoonful of instant tea and then completely ruined it by adding sugar. Ice cubes clinked against the glass as he returned to the porch and sat on the step once again. He watched from the corner of his eye as she took a sip.

"Better?"

Her sigh would have been answer enough, but she followed it up with a small nod and a quiet thank-you, which she murmured after she drew her legs up and slowly tucked her skirt around her knees. Cale stretched out and leaned his elbows on the step behind him.

The sun had begun its descent a while ago. Clouds were moving in from the east, but it was clear in the west, where the lower edge of the sun brushed the mountaintops in the distance. Soon, it would quietly disappear for another night.

Other than the clink of ice cubes as he and Miranda raised their glasses to their lips from time to time, the quiet was broken only by the inharmonious concert of crickets chirruping from their hiding places nearby, and leaves stirred by an occasional breeze. It wasn't Beethoven or Bach. It wasn't even Billy Joel. In its own way, it was just as entertaining and even more relaxing.

"Rough day?" he asked.

He took another swallow of tea. Eventually, she did too. Staring straight ahead, she said, "I really am sorry about tonight, Cale. Until I got back to my house half an hour ago, I'm afraid I'd completely forgotten I'd asked you to go for a drive with me this evening."

"I think the reason you Southerners like your tea sweet is because you don't sugar-coat anything else."

She turned her head so fast, her hair swung to the front of her shoulder. She stared wordlessly at him, her eyes round, her lips parted slightly, as if unaccustomed to and consequently mortified by her lack of tact.

An unexpected warmth surged through Cale. "That's better."

"I'm glad y'all think so. My mother would be appalled."

"She would also be relieved to see a little color on your cheeks."

For a moment, he saw a spark of some indefinable emotion in her eyes, as if an unspoken pain had come alive inside her. He would have listened if she'd wanted to talk about it. When it became apparent that she wasn't going to do that, he said, "Have you eaten?"

Miranda shook her head. When she'd first arrived, it had taken everything she had to keep tears from spilling over. The moisture was gone now, as if evaporated by the onrushing breeze. She really should be going too. "I appreciate the offer, but I have food at my house."

"Yes, but do you have peanut butter and jelly and three-day-old bread?"

She smiled in spite of herself.

He gestured toward the house with his free hand. "Come on. I hate eating alone."

He disappeared inside, leaving her to decide whether or

not to follow. Staring at the mountain peak in the distance, she rose to her feet.

Cale's back was to her when she entered the kitchen. Leaning in the doorway, she hugged one arm close to her and finished the rest of her tea. She felt exhausted. Evidently, she wasn't too tired to notice the width of Cale's shoulders, or to appreciate the ripple and play of muscle across his back as he spread peanut butter and jelly on bread. Caleb Wilder was one man who looked as good walking away from a woman as he did walking toward her. He was lean, muscular, and solid. She couldn't fault the way his jeans fit, that was for sure.

She gave herself a self-deprecating shake and managed to drag her eyes away before he turned around and caught her looking. He handed her a chipped plate that contained a peanut butter sandwich sliced in half. She noticed he'd left his whole. Sauntering to the other side of the room, he leaned against the old refrigerator, crossed his ankles, and took a large bite. He seemed sure of himself and of his rightful place in the universe. His attitude put her at ease.

He was right about the bread. It was dry, but the peanut butter was thick, the jelly sweet. It was high in fat, high in sugar, basically terrible for her. It was exactly what she needed.

Feeling stronger, she pushed herself away from the doorway. Carrying her plate in one hand, her remaining sandwich in the other, she strolled around the room. There was an old enamel coffeepot on the stove, a trivet on the counter, an iron skillet turned upside down in the sink. A pair of work boots sat next to the refrigerator, and a faded kitchen towel was tossed carelessly on the narrow strip of countertop next to the stove. The touches were masculine, like the man who'd put them there. "I like what you've done to the place."

He washed his sandwich down with weak iced tea before casting a skeptical look around. "Are you saying early squalor suits me?"

She liked his dry sense of humor too. "It might have been

decorated in early squalor before you cleaned it up, Cale, but not anymore.''

"Having glass in the windows is a tremendous improvement."

She eyed the window nearby. "Clyde says the local kids are the reason he stocks plenty of glass. According to him, they keep him in business."

"Clyde tell you all that during one conversation, did he?"

Miranda really hadn't expected to smile tonight. "I take it you were here when Clyde replaced the glass this morning."

"We came face-to-face, but we weren't formally introduced."

"People up here don't stand on ceremony."

"Yeah? Well, if understatements were gold, people up here would be rich."

Again, she almost smiled. She finished her sandwich, set the plate on the table, then strolled into the next room. An old curtain separated it from the downstairs bedroom. From what she could see, the entire house had been thoroughly cleaned. The living room, or front room as the people in Dawsons Hollow called it, was small. It contained a sofa that was so threadbare, any pattern it might have once had was no longer discernible. An antique rocking chair sat in front of the room's only window, a man's shirt draped over the back. Running a hand along the weathered windowsill, she said, "Clyde may not say much, but he's a very kind man. He's loved Ruby from afar for years. Although she doesn't give him the time of day, I for one don't know what I'd do without him. He fixed my porch steps and patched my roof one year after a terrible storm. And he replaces all the glass the teenage boys so enjoy breaking."

Cale watched Miranda from the doorway between the kitchen and living room. She moved with an easy grace he'd noticed before. He could have blamed the change in the beating rhythm of his heart on that soft lilt and that Southern accent, but he was pretty sure there was more to it than that.

He was curious about Ruby, but it wasn't Ruby he wanted

to learn by heart. Walking casually into the room, he said, "Teenage boys were responsible for breaking these windows?"

She answered without turning around. "There's just something boys seem to love about the sound of shattering glass. My brother, Alex, was the same way. The year he turned twelve, he got a BB gun for Christmas. The number *twelve* was symbolic because he lined up twelve of our mother's most cherished Waterford champagne flutes on the edge of the fountain. Doing an about-face that would have earned him a place in the front row in drill practice in military school, which just happens to be a punishment my parents threatened, he took twelve paces, turned, and took aim."

Cale liked listening to her talk, as fascinated by what she said as by the way she said it. "Was he a good shot?"

She still looked weary, but her voice held a smile as she said, "He nailed the first eight without missing. By the time our little sister tattled to our mother, who started yelling long before she reached the garden, Alex had shattered three more."

"Did they decide against military school?"

"They're very patriotic, and I don't think they wanted to put our country through that. Besides, Mother came up with a much more cruel and fitting punishment."

"What could be worse than military school?"

"Every Christmas Eve, she proposes a toast using the sole remaining glass and her longest long-suffering sigh."

A smile stole across her face, drawing him much the way a lighted window drew a weary traveler. "What does your brother do today?"

"He's an attorney in Atlanta. He has aspirations to become the future Honorable Alexander Graham Sinclair."

"Your parents must be proud."

"Relieved is more like it. Still, about twice a year, he manages to do something outrageous to get a rise out of them."

"Are they proud of you too?"

"They're proud, but they worry about me."

"Falling in a gopher hole is a big concern for most parents."

Instead of smiling as he'd expected, she took a shuddering breath. "They're more worried about what I do for a living." When she spoke again, her voice was lower, deeper, and darker. "A little girl drowned today. That's why I was late."

God. No wonder she looked exhausted. And so hauntingly sad. "Was she one of your patients?"

She shook her head. "She lives—lived—near a little town called Tallulah Falls. Her parents are former New Yorkers who moved down there to give her and her sister a better life." Miranda's voice broke at that.

Situations like these always made Cale feel completely inadequate. He didn't know whether to stop her or encourage her to go on. So he simply remained quiet.

Taking another shuddering breath, she said, "They own a resort there. The girls were outside playing while the parents did yard work, and the little one came up missing. Her father found her and immediately began administering CPR. One of their guests had heard of me. They called. And I went."

"How long had she been in the water?"

"Twenty-five minutes."

Christ. Cale wondered if they expected her to part the Red Sea too, or turn water into wine. If it had been Danny, he would have done the same thing. Did that mean he believed? Recalling his own bruised ribs and Benjie Winters's injured eyes, Cale just didn't know.

No wonder Miranda's parents worried. Caring for these people took an enormous toll on her. "What does it feel like, Miranda?"

The watery eyes she turned to him held a question and prompted him to add, "This power people say you have. What does it feel like?"

"It feels like an echo."

Answers like that reminded him of the reason he'd never made room in his life for superstition. An echo could be heard, not felt. What was an echo, really? A vibration of sound waves moving through the distant canyons or valleys.

Cale didn't know if he believed anybody could feel an

echo, but there was one thing he was certain of. Miranda cared deeply for her patients. She was aching for the family of a little girl she didn't even know. Perhaps that was why Caleb Wilder, a man who found it difficult to express his emotions in words or deeds, placed a gentle hand on her cheek as if it were the most natural thing in the world.

The simple touch of Cale's work-roughened hand sent fresh tears to Miranda's eyes. She blinked them away, feeling fragile, as if the warm mountain breeze streaming through the open window could shatter her into a thousand pieces and then scatter them like dandelion fluff.

"I don't want to feel weak," she whispered.

She wanted to lie down. She wanted to curl into a ball and go to sleep. She gazed into Cale's eyes.

As she took a tentative step closer, she heard the air whoosh out of Cale's lungs. His gaze strayed to her mouth and he sucked in a ragged breath. His hand fell away from the side of her face, but he made no move to set her away from him.

"You're stronger than you realize, Miranda. And you still have time."

"Time?"

This close, his eyes were a deep, vivid blue, this late in the day, his voice a husky baritone. "Time to turn away, time to lower your chin, time to tell me no."

Another step brought her within inches of him. "I was trying to give *you* time turn away, time to raise your chin, time to tell *me* no."

He made a sound in the back of his throat, and then, as if they both knew they were out of time, out of diversions, out of reasons to resist, he lowered his face to hers. His lips touched hers so gently, so sweetly, she very nearly cried out. She didn't sway toward him. Her emotions were simply too raw to take that big a risk with her heart tonight. She left her lips on his though. For just a moment.

And then she slowly pulled away.

Cale drew back a few inches and let her go. It wasn't

easy. He wanted another kiss, another connection, a hell of a lot more than either of those things.

She'd strolled as far as the door when he pulled himself together enough to follow. "Thank you for supper. It was exactly what I needed." Her accent was enchantingly Southern, *suppah* for supper. "And you were right. It was better than eating alone."

"You saw the way I knocked myself out preparing it, Miranda."

She glanced over her shoulder, and they shared a smile.

"Are you sure you're up to driving home?" he asked.

"It's only a mile."

Although there were still dark smudges underneath them, her eyes were clearer. She was going to be all right. They strolled to her car side by side. Because he was a gentleman, he opened her door. Because he was a man, which, among other things meant that he liked to have the last word, he said, "You still owe me a drive."

She settled herself onto the rich leather seat, but she didn't turn the key in the ignition. And Cale didn't close her door. Instead, they talked—about the weather at first, then about how dark the sky was and how the air smelled faintly of rain. He told her about his students back in Columbus, and a remedial English teacher who had a raging fear of spiders. And she told him about a professor she'd had in college who'd believed he was a reincarnated Civil War soldier. They talked for a long time, Cale's left hand on the car door, hers resting softly on the steering wheel. Cale mentioned Danny and his quest to learn the identity of his natural father. Miranda hadn't heard of any Stanoways living in these hills, but she suggested he check with some of the people who had been here all their lives.

It was ten o'clock before she made noises about leaving, ten-thirty before she actually started her vehicle and he closed the car door. Cale would never know what possessed him to ask, "Are you going to be busy all weekend?"

It was probably her social graces that kept her from mentioning the surprise that was surely evident on his face.

"Actually," she said, "I'm going to the dance at the Livery tomorrow night."

"Alone?" God, he was no good at this whatsoever.

The next time he met her gaze, she was trying not to grin. "I always help Ruby and a few of her friends set up. Admission's free, and it's fun. Folks come from all over the mountain. Someone hauls out a fiddle, and before long everyone's hooting and hollering and dancing up a storm. You should come."

"Maybe I will."

"Maybe I'll see you there, then." She said it with a smile. This time, Cale noticed the smile reached all the way to her eyes. "Good night, Cale."

Cale. The sound of his name felt almost as intimate as a kiss. He heard her driving away long after she disappeared from sight. Although a thick layer of clouds obscured the moon and every star in the sky, Cale took a chair out to the porch and sat for a long time, just as he had the previous night.

Day by day, he was changing. Some of the changes were subtle, others weren't. In every way that counted, it had been a married man that had landed that airplane in the rocky meadow less than a week ago. A married man who had felt dead from the neck down.

One tender, brief kiss had jump started his libido. Maybe Miranda was a healer after all. Or maybe all women were healers when it came to matters of the heart. He didn't feel numb anymore. In fact, he felt more alive than he had in a long, long time.

He didn't have a clue what he wanted to do about it. The throbbing rhythm of his heartbeat whispered, "Liar."

Daniel rounded a corner, breaking into the clearing on a run. He'd spent the entire morning working with Cale on that dirty old truck. He'd never understood how a man could garner so much satisfaction while getting so much grease underneath his fingernails. Daniel admitted that the 'sixty-seven Ford didn't look too bad. It was big and boxy, and according to Cale was going to handle like a Mack truck. Evidently, that was a good thing, because Cale had been whistling all morning. Shortly before noon, a man named Clyde had shown up with four used tires in the back of his truck. Cale had acted like a kid on Christmas.

Daniel had left to see to the raccoon shortly thereafter. He'd hung around the cabin long enough to feed the chubby little animal twice. Daniel had eaten some of the food his father had sent back with him and polished off what remained of the lemonade Ruby McCoy had left the day before. Full, Daniel washed the dishes in water he dipped from the creek. His money in one pocket, the picnic basket in one hand, he set off for town.

He felt good. Strong, nourished, rested. He wasn't certain what brought him to the gate near the sourwood tree. He supposed he was drawn to the garden's beauty. It was peaceful there. It was one of the first things he'd noticed when he'd arrived on the mountain. Those first few evenings he'd hidden. No more. Today, he stood in the open near the white picket fence.

The pretty lady with the long, golden-brown hair was working in the garden and noticed his presence almost immediately. She was kneeling on the ground, doing something to the strange-looking plants. Glancing sideways at him, she shaded her eyes with one hand, then rose to her feet without hesitation. And smiled.

Daniel's throat felt thick and threatened to close up. Sometimes, when he least expected, it hurt, kindness.

Miranda brushed her hands together, then moved on to brush the dirt off the knees of her jeans. Straightening, she crossed her arms and studied Caleb Wilder's son. The boy hung back near the sourwood tree. He wasn't hiding, yet he seemed reluctant to come any closer. "Nice day," she called.

He nodded once, his only concession to civility before glancing at the ground at his feet.

"I wasn't sure you would stop by my mailbox tonight."

He turned his head sharply, making a sweeping perusal

of her empty mailbox. "I didn't come for a handout. I came to return the picnic basket to your friend and to look for a job."

She eyed the wicker basket dangling from his left hand. "Would you like me to return that to Ruby?"

"I'll do it. I know where she lives."

He was obviously proud. That kind of stubborn pride was rare in someone so young. Pointing through the trees, Miranda said, "If you follow the path, it's a shortcut to Ruby's."

She expected him to turn on his heel and leave. Instead, he gestured to her garden with his free hand. "I've never seen plants like these."

Miranda studied the row of boneset at her feet. "I suppose it isn't a typical garden. A lot of these natural remedies so popular today were grown and used by our grandmothers. Well, maybe not my grandmothers, because neither of them, or my mother either for that matter, believes it's proper for a lady to get her hands dirty."

"Then who taught you to grow things?" Daniel asked.

Pushing a lock of hair away from her face, Miranda stifled a yawn. She hadn't slept well last night. It wasn't a nightmare that had kept her awake but the haunting memory of that little girl's still face. "A dear old friend showed me when I wasn't much older than you are now."

Last night's rain shower had softened the ground, making it perfect for weeding. She'd spent the last two hours doing just that. It was relaxing work. Healing work, Verdie used to call it. She used to say that no matter how bad things were in the rest of your life, you could always make sense out of pulling weeds.

"Why is it," she asked, strolling closer to the boy, "that weeds grow twice as fast as my plants?"

"Weeds have been adapting for a million years. They're much hardier than your medicinal plants." He glanced away shyly.

Daniel Wilder was obviously extremely bright. He didn't

seem particularly pleased about that. "Daniel? You mentioned that you're looking for a job."

He nodded very cautiously.

"I could use somebody to help me with the weeding and hoeing. I'd pay you."

"How much?"

She named an amount.

"Is that per hour? Or total?"

She hid a smile. "Per hour. I know it's not a lot, but that figure includes as much homemade bread and smoked game and milk you and your raccoon need."

He seemed to be considering that. "When would you want me to start?"

"Tomorrow's Sunday. How about Monday morning? Nine o'clock."

He nodded, and she stuck out her hand. Daniel stared at it for a moment, then slowly placed his in hers. Mumbling a hasty good-bye, he hurried to the garden gate.

Miranda watched him walk away. Something about Caleb Wilder's boy made her smile. Whether it was genetic or not, he was like Cale in that way.

Ruby McCoy's pretty blue house was right where Miranda had said it would be. Since Ruby wasn't home, and therefore he couldn't thank her in person, Daniel left the basket, along with a bouquet of wildflowers he'd picked along the road, on her front porch. After that, it took only minutes to reach the village-limit sign. The doors were open on the big wooden building on the corner. The sign overhead read NELSON'S LIVERY. Someone was sweeping the floors, sending a cloud of dust onto the street. Daniel gave it a wide berth, striding to the edge of the street. From there, it was just a stone's throw to Pratt's Grocery Store.

As far as he was concerned, the old-fashioned cowbell that signaled his arrival into the store was completely unnecessary. Folks up here watched one another like hawks. Consequently, everybody within a hundred-yard radius knew he was there long before the bell over the door jangled. He'd hated to be stared at back home. Up here, Daniel ignored the censure. He had money. He had a job. He had a place to stay. It they wanted to stare at him, fine.

He chose his groceries carefully, making two passes up and down every aisle. Feeling strangely elated, he placed his selections on the counter, where a heavy woman with humorless eyes slowly began ringing up his items.

"You're new around here." The woman eyed him up and down while a man who looked a lot like Willow but much older, thirty at least, looked up from a carton of canned goods he was placing on a nearby shelf.

Since it wasn't a question, Daniel didn't see any reason to offer more than a passing nod.

"Willow!" The woman yelled so loudly, Daniel jumped. "Git in here and bag these groceries."

He brightened the instant he saw Willow slip through a door on the other side of the counter. She glanced at him, gave her head a small shake, and immediately glanced away. For some reason, she didn't want anyone to know they'd met. Daniel played along.

"What's your name?" the woman at the cash register asked.

"Daniel Wilder."

"Wilder." The woman's eyes narrowed so much, they disappeared. "Ain't that the name of the man who crash-landed his airplane earlier this week?"

Daniel was halfway through a small nod, when Willow spouted, "Paper or plastic?"

She opened both hands in a gesture Daniel interpreted as a request to meet her east of town in ten minutes.

"Plastic," he said, and then, to the older woman, "Yes."

"He your father?"

Again, his answer was a simple nod. While the older woman rang up the rest of his groceries and Willow bagged them, Daniel reached into his pocket for the wallet where he kept his mother's picture and all the money he had to his name. He could feel Willow's eyes on him, but he didn't look at her again. Taking a bag of groceries in each hand, he left the store.

He started down the street in the direction Willow had indicated, searching for a secluded place to wait. Three teenage girls were eating ice-cream cones at the Tastee Treat across the street, and an old man was watching him out the diner's big window. The search for privacy continued. Two young boys who had tipped a bicycle upside down in front of the first house he passed looked up at him shyly. One had a bandage over one eye. He worked the pedal with his hand while the other held a stick to the spokes.

Daniel didn't pay either of the old cars that passed him much attention, but when he caught a glimpse of an old blue Ford pickup truck pulling into a driveway on the outskirts of town, it required a conscious effort to continue in a leisurely fashion.

Making no sudden moves, he veered to the right and wound up along the edge of a narrow clearing. He could see the sourwood tree. He could see the old Ford pickup truck too. He wasn't surprised Cale had gotten it running. His dad had always been a genius with engines, but Daniel was a little surprised at the sight of Cale knocking on Miranda Sinclair's door. His dad stood back, hands on his hips, one foot on the first porch step, waiting for Miranda to answer.

"Do you think they're gonna do it?"

Daniel jumped straight into the air. "Damnit, Willow!" He dropped one bag of groceries as he spun around. "Are you trying to scare me to death?"

Willow, who had been busy peering through lacy foliage, turned her head very slowly.

Daniel picked up his groceries and took a backward step. It wasn't fear that made him leery. It was just that he was a guy, and every male on the planet recognized the look of a female gearing up to speak her mind.

CHAPTER ELEVEN

Daniel doubted that Willow Pratt weighed more than ninety-seven pounds. Every last one of those ninety-seven pounds had bristled. "I as good as told you I was coming. I suppose it's my fault you didn't hear me approaching."

"I . . ."

"Not that I didn't make plenty of noise. Besides, I'm not the one spying for a change."

"I wasn't spying."

"You saying your father knows you're here?"

"Well, no . . ."

"I see. You saying y'all weren't watching him hit on Miranda?"

"He's not hitting on Miranda. Willow, he's thirty-six years old. And it doesn't even look like she's home."

She made a sound by releasing a breath of air through a tiny opening between her lips. Daniel would have been hard-pressed to say what letter it began with. "I hear tell men are never too old to, well, you know. And I would appreciate it if you wouldn't swear."

Daniel simply stared at her.

"What?" she asked.

"Never mind."

She jerked her chin into the air and stomped away. "Show me one boy who doesn't say *never mind* when he knows he's licked in an argument." She spun around, glaring at him. She wasn't wearing much makeup today, and her hair was in a high ponytail. Her outfit consisted of a pair of cut-off overalls and a cropped green shirt. How anybody managed to look so young, and kind of cute really, and still be so infuriatingly intimidating was beyond Daniel.

"While you're at it," she said huffily, "show me one man who doesn't think he's always right."

Daniel was in the process of staring her down, when he heard Cale's truck start again. What *was* Cale doing at Miranda's anyway? He sighed. "Just one man?"

Willow's smile came as a surprise, even if it did spread across her face a quarter inch at a time. "Have you seen your dad's airplane yet?"

She barely stuck around long enough for him to shake his head. Daniel had little choice but to follow. She led the way to a narrow path that looked as if it got little use. They followed the trail in silence, sidestepping rocks and fallen branches. After traveling the equivalent of five or six blocks, they came to a clearing. And there was Cale's plane.

The propeller was bent, one tire was flat, and the windshield was cracked. The enormity of what might have happened hit Daniel head-on. "Damn, Willow."

"I know," Willow said. "He's either an amazing pilot or real lucky. But I mean it. I don't mind cussing, but I really can't tolerate swearing."

"Is it against your religion or something?"

She scoffed. "It's against my nature. Indians don't abide by swearing, you know."

"You're part Indian?" Other than her dark hair, she didn't look it.

"I might be. The Onondaga Indians once lived in these hills, so it's possible. I've read a lot about them. Bet you didn't know that Native Americans believe in their own messiah. They won't tell non-natives his name because so many of them use it in vain.''

"What do you mean, they have their own messiah?''

"What do you think I mean? They called him their Peace-maker. He was last seen paddling a canoe down a river toward what's now Canada about the same time Jesus was walking on water on the other side of the world.''

His silence drew her attention.

"Aren't you going to argue?''

Daniel shook his head. He'd never known anybody with so much knowledge about things he'd never heard of. He lowered the sacks of groceries to the ground and flexed his fingers. "I've taken dozens of standardized tests, and a dozen more specialized ones. When the results came in, they put me in a program for the gifted and talented. You're lucky. If they taught this in school back in Ohio, I wouldn't be half as bored.''

All her breath came whistling out between her pursed lips again. "Nobody's ever said I'm gifted or talented, that's for sure. Most folks up here are disappointed in me. And they don't teach this stuff in schools here either. Other than showing up for the first Thanksgiving and the occasional Indian uprising, which were perfectly justified if you ask me, Native Americans are hardly mentioned in school. A lot of things white people aren't proud of get left out.''

"Is that what you want to be when you grow up?'' he asked. "A teacher?''

She reached for one of the bags at his feet. "I wanted to be a medicine woman. You know, a healer, like Miranda, but I just don't have the healing touch like she does. Mrs. Arrowood calls me into her office about once a week to lecture me on the importance of a good attendance record. I always show up on test day. I read everything I can get my hands on, and I ace every test, so there's not much she can say. First chance I get, I'm leavin'. Nobody believes me, but I'm gonna do it one of these days.''

That's what Daniel had done. Only his dad had followed. He hadn't expected that to mean anything, but it did. He wondered if anybody would follow Willow if she left. "Was that your mom back there in the store?"

She pulled a face.

"Will she care if you go?"

"Other than asking me a hundred questions about where I've been or what I've done, my mother doesn't give me the time of day. The only one who'd mind is my oldest brother, J.R., because then he wouldn't have anybody to boss around. He acts like he's my father. What about you? Your dad boss you around a lot?"

Daniel picked up the other bag and stared at the airplane that had been his father's pride and joy. "He's not like that. But he's my adoptive father. I came to this mountain to find out who my biological father is."

"What makes you think he's here?"

"My mom talked about Dawsons Hollow. Just before she died. And my birth certificate lists Rabun County as the place I was born."

"Do you look like your mom?"

He shrugged. "She had red hair and green eyes."

"Was she pretty?"

His answer was a slow "Yeah."

"You must take after him, then. Your father."

Daniel turned his head slowly. And Willow grinned. "I didn't mean that the way it sounded."

He didn't give in and smile in return. A boy had to have *some* pride. Willow could be a real brat when she wanted to be, but he had to admit he enjoyed pitting wits against her. "Do you know most of the people in these hills?"

She nodded.

"Well?"

She cocked her eyebrow. "Well, what?"

It felt good to have the upper hand for a change. "Do I look familiar or don't I?"

Willow knew folks up here thought she was just another one of those wild Pratt kids. They sure didn't think she was very smart. Maybe they were right, but she knew a golden opportunity when she saw one. She gave Daniel Wilder a thorough once-over, just like he'd wanted. He was tall. Of course, most everybody looked tall to her. His chin was still boyish, but the rest of his face was all angles and planes and interesting hollows.

She held her arm up to his. "Nothing unusual about the shade of your skin or the color of your hair. You're cuter than most of the boys I know though."

"You think so?"

Willow crossed her arms and tapped one hiking boot on the moist dirt below. Boys were so obtuse. Even brilliant boys.

"You look vaguely familiar."

She had his undivided attention. "Who do I remind you of?"

"I don't know. I said it was vague. Don't worry. If it doesn't come to me on its own, I'll hug a tree until it does. I've gotta go."

"Already?"

She paused, torn. He didn't want her to go. She gave him a broad smile for that. Handing him the sack of groceries she'd bagged for him a little while ago, she said, "I have to get back to the store before J.R. suspects something."

"Can you come back later?"

Later? Did he mean it? Most boys didn't like her. Oh, they liked looking at the front of her shirt, and a few of them had tried to feel her up, but once she'd threatened them with her knee, none of them much cared whether she stayed or went. And the few times she'd tried to tell them about some of the stuff she read about, they got these blank looks on their faces. Daniel Wilder was different. He listened when she talked. Imagine that.

"I'm baby-sitting the Sprague kids while Lavender and Randy go to the dance at the Livery tonight. Tomorrow's Sunday. J.R. has to go after supplies, and my mother sleeps all day. Meet me here at ten."

While Willow had been talking, Daniel's gaze had strayed to the airplane. He juggled the grocery bags into one hand and tried not to think about what would have happened if that meadow had been ten feet, hell, two feet shorter. It took a moment for something Willow had said to sink in. Dazedly, he said, "What do you mean you'll hug a tree?"

He turned around as he spoke. But Willow was already gone.

"You look real perty tonight, Miranda."

"Thanks, Angus." Since anybody who'd ever danced with old Angus Warner knew better than to let her guard down, Miranda smiled at him but kept her feet safely out of his way.

"So perty, it's taking my mind clean off my sore finger."

"That's nice," she said before the line of women went one way and the line of men went the other.

"Hi, Miranda," Doug Benson, her next dance partner, said, falling into step beside her. "You look real pretty tonight."

And so it had gone all evening. The air was warm, the dance floor was crowded, and spirits were high. There was nothing unusual about that. Ruby had started the event eight years before in an effort to instill a feeling of closeness among the people in and around Dawsons Hollow. Judging by the noise level alone, it had been a huge success.

From the corner of her eye, Miranda caught a movement near the door. Oh. It was only Earl and LeRoy Pratt heading over to the Bootlegger. There was nothing unusual about that either. George Benson had done everything in his power to keep Ruby from having her dances in the beginning. He'd claimed the building was unsafe, but really, he'd been worried it would give his Saturday night regulars a better place to go. Ruby, being Ruby, had found a way to appease them both. The Livery had a wooden floor, which was perfect for dancing, but no bathroom. So she'd struck a deal with George. Now anybody wishing to use the facilities strolled across the street to the Bootlegger. Nine times out of ten, the men had a shot or a beer as long as they were there.

The second Saturday of every month was George's biggest night of business.

"You're lookin' pretty tonight, Miranda."

She nodded her thanks and pasted a smile on her face as Brad Sprague swung her into a neat little two-step. They talked about this and that, and when the song ended, she thanked him for the lively dance, then made her way to the punch table. Anybody watching could see the regret in Brad's eyes as he watched her go. There wasn't anything unusual about that either. A lot of the local men wished Miranda would give them more than one dance.

"Well, will wonders never cease." Ruby ladled punch into a paper cup just like she always did, but the twinkle in her eye was brand new.

Miranda looked all around, trying to pinpoint the origin of Ruby's know-it-all attitude. The old livery stable had been converted into a hall before electricity had made it up the mountain. The gaslights on the walls were turned down low, just as they always were. The same four men played the songs they always played. For the most part, the same people were in attendance. They were even sitting in their usual places. Miranda might have spent twice, three, four times as long getting ready tonight, trying on and discarding practically every outfit in her closet before settling on an ordinary pair of khakis and a sleeveless dark purple shirt, but Ruby couldn't have known that. So what had she been referring to?

"Hello, Miranda."

Ahha.

Miranda turned around slowly. Just as slowly, she smiled. "Hello, Cale." She could have blamed her shortness of breath on the last dance, but she was too honest for that.

"Looks like the party started without me."

There was a current in his voice, like a taut rope being played by one finger, strumming it into a low, deep hum. He glanced over Miranda's shoulder. "Hi, Ruby."

" 'Bout time you got here. Would you care for a glass of punch?"

"Maybe later." His gaze dropped to Miranda's. "Care to dance?"

Ruby leaned across the table, taking Miranda's paper cup. In a voice barely loud enough to hear, she said, "Now you can stop watchin' the door."

Now, *that* was unusual. Leave it to Ruby to notice.

Miranda led the way to the edge of the dance floor just as the local boys settled into a slow song. She and Cale started out in the traditional manner, her right hand in his, her left hand resting lightly on his shoulder.

"I was beginning to think you weren't coming."

"I almost didn't."

His breath stirred her hair. And she very nearly sighed. Every time she got near him felt like the first time. Her breathing became shallow, her pulse sped up, and her thoughts turned as hazy as a long-forgotten dream.

"Why did you?" she asked.

"There's a question." His hands slid to her waist, and she knew why. That one brief kiss the previous night had brought something to life inside him too.

"Did you pay Moot a visit?" she whispered.

"As a matter of fact, I just came from there."

"No luck?"

Breathing in the scent of her shampoo, Cale closed his eyes and spoke close to her ear. "An effort in futility. Why didn't you tell me that talking to Moot involves pursuit?"

Her laughter was low and sultry, thrumming the chord that had been vibrating deep inside him ever since last night. He let the amateur band set the pace, letting the slow burn deep inside him set the mood. He and Ellie had always been a perfect match. He and Miranda were a perfect fit. He couldn't explain it, but his hands fit the small of her back so naturally, he didn't remember gliding them there.

She asked questions about his visit with Moot, and Cale described his conversation with the old codger, although *conversation* wasn't really the right word. Cale had asked a lot of questions, at the top of his lungs no less, and Moot had done a lot of nodding as he pointed out foliage and talked about natural remedies while Cale tried to keep up with him.

"Then he didn't leave you with any helpful information?" Miranda asked.

"He left me with all kinds of helpful information. For instance, did you know that a prickly-pear-root poultice is a sure cure for infection?"

He heard the smile in her voice as she said, "I might have heard that somewhere, yes."

Cale really hadn't intended to attend the dance tonight. He'd even stopped by Miranda's to tell her before setting off for Moot's place on Possum Road. She hadn't been home. And now Cale was dangerously close to pulling her against him. Her scent, her warmth, her touch, were all wreaking havoc with his senses, making him feel big and strong and invincible, making him consider throwing caution to the wind. "You look beautiful tonight."

Closing her eyes, Miranda breathed in the scent of man and clothes left outside to dry. She'd lost track of how many times the local men had said she was pretty tonight, so there was absolutely no reason she should feel beautiful simply because Cale had said it.

"This is nice. And to think I didn't plan to attend the dance tonight."

He'd said as much earlier. This time, something in the tone of his voice made her open her eyes. "Why is that, Cale?"

"Damned if I could stay away."

"You tried?"

He made a sound only men could imitate. "I set off for a walk in the opposite direction."

He didn't say "How I ended up here is beyond me," but he might as well have. Well, didn't that beat all? While she'd been watching the door for his arrival all evening, something she absolutely never did, he'd been trying to keep his distance.

She brought her chin up slightly. "Nobody's forcing you to dance with me, Cale."

"That's where you're wrong." Too late, he realized what he'd said.

She'd bristled, her back as straight as a board.

"I didn't mean that the way it sounded, Miranda."

"And how did y'all mean it?" The warmth in her eyes had been replaced with a flash of temper.

He'd insulted her. He hadn't meant to. He was trying to decide how to apologize, when he felt a tap on his shoulder. Before he knew how it had happened, Miranda had stepped out of his arms without so much as a backward glance and into the arms of a young man with curly blond hair and a shy grin. And Cale was left standing on the edge of the dance floor, watching.

"Don't take it to heart," a middle-aged man with a barrel chest and graying hair said. "Our Miranda never gives any of us more than one dance. She sure is pretty, isn't she?"

Cale scowled. He wasn't jealous. Hell, no. Apparently, Miranda was just keeping things even. She'd given him his brief dance and then moved on. He couldn't very well fault her for that.

Her current dance partner was light on his feet. He spun circles around the other dancers, so it was really no wonder Miranda seemed to be enjoying herself. There was certainly no law against that.

Cale gritted his teeth.

When the song ended, the fiddle player called all the old-timers to the floor. While everyone else watched the bib-overall crowd take turns dancing a bluegrass jig, Miranda and her dance partner strolled to the other side of the floor.

Cale decided to take Ruby up on that glass of punch. Since Ruby looked a little too knowing for his peace of mind, he carried his punch back to the edge of the dance floor and took a large swallow. It was cold and hit the spot. He could have used something stronger.

"So," a man he didn't know said without looking at him. "You have a thing for our Miranda too."

Cale glanced at the man's profile. His face looked a lot like other men's faces. His nose was long and straight, his face slightly ruddy, his eyes an indiscernible color, probably blue or gray.

"You have family in these parts?"

Cale's gaze strayed to a table twenty-five feet away, where Miranda was talking to the tired-looking young mother-to-be he'd seen his first day in Dawsons Hollow. "No, at least not that I know of."

"What are you doin' here, then?"

Now, there was a question. Here in the mountains? Cale knew the answer to that one. Here at this dance? That reason was even more complicated.

When Cale failed to answer, the man looked up at him and said, "The name's Emory. Emory Sturgis. That man hovering close to Ruby there is my brother, Clyde. That girl over there with Miranda is my youngest, Lavender. She's the wife's and my seventh child. That baby she's expectin' will be her seventh. The seventh child of the seventh child is said to have great powers, you know."

So Cale had heard.

In his late fifties or early sixties, Emory Sturgis had a balding head and a hardy paunch. His eyes were clear, however, and his gaze direct. Like Ruby, he had the look of a person who knew a great deal about a lot of things. It occurred to Cale that he might be able to salvage a small part of the evening after all.

"I'm from Ohio, but my wife was from the South."

"Was?"

"She died almost nineteen months ago. I think she lived here for a little while. Ever hear of a girl—"

"Sorry to hear that. She was from the South, you say?"

"Yes, her name was—"

"Southern people are—"

"Ellie. Ellie Stanoway—"

"God's people," Emory said.

Cale wondered what the hell that had to do with anything. All right, he would take the bait. "And what are Northerners?"

"It's funny you should ask, because Northerners, well,

they aren't. Not that there's anything wrong with them, mind you. Had a coupla friends from up north when I did my stint in the army. Me and those boys went into town every chance we got. Sowed some wild oats in our day. 'Course, that was before I married the wife. Haven't heard from any of 'em in years. Not my wife. I hear from here all the time.'' Emory guffawed. ''Anyway, one night me and the boys decided to . . .''

Cale crushed the paper cup in his hand. The evening was going from bad to worse. He'd inadvertently insulted Miranda. And to top it all off, the only past Emory was interested in was his own. Twenty minutes later, Cale knew more than he needed to about the Sturgis clan and nothing about the summers Ellie had spent in the Blue Ridge Mountains. When Emory finally came up for air, Cale understood why the man's only brother, Clyde, didn't say much. Hell, nobody could get a word in edgewise.

''Where'd you say you're from again?'' Emory asked.

''Ohio.''

''You here to stay?''

Cale hadn't realized his gaze had strayed to that nearby table until Miranda looked up at him. Still miffed, she quickly looked away.

''Pretty little thing, ain't she?'' Emory declared proudly.

Cale was all set to agree with him, until he realized Emory wasn't referring to Miranda.

Lavender, pretty?

Cale had seen Lavender Sprague his first morning on the mountain. He'd taken one look at the way her straight, dark-blond hair was parted down the middle and pushed behind her ears, and he'd written her off as plain. Her eyes were brown, her lips too wide for her narrow face. Miranda glanced up at him again, and a jolt of sexual attraction came out of nowhere with so much force, Cale had to remind himself to breathe. Lavender's eyes were filled with awe of a different nature. The girl gently placed Miranda's hand on her swollen abdomen; the way Lavender's smile softened her face changed the way Cale measured beauty.

"Well?" Emory prodded. "Are y'all here to stay, or aren't ya?"

Miranda turned her attention back to Lavender Sprague. Dazedly, Cale returned to his senses. "No, my son and I are staying here only temporarily."

"I hope you aren't thinkin' of trying to take Miranda away from us."

Take her away from these people who listened to her every word and believed the sun rose and set on her shoulders? Cale was glad Emory didn't seem to expect a reply, because he had no idea what to say. He liked Miranda. There was nothing unusual about that. Everybody liked Miranda. Okay, he was attracted to her too. Hell, maybe every male on the mountain was attracted to her. Why wouldn't they be? She treated their illnesses and injuries, showering her patients with kindness and compassion. Who wouldn't respond to that?

"Come on over to the table and meet the family," Emory said.

Cale was halfway to the table, when a woman he hadn't met said something to Miranda, and the two of them made their way to the other side of the room. Emory was making introductions. Cale told himself he wasn't disappointed and tried to pay attention.

The family consisted of Lavender; her sullen-faced husband, Randy; two older brothers named Greg and Mike; Greg's wife, whose name escaped Cale; three sisters who had left the mountain but had been mentioned anyway; and Emory's wife, Lucille. Cale knew that didn't add up to seven, but he didn't bring it up for fear that Emory would launch into a lengthy explanation. As it was, Lucille was wringing her hands, and Emory was engaging his sons in conversation. As if he couldn't stand another minute of it, Emory's son-in-law Randy jerked to his feet.

Lavender looked up at her young husband. "Where are you going?" she asked.

Randy glanced away. Cale couldn't tell if he looked guilty or uninterested or just plain tired.

"I need some fresh air."

"Miranda thinks this one will be a boy," Lucille said a little too brightly. "Another boy, Randy. Wouldn't that be nice?"

Cale doubted he was the only one who had noticed Randy's dull expression.

"We'll do what we can," Lucille said. "Isn't that right, Emory? I'm gonna come by every day to help until you get home from the plant, Randy. As soon as Lavender has the baby, things'll get back to normal, you'll see."

Cale recognized a family in trouble when he saw one. He should. He was part of one. Problems. Everybody had them. Cale, Emory, Ruby, a girl with too many children, and her husband with too much responsibility. With a nod to the Sturgis clan, Cale excused himself.

Emory Sturgis watched him go, thinking that for a Northerner, Cale Wilder wasn't too bad. His name suited him. Not Cale. That was the damnedest name he'd ever heard, but Wilder, now, that suited him real well, because that was how the man moved, wild, like a panther, confident and quiet and strong. The band started up again, and folks clapped their hands and stomped their feet. There was so much danged commotion, Emory could hardly hear himself think. That didn't stop him from turning to his wife and saying, "You ever hear of anybody by the name of Ellie Stanoway, Lucille?"

Thirty-five years of marriage had made Lucille Sturgis blessedly deaf to the incessant drone of her husband's voice. But there was something about the name Ellie Stanoway that tugged at her memory. Ellie. Ellie. No, she'd never met anyone by that name. But Stanoway, now, that sounded vaguely familiar.

Lucille was on the verge of placing it, when she saw her son-in-law tip his head down so that Shantelle McCausy, the little bleached blonde who'd had a crush on Randy and every other male within one hundred miles, could whisper something in his ear.

"Randy?" Lavender called.

"What!" For a moment, Randy looked remorseful at

having used that stern tone, but his gaze swept his wife's protruding stomach, and the remorse turned to determination that chilled Lucille clear to the bone.

"Remember how we used to dance to this song back in school?" Lavender asked.

Randy's gaze softened, and Lucille breathed a little easier. "Yeah, I remember."

The smile Lavender gave her young husband sent tears to Lucille's eyes. Randy was a good boy, but he was young, barely twenty-five, and Lucille knew he was feeling the burden lovin' had brought with it.

"Where are you going?" Lavender called.

Randy said, "Thought I'd wander over to the Bootlegger for a beer."

Lucille looked around in time to see Shantelle slip out the side door. Lavender might have been Randy's wife, but she was Lucille's baby. And Lucille was worried about her. Except for her rounded belly, Lavender was terribly thin. Her skin was sallow, and the dark circles beneath her eyes seemed to be a permanent part of her face. She'd already buried two babies, and Lucille didn't know what Lavender would do if this one died too. If the worst happened, she was going to need her young husband at her side. But what could she, Lavender's mama, do?

"Wait up there, sonny," Emory said, sidestepping a vacated chair. "I'm feeling a might thirsty myself."

Lucille and Lavender shared a long, heartfelt sigh. "It's going to be all right," Lavender said. "Daddy's got him."

Lucille nodded and gave her daughter what she hoped was an encouraging smile. Lots of folks said Emory Sturgis talked just to hear the sound of his own voice. God knew it had worn on her nerves over the years, but there was a lot more to that man than hot air. Always had been. Most days it took her hours to sift through everything he said. Tonight was going to be no exception, for there on the edge of her memory she saw an image of a young woman with long red hair and sad green eyes.

"Mama," Lavender said, "I'm gonna go get some punch. Want some?"

Lucille jumped to her feet. "You sit, sugar. I'll fetch us each one." She put the nagging memory out of her mind and bustled away to see to her daughter's needs.

The band members were packing up when Miranda called good-bye to Ruby, and to Clyde, who always stuck around to make sure Ruby got home safe and sound. The practiced eye she cast all around as she left the building was so automatic, she barely knew she was doing it anymore.

Other than a few cars that were still parked in front of the Bootlegger, Main Street was deserted. She strode to her Explorer, unlocked the door, and got in. She'd started the engine and was pulling out of the parking space, when Ruby bustled through the Livery's door, Clyde close behind. As far as she knew, it was the only time the two of them were ever alone.

Once, Miranda had asked Clyde why he didn't give up. After all, Ruby had made it clear that she intended to spend the rest of her life alone. In his own quiet way, Clyde had said he was just letting nature take its course.

Nature, Miranda thought, turning onto Main Street and heading toward home. The ebb and flow of life. It could be as gentle as the dawn of a new day, as temperamental and powerful as a flash of lightning, and as poignant as an entire congregation joined in prayer. Until she'd felt Cale's arms go around her during that one brief dance tonight, Miranda had forgotten how powerful desire could be. She'd wanted more tonight, more than a slow dance beneath the watchful eyes of a roomful of people. Cale's reasons for resisting weren't so different from Ruby's. Just because he made her feel beautiful didn't mean he owed her anything. She had no right to judge him.

It wasn't as if she were falling in love with him. She didn't know him well enough for that. He'd put his arms around her during that dance, and she'd let him, for the plain and simple reason that it had felt good. She wasn't going to turn all poetic and imagine that she'd found heaven in his arms or a haven in the nook between his neck and shoulder, where she'd rested her cheek for a few minutes. There had been nothing heavenly or poetic about any of it. That exasperating Northerner didn't love her. He couldn't.

But she could love him if she wasn't careful.

A possum's eyes shone yellow in the glare of her headlights. It lumbered into the weeds as she turned into her driveway. Loose gravel crunched beneath her tires. Her headlights flickered over the exasperating Northerner sitting on her front porch.

CHAPTER TWELVE

An owl hooted in the distance as Miranda pulled to a stop in her driveway. Her door clicked open and then closed again, her shoes barely making a sound as she rounded the front of her car. She didn't say anything, and neither did Cale, although he did rise to his feet as she neared. They stared at each other for a few seconds, him on the first step, her on the grass below.

Cale found his voice first. "Go ahead and say it. I've got it coming."

"What is it you think I should say, Cale?"

He settled his hands on his hips and studied her. "Oh, I don't know. Look what the cat dragged in, maybe. Or you could tell me to get off your porch and never come back."

The man was a pro at sending mixed signals. "I need an update, Cale. Is that what you want me to say?"

Keys in hand, she walked toward the steps. He shifted to one side as she passed, but only slightly, so that her body came within a hairbreadth of his.

"What I want. Now, that's a good one."

Miranda simply did not understand this man. Resigning

herself to that fact, she said, "Have you been sitting on my porch long?"

"An hour or so."

"I assumed you'd gone over to the Bootlegger." She opened the screen door, then fit her key in the lock in the heavy inner door.

"I thought about it."

From the sound of his voice she could tell he'd turned and was coming closer.

"But I didn't see much sense in doing two stupid things in one night."

"Did you do something stupid tonight?"

"A size-eleven shoe isn't easy to chew up or spit out. I'm sorry, Miranda."

"There's no need, Cale."

"That's where you're wrong. I have plenty of need."

She glanced sideways at him, thinking that wasn't what she'd meant. His expression told her he knew it. "I wasn't asking for a commitment, Caleb. It was just a dance."

"It wasn't just a dance, dammit. Not to me."

"Then what was it?"

"I think the answer's simple."

She shook her head. "There's nothing simple about you. Not who you are, not what you are, not where you've been or where you're going. Losing your wife was horrible for you. I understand that. No one should have to go through what you're going through. Suddenly, you've become a single man again, and you don't know how you're supposed to act."

"Thanks for the recap."

Leaving the key in the lock, she closed the screen door and leaned against it. "I realize," she said quietly, "that I might have sounded a trifle knowing and perhaps even slightly condescending."

Cale knew he was staring. He couldn't help it. He'd gone there to apologize, not to extract an apology from Miranda. And yet that was what she'd done, giving him an exoneration of sorts in a voice soft and warm enough to slip into. In a simpler time, he would have pulled her against him, and—

Hell, she was right. There was nothing simple about this.

The sound of an approaching car drew both their gazes. Within seconds, Clyde Sturgis's truck came and went from view. They heard it slow down at the corner and fade into the distance.

"Clyde's taking Ruby home," Miranda said.

"Are they . . ."

"A couple?" she asked. "No. They care about each other. I'd even venture further and say that Clyde loves her and probably has most of his life. She might love him too, although she won't admit it."

"Why?"

"I think she's afraid."

Cale remembered when Ruby had mentioned that people claimed she was cursed. He didn't believe in hexes and voodoo and black magic, but he understood fear. "She's afraid to love again. Is that it?"

"The loving is easy. She's afraid to lose again."

Cale understood that too.

"Ruby and her husband, Harlan, grew up on the mountain. Like a lot of people in these hills, they married young. Back then, women didn't have careers. They said I do and then waited for the first baby to come along. Ruby and Harlan waited. And waited. Today, a couple would go to a fertility specialist, but times were different then. Finally, after ten years of yearning for a child, she became pregnant. Folks say Harlan danced a jig when he first found out. She delivered a healthy boy. Ruby says he looked just like his daddy."

Miranda paused for a moment, and Cale said, "The baby died?"

She nodded. "Shortly before his first birthday. Back then they called it crib death. Today, it's called SIDS. The enormity of the loss is incomprehensible no matter what it's called. I didn't know Ruby then, but Lucille Sturgis once told me that Ruby cried for the better part of the following year. She and Harlan were never able to have another child."

They were both silent for a moment, respecting the tragic loss even all these years later. "Is that why folks up here say she's cursed?" Cale asked.

"No one can understand everything that happens in this world, but this much I know for sure. Ruby McCoy has lived through more than her share of tragedy, but she's not cursed."

"I take it her husband died too?"

"Harlan had cancer. They went all the way to Boston for treatment. That's where they were when I first came to Dawsons Hollow. By the time I met her, she was all alone. She clucked over me like a mother hen, and I bullied her into going on. Guess you could say we clicked."

"And Clyde Sturgis?"

"Clyde's a good man. I don't have his patience. I couldn't stay in the shadows the way he has, accepting crumbs."

Closing his eyes, Cale knew Miranda was trying to tell him something. She'd wandered to the railing and was staring into the night. After a moment of careful deliberation, he came closer and said, "Basically, you're saying you won't allow yourself to be the proverbial sacrificial lamb, and you won't allow me to be either."

"It's not up to me, Cale."

He placed his hand on her shoulder, turning her around to face him. "Are you saying it's up to me?"

He kissed her before she could answer. It happened fast, but Miranda still should have seen it coming. Her breath rushed out of her, her eyes fluttered closed, and she swayed toward him slightly. It was all the encouragement he needed. His arms shot around her, and his mouth moved over hers, his lips warm, moist, hungry.

This was what she'd wanted at the dance earlier, a senses-spinning-out-of-control connection. It wasn't a kiss about the past or the future. It was a kiss for the moment between a man and a woman teetering on the edge of today, a kiss between two people who weren't pretending that the wind was singing through the cottonwoods or that there was magic in the shadows where moonbeams brushed the earth.

Their lips parted, clung, parted again. They took collective breaths and opened their eyes. His arms were still around her, his face inches from hers.

"I did that because I wanted to," he whispered. "Not because I had to. Just so there's no confusion."

He backed up as he spoke, his hands skimming her hips, then slowly finding their way into his pockets.

"Yes, well," she murmured, "that certainly cleared that up."

The porch light cast shadows beneath his eyes, at the base of his neck, and in the folds of his shirt. It was midnight. The witching hour. Perhaps that was why he smiled. His mouth was made for rakish grins, the bottom lip slightly thicker than the top, the corners meeting a shallow crease, slightly insolent, terribly attractive.

"I heard everything you said, Miranda. I even heard a little of what you didn't quite say. You're not asking for a commitment, and I'm in no place to offer you one. But you deserve more than a one-night stand. You're right about me. I don't know how I'm supposed to act now, how I'm supposed to feel. I'm a single man but not a never-been-married one. I'll never be that again. Unfortunately, I don't know where that leaves us."

His voice had been little more than a rasp in the quiet night, his expression so serious, Miranda couldn't help thinking it was a shame that people always seemed to grow the most from the difficult things in life. Where did that leave her and Cale? "Between the proverbial rock and a hard place?"

Cale shook his head. He'd been burrowed underneath that proverbial rock she'd mentioned for months now. And the hard place, well, he was trying valiantly not to think about that. He wanted her. She wanted him too. He'd felt it in her kiss, saw it in her eyes, heard it in her sigh.

What now?

He glanced at the sky. "It's late."

"Yes."

He took a backward step and then another.

"Good night, Miranda."

"Cale?"

He was halfway to the road when he glanced at her over his shoulder. Her hair looked almost golden beneath the glow of the porch light, her eyes, as always, artful and serene as she said, "When I first saw you sitting on my porch, I considered apologizing to you. Lord knows I probably should have. Why is it so much easier to ask for permission than to ask for forgiveness? You've probably figured out that I'm not terribly sweet."

His grin was slow but sure. "That's one of the things I find so damned appealing about you. That, and how half the men on this mountain are in love with you, and yet I'm the only one you let kiss you."

"At least y'all haven't let it go to your head."

Miranda carried the sound of Cale's laughter inside with her. She listened at the screen door as his chuckle turned into a mellow whistle. She had a feeling it had been a long, long time since Caleb Wilder had whistled. Peering at her shadowy garden, Miranda thought that perhaps there was magic in those moonbeams after all, and music in the gentle sigh of the wind in the trees.

"Cale?"

On the bathroom floor, Cale's whistle trailed away. He was wedged in the narrow space between the sink and bathtub, his neck at an angle God couldn't have intended.

"Er. Dad? I did the dishes."

Cale had been trying to install the water heater when Danny had shown up shortly before nine, a pillowcase filled with soiled clothes slung over his back. Cale had stopped what he'd been doing and prepared a big breakfast of fried eggs and bacon and toast. They'd talked now and then, but much of the time they'd been quiet. For the first time in months, the silence had felt almost companionable. After breakfast, he showed Danny how to use the old-fashioned washer, then Cale went back to his plumbing project in the bathroom.

One hand on the wrench, the other on the stubborn pipe fitting, Cale said, "You didn't have to do the dishes, but thanks."

"I hung my clothes over the line too."

"The washing machine finally finished, then?"

"That's not a machine. It's a monster. Washing clothes in raging rapids would be safer."

Cale chuckled at that.

"I started the next load of your stuff too," Danny said.

In some ways, the past year and a half had made them both self-sufficient, at least when it came to the wash.

"And I'm leaving."

A dozen questions sprang to Cale's mind. God knows he'd asked them all before. A few months ago, he would have voiced them all too, and Danny would have responded with a quelling glare and silence. The harder he'd pulled, the more Danny resisted. Today, Cale relinquished his hold on the fitting that had been so close to coming loose and calmly said, "You planning on coming back in time for lunch?"

"You want me to?"

"It's up to you."

"Maybe I will, then."

Cale smiled.

Danny didn't seem to know where to look. "Well, see ya."

After the screen door bounced closed, Cale returned to the water heater. He scuffed his knuckles two more times, but a half hour later, the water heater was humming away from its perch between the sink and bathtub, and Cale was whistling again and admiring his handiwork.

The old tank-style washing machine chugged and whirred so loudly, it lured him from the antiquated bathroom. Stopping on the back step, he leaned over the machine, only to jerk backward when the thing lunged at him.

The load of clothes must have been unbalanced. Finding a sturdy stick on the ground, he poked it into the water. A serious mistake, because the machine yanked it out of his hands and proceeded to eat it. No wonder Danny had said the thing was dangerous. Cale unplugged the machine, retrieved the stick, and, plunging his arms into the sudsy water, redistributed the clothes.

He scooped a shirt he'd worn last night off the pile at his feet and dried his hands. Slowly, he brought the shirt to his nose. It smelled of spring flowers. It smelled of Miranda.

Funny, he hadn't consciously associated her with the perfume she'd been wearing, but her scent brought back everything about her—how she'd smelled, how she'd looked, how she'd felt in his arms.

Miranda Sinclair was a unique woman, strong yet tenderhearted, quiet and stubborn and smart. And passionate. God, yes, she was passionate, swaying toward him, sighing deep in her throat, opening her mouth beneath his. He'd been drawn to her from the first, and she knew it. She wasn't asking for a commitment, but she wouldn't accept an overture from him until he was ready. In other words, there would be no denying, hiding, or sugar-coating his feelings. Either he was ready to move on. Or he wasn't.

He remembered when she'd said she'd been precocious as a child. Just last night she insinuated that she wasn't always sweet. A steady diet of sugar would get old. He brought the shirt to his nose again and inhaled her scent. A steady stream of her kisses sounded damned appealing.

Church bells sounded in the distance. After plugging the washing machine back in, he made a pass through the small house. True to his word, Danny had stacked the clean dishes upside down next to the sink. The boy wouldn't be back for a couple of hours at least. That left Cale with two hours and nothing to do.

He washed his hands in lukewarm water, ran a comb through his hair, and decided to take a walk and see where he ended up.

* * *

"It weren't until after the war that ever'thin' started to go to hell," Angus Warner insisted. "Before that, ever'body was poor. Nobody knew no different, ain't that right, Elmer?"

"Everybody except Moot. And the Pratts, mebbee."

"Yup, yup, you're right. Ever'body except them. Anyway, during the war . . ."

Cale shook his head to clear it and tried to follow the conversation. They'd only reached the war years. What had he done to deserve this?

What he'd done was stopped at Angus's porch and said hello.

He'd gone to Miranda's first. Her Explorer was gone, her house closed up tight. Ruby hadn't been home either. Now, an hour after he'd wandered down a side street in Dawsons Hollow, he was sitting on an old folding chair amid a growing pile of wood shavings while Angus whittled and reminisced about the past.

He'd almost fallen asleep a couple of times. Not that Elmer and Angus noticed. They didn't seem to expect more from him than an occasional unh-unh or uh-huh. They'd complained about taxes, the national deficit, teenagers, and the price J. R. Pratt charged for a can of beans. If there was one thing these small-town people had, it was big opinions.

Angus's voice droned on in the background. Cale was more interested in the piece of wood the old man was transforming in his hands. Stroke by stroke, shaving by shaving, an animal was emerging.

"You sure you never heard that name Stanoway?" Elmer was scratching his scraggly beard.

Cale homed in on Ellie's maiden name.

"Perty sure," Angus said. "You're thinkin' of Galloway."

"Who?" Elmer asked.

There they went again. Cale's gaze returned to the wood carving in Angus's gnarled, bandaged hand.

"Galloway. You remember them. They lived up on Possum Road in the old Campbell place back in the fifties."

"The Hurleys lived in the old Campbell place. The Galloways lived in the old Thompson place."

"Oh, that's right."

"Whatever happened to old man Hurley anyhow?"

"He and the wife got a divorce." Angus pronounced it *dee*-vorce. "Claimed she finally got fed up with his drinkin' and left him. Unusual for a woman to do that back then. Nowadays, well, it's a different story. Too bad too. Families getting torn apart right and left. It's a cryin' shame, that's what it is."

Cale shook his head. Ask an old person one simple question, and you ended up with a boatload of useless information. "Then neither of you remembers any Stanoways?"

"Cain't recollect any, no. If you want, you could always ask Jed at the next poker game."

"Jed?" Cale asked dazedly.

Angus and Elmer exchanged a knowing look behind Cale's back. "That's right, sonny. You remember Jed. Pert near ran over you and Miranda a couple of nights back. Some of us menfolk get together over at the Bootlegger Thursdays for some spirits and poker. You can join us if ya want to."

"Maybe I'll do that," Cale said. Staring at the wood carving in Angus's hand, he said, "Angus, do you ever carve anything besides panthers?"

"Like what?"

"Oh, I don't know. Birds, maybe?"

Elmer and Angus were both peering at the panther Angus was finishing. "What sort of birds?" Angus asked.

Cale told him. And Angus sputtered, "Why on earth would anybody want one of those?"

Cale said, "I'd pay you."

"You would?" Elmer asked.

"How much?" Angus said at the same time.

Cale named an amount. Angus reached for another piece of wood, the war years all but forgotten.

"Did you remember yet?"

Daniel's question was met with Willow's fierce glare.

How was he supposed to know you couldn't talk while somebody was hugging a tree?

The look of concentration on Willow's face was almost comical. No dummy, Daniel kept the observation to himself and held very still. Briefly, her expression changed. She was either having an embolism or she was figuring out who Daniel reminded her of.

She heaved a huge sigh, opened her eyes, and released the tree. "Let's go."

"What do you mean, let's go? We can't go until you remember."

"Well, I don't know, all right? These things can't be forced. You of all people should know that."

How in the hell was he supposed to know that? He made a sound he'd heard Cale make moments before his temper went through the roof, then turned on Willow. He was all set to cuss up a blue streak, when she laid a hand on his arm and gestured for him to hold still.

They were standing on the edge of a clearing. Twenty feet away, dozens, maybe even a hundred or more butterflies fluttered among the wildflowers. "They're blues and coppers mostly," Willow whispered. "Aren't they a sight to behold?"

She reached for the camera hanging around her neck and snapped several pictures. She'd taken pictures of everything. Trees, rocks, birds, him.

Lowering her camera to hang from the strap around her neck, she whispered, "The ancient Greeks believed the soul left the body after death in the form of a butterfly. Their symbol for death was a beautiful girl with butterfly wings, named Psyche."

Daniel's irritation evaporated into thin air. Willow Pratt knew things. Important things, inconsequential things, interesting things, funny things, strange things. Nothing unnerved her. When she talked, Daniel listened. Now and then, she asked questions, but she was just as content to answer his. And Daniel had a million of them—about the mountain, about the people of Dawsons Hollow, about the books Willow read. He was considered brilliant. As far as he was concerned, Willow was smarter. Hell, she knew stuff about everything. She didn't always use proper English and grammar, but she had a wellspring of knowledge that surprised the hell out of him. And yet she wasn't full of herself. She didn't define herself with her intelligence the way his fellow classmates back in Ohio had. Best of all, she didn't define Daniel by his. He actually felt normal around her. He liked her for that.

"I have to get back up to my cabin. The raccoon will be getting hungry."

She fell into step beside him. "You ever get tired of having to do that?"

He shrugged. They walked along in silence after that. That was something else he liked about her. She was as comfortable with silence as she was with sound. He didn't know any other girls like that.

He reached the place where the trail forked on Hickory Gap Road. From there, it was little more than a hop, skip, and a jump to his place. He led the way inside, stopping at the edge of the box. The raccoon started to chatter the instant he saw Daniel.

"He knows who you are," Willow exclaimed.

"Yeah."

"Poor thing, being stuck in this here box all day." At Daniel's stricken look, she rushed on to say, " 'Course, it's gotta be better than starvin' to death."

Daniel breathed a little easier. Taking charge with quiet assurance, he prepared the raccoon's bottle and reached for the small animal.

Willow watched, eyes narrowed, arms crossed, one foot tapping the plank floor. "What's his name?"

"How should I know?"

"That's what I thought."

"What's what you thought?" Daniel asked.

She shrugged one shoulder and slanted him a look that told him he wasn't going to like what she had to say. Not that that kept her from saying it.

"You didn't name him because you knew it wouldn't be right. Because you can't keep him. At least not forever."

Daniel had thought about that, but he'd never actually put it into words. It sounded as bad out loud as it did in his head. In a sense, he'd saved the creature's life. But for what? Raccoons weren't pets.

"He's cute and cuddly right now," Willow said. "But when he grows up, instinct is going to take over. You know, foraging and mating and stuff. If you keep him locked up, he'll never learn how to take care of himself."

Daniel studied the small animal. His coat was thick and gray and soft, his belly so round, it was comical. Daniel swore the little guy had doubled in size in the week he'd been feeding him.

"Right now he trusts you," Willow said. "What about when he's older and he comes face-to-face with a hunter? If that happens, his trust in man is gonna come in about as handy as pockets on a space suit."

She must have read his stricken look again, because she said, "Don't worry. The right solution will present itself. It's gonna be up to you to recognize it when it happens."

Daniel nodded gravely, the weight of responsibility heavy on his shoulders and on his mind.

"Wilder?"

A light flashed, a camera clicked. "Damnit, Willow."

"Unh-unh-unh."

"Yeah, yeah, I know. Swearing goes against your nature." Daniel was still seeing shards of light when he sputtered to himself that Willow Pratt had the most exasperating nature he'd ever come across. He didn't even know why he liked her.

Yeah, he did.

"How much longer is that animal gonna take to eat?"

"He's almost done. For crying out loud, Willow. You could use a little patience."

She spun around and peered out the window. "That's another reason I know I'll never be a healer like Miranda.

I don't have any patients." When she spelled it, Daniel rolled his eyes.

She wouldn't earn a living doing comedy either.

She clicked another picture of him. When he started to protest, she said, "Maybe I'll be a world-renowned photographer. Quit complaining. If I study your picture long enough, maybe I'll figure out who you look like. Hurry up. We only have all day."

Daniel put the raccoon back in the box. It was strange how somebody who didn't use proper English had such a way with words.

"Looks like you're making progress."

Daniel straightened, grimaced slightly at the pull of muscles in his back, and nodded at Miranda Sinclair. His hands were covered in dirt. There wasn't much he wouldn't have given for an opportunity to wash them.

"Have you had enough for one day?" she asked.

He jabbed the hoe into the soil one more time. "I'm not done."

"Gardening is never done. That's why it's so soothing. It's like an old friend who's always there. A storm's brewing. You've done the weeding and hoeing, now nature's going to do the watering. Want to come inside for a little while? Have something to eat and drink, wash your hands."

Wash his hands?

Daniel followed her to the porch. While she unlocked the door, something he hadn't seen anybody else up here do, he surveyed the rows of plants he'd hoed and weeded. Personally, he hadn't found the task particularly soothing, but there was a sense of satisfaction in looking at the progress he'd made.

The door swung open. Leading the way inside, she said, "The bathroom's this way."

By the time he emerged from the bathroom, his face was clean-scrubbed and he'd gotten the dirt out from underneath his fingernails. He found Miranda in the kitchen, spreading mayonnaise on bread, several dollar bills on the counter nearby.

"We didn't discuss the method of payment," she said. "I hope this is okay."

He slid the money into his hand. "Cash works for me. Thanks."

"Hungry?" she asked.

Daniel was usually hungry, but he didn't want to overstay his welcome.

"Silly question," she said as if he'd answered. "Aren't teenage boys always hungry?"

He was still trying to formulate his reply, when she handed him a plate containing two thick turkey sandwiches sliced diagonally, the way his mom used to. Turning to the refrigerator, she said, "Would you like milk with that, or lemonade?"

He had to chew fast and swallow in a hurry. "Lemonade, please."

Miranda smiled to herself. A boy with manners in this day and age ... his parents should be commended. She made a mental note to mention it to Cale the next time she saw him, whenever that might be. Stacking everything she and Daniel would need on a tray, she carried it to the table. Years of practice made the positioning of place mats, glasses, cutlery, and napkins automatic.

Finished with the task, she noticed Daniel looking at the artwork hanging in the kitchen window. "Pretty, isn't it? It's called a dream-catcher. It's believed to hold nightmares at bay."

"People up here are superstitious."

She nodded and motioned to the table. "I spent most of the morning immunizing children. I don't know about you, but I'd like to sit down."

He sat across from her at the ceramic-topped kitchen table. "Do you believe in superstition?" he asked.

Miranda took a sip of lemonade and tried to decide how to explain what she believed. "Most folklore dates back hundreds of years. People used to believe that washing in fresh rainwater on the first day of June removed freckles. Back when people didn't bathe very often, it probably seemed that way."

Daniel started on his second sandwich. Miranda continued. "To this day, some people still turn their shoes bottom side up before going to bed to cure cramps in their feet. Lo and behold, when they wake up, the soreness is gone."

"Not because of the position of their shoes," Daniel said levelly. "Because they stayed off their feet all night."

"The reason they feel better doesn't matter, does it? The proven worth of most of these remedies is scientifically based. The active ingredient in oak-stump water, the old-fashioned treatment for removing warts, is tannic acid."

"No kidding."

She smiled. Something went warm deep inside Daniel. And he smiled in return. Talking to Miranda was nice. Maybe it was her accent. Everyone up here had a Southern accent, but hers was more refined, cultured. His mother's had been like that, only she'd claimed living up north had wrung all but the most minute traces of it out of her.

"Would you like another?"

Daniel had been so lulled by Miranda's voice, he hadn't realized he'd finished both sandwiches. "No, thanks." He pushed his chair out and stood.

It wasn't until he'd picked up his empty plate that Miranda noticed the red splotches and blisters on his hands from hoeing. She touched him with the pads of three fingers. They both went momentarily still. Thunder rumbled in the distance, and goose bumps skittered up Miranda's arms.

Either he heard the shuddering breath she took, or he noticed how pale she'd suddenly gone, because he said, "Are you okay?"

She nodded, glancing through the dream-catcher and out the window at the darkening sky. "Storms unnerve me, that's all."

From his position, Daniel could see the dream-catcher in the kitchen as well as two more in the living room. She kept her doors locked, and she'd placed dream-catchers in every window. He remembered thinking, first time he'd seen her that there was something ethereal about her. He didn't know what she was afraid of, but somehow he thought it had to do with the way her inner strength combined with her fears.

"Do they work?"

She smiled at that. "Sometimes. I've read volumes about dreams and what they mean. There's a place in folklore for them too. It used to be said that dreams of locked doors invited measles or croup unless serious precautions were taken. Of course, that was before vaccines."

"What about recurring dreams?" Daniel said, thinking about the dream he'd had again last night in which he saw his mother and a gentle doe watching him from a distant cloud.

"That's one point where psychologists and superstition meet. Both agree that recurring dreams are windows to the soul. Come on," she said. "I'll give you a ride up the mountain before that storm hits."

"I brought the raccoon with me to my, er, dad's house this morning. I can make it that far before the rain starts."

"Are you sure?"

Shy again, Daniel nodded. Before Miranda could argue, he was gone.

A series of shudders overtook her. She didn't understand it. The thunder wasn't even close yet. Normally, she didn't get this jumpy until it was right outside her door.

She practiced her deep-breathing technique. Calmer now, she hurried outside, where she put the hoe away and closed up the shed. In the distance, she could see the clouds closing in. A raging storm was approaching. Miranda felt its pressure. Her skin prickled, her eyes darted back and forth. She shook it off and went inside to bottle the peppermint oil a colleague had shipped from his mint farm in Michigan.

She was screwing on the droppers and lids, when Ruby bustled in. The thunder was close now. And Miranda's bottom lip had an indentation so deep, she tasted blood.

"Landsakes, these summer storms are unpredictable."

Miranda's heart swelled with feeling. Oh, Ruby. Dear, kind Ruby.

Lightning snaked out of the sky, and thunder shook the earth with so much force, Ruby almost dropped the mail she'd picked up on her way past Miranda's mailbox. Handing the mail to Miranda, Ruby said, "Looky what I found sitting on top of these letters."

She handed over a small carving the size of her fist. "Any idea who it's from?" Ruby asked.

Turning it this way and that, Miranda almost smiled. "I believe it's from Cale."

"Well? You gonna make me guess what it means?"

Miranda's smile was real now. "I do believe a chicken has just been exchanged."

CHAPTER THIRTEEN

Miranda sat in front of her computer, hands poised over the keyboard. The thunderstorm had ended hours earlier. Ruby had gone home, and Miranda decided to use the quiet time to put together the report and newsletter her mother would distribute to the fine, affluent, world-conscious people downstate. She'd written and deleted the first paragraph four times. Currently, she was staring at a blank screen.

She seemed to be having a slight problem concentrating.

Birds had chirruped after the storm, feasting on worms, splashing in puddles. The garden was quiet now. It was too early for animals of the night, and those that weren't nocturnal had crept off to their dens and nests and thickets. A long time ago, it had been Miranda's favorite time of the day.

She pushed her chair out and stood, pausing long enough to pick up the carved chicken that had captivated her attention along with her sense of whimsy. The piece said a lot about Cale's sense of humor. It said even more about the man himself. Caleb Wilder was a man whose actions spoke louder than words. Throw in the fact that his smiles made her dizzy and his kiss made her want another, it was no wonder she couldn't concentrate on her newsletter.

The Aubusson carpet was soft beneath her sandals as she strolled to the other side of the room. Realizing she'd brought the carved chicken with her, she placed it on the rustic little table Randy Sprague had made for her as payment for her help delivering his and Lavender's last baby. The table didn't blend with her finer furniture, but she didn't care. She liked the way her living room looked, the refined pieces mingling with handmade treasures.

The carved chicken fit right in. She recognized Angus Warner's handiwork, although this was the first time she'd ever seen a carving that wasn't a panther or a bear or a badger.

Suddenly, there was a loud squawking and flapping outside her window. What in the world? She lifted the curtain aside, pleasure spreading through her at the sight of Cale leaning casually against her gate.

It normally took a lot to ruffle a sparrow's feathers this time of the evening. Sauntering out to her porch, she pointed to the sourwood tree. "Any idea what startled them?"

Cale uncrossed his ankles and straightened, as if he had all the time in the world. "I don't think they liked something that went sailing into their tree."

Every few years a sparrow hawk discovered her garden. She didn't see any sign of a larger bird tonight. "What might that have been?"

"I don't know for sure, but it's possible it was a stone."

"You threw a stone at innocent birds?"

"It isn't as if I hit any of them."

Of course not. He'd simply been making an entrance. She had to hold back her grin.

He gestured to the carving she'd brought outside with her and slowly started toward her. "I see you found my gift."

"Am I to assume this chicken is a sign that your intentions are honorable?"

"Oh, I don't know." He came closer. "I wouldn't say my intentions are"—and closer—"completely honorable."

The man was part rascal, part rogue, all male. He'd reached the steps and was looking up at her, his gaze steady, his eyes a deep, vivid blue.

"Would you like to come in?" she asked.

"Not tonight. Have you eaten?"

At her nod, he said, "In that case, I won't invite you to dinner. On to Plan B. Could I interest you in a movie?"

"Your gentlemanly side is very becoming. I'll get my bag."

"Don't be long. It's been a while since I've exercised my gentlemanly side. I'm not sure how long it'll last."

It lasted all through the shoot-'em-up, blow-'em-up, good-guys-were-victorious late movie they saw down in Toccoa. Cale had held her door each time she climbed in and out of his old pickup truck. Miranda was more taken with the way he held her gaze. There was warmth in his eyes and a lazily seductive gleam that wrapped around her in a way she wasn't sure she'd ever felt before. Every time his gaze strayed to her mouth, her thoughts turned hazy. She'd dated other men years ago—at first to prove to herself that she was still a whole woman and later for the simple reason that she enjoyed getting a man's perspective. Not one of them had ever made her senses reel by just looking at her.

Only Cale did that. But it was more than the way he looked at her. It was the questions he asked and the way he listened to her responses. Sitting across from him, she'd discovered she could laugh freely with him, something she'd been doing a lot since they'd claimed the corner booth in the nearly empty truck stop just west of the South Carolina border. Never mind that it was almost midnight. He'd ordered a huge serving of sausage gravy over mashed potatoes, then sat there and finished every last bite. The man had impeccable manners and terrible food choices. He also told incredible stories of his younger days, each one more humorous than the last.

If he didn't stop, she was going to put out a rib laughing. One hand pressed over her rib cage, she whispered, "I'm begging for mercy."

He'd pushed his plate away a while ago. Now, elbows

on the table, hands clasped loosely beneath his chin, he said, "Believe me, it wasn't my intention to make you beg for anything."

Just like that, the awareness that had been hovering beneath their laughter became a living, breathing, tangible being. She looked directly into his eyes and quietly said, "And what are your intentions, Cale?"

His intentions? Until that moment, they'd been crystal clear. He'd intended to take things slowly, one day at a time, to get to know her, and her him. "It just occurred to me that I've done most of the talking tonight."

She shrugged. "I don't mind."

He studied her unhurriedly, feature by feature. Earlier, he'd caught her staring at his hands. He wondered if she knew she did it. Somehow, he doubted it. He remembered when she'd told him that all she'd seen of her attacker was the shape of his head and his awful hands. Until he'd met her, he'd never given rape a lot of thought. Day by day, he was coming closer to understanding the lasting effects that kind of violent act had on a woman. Even if he hadn't known what the violence had been, he believed he would have sensed that there had been something. Maybe the battle weary recognized one another, connecting on a soul-deep level.

Tonight, she didn't look battle weary, not in the least. Her face was nearly a perfect oval, her features just irregular enough to be arresting. She'd twisted her hair high on the back of her head and secured it with several strategically placed pins. Of course it didn't stay there, at least not all of it. Loose tendrils brushed her eyebrows, her jaw, and neck. Her amber-colored silk shirt brought out the gold highlights in her hair. Laughter had given her light brown eyes a luminous sheen. A man didn't have to look far to find the reason for the glimmering intensity in their depths. Sultry and warm and more than a little brash, she was as aware of him as he was of her. It made being a gentleman damn difficult.

That awareness continued to shimmer between them long

after he paid for his meal and her coffee. It was there during the ride back to her place. If it changed slightly when he turned off the engine in her driveway, it was only because it intensified in that moment in the quiet, in the dark.

Humming "One Hundred Bottles of Beer on the Wall" wasn't going to cut it tonight. If he'd been fifteen years younger, he would have dragged her closer and worked around the steering wheel and shifting lever. But he was a man now, and Miranda was a woman who deserved better than what he could give her in the cramped interior of this old truck.

Calling on the last reserves of his willpower, he opened his door, strode around the front of the truck, and opened her door. They walked to her house in silence. Searching through her oversize purse for her key, she said, "Now would you like to come in?"

"I'd like to. But I'm not going to."

Keys forgotten, she looked up at him with so much open longing, he wanted to chuck his conscience. "If I walk through that door tonight, I'm going to lose the last shred of my control." He eased slightly closer. "And I don't have protection. So unless you have something . . ."

"No, I'm sorry, Cale, but I don't."

A smile stole across her face. She didn't look sorry exactly. She looked adorable and precocious, and oh, hell. He pulled her to him and kissed her.

Need poured through him, hot and heavy. His mouth moved over hers, capturing her initial yelp of surprise and then her deep moan of pleasure. He wrapped his arms around her, his hands roaming her back, pressing her to him. Her silk shirt was smooth beneath his callused hands, gliding over warm skin underneath. He memorized the contours of her body, the delicate ridges of her spine, the flare of her hips. He'd seen her pick up forty-pound children, and yet she felt fragile in his arms, and winsome and lithe. And willing. God, yes, she was willing.

Miranda slid her hands up and down Cale's broad back, memorizing the breadth and texture of muscle, cotton, and skin. He molded her to him, sliding a thigh between hers. She felt his response, his need, his desire, heard his moan. All the while he kissed her, she kissed him back, his mouth, his cheek, his chin. He'd been clean-shaven when he'd arrived. Already, his cheeks and jaw were rough beneath her lips.

Running her hands up his back one more time, she whispered, "You're a bundle of knots, tied so tight, I'm not sure I'd be able to undo them."

He laughed, the sound a deep rasp that was more frustration than humor. "You're wrong. You've nearly undone every inch of me."

"Nearly?"

His next chuckle was a carbon copy of the last. He wanted her. She knew it. He knew she knew it. They were going to make love. Judging by that kiss, soon.

He drew away slightly.

Soon. But not tonight.

"What are you doing tomorrow evening?" he asked.

It took a moment for her mind to clear enough to remember. "I usually make house calls on Tuesday evenings."

He nodded. And she dared to say, "You're welcome to come with me if you'd like."

"How long does it take?"

"I'm usually finished by dark."

Their gazes met, held. Each in their own mind imagined what they might do after dark.

He kissed her again swiftly, then set her away from him. "Until tomorrow, Miranda."

Yes, until then. "Good night, Cale."

On her own a few minutes later, the doors locked, her house quiet, Miranda strolled from room to room. Talking to Cale had eased the knot of tension that had claimed the biggest share of her stomach since before the storm had hit that afternoon. For a few minutes, the passion in his kiss chased it completely away.

For some reason, the tension threatened to return. She slipped a Beethoven disc into the CD player. Listening to the beautiful strains of music, she changed into her nightgown and prepared for bed. It was late, and she had a lot to do in the morning. When she felt relaxed enough to sleep, she turned off the music, checked the doors, turned out all the lights except the one she kept on in the hall, and slipped between sheets scented of lavender.

Lying in the drowsy warmth between sleep and wakefulness, she recalled the stories Cale had told her. She was in the middle of a smile when she drifted asleep.

Thunder rumbled in the distance. Someone whispered her name.

No. Please. No.

Miranda's head thrashed, the covers tangling around her legs. Beneath her closed eyelids, her eyes darted back and forth.

Fear. It had a sound, a touch, a scent. But it had no face.

She felt his hands. An instant later she saw them in a blinding flash of lightning. She ran. He reached for her, his hands snagging her clothes.

No. Please.

She tried to breathe but couldn't. Tried to scream, but the sound stuck in her thick throat. Hurry. She ran faster and faster. But not fast enough. He clawed at her with thòse horrible hands. She wrenched away, running blindly through the pouring rain. Mud muted her footsteps and his, but she knew he was there, closing in on her. His fingers gripped her shoulder. Again, she struggled free, but his hands dragged her back. They fell to the ground.

No. Noooo.

He touched her.

Finally, she screamed.

* * *

She awoke, bolted upright, chest heaving, mouth still open from her own wrenching scream. Heart pounding, Miranda flipped on the light.

Breathe.

She was in her own four-poster, safe. It was dark beyond the gauzy curtains and handmade dream-catcher in her window, but here in her room, soft lamplight reached into the corners, touching upon the white wicker chair, the cherry dresser, the antique chest covered with silver-framed photographs of the people she loved.

She was loved. And she was safe.

That's it, breathe.

There was no thunder or lightning. It wasn't even raining. It had only been a dream. The hands weren't real. They had been once, but no more.

It had been a dream. A nightmare.

Bringing her knees up close to her body, she wrapped her arms around them. She sat that way, coccooned beneath her blankets, until her heart rate had slowed and the fear had subsided.

The hour hand on her bedside clock reached steadily toward the three. She'd been in bed only a matter of hours, but she knew it would be a long time before she was able to go back to sleep.

She'd made peace with the night years ago. In those rare instances when this happened, she'd learned not to fight her insomnia. She'd learned to trust that the night would pass and morning would come.

Donning her robe, she tied the sash, swept her hair out from under the collar, and padded to the chest across the room. She peered at the photographs one by one. There was one of her parents, taken on their cruise last year, an old photo of her and Gwen and Alex, as well as the photograph they'd posed for as a gift for their parents last Christmas. There was a picture of Ruby, another of Moot Nelson, and still another of all seven of Lucille and Emory Sturgis's kids in younger days. She'd snapped the picture of Clyde Sturgis shortly after coming back to the mountain. Another time she would take a moment to appreciate the others. Tonight, the frame she reached for contained a photo taken before she'd left the mountain the first time.

Nora.

Miranda carried the picture out to the kitchen, where she filled the teakettle with water and started the stove. She'd never developed a taste for chamomile tea, and this wasn't an occasion for anything sweet or artificially flavored. When the kettle boiled, she reached for the Earl Grey.

Breathing in the steamy aroma, she carried her cup to the table and took her first sip, then settled down to finish the pot and gaze at the old picture. It was a black-and-white photo of the two of them, taken the first week Miranda had arrived in Dawsons Hollow along with several other members who'd joined the work-charity organization set up through the churches downstate. Do-gooders, the mountain folk called them.

Nora had been visiting her aunt that summer. She and Miranda became friends the moment they met. In the photo, their arms were around each other, their heads bent close together. Miranda looked young, robust, the epitome of a girl on the brink of womanhood, a girl who intended to save the world. Nora was a few years older and pale. She'd come to the mountain, hopefully to heal following a grave surgery. There were dark circles beneath her eyes in the photograph and dark shadows within them.

A month later, Miranda's eyes had looked the same.

It was Nora who'd found Miranda, bruised, bleeding, terrified after the rape, Nora who held her, cried with her, helped her up, Nora who took her to Aunt Verdie. Both Nora and Verdie stayed with her while the doctor on staff in the ER examined her, and later, while the police shuffled from one foot to the other and asked their probing questions. Afterward, Verdie and Nora took her back to their cabin in the hills on Old Crooked Road. To this day, Miranda could remember how her legs had shaken as she'd gotten out of the car and wobbled into the tiny bathroom inside the cabin.

She'd climbed into the bathtub fully clothed, turned on the shower, and sat down, cross-legged. Water went everywhere. She'd failed to draw the shower curtain. She sat that way forever, the water pelting her face, her hair.

She'd taken a shower in the hospital after the doctor and nurses and police had left. She'd scrubbed every inch of her body, but it wasn't enough. When it became apparent that Miranda was going to scrub her skin raw, Nora climbed in with her, shoes, clothes, and all. Crooning unintelligible words of comfort, she'd washed Miranda's hair over and over and over, because he'd touched her hair. With those horrible, clawing hands. Finally, Nora wrapped her arms around Miranda and just held her, the water blessedly hot and loud. So loud, it almost drowned out the voice in Miranda's head.

"So pretty. Don't cry. I'm the best there is. You'll see. So pretty."

She'd taken hundreds of showers those next few months. It was a long time, more than a year later, when she discovered that she could take a quiet bath. The counselor she'd seen back at school the following year said it probably had something to do with the fact that it had been raining during the rape. There was a correlation between the cold rain pelting her face, the mud at her back, the filth in his whisper, and the hot, cleansing shower.

The first time she'd taken a bath, she'd felt empowered. Of course, Nora was gone by then. Miranda picked up the framed photograph. Gone, but not forgotten. Never forgotten. Forgetting Nora Cook would be like forgetting a part of herself.

Miranda drained the last of the tea in the pot into her cup. She felt better. Thinking about Nora always made her feel better, a little weepy perhaps, but better. She carried her tea with her to her tiny living room with the beautiful Aubusson rug, the overstuffed chair and sofa, and handmade tables, lamps, and knickknacks. One knickknack in particular caught her eye. She ran the tip of her finger over the crude lines of the wooden chicken. From there, she wandered to the window. Lifting the lacy curtain away, she peered out into the night. It wasn't raining. That was strange. Until a week ago, it had been a long time since she'd had the nightmare. That night, she'd blamed it on the storm and on the injured stranger sleeping in her spare room. She *had* been feeling edgy before the storm this afternoon. But the thunderstorm was long gone. Sometimes, a violent movie brought on the dream. The movie she'd seen with Cale earlier had been loud and predictable. There had been plenty of explosions and bullets flying, but nothing graphic or gory that would bring back the nightmare.

What else could have reminded her of that terrible clawing fear? It didn't make sense. A long time ago, she'd faced the fact that she had little control over a great deal of her life. Turning in a half circle, she found herself staring at the computer. Just because she didn't try to control her life didn't mean there was nothing she could do to bring a semblance of order to it. She returned the photograph to her bedroom and the teacup to the kitchen. Never mind that it was the middle of the night. The pot of tea she'd sipped was kicking in, giving her a good caffeine buzz.

She flipped on the computer and got down to the business of writing the newsletter for the fund-raiser that would bene-fit the clinic, and ultimately the quiet, good, impoverished people living in this remote town in the Appalachian Mountains.

"Y'all come back now."

"We will, Happy," Miranda called as Cale pulled away from the charming mountain cottage on Hickory Gap Road.

Once they were out of sight, Cale said, "I thought I'd seen everything."

"You've never met a man named Happy?" Miranda asked.

As a teacher, he'd come across students with nicknames far more unusual than Happy. "I was referring to Happy's thirty-two-year-old mule bearing the same name. This was the first time I've ever heard of a mule that old, let alone been formally introduced to one.''

"Happy's wife died years ago, and their only son left the mountain shortly thereafter. He never comes back. That mule is the closest thing to family that old man has. Every so often Angus reminisces about some of the antics he and Happy pulled growing up up here. According to one story, Happy . . .''

The air streaming through the open windows smelled of early summer, still warm from the sun, still fresh from yesterday's rain. They were halfway down the mountain when Miranda finished telling Cale about Happy's past. Cale was doing the driving. Tonight, Miranda was doing the talking.

He'd driven down to Clayton first thing that morning on the off chance that he might find information regarding Ellie's past or Danny's birth in the county records. Other than an exact replica of the birth certificate he kept in the safe back in their house in Columbus, Cale found nothing. The trip wasn't a total waste. While he was there, he'd stopped by a corner drugstore and made an important purchase.

Tonight, Miranda had introduced him to several more people who'd lived here all their lives. He'd met a blind man named Tinker and his wife, Flora, and his two spinster sisters, Maxine and Madeline, who lived next door. Tinker had thought the name Stanoway had a familiar ring but couldn't place where he'd heard it. It was a start, but a damned small one.

Miranda had checked on Lavender Sprague on their way. Her two little boys were fighting, the baby was crying, frettin', Lavender called it, the three-year-old was cranky, and Lavender's young husband wasn't around. It was no wonder she looked tired. Cale wondered why Miranda did.

When he'd mentioned it, she'd said she'd been awakened in the night, and as long as she was up had typed up a newsletter and a report. He'd wanted to probe deeper, but she'd changed the subject, sharing tidbits of history and interesting facets of these people's lives.

She wasn't normally this talkative. As far as he could tell, that was the only thing different about her tonight. She wore no earrings, no combs in her hair, no jewelry. Her dress was yellow, a color she wore often. This one was sleeveless and long, secured in the back in a series of crisscrossed ties. Cale spent a great deal of time wondering how a man went about undoing them.

"Your son is proving to be a great help," she said in yet another foray into unrelated topics. She must have noticed his severe expression, because she grasped the long strands of her hair that were tangling in the breeze and said, "Lavender was right."

Cale took his eyes off the road long enough to ask, "About what?"

"She said you look like you've just taken a bite of a rotten pickle."

He shook his head. All right, maybe he was mistaken and was imagining the weariness around Miranda's mouth and the vulnerability in her eyes.

"He weeded and hoed a good share of my garden yesterday."

"Who?" Cale asked.

She shot him an arched look. "Daniel. Isn't that who we were talking about?"

Him and a few dozen others, Cale thought.

"Since it was too wet for gardening today, he ran copies and errands. He even found and fixed the glitch in my computer system. He knows a lot about computers."

Cale didn't mind talking about Danny. In fact, normally, his son was his favorite topic of conversation. But it wasn't like Miranda to talk nonstop. He pulled into her driveway and cut the engine. "Am I making you nervous, Miranda?"

"What? No, not at all." A trace of apology in her voice, she said, "Some people get quiet when they're tired. I get wound up. Have I been boring you to tears?"

"If you're tired, maybe I should go home."

"Is that what you want?"

"What do you want?"

She chewed her bottom lip, as if considering the question. "I was hoping you would come in."

Cale's reach for her hand was automatic. Smoothing his thumb along the inside of her wrist, he brought her hand to his mouth and kissed the skin he'd just touched.

Slightly breathless, she said, "Was that a yes?"

He slid his hand into her hair, drawing her closer. "Just so there's no confusion, this is a yes."

And he kissed her. He'd done it before, and yet every time felt like the first time. When the kiss ended, their brains were thick but not with confusion.

It took her a minute to locate her key and open her front door. Inside, she leaned down to turn on a lamp and said, "Would you like something to drink?"

"If you're having something."

"And if I'm not?"

God almighty, he'd never known another woman quite like her. "Then I'd rather have more of this."

He met her in the center of the room. His hands went to her shoulders, his mouth to hers.

Miranda wrapped her arms around Cale's waist and held on. His kiss was a delicious sensation. If it had been any other time, any other man, she would have held back. But this was Cale. Not her Cale. She wasn't that naive. The fact that he wasn't hers, not in the real sense of the word, not in his heart, didn't matter. She'd lost a part of herself when she'd been eighteen. His loss had been more recent but no less severe. She didn't want to deal with yesterday, with doubts and regrets and pain, nor with tomorrow, with worries and logic, sadness and more pain. For this one night, this one moment, there was only him and her, a kiss deepening, a touch leading to another, a sigh leading to total abandon.

She heard a sound outside the circle of Cale's arms. It took a moment to identify it as the ringing of her telephone. By the third ring, it penetrated Cale's cloud of passion too.

He dragged his mouth away from hers. "Do you have to answer that?"

"It could be a patient."

She stepped out of his arms and hurried to the desk in the little alcove in her dining room. "Sinclair residence." Her eyes widened, her gaze going automatically to Cale. "Yes. He's here. One moment, please."

Cale was watching her. "It's for you. Your friend Sam Kennedy."

Thoughts fragmented, Cale took a step in Miranda's direction. "I gave Sam your number in case of an emergency. I hope you don't mind."

"Of course not. Then this must be important."

When Cale still failed to move, she gestured with her hands. He came to his senses. Grabbing the phone with one hand, he slid the other hand into his pocket, his fingers coming into contact with a small square package. He sighed. "Yeah, Sam, I'm here."

He concentrated on Sam's deep voice. He had to listen intently, because he was having a hard time thinking clearly. It was a common phenomenon occurring when all the blood left a man's brain and gathered in a place directly south of there.

"No. I mean yes, of course." He made a series of humming sounds. "Delvecchio really said that?"

Cale continued to listen, his temper flaring. Sam gave him the general rundown of the situation that was arising back home. Cale asked a question or two to clarify things, but for the most part, he listened.

He could see the back of Miranda's head. She'd curled up on one end of her sofa, her back to him. He wondered where the woman got her patience, her calm acceptance.

When Sam was finished, Cale said, "What I wouldn't give for five minutes alone in a dark alley with that little weasel."

"You and me both. What are you going to do about him?"

"I don't know yet."

Sam asked how Danny was, and if they'd made any progress finding the answers the boy was seeking. And Cale answered honestly. Just before hanging up, he said, "Thanks, Sam. One of these days, I'm going to be able to stop telling you that."

He stood perfectly still, lost in thought, after the connection had been broken. He surfaced slowly, then returned to the living room, talking as he went.

"Apparently, Danny's counselor is sticking his nose where it doesn't belong. The man has the compassion of a piranha."

Silence.

"Miranda?"

Skirting the sofa, he discovered the reason for her silence. Her feet were tucked underneath her dress, her head tipped slightly, resting on a pillow, her eyes closed. Miranda Sinclair was fast asleep.

He lowered himself to the cushion next to her and glanced at his watch. It was only nine-thirty; he'd been on the phone for only ten minutes.

He spoke her name softly. She moaned, looking fragile, her eyes moving beneath her lids. "Miranda?" he said again.

She sprang forward so suddenly, he jerked backward.

Eyes instantly wide, her fear was so real, Cale felt it, her dread so profound, it suffocated him as well as her. She dragged in great gulps of air. "I fell asleep."

"Yes."

Silence.

"You were having a nightmare." He was beginning to understand why she'd looked so weary today.

"No. I was about to have the nightmare."

"How long has this been going on?"

"Since the rape."

That wasn't what he'd meant. "Did you have a nightmare last night too?"

She nodded.

"Why didn't you tell me?"

She glanced at him then quickly away. "I was afraid you'd think it was because of"—her voice lowered in volume—"us."

He jumped to his feet. "Damn right I think that."

"Then you're wrong."

Cale wasn't accustomed to being told he was wrong. "Do you relive the rape? In your nightmares?"

"Not the actual rape." She'd spoken quietly, but that wasn't what drew him closer. "I relive the fear. For a long time, it was as inescapable as he had been. During those first months following the rape, I had a nightmare every time I closed my eyes. The hot spray of the shower was the only thing that helped. I thought I was going crazy. I was sure of it. Nora's Aunt Verdie saved me."

"How?" Cale hadn't realized he'd moved closer until he was looking deep into her eyes.

"One day, she handed me a hoe, gave me seeds to plant, weeds to pull. Said if I was going to take six showers a day, I might as well have some dirt to scrub off. Gradually, the garden became more enticing than the shower. I don't understand what's driving me to have nightmares all of a sudden, Cale. But it isn't you."

"How do you know?"

"Because I'm not afraid of you."

"But—"

"You're going to have to trust me on this. If it's proof you want—"

"Yes?"

Miranda had to think fast, or he was going to leave. She couldn't explain it, but she didn't want him to do that. She didn't want to deal with painful memories or difficult explanations. Cale was a seeing-is-believing sort of man.

"We could conduct a little experiment."

"An experiment?"

She took the fact that she had his undivided attention as a good sign. "You could kiss me again."

Emotion welled up inside her at the expression on his face. "I don't see how that could help."

"I don't see how it could hurt."

He took her face in his hands and kissed her deeply, reverently. Almost instantly, the reverence changed, turning to passion and need. "Now do you believe me?" she asked when the kiss ended.

"I'm beginning to."

"Then it seems we should continue with the experiment."

Hand in hand, they made their way to her bedroom. Cale had slept in the room at the end of the hall the night he crashed on the mountain, but this was the first time he'd been in Miranda's room. She turned on a lamp, opened a window, and he had a hazy impression of lacy curtains and expensive, feminine furnishings. The bed was a four-poster, the dresser probably made from cherry. Dozens of framed photographs sat atop an antique trunk. He was more interested in the living, breathing woman a few feet away.

"What are you thinking?" she asked.

"I've been wondering how I was going to loosen the sash crisscrossing down your back."

Holding his gaze, she reached behind her and slowly, deftly, unlaced the tie. A heartbeat later, the yellow fabric swished to the floor, and Cale had his first glimpse of pale skin covered only by thin strips of satin and lace.

He toed out of his shoes, tugged his shirt out of the waistband of his jeans. He undid his belt, unhooked the top closure of his jeans. Her bra came off easily, her breasts soft and lush in his hands. Wrapping his arms around her, he lowered them both to her bed. He stretched out beside her, legs tangling, hands seeking, lips joining.

A breeze stirred the lacy curtain, scenting the air with honeysuckle, raising goose bumps on her arms. She was soft where he was hard, cool where he was warm, beautiful everywhere. He wanted to roll her underneath him and take her as men have taken women since the dawning of time. He wanted to stake his claim, his dominance in the most primal, elemental of ways. But another man had taken her that way once, brutally, heartlessly. Rape was a vulgar act of violence. Cale couldn't bear to remind her of any of that.

With his need building to the brink of no return, he rolled to his back, bringing her with him so that she lay on top of him, her breasts pressed to his chest, her legs straddling his.

She opened her eyes, her gaze so soulful, he couldn't breathe. Taking her face in his hands, he held on to his desire with everything he had. He kissed her hard and deep, and in a voice laden with desire, he whispered, "Miranda? Why don't you take it from here?"

CHAPTER
FOURTEEN

"You want me to take it from here?" Surely, Miranda's expression mirrored her surprise.

Cale's face was all sharp angles and hard planes, his jaw clenched as if in pain. "I think it would be best this time, don't you?"

This time? Something softened around her heart. The man of action was being noble. She considered telling him it wasn't necessary. Just because she hadn't made love in a long time didn't mean she was afraid. Quite the contrary. She wiggled her hips the tiniest bit, in case there was any doubt.

His face tensed even more.

She wasn't afraid of sex. She had been once. After the rape, she'd been afraid of everything. Strangely, she'd been more afraid of the dark, even then. She'd never told either of her boyfriends in college why she'd wanted the light on. She'd been nervous about sex all those years ago, but the real fear had been of violence and force. The first time she'd thought she would be terrified, that she would panic. She had done neither. It hadn't been particularly painful or enjoyable. It had simply been. The second time had been easier.

She hadn't been promiscuous. In fact, she'd discovered the complexities of sex, first with a boy she'd trusted, and later with a boy she'd thought she loved.

Caleb Wilder was no boy. She trusted him more than she'd ever trusted anyone in her entire life. Perhaps the reason she wasn't afraid of having sex with him was that with Cale she felt that she was making love. "How many times do you think we'll . . ."

His eyes were still closed, his teeth still clenched. "Tonight? You want an exact amount or a ballpark figure?"

She felt a smile coming on. "Take your pick."

"I was thinking somewhere in the range of more than once and less than five. Any more might kill me. I am only human, after all."

"For a noble man, you have big—"

He quirked one eyebrow. And she smiled. "Allow me to rephrase that. For a noble man, you have extremely high expectations."

She shifted away from him slightly, then slowly glided to her side. Reaching between their bodies, she covered the front of his jeans with her hand. Oh, my. She'd been right the first time. "We wouldn't want this to kill you, now, would we?"

He sucked in a ragged breath. "Miranda?"

"Yes, Cale?"

"It's going to kill me if you don't do that again."

"We can't have that." She touched him, stroking him through the heavy fabric until he mumbled that now she was killing him with kindness. Still, he let her have her way. Not that it didn't cost him. His fingers were clasped into fists at his sides.

"Relax," she whispered.

His stomach muscles contracted as she reached across his abdomen. Taking his left hand in hers, she brought it to her mouth and kissed each white knuckle. He relaxed his hand, opened his eyes, and traced the shape of her mouth with the tip of one finger.

She nipped it with her teeth, then slowly drew it farther

into her mouth, her gaze on his all the while. "Just so there's no confusion," she whispered.

Miranda smoothed a hand down Cale's chest, his abdomen, pausing at the opening of his jeans. One of them was wearing too many clothes. "Cale? If y'all are going to get anywhere near that ballpark figure you named, perhaps we should both take it from here."

"Are you telling me to put my money where my mouth is?"

She closed her eyes and sighed. Oh, no, she had another place in mind for his mouth. As if reading her mind, he whisked her panties away and removed his remaining clothes. He stretched out on his side next to her and touched her as she touched him; kissed her as she kissed him; pleasured her, learning her secrets as she learned his.

The bedsprings creaked slightly as Cale shifted, bringing Miranda with him to its center. He didn't know why a man was attracted to a certain woman. He would leave the analogies and the reasons and scientific explanations to the poets and philosophers and scholars. Why didn't matter. It was as if these past months of despair, and these past days of anticipation, had led him to this point in time, to this place, to this woman.

She was a vision, a fantasy, only better, because she was real: her hands, her lips, her sighs and moans and cries. Cale wanted to go slowly. She would have nothing to do with any such thing, urging him on with whimpers that let him know her need was as strong as his own. By the time he saw to protection and made them one, all such thoughts had fled his mind. Already he could feel the tremors inside her. She gazed up at him, her eyes soulful and deep. Her Mona Lisa smile undid the last of his restraint.

It was the closest he'd come to heaven in a long, long time.

Miranda awoke slowly, the joy as much in the waking as it was in the sleeping. Unless she was having a nightmare, she always came awake in degrees. First she moved her legs, then she opened her eyes a fraction of an inch, finally she rolled over to her back. This morning, she did it more carefully than usual. She wouldn't have had to, because she was in bed alone.

Where was Cale?

She opened her eyes the rest of the way and sat up. It was early, not quite five-thirty. The sky was just starting to lighten, the horizon beyond the dream-catcher streaked with gray and pink and blue. She stretched, pausing at the pull of muscles she hadn't used in quite that manner in a long while. She took a deep breath, inhaling the scent of strong coffee all the way to the bottom of her lungs. Not quite sure what to expect, she slipped out of bed and donned her robe. In the bathroom, she ran a warm cloth over her face and a toothbrush across her teeth and a comb through her tangled hair.

She checked the kitchen first. And then the living room. Catching her first glimpse of Cale through her living room window, she wrapped a hand-woven throw around her shoulders, poured a cup of coffee, and padded barefoot out to her little front porch.

The birds, always noisiest this time of the morning, covered the creak of the screen door. For a few moments she watched Cale, undetected. His white T-shirt was easy to see in the shadows in her garden. He strolled away from her, following a curving path that connected her herb garden to the area where her flowers grew in glorious profusion.

He moved with an easy grace, a kind of loose-jointed swagger that could have earned him a lot of money on a runway somewhere if he ever needed the work. As handsome as he was, she doubted he would appreciate the tip. Perhaps handsome was too tame a word. The new furniture in her father's study down in Atlanta was handsome. Her brother was handsome. Cale was so much more.

He seemed to accept her as she was—flaws, eccentricities, strengths, and weaknesses. Not everyone did. Much of her formative years had been by the book. She'd attended private

schools, studied dance and art, taken violin and piano lessons, attended the opera, shopped abroad. In many ways, it
had given her a deep appreciation for talent and the finer
things in life. Even then, much of it had bored her. She'd
once overheard her mother explaining to one of her teachers
that her elder daughter just wasn't content painting between
the lines. That was one of the things Miranda liked about
Dawsons Hollow. The boundaries between what she did and
who she was were blurred.

She and Cale had talked long into the night. About life,
her family and his, the problem his friend had called about.
Neither of them mentioned the future. Miranda knew better
than to ask for promises. She wasn't ready to break the
tenuous connection that had formed between them. For now
at least, she wanted to strengthen that connection. She knew
how to live for the day, for the moment. And for this moment,
she wanted to feel Cale's arms around her again. Back in
college, sex had become a pleasurable experience. And yet
it had been relatively easy to live without it all these years.
It wasn't that she hadn't known what she was missing.
Perhaps what had been missing was this particular man.

She took a long sip of steaming coffee at the top of the
steps, and another at the bottom. Noticing a movement, she
turned, then paused as she saw Cale on the garden path.
Slowly, they both smiled. "How long have you been
awake?" she asked.

Cale eyed her coffee. "Long enough to finish a cup of
that."

Actually, he'd first wandered outside when the sky had
still been gray. A mist had hung over the tops of the trees,
shrouding the first rays of sunlight that crept discreetly over
the mountain. As one second had followed another, the night
weakened, and the sun gained strength, warming the mist
until it thinned to transparency and magically disappeared.
Columbus didn't have dawns like this. Here, the sun scaled
the mountain peaks in a single bound, its rays bursting
through the atmosphere in lines perfectly straight and uni-
form until they touched the earth. There, they bent, flickering

and softening, turning a single drop of dew into something more beautiful than the most precious diamonds in the world. Those same glimmering rays of sunlight cast lacy shadows beneath the spiderwebs between plants and dappled the ground below with intricate patterns.

He wasn't normally a morning person. He'd used the time alone to think. He'd strolled along the curving path, and for a moment, when he'd inhaled the scent of lavender growing several feet away, he'd been transported back in time to a few summers ago, when Ellie had still grown it in their garden. Every year she'd planted a few herbs and a few flowers, but he'd never spent time in a garden such as this one.

"That's vinca," Miranda said, pointing to a low-growing lush bed of flowering plants near his feet.

"I didn't know you grew so many flowers."

"When I first set up practice in Dawsons Hollow, the kids called me the butterfly lady. Gradually, they figured out that I didn't draw the butterflies. My flowers did."

Her voice held the soft Southern drawl he liked so much.

"Of course," she said, "most of them are grown now with kids of their own."

He wondered why she didn't have kids. That was hardly a question a man asked a woman so soon after he'd spent the better part of the night making love to her, especially when the man had a life, a job, and responsibilities elsewhere. In the dawning light of a new day, he wondered where that left them.

"Your garden is amazing, Miranda." What he meant was, she was. Even in his younger days, Cale hadn't gone for one-night stands. Consequently, he'd never gotten adept at handling the dreaded morning after. She smiled at him as if she knew it, everything about her as pretty as a summer day.

Taking another sip of coffee, she said, "The medicinal plants are for my patients. The flowers are for me. Now who's making who nervous? Or should I say whom?"

He did a double take. She only grinned.

"I don't want to mar your reputation."

"I appreciate that, Caleb." She peered at the eastern sky. "It's not even six o'clock. There's still time."

"Time?"

She sauntered closer, the early morning breeze pressing her thin robe to the contours of her body not covered by the blanket she used as a shawl. "I believe we're one shy of the finale."

It took him a moment to comprehend her meaning, but only one. His body heated, along with his thoughts.

"Shy, Miranda? I believe you're going to have to come up with another word."

He held out his hand, and she took it. He'd expected her to lead the way toward her house. Instead, she led him to a secluded little area where flowers grew lush, and tall fronds and thick leaves and trailing vines blocked the view from the gate and the road. It was like a secret garden, so private, he hadn't known it was there.

"See that wild rambler?" Miranda pointed to a prickly rose vine climbing up the side of her potting shed. "When I first bought this place, I tried to dig it out. It grew back. One year, I thought I'd killed it, but sure enough, come spring, there it was, bigger and stronger than ever. Finally, I let it have its way. It grows wild, defying its boundaries, resistant to rust and insects and a vast array of diseases that plague its hybrid cousins."

"Strong and healthy and free," Cale said. "And beautiful. Like you. Did you bring me to this secluded corner to show me your roses and your potting shed, Miranda?"

"I think we both know what I have in mind, Cale."

He was right. She didn't possess a grain of shyness, at least not around him.

Whisking the woven throw from around her shoulders, she spread it on the ground over the bed of blooming vinca. Together, they sank to their knees, and then to their sides. They murmured kisses and groaned softly, right there in her garden, the rambling rose nearby, the scent of a hundred flowers wafting on the warm, muggy morning air.

Last night they made love beneath lamplight, and later, in the dark. This morning, they murmured and sighed in the glorious pale light of dawn. He undressed her and caressed her, then had to lie back and catch his breath when she did the same to him. She was no wallflower, no shrinking violet. She was as vibrant as the air they breathed, more beautiful than he'd imagined a woman could be.

They'd learned a lot about each other the previous night. Now they knew where to touch and kiss, and yet they still discovered new ways to pleasure each other. Birds twittered, completely uncaring what was happening on the earth below. Hands on either side of Miranda's face, Cale kissed her as if he could never get enough. And when the kiss ended, he joined them again and gave up all pretense of being able to think.

The garden was as alive as they were. It was an idyllic spot, a private interlude between one man and one woman. And it was the grandest grand finale, more like the Fourth of July and Thanksgiving all rolled into one.

"They know," Cale said.

Miranda licked the ice cream that was fast melting down the side of her waffle cone. "It certainly looks that way."

It was Thursday evening, a half hour before he was due to join Angus and Elmer at the Bootlegger for a friendly game of poker. Cale had been on his way to Pratt's Grocery Store, when he'd noticed Miranda closing her clinic for the day. He'd met her on the grassy slope out front and had invited her to have ice cream with him. It had been completely innocuous. Honestly, he hadn't so much as touched her within sight of all the busybodies in this town.

"I don't understand it," he said, his forgotten banana split melting in the evening sun. "I didn't see a living soul when I headed back to my cabin yesterday morning. I was just as careful today. And yet they all seem to know. Danny is just beginning to open up to me again. Although he isn't staying with me all the time, he comes by often. I don't know how he would react to the idea of another woman in my life. I'm just as worried about you. You have to live and work with these people. I didn't want to do anything to harm your reputation."

Miranda looked at him, her expression unreadable. "The people of Dawsons Hollow don't know anything for sure, Cale. They heard that you asked Angus to make a carving for me, and they've put two and two together. Not much happens in Dawsons Hollow. Speculating about us is more interesting than watching the air leak out of their tires."

"You really don't mind, do you?"

He followed the course of her gaze to the diner's only waitress, Priscilla Moore, who was watching from behind the checked curtain. Miranda waved at Buckie Gillespie, the filling station attendant on the corner, but she saved her smile for Cale. "Every once in a while I hear that somebody's been whispering about me behind my back. I've known doctors and nurses, and even a plumber once, who've told me to my face that I'm a fake and a quack. Compared to that, a little idle curiosity feels pretty tame." She pointed to the dish in front of him. "Are you going to eat that?"

Cale shifted on the bench and simply stared across the picnic table at Miranda. She had a tranquillity few people possessed. It was a rare gift. He felt honored to be in her presence. It wasn't honor and it sure as hell wasn't honorable to suddenly imagine her naked.

She really hadn't said anything lust-arousing. Perhaps sitting across the table from a beautiful woman who was doing nothing to try to disguise the open longing in her eyes was reason enough to cause a man to consider forfeiting a poker game for a more one-on-one activity. This particular woman had a dozen reasons, all of them good, for maintaining a careful distance from him. And yet she'd opened her arms to him these past few days, accepting him without question or judgment or drama.

"You're an amazing woman, Miranda."

He'd said it before, but if it were possible, he meant it

even more now. The people on this mountain respected her
and cared about her, and so did he.

"I wish I hadn't promised Angus that I'd join him for
that poker game."

"What are you doing after the game?"

A few ideas came to mind. "Would you like to hear it
word for word?"

"Actually, I think I'd like that very much. Hold that thought.
Right now there are a few things we both need to pick up at
Pratt's."

Nothing intimidated her. He liked that about her. He liked
a lot of things about her.

They tossed their ice cream into the trash can and sauntered across the street to the store. He could hear the noisy
freezer motor on the far wall, but otherwise, the store was
unusually quiet. Cale expected to find it deserted. Once his
eyes had adjusted to the dim interior, he was surprised to
discover several of the Pratts as well as a handful of shoppers
inside.

Miranda said hello to the younger two Pratt boys. When
he'd seen them before, they'd been all attitude, mostly bad,
from their tight blue jeans to their scraggly goatees. He'd
expected them to snicker, perhaps leer at Miranda. Strangely,
they seemed ill at ease. They nodded at Miranda, glanced at
each other, mumbled something to J.R., their oldest brother,
about getting back to work on LeRoy's truck, then hightailed
it out of there. Apparently, Miranda viewed it as normal
behavior, because she took a basket and started up the first
aisle as if nothing unusual had occurred.

Somebody she called Mrs. Arrowood struck up a conversation with her before she'd made it halfway down the first
aisle. It was a good thing no one seemed to expect Cale to
talk, because the smile Miranda cast him as he walked by
rendered him speechless.

He went about selecting the items he needed. Trying to
choose between regular potato chips and barbecue-flavored
ones, he happened to glance toward the front of the store.
Ruthie Pratt was standing behind her register, staring at

Miranda, her face more pinched than usual, the look in her eyes hard as stone.

Not everyone in Dawsons Hollow liked Miranda Sinclair.

Of its own volition, his gaze shot to the refrigerator case J. R. Pratt had been filling a few minutes earlier. J.R. was looking at Miranda too. If the expression on his mother's face had been difficult to decipher, the one on J.R.'s was impossible. It made Cale damned uneasy.

J.R. glanced at Cale just as the cantankerous freezer motor burst on. The other man started, then returned to his task, arranging milk cartons on the shelves. The next time he looked at Cale, his features were arranged in a careful mask.

By the time Miranda had managed to break away from Mrs. Arrowood, Cale had paid for his groceries and had headed outside.

Swatting halfheartedly at a mosquito buzzing his ear, he tried to remember what he'd been told about the Pratts. The little he'd seen and heard of Ruthie Pratt, he didn't like. She was lazy and bossy, not exactly mother-of-the-year material. Other than J.R., the oldest, the kids seemed to run wild. The boys favored black shirts and loud engines. They weren't the kind of people he'd want to meet in a dark alley. The youngest, and only girl in the bunch, spied on people, skipped school on a regular basis, and just happened to be Danny's only friend.

Great.

After giving the matter careful thought, Cale decided he wasn't worried, at least not about that. Daniel had a good head on his shoulders. Always had. Even when he'd hit rock bottom, the boy hadn't run away to join a gang or a cult. He'd run away to live alone in a remote cabin in the mountains in a quest for the truth. No matter what else happened, Danny was Cale's first priority.

A noisy old car rumbled by, the driver taking his half of the street out of the middle. Cale recognized Jed Hershey, the old coot who'd nearly run over him and Miranda last week.

"It looks as if your poker game is about to begin." He

hadn't heard Miranda join him outside, and yet the sound of her voice didn't startle him. When Jed had pulled into a parking space in front of the saloon, she said, "I think it's safe now, don't you?"

Cale glanced to the left but made no move to leave.

"For a man who's about to play cards and drink whiskey, you don't look very happy."

"I suppose that's less offensive than saying I look like I've just taken a bite of a rotten pickle."

"Lavender said it. I just passed it on." Her smile nudged him from the inside.

"What do you know about the Pratts?" he asked.

She shifted her grocery sack to her hip. "Ruthie owns the grocery store. She appears to have money. They live in that house right up there." She pointed to an imposing-looking structure high on the hill.

"What about Mr. Pratt?"

"Jonas was a bit of a legend up here, you know, high school quarterback, the boy voted most likely to, that sort of thing. I guess he was considered quite a catch."

"And he married Ruthie?"

If she noticed the dismay in his voice, she didn't comment. "People say Ruthie was pretty in her day, before her scowl became a permanent fixture on her face."

"What happened to him?"

"I don't remember much about him. Every once in a while, somebody will mention the time he went white-water rafting or mountain climbing. Apparently, he fell into a ravine and died shortly before Willow was born."

Tragedy, Cale thought. Sooner or later, it touched everyone's life. "Are you telling me the widow Pratt has a good reason to scowl?"

"Maybe, but she has no right to treat those kids the way she does. Every child conceived is a blessing, and she's been blessed seven times."

There was that number seven again. "Are you superstitious, Miranda?"

"I don't throw salt over my shoulder, if that's what you

mean. Chinese philosophers believe that a stone overturned in a babbling brook at the bottom of the world is eventually felt all the way around on the other side of the planet.''

"You're saying everything happens for a reason."

"I believe everything that happens is a response, either directly or indirectly, to something that happened a moment ago, a year ago, even hundreds and thousands of years ago."

It was nearing eight o'clock, that quiet time of the evening when the sun was less intense as it slowly dipped toward the west, as if uncaring that it was about to lose its glory for another day. It was no competition for the serenity on Miranda's face. Cale had a feeling the fine folks of Dawsons Hollow would be discussing the two of them over breakfast at the diner the following morning, which was another reason he needed to talk to Danny.

Elmer and Angus rose from their bench in front of the barbershop. After casting a look his way, they ambled, bow-legged, into the saloon. Reacting to the silent cue, Cale and Miranda strolled toward the Bootlegger. Only the children who were too busy playing kick the can down the street failed to stare. When Cale and Miranda reached the grassy knoll between the bar's front door and the street, he leaned closer. "If it's gossip they want, we might as well give them something to talk about."

He'd whispered the words, and then he whispered a kiss in the little hollow on her cheek. Miranda held perfectly still. There was something poignant and gentlemanly about the brush of a man's lips on a woman's cheek. Gentlemanly or not, it snuck up on a woman, tricking her, leaving her feeling weak in the knees, leaving her wanting more than a brush of lips, more than a whisper, more than one brief touch.

"Are you going to stop by later, Cale?"

"I'd like that, but I'm going to talk to Jed Hershey, and then I'm going to drive up to Danny's cabin and talk to him. I can't make any promises, Miranda."

Miranda wasn't asking for promises. Watching Cale stroll away and disappear inside the Bootlegger, she thought it

was a good thing. It was also a good thing more men didn't
know what a kiss on the cheek did to a woman's heart. A
gesture like that could lure a woman dangerously close to
falling in love.

It was ten-thirty when Cale pulled into the lane leading
to Danny's cabin on Hickory Gap Road. He found the front
steps by the light of the moon. After that, he had to rely on
his other senses.

"Danny?" He groped his way to the dilapidated front door.
"Yeah?"

Cale jumped and tried to see inside the dark cabin. "Do
you have a lantern or a candle?"

"The light seems to draw mosquitoes."

Cale took a careful step inside. "Stinking nuisances, aren't
they?"

Cale thought he heard Danny mumble something agree-
able. "What are you doing here?"

Of course, he could have been wrong. "There's something
I want you to hear from me. What do you say we sit on
your porch? If the mosquitoes discover us, at least they
won't be inside."

An animal chattered from the other side of the room.
Daniel spoke to the raccoon. The next thing Cale heard was
the rustle and clink of crushed ice Danny must have picked
up in town. Moments later, he joined Cale on the leaning
front porch. "Watch that top step. It's rotten."

Cale found himself face-to-face, nearly eye to eye with
Danny, who had two Pepsis in his right hand. Accepting the
aluminum can the boy held out to him, Cale sat on the rough
plank boards, his feet dangling over the side. Danny lowered
himself to the other side of the steps, then promptly popped
the top of his Pepsi can. Cale did the same. Both tipped the
cans back and took a long swig.

"Did you discover something?" Danny asked. "About
Mom?"

What? Oh. Cale shook his head. "I have to find another

place to begin, another way to search for information. I checked the county records, and I've asked several people if they remember a girl named Ellie Stanoway.''

''Nobody remembers?''

Cale shook his head. He'd brought up the subject during the poker game earlier. The old cronies had been more interested in what was happening between Cale and Miranda. After Cale's second vague response to his probing questions, Angus had slapped the deck of cards on the table and started dealing. There had really been very little time to talk after that. Those mountain men played cards as if their lives depended upon it. Five-card stud, jokers wild, jacks or better to open. Cale had spent most of the night making sure Jed anted up and Angus didn't deal from the bottom of the deck. He'd lost ten bucks, but it hadn't been a complete waste of time. Jed didn't remember anyone named Ellie, but when Cale had used her full name, a light of recognition had flickered far back in the old man's eyes.

Taking another swig of cola, Cale said, ''I'm going to pay Jed another visit tomorrow. If that doesn't pan out, I'm going back to Columbus.''

''You're leaving?''

''I'm coming back, and when I do, I'm going to bring more clothes and supplies, and the box of your mother's papers and mementos. Maybe we'll find clues in something she saved. I was hoping you'd come with me.''

Danny seemed to be considering it. In the end, he said, ''I have to stay here and feed the raccoon.''

Cale didn't want to leave Danny behind, completely on his own in the remote hills of northeastern Georgia. It was damned hard to corral a kid who didn't want to be corraled. How many times had Cale tried it back home? Short of locking him in his room and barring the windows, there was little Cale could do. That didn't mean he liked it. No matter how adult Danny felt, he was only a fourteen-year-old kid. Cale noticed the boy had accepted the groceries he'd been leaving on the cabin's slanting porch. And while he felt better about that, he still couldn't just drive off and leave the boy to his own defenses. If Danny refused to come with him, he'd think of some other way to be sure he was taken care of. But he let the subject drop for now.

"Do you still think about her?"

The question came out of the blue, and yet Cale knew precisely what Danny meant. "Every day."

"Do you ever dream about her?"

"I haven't lately." And then, because it just occurred to him, he added, "Do you dream about her, son?"

Danny's nod was barely discernible in the dark. Even so, Cale's gaze was drawn to his son's profile. Danny Wilder was growing up. He looked more like a man with every passing day. There was something vaguely familiar about the angle of his chin and the shape of his forehead. Cale had seen those features in someone else. But who?

More shaken than he cared to admit, Cale said, "What do you dream?"

"It's always almost the same. She's standing on a cloud with a deer. I think it's the one that died the same day she did. At first, the cloud is far away. As it moves closer, I see Mom's expression. Remember how she used to look when she was holding a three- or four-pound baby who shouldn't have survived but somehow did? That's the way she looks at me in my dream. Last night, she said something. I couldn't make out all of it, but she told me the truth was close at hand. That's why I thought you'd uncovered something. If you didn't come up here because you'd discovered something about my biological father, why are you here?"

The swig of Pepsi Cale took served two purposes. It garnered him a little time, and it helped wash down the lump that had jammed sideways in his throat. "It's not about your mom. It's something else."

"What?"

Cale had come to tell Danny about Miranda. Now he wasn't so sure it was a good idea. It had been a long time since Danny had confided in him, and Cale didn't want to do or say anything that would send them back to the way they'd been a week ago, a month ago, or a year ago. "Never mind. It'll keep."

"Now it's going to bug me if you don't tell me."

Cale's heart brimmed with feeling for his son. "I'm seeing someone."

"You mean Miranda."

So much for trying to ease into the delicate subject. "Yes."

Just like that, Danny's countenance changed. He didn't even try to disguise his derisive snort. "What do you want? My permission?"

Cale wanted the easy camaraderie back. He wanted his son to understand. He wanted Danny to know how much he loved him. Somehow, since Ellie had died, that had been even more difficult for Cale to put into words. Without her, they were like spokes without a hub.

Cale knew he couldn't rely on Ellie to smooth things out, to keep him and their son connected. No matter how difficult it was for him to put his innermost feelings into words, he had to if they were ever going to be a family again. "You and your mom were an established unit when I met you. It didn't take me long to fall in love with her." He cleared his throat. "You either. You're my son, Daniel. In here." He placed a fist over his heart. "I don't love a lot of people. You're one of the ones I do." Cale clamped his mouth shut, wishing he weren't doing this so badly. He'd started this, and by God he was going to continue. "No matter who planted the seed, to me you'll always be my son. Among other things, that means I'll always be honest with you. I've been spending time with Miranda. People up here like to gossip, and I wanted you to hear it from me."

They were both silent for a long time, the only sounds the buzz of mosquitoes, the chirrup of crickets, and the occasional slurp of soda guzzled straight from the can. Wiping his mouth on the back of his hand, Danny finally said, "What about Mom?"

What in the world could Cale say to that? He sighed. "I loved your mom. I always will. I don't know how I feel about Miranda. I guess that's not entirely true. I like her, and I respect her."

Danny crushed his empty can, then rose to his feet.

"Do you believe me?"

Danny shrugged. "Like you said. You don't lie."

Cale thought that was something, at least. He climbed to his feet. "Are you working for Miranda tomorrow?" he asked.

"I'm supposed to."

"You might as well bring the raccoon as far as my place again."

"I'll see." Without another word, Danny went back inside.

Cale strode to his pickup truck. He glanced over his shoulder just before pulling onto Hickory Gap Road. A match flickered inside the cabin, the light gaining strength as Danny touched it to the wick of a candle. It must have been feeding time for the raccoon.

In the flickering glow of candlelight, Cale once again got a glimpse of his son's profile. Ellie had been petite, her nose small, her face slightly round. Danny's profile was striking and strong, his forehead low, his cheeks and jaw lean. And vaguely familiar. Cale had seen a hundred people since coming to Dawsons Hollow. Was one of them the man Danny was looking for?

What would Danny do when they found him? Where would that leave Cale? It left a bad taste in his mouth, a bad feeling in the pit of his stomach.

Cale's hand was raised to knock when Miranda turned the lock and opened the door. Just like that, his apprehension gave way to something a lot more enjoyable.

Her hair was down, her feet were bare. The shimmery fabric of a light green pantsuit that swished with her every move covered everything in between. "How did it go?" she asked.

He stepped over the threshold. "Jed Hershey cheats."

She smiled. "I've heard that. And with Daniel?"

She closed the door, the movements causing the dream-catcher to swing back and forth. "I told him I'm seeing you."

"How was he?"

Cale shrugged. "He reacted about the way I expected."

"I'm sorry, Cale. I never intended to do anything to come between you and your son."

Feeling as if he'd been dragged through a knothole backward, Cale closed his eyes. "I'm sorry about a lot of things, but I'm not sorry I met you. What have you been doing tonight?"

So, Miranda thought, he didn't want to talk about his relationship with his son. "I've been catching up on my reading. It seems naturalists in India are making interesting discoveries concerning the occurrence of nightmares and their correlation to certain foods."

Cale took a step closer. "Are you saying there might be something more effective in warding them off than threads woven together and tied with knots?"

Tilting her head slightly, she looked him up and down. "I've already discovered something more effective than dream-catchers."

His next step brought him within inches of her. "What have you discovered?"

She went up on tiptoe and whispered, "I've discovered you."

They shared a smile, and a kiss that turned into another, and a touch that turned into a caress, and a sigh that blended with the wind in the trees.

They walked together to her bedroom. Suddenly, he reached for her and kissed her, her back pressed against the wall, his body pressed to the entire length of hers. Their clothes came off in a frenzy, as if she shared his burning need to be closer. Skin to skin, chest to breast, man to woman. It still wasn't close enough.

Miranda had thought she'd discovered the intricacies of sex in college. She thought she'd discovered the complexities of it last night. Tonight, she discovered a few things about herself. For instance, she had a voracious yearning for Cale's kisses. And she reveled in touching him and being touched in return. And there was one more thing she discovered she loved. She loved looking into his eyes as he made love to her, loved the emotion and rapture on his face.

"Cale?" she whispered on a shudder that matched the one taking place deep inside her. "Open your eyes."

He did, and he gazed deep into hers.

"What do you see?"

"I see an incredible woman." He began to move. "I see you, Miranda."

She smiled and discovered that the time for talking had come to an end. She discovered him two more times that night. Lying in her bed much later, blissfully sated, Cale felt that while she'd been discovering him, he'd been *redis-*covering something infinitely precious. Life.

CHAPTER FIFTEEN

"You mad at anybody in particular?" Ruby asked Daniel. "Or do you just feel like sulkin'?"

Daniel was being paid to hoe Miranda's herb garden. There had been nothing in the job description about answering annoying questions. Jabbing the hoe into the soil four times, he mumbled, "What's it to you?" so far under his breath, it wasn't even a whisper.

"Miranda is the closest thing to a daughter I've ever had. That's what it is to me."

He lost his momentum, the blade of the hoe coming precariously close to a plant's stem. He'd thought Willow had been exaggerating when she'd said Ruby had supersonic hearing.

"Tell me, Daniel, are you the type who blames other people for his problems?"

Daniel knew a trick question when he heard one. And he knew better than to answer.

Ruby McCoy didn't seem to expect a reply. "All right," she said. "As long as I'm giving you food for thought, think about this. Who led who to these hills?"

Giving up all pretense of trying to work, Daniel gave

Ruby a quick glance. She was thin to the point of looking gaunt, one of those people who seemed downright homely at first glance. She wore faded flowered housedresses most of the time, and had probably earned every one of the wrinkles in her face. Her hair was threaded with gray, her eyes the darkest brown he'd ever seen. It so happened the expression deep inside them made it worth a person's while to take a second look.

It wasn't her fault he was in a lousy mood. The hoe suddenly felt as heavy as his guilty conscience. "He came here because of me."

Seemingly satisfied with his honesty, she folded her arms and gestured with one bony shoulder toward the house. "See that picture window there?"

Daniel glanced at the window and wished he hadn't. Cale was pacing up and down the sidewalk directly in front of the window, talking on Miranda's cordless phone. Miranda was digging up the roots of weird-looking plants nearby. They shared a smile every time he passed. Each time he saw it, an invisible fist squeezed a little tighter around Daniel's throat.

"Last summer a mourning dove flew into it so hard, we were sure he cracked his beak," Ruby declared. "At first, Miranda thought it was a fluke, but it happened again and again. She tried shooing him away. He just kept coming back to the window. Doves mate for life. Something must have happened to the little gal he'd set up roost with. All day long, he kept beating his beak against the glass. Miranda wanted to help, but what could she do? She could have opened the window, but what then? He would only have injured himself worse trying to get out."

Daniel went back to work. He figured Ruby would get to the moral of the story if he listened long enough.

"People wanna help when somebody they care about loses someone they love. About the only thing that's helpful is to remain steadfast, close but not too close, while we beat our heads against the picture window of life."

"What happened? To the mourning dove."

"Finally gave up and flew away. Coupla days later, we saw him sitting on a low branch in the sourwood tree, a pretty little dove at his side."

"Are you trying to tell me Cale, er, my dad's mourned long enough?"

"Willow told me you were smart. Your dad looked pretty beat up when I first saw him. And I don't mean from landing his airplane. I'm talkin' about on the inside. He's lookin' happier these days. If it'll make you feel better, I s'pose we could always hit him over the head with a shovel."

Daniel fought valiantly not to smile. And lost.

For some reason, his gaze was drawn to Cale and Miranda again. His dad punched a button on the phone, then said something to Miranda. Daniel was too far away to hear, but he was close enough to see the expression on Cale's face.

"He used to smile at my mom like that."

Ruby grasped the hoe's handle a few inches below Daniel's fingers. "This would work almost as good as a shovel."

Daniel didn't bother with a reply. Wrestling the handle out of her grasp, he said, "Miranda's paying me by the hour, and I'd just as soon give her her money's worth."

"You have good work ethics. Like your daddy. Before you go sputtering how he ain't your real daddy, let me just say that it don't matter. It ain't what we're born with that counts. It's what we do with what we're born with. The most important things are picked up from good example. Someday you'll see all the traits you've garnered from the man who's raised you."

Daniel glanced over his shoulder. Cale had been talking to Sam Kennedy earlier. He'd punched in another phone number. His eyes had narrowed, his lips thinned, his jaw set.

"I wonder who he's talking to now."

"Heard him tell Miranda he was gonna call somebody named Bud."

The only Bud Daniel knew was Bud Delvecchio. "Really? Why?"

"Seems the man's been makin' threats, carefully worded mind you, but threats just the same."

So that was why Cale had asked Daniel a hundred questions about his dealings with the counselor at school. "Who is Delvecchio threatening?"

"All I know is what I overheard, but from the sound of things, this Bud's got his tail in a knot over you. Seems he considers you his prodigy, his claim to fame. Cale's been on the phone for hours, talking to other parents whose kids go to your school. This Bud person's pursuing something called a doctorate. Now, I ain't sure what that is, but your running away and dropping out of school isn't the means to the end he was looking for."

"What's Cale, er, my dad, talking to him about?"

"Your daddy's smooth. He's setting up an appointment to meet with him. Somehow, I don't think Bud's expectin' the reaming Cale's got planned for him, do you?"

Daniel's chest felt heavy. Not with sadness, with pride.

"I wouldn't mind seeing that," Ruby said. "Would you? Whew. The sun's hot. What do you say we take a break? Yeah, that's what we'll do. I'll get us some lemonade, and we'll take a breather on the porch. It'll be easier to eavesdrop from there."

Daniel gaped at her.

"What?" she quipped. "You think the good Lord would have given us two ears if he didn't want us to use them?"

Ruby bustled away, disappearing inside the house. Daniel followed but more slowly. So far, he'd managed to keep from having much contact with Miranda. She smiled at him as he neared. It was all he could do not to look away.

"I'm finished with that area," he said, keeping his voice low so it didn't disturb Cale, who had moved a few paces away. "What do you want me to do next?"

Miranda leaned back on her haunches. Although he tried to hide it, she could see the belligerence in the set of Daniel's jaw. A few days ago she'd thought they were becoming friends. Now that Cale had told the boy about her, he viewed her as a usurper. Rather than pushing, she left him to his feelings.

She swiped the back of her hand across her brow. "I've gathered nearly enough echinacea." Snagging a metal pan from the ground nearby, she said, "Those dandelions next to the steps are perfect. I could use two or three handfuls of stems."

The only things that moved were his eyes, and then only to widen. Holding the pan in a manner that left him little choice but to take it, she said, "Break the stems off close to the ground if you can. And then pop off the flowers."

"What do you do with all this?"

"Echinacea is made from cone flowers. It's a natural antibiotic. Most people view dandelions as the most dreaded of weeds, but really, the stems contain potassium, calcium, and several vitamins. I prescribe it to patients who have gallbladder, spleen, urinary, and kidney ailments. It's also useful in treating acne, arthritis, asthma, and low blood pressure."

Daniel's fingers brushed hers as he took the pan. The gentleness in Miranda's fingertips sent a lump to his throat. It must have done the same to her, because she lowered her hand as if in slow motion.

"Daniel! Daniel! Oh, my God, you've gotta help me!"

Daniel and Miranda both jerked backward. Willow was racing toward them, black tears streaking her face. Miranda and Daniel met her on the path. Cale turned the phone off and followed just as Ruby rushed onto the porch, a tray of lemonade in her hands. "Girl, what is it?"

"A mother raccoon. She's caught in a trap. And her babies—" Her voice broke on a sob. "I ran all the way here, Daniel, because I knew you'd know what to do."

Daniel turned to Miranda but spoke to Willow. "I'm supposed to be working—"

"Go," Miranda answered with enough vehemence and just enough emotion to make disliking her damn difficult.

Willow had already spun away in the direction she'd just come from. Daniel set off on a run. Cale moved to follow, but Ruby laid her hand on his arm. "Give the kids a chance to handle this. If they need you, they know where to find you."

Willow looked back only once. Seeing Daniel, she slowed down a little, letting him catch up. She started to talk as soon as he was within hearing range. "Monsters. That's what some people are. How could anybody be so cruel?"

Twigs snapped, hitting them in the face as they rushed headlong through the thick underbrush. "I couldn't go to school today, I just couldn't. It was as if I knew there was someplace more important I was supposed to be. So I went for a walk."

When Daniel got upset, he got quiet. Willow was just the opposite. "I thought I'd swing up to Lavender's place and see what she was doing. Before I'd gone far, I heard a horrible sound, somewhere between a screech and a scream. At first, I thought it was human." She'd stopped crying, but her voice was still shaky as she said, "It was a mother raccoon."

Daniel estimated that they'd gone a little over a half mile. Although he couldn't see it, they weren't far from Cale's cabin. Willow was light on her feet, agile, moving effortlessly around trees and boulders and fallen logs. Daniel was fast, but he had to work to keep up.

"This way," she said, veering sharply to the right.

Daniel's skin prickled, goose bumps snaking up and down his arms and shoulders. He'd felt this way before. That day he'd stumbled upon the baby raccoon, so close to death it hadn't even been moving. Today, he knew what the feeling meant, and dreaded what he would find.

Willow stopped so abruptly, he ran into her back. Regaining his balance, he stepped around her. The sight awaiting him turned his stomach.

The mother raccoon looked up at him, utter desolation in her black eyes. Her front leg was stuck in a trap and was bleeding profusely. Six feet away, her two babies lay dead.

"Whoever did this," Willow whimpered, "must have known the mother came this way. That's why the trap was set here. It looks like he waited for the babies to come looking for their mama, then slaughtered them in plain sight of her. It must have just happened before I got here. That's why she was wailin'. She hasn't made a sound since.''

A sob lodged in Daniel's throat. The poor creature was nearly out of her mind in pain. The more she writhed, the deeper the trap cut into her leg.

Trying to portray a calm he didn't feel, he unbuttoned his shirt. "Willow, you can get around these hills faster than anyone I know. Run back to my dad's cabin. Bring the raccoon.''

"What are you going to do?''

His shirt was in his hands now. "I'm going to get that poor raccoon out of that trap.''

"She's out of her mind. She'll bite you and slice you with her claws.''

"I'll be all right. Go.''

Without another word, she hurried away to do as Daniel said. Alone now, Daniel knew a moment's panic. He wanted to call her back. But he couldn't. This was for him and him alone to do. "Easy,'' he said as much for his sake as for the poor creature's. Shirt in hand, he approached the animal. "What's happened to you stinks. I know. I didn't do it. Guess that doesn't matter much to you, does it?'' he crooned to her, creeping closer all the while. "I wish I could undo it. You and I both know I can't. I can help you get out of that trap. If you let me.''

She hissed at him. Sweat broke out on his brow. "Hell, I'm sweating bullets and shivering at the same time. I know, I know. You'd trade places with me in a heartbeat.''

The closer he came to the dead babies lying in their own blood, the more cold seeped into his chest. Circling around so he wouldn't have to step over them, he averted his gaze. Once again making eye contact with the mother, he continued to talk, his voice a low hum, the words unintelligible, the words themselves unimportant. At first, she hissed and lunged for him whenever he got within three feet of her.

Each time, the trap cut deeper into her leg, and she writhed in pain.

Rivers of sweat ran down Daniel's face and neck. His hands shook, but his voice remained steady and deep. He eased closer. Finally, she stopped writhing and hissing. Maybe she was too weak to fight anymore. Or maybe she'd stopped caring whether she lived or died.

Daniel heard twigs snapping and leaves rustling. "Willow," he said in the same voice he'd used with the raccoon. "That you?"

"Yeah, I've got him."

He didn't break eye contact with the injured raccoon. "I wish I were more of an outdoorsman," he said. "Until a couple of weeks ago, I was a city boy through and through. What I knew of the outdoors came from books. This trap doesn't look too complicated. If you'll let me, I'll pry it open. Once you're free, that leg can start healing. What do you say?"

She made one last feeble attempt to lunge at him, swiping at the back of his hand. Drops of blood rose to the surface of his skin, then slowly trickled toward his wrist.

"Willow, don't say anything. Just bring the orphaned raccoon over here. Put him down next to the others and then back up real, real slow."

Using his shirt as a shield between his skin and the sharp teeth on the trap, he eased the mechanism open. The poor creature whimpered in pain. When she was free, Daniel released the trap and backed away.

The mother licked her wound. Limping pitifully, she made her way to the babies. Willow came to stand beside Daniel, her shoulder touching his arm. They stood in silence, watching, waiting. When Daniel was little, other kids had warned him not to touch a baby bird that had fallen from its nest. They'd insisted the mother would smell the human scent and desert her chick. Years later, he'd learned that wasn't true. Birds had very poor senses of smell and wouldn't desert the baby as long as it wasn't too seriously injured. Raccoons were different. They had a keen sense of smell. Daniel didn't know what the mother would do.

She sniffed the still forms of her offspring. Frantic, desperate, she chattered something, then nudged them, each in turn, with her nose. The raccoon Daniel had been feeding for more than a week mimicked the mother's movements. Daniel held his breath.

They studied each other, the large, injured creature and the helpless small one. Perhaps they each picked up on the other's fur the scent of the boy who had helped them. Or perhaps it was just a matter of like accepting like. The grief-stricken mother nudged the orphan, and the orphan nuzzled the mother. She chattered something in raccoon talk. Daniel couldn't understand it of course, but to him it sounded mournful, sad. And yet, when she limped slowly away, the baby followed.

Willow sniffled quietly, but she didn't speak until the raccoons had disappeared into the woods. "Didn't I tell you something would present itself?"

Daniel turned his head to gape at her. Leave it to her to say "I told you so" at a time like this. And yet, if she'd said anything else, he doubted he could have held back the emotion that had welled up inside him.

Willow flitted away from him. Spying a fallen branch, she picked it up, testing it for strength. Next, she lowered herself to her knees and began to dig. Realizing her intent, Daniel joined her. Together, they dug a shallow grave and buried the baby raccoons in silence. When they were finished, Daniel rose to his feet and in a fit of temper yanked the trap from the stake holding it in the ground.

She sighed. There were plenty more traps in these hills. "You saved two lives today, Daniel. If I had your talent, I'd get off this mountain for sure."

Daniel thought about the phone call his dad had made to Mr. Delvecchio. He tried to imagine what it would be like to have nobody on his side. Measuring his words carefully, he said, "I didn't do this alone, Willow. If it hadn't been for you, I'd still be picking dandelions at Miranda's."

"But—"

"You're the one with the ability to see an opportunity as it unfolds. If you want it bad enough, you'll get off this mountain."

Willow blinked several times and swallowed the lump in her throat. Still, she came close to blubbering. No one had ever had so much faith in her.

"What?" he said. "No smart comeback?"

She was too choked up to speak. He grinned down at her playfully, and she swore something shifted in her chest. She'd never had a best friend before. Rather than saying something that might embarrass her, she turned and led the way to the path.

Cale stood at Miranda's screen door. His hands were in his pockets, his eyes trained on the gate Danny had forgotten to close when he'd left a little while ago. He could hear Miranda moving about in the kitchen. Dishes clattered, drawers squeaked, cupboard doors thudded.

Danny and Willow had returned from the woods hours before. After washing up, Danny had given a brief rundown of what had happened with the trapped raccoon. Willow had rolled her eyes, then launched into a descriptive rendition of the entire episode. She was an avid storyteller, and when all was said and done, Cale had a vivid mental picture of what had happened. He was proud of that boy. He'd told Danny so. Danny's Adam's apple had wobbled a little as he mumbled a quick thanks, but Cale knew he'd been pleased with the praise.

Cale was feeling pretty wobbly himself. It was as if he were slowly awakening from a nineteen-month-long nap. In many ways, Danny had been a boy when Ellie died. Now Danny was damn close to becoming a man. Cale had seen signs of it for weeks, but the way Danny had dealt with the trapped raccoon incident that afternoon had opened Cale's eyes.

"Is it growing, Cale?"

His brow furrowed as he glanced over his shoulder. "Pardon me?"

Miranda leaned down and carefully placed a tray on a low table. "The grass. You are watching it grow, aren't you?"

"I suppose you know you're very funny."

"Everyone has their gifts."

Whether she knew it or not, Miranda's gifts included far more than her sense of humor. She had poise and class and a unique brand of Southern-belle charm. Cale took a sip of iced tea. She was a damn good nurse practitioner, treating young and old, male and female, skeptics and believers, babies with colic, old men with rheumatism and angina. She hadn't, however, mastered making a decent glass of iced tea. That was okay. Too much perfection would get old.

"Did I tell you Danny has agreed to ride back to Columbus with me in the morning?"

"You might have mentioned it. Six or seven times."

Cale turned around, and damned if he didn't smile. Miranda didn't pull many punches. Most of the time, she spoke her mind in her own quiet way. She was ardent and passionate when she was awake and a blanket hog when she was asleep. He tried his damnedest to give as good as he got. If the shadows in her eyes he glimpsed from time to time were an accurate indication, he was afraid he didn't always succeed.

"Is something wrong?" she asked.

Cale shrugged. "I guess I could take a lesson from Willow when it comes to talking. That girl has a way with words."

"Did you see the way she looked at Daniel?" Miranda asked.

Cale pulled a face. "I wonder if I should talk to him about that."

"You haven't talked to him about sex?"

"Ellie was a nurse and a few years ago gave him the medical equivalent of who puts what where. I've been waiting to give him the man-to-man version."

"Daniel's fourteen?" She strolled past him with a stack of books, leaving behind her subtle flowery scent.

"He's almost fifteen." Cale took a deep breath and nearly sighed at the memory that scent evoked.

"What are you waiting for?"

The heat gathering in the very center of him lowered his voice an octave. "I guess I'm waiting for my father to tell me."

She hesitated but only for a moment. Returning the books to the proper shelves, she said, "I'd say you've done an admirable job figuring it out on your own."

Although he couldn't see her face from where he stood, he was pretty sure she was smiling. His quick trek across the room wasn't a conscious decision. Laying a gentle hand on her shoulder, he turned her around to face him.

She was grinning all right. He kissed her lips, smile and all. When he lifted his face from hers, she whispered, "You don't need to take speech lessons, Cale. Your actions speak loud and clear."

This was one "conversation" he would have liked to continue. But Danny had hiked up to his cabin for his clothes and would be returning to Cale's place for the night. "Do you have any idea how much I'd like to stay awhile, Miranda?"

"I think I do. But I also think you're looking forward to putting Daniel's counselor in his place."

He shrugged because she was right. It was something he should have done a long time ago. Day by day, he and Danny were bridging the gap that had cracked and widened between them since Ellie's death. They still had some work to do, but they were closer than they'd been in a long time. In a sense, they were both healing. For Cale, Miranda was largely responsible. She gave of herself freely—her humor, her passion, her advice. She asked for nothing in return. That was what was bothering him. He'd been on the verge of that realization for days. A no-strings sexual relationship was most men's fantasy. But what about Miranda? Was sex enough for her? Or did she secretly want more?

Sex. The pull of a man to a woman. A boy to a girl. He cringed. "I really need to talk to Danny. I'm just not sure where to begin."

"You could always tell him what my mother told my older brother. That if he kisses a girl, he'll go blind."

If it had been Miranda's intent to ease his tension, it worked. "I think I'd like your mother."

"I would reserve judgment if I were you. Don't get me wrong. I love her to pieces. My father insists my drive came straight from her. She's a whirlwind, and she likes things her way."

She took her keys off the peg on the wall, scooped her purse off her desk, and grasped in one hand three of the small jars she'd filled that very afternoon, talking all the while. "The saying 'If you want something done, ask a busy woman to do it' was most likely coined after my mother."

They strolled out to Miranda's porch. After locking her door, she led the way down the steps. Following close behind, Cale said, "The picture you paint of your family is interesting. A strong, silent father, an equally strong, loving, opinionated mother, a smart, outspoken, slightly conniving older brother, and a precocious younger sister. It's no wonder you turned out quiet and stubborn and strong. In a lot of ways, you're like the mountain. I can't picture you anyplace else."

They'd reached the edge of her driveway. "Thank you," she said. "I think."

He shrugged a little sheepishly. "There's a reason I'm normally a man of few words."

She unlocked the driver's side door. "It's extremely open-minded of your parents to support your decision to set up a practice here, after what happened to you all those years ago."

When she didn't comment one way or the other, he turned to look at her. She was staring straight ahead, one hand on the car door.

"They must have been scared to death for you at first."

She hiked her skirt up far enough to allow her to hoist herself onto the driver's seat. Still, she didn't offer him any insight.

"If I had a daughter who had suffered the horror you

suffered, I don't think I could let her out of my sight, let alone return alone to the scene of the crime.''

Cale was holding the door now; Miranda was staring straight ahead. ''They probably wouldn't have if they'd known.''

She'd spoken so quietly, Cale thought he'd heard wrong. ''How could they not know?''

She turned her head and looked directly into his eyes. ''I never told them.''

He knew he was staring, mouth gaping. He couldn't help it. Surely, she had a good reason for keeping such a secret from her family. What reason could possibly be good enough? It was none of his business. She'd made no demands on him, and he had no right to make any on her.

''Why, Miranda?''

CHAPTER SIXTEEN

Miranda strummed her fingers on the steering wheel. Why? Cale had asked. Why had she never told her parents about that horrible day?

She glanced at her garden, at her pretty white cottage with its inviting little porch, at her potting shed with its stained glass window and the wild rambling rose climbing to its roof. In many ways, this place was her haven, her sanctuary, separate from what had happened to her all those years ago. Other than the police and the doctor and nurses she'd seen in the emergency room, she'd told only three people from the mountain about the horror and trauma of her rape: Ruby, Verdie, and Nora. She hadn't talked about it to anyone other than Cale in a long time. Except for one day every June, she rarely thought about it anymore. Until recently, that is.

There were a lot of things Miranda didn't understand, a lot of whys she couldn't answer. She and Cale had shared so much in the short span of time he'd been here. She wasn't delusional. She knew he wouldn't stay forever. He'd sailed into her life, changed it in a positive way, and would leave again, perhaps soon. She dreaded that day, but she would handle it. If there was one thing facing tragedy taught people, it was that life went on. Often not smoothly, and rarely easily, but it went on just the same.

She didn't feel the need to explain herself to many people, and yet she wanted Cale to understand her reasons, the decisions that had brought her to this point in time and had helped shape her into the woman she was today. It would be an important conversation, too important to have while sitting in her Explorer with the sun beating mercilessly down.

"Cale? Why don't you get in? I'll give you a ride to your place. And I'll try to explain."

He did as she said, climbing into the passenger seat without saying a word. They drove in silence over the curving, climbing, sun-dappled road. She pulled into his driveway, and by unspoken agreement, they got out and began to walk.

Before they'd gone far, she began. "Both my parents come from old money, honestly earned. They believe in America, God, education, and hard work, not necessarily in that order. My brother and sister and I were raised with a silver spoon in our mouths, and a hand flattened firmly along our backs, propelling us forward."

Cale and Miranda had strolled to the backyard. Ducking underneath the low-hanging clothesline, she continued. "My mother graduated from Radcliffe, my father from Harvard. Mother uses her degree to aid her many charities. Daddy's name is world renowned in research medicine."

Cale had grown accustomed to the Southern cadence in Miranda's voice and was thoroughly enjoying its cultured lilt. But he didn't see how anything she'd told him so far could have prevented her from telling her parents the truth. The teacher in him raced ahead, formulating questions. The part of him who knew her waited for her to continue.

"I attended private schools, skipped an early grade, and graduated from high school with high honors a month before I turned seventeen. I'd always been interested in medicine, and it seemed natural that I would attend the same university my parents had attended. There was only one problem. I was rebellious of staunch old matrons in orthopedic shoes and old men with no necks and less vision telling me how to behave and what to think. So much of their medicine, commonly referred to as modern medicine, is paperwork and politics. I know it serves an important purpose, but it wasn't the kind of medicine I wanted to practice."

Her silence prompted Cale to ask, "How did that go over with your parents?"

She smiled, and he got a glimpse of the imp she'd once been. "Does the term *like a lead balloon* mean anything to you? Alex was studying pre-law at Yale, Gwen had set her sights on Brown University, and I wanted to join the Peace Corps. I figured two out of three wasn't bad, but they didn't see it that way. Finally, we compromised. I'd seen an advertisement for a church organization looking for volunteers who wanted to work in the Appalachian Mountains. By then I was eighteen and had four semesters of college behind me. It was fall, and Daddy had accepted a one-year position to head up a research team in England. He, Mother, and Gwen went abroad. Instead of returning to school, I came up here. I connected with this place at first sight. More than anything, I felt an immediate bond with Verdie Cook, an old granny-woman, and her great-niece, Nora."

Miranda grew silent. Her choice had proven powerful and dangerous, the consequences more far-reaching than an eighteen-year-old girl could have imagined. That one decision had changed the course of her life.

"Then, that man, that pervert spawned in the bowels of the earth, attacked you when your parents were in England?"

She nodded slowly. "Earlier that very week, my mother had called to tell me that my father's research team was on the cutting edge of a discovery that would contribute to the cure and treatment of a form of cancer. By the next morning, his name was in newspapers and medical journals all over the world. They were flying to France to speak with a research team there and would be returning to England the following week. They were in France the night I was attacked. All I wanted was to go back home, to go back to the way things used to be when I slept in my canopy bed and read books about crystal pentagrams and Tibetan prayer wheels and imagined which boy would be my first lover. But I couldn't go back to any of that. Calling my parents home wouldn't have changed what that man had done to me.''

Beneath Cale's closed eyelids, he could see a young girl, her golden-brown hair caked with mud, her face streaked with tears, her body with blood.

"The irony of it," Miranda said, "is that my mother and father would have come home if they'd known. My dad would have walked away from a discovery that has since aided in the treatment of a hundred thousand people."

"But you didn't confide in them."

Miranda shook her head. "In many ways, I was beyond thinking coherently, rationally, by then. I was beyond a lot of things. I was afraid of everything and everyone except Verdie and Nora. By the time I was stronger emotionally, my mother called again. She sounded different, her voice edged with only the barest veneer of control. My dad had suffered a heart attack. Mom assured me that everything was going to be all right, and I didn't need to come to England. Were we of the same mold, or what?''

"*Was* everything all right, Miranda?"

There was a question. Although she'd later learned that it had been touch-and-go for several days, her father had survived, and so had Miranda. But she hadn't been all right for a long, long time.

"Daddy took a leave from his research and recuperated on the other side of the ocean. On this side, I huddled in fear. I literally thought I was going crazy. By the time they moved home six months later, I was beginning to feel stronger. I'd made several important decisions. One of them was to transfer to the University of Georgia in Athens and work toward a master's degree in nursing so I could become a nurse practitioner."

She fell silent again. It was a different Miranda Sinclair who had walked onto the college campus after leaving the mountain. Some of the changes were minuscule, difficult to fully grasp. Others were so blatant, it was a wonder nobody had guessed the cause. But no one had.

Cale's sigh brought Miranda from her memories. She turned her head in order to look at him and was struck all over again by the rugged lines of his profile, his masculine chin and cheekbones, the five o'clock shadow.

"Are you and your parents close, Miranda?"

Of all the questions he might have asked, she hadn't expected that one. "In many ways we're extremely close. But there's an invisible line we haven't been able to cross."

"Are you ever going to tell them?"

Again, Miranda sighed. "I've been thinking about that a great deal these past several days. I've been wondering if perhaps that's the reason the nightmares have returned. It's going to hurt them."

"Believe me," Cale said. "As a parent, I would want to know."

Yes, Miranda thought, so would she. Just then, footsteps sounded on the front porch. A door opened and slammed shut. Daniel was back. She started toward the driveway. "Perhaps I'll see you when you return."

Cale called her name softly, halting her steps. "If all goes well, I'll be back by the weekend. And I will see you again, Miranda. Just so there's no confusion."

His declaration warmed her in ways she hadn't expected. She wished— She brought herself up short. She hadn't wished for things to be different in a long time. It wouldn't be wise to start now.

Miranda traced the pattern on the dream-catcher in her kitchen window. Around and around and around. She felt restless and had most of the day. She'd made her house calls after she'd left Cale's cabin, then paid Ruby a visit. Ruby had noticed her restlessness, and of course she'd mentioned it.

What could Miranda say? She needed to keep moving, that was all. She'd worked late, scrubbing her house until it shone, organizing her shelves containing her natural remedies. By the time she took a hot shower, it was after midnight, and she hoped she was calm enough to sleep. Crawling between her lavender-scented sheets, she fell into a dreamless sleep. Hours later, she began to thrash.

In the corner of her mind, she saw the silhouette of a man. Hands, caked with mud, reached for her. She ran. He caught her, groped her. No. Nooooo.

Slick with sweat and sick with fear, she bolted upright, her heart racing, her scream stuck in her throat. A sense of cold had settled over her, along with a sense of dread. Sickened, she tried to swallow, tried to concentrate on taking one deep breath and then another.

Wrapping her arms around her bent knees, she rocked back and forth. Beyond the dream-catcher in her window, the moon was high in the star-studded sky. She sighed. There wasn't a storm cloud in sight. No thunder or lightning or rain. Why had the nightmare returned? Why now, after all these years? Was it guilt because she hadn't told her parents? Or was it something else?

When she was calm enough, she got up, donned her robe, and padded out to her kitchen to brew a pot of tea.

Smells wafted from the cafeteria, mingling with the scent of floor polish and books and copy machine ink. Cale was early, just as he'd planned. Bud Delvecchio wasn't in his office. Good. That meant the two men would meet in the outer office, where Bud would have the disadvantage of having to look up at Cale, knowing he was staring at the bald spot on top of his shiny little head.

The outer door opened and Bud entered, only to stop short as his eyes met Cale's. "This way." He wasted no time leading the way to his stuffy office, where he immediately took his rightful place behind his cold metal desk. "I take it you've brought Daniel with you."

Cale nodded. "He's in the principal's office."

This wasn't the first time he'd had a meeting with Bud

Delvecchio, but this was the first time one had involved his son. The omission had been a grave injustice to Danny. In Cale's defense, he'd known that Bud Delvecchio looked down his nose at students who were troubled, poor, or struggling, but he'd thought straight-A students were safe. Now that Cale had spoken with several of those A students and their parents, he knew better. The man was condescending and self-serving. If he had any good traits, he hid them well.

"I don't like using scare tactics," Bud said, "but whatever works, eh?"

By scare tactics, he undoubtedly meant his intention to make note of Danny's absences as well as Bud's threat to turn Danny's name over to the authorities. Ohio law dictated that a student between the ages of six and seventeen must attend school unless special provisions for home schooling were made. A series of unexcused absences in Danny's permanent record could ultimately be a deciding factor in his acceptance into certain colleges. In an earlier century, Delvecchio would have been the kind of headmaster who believed in public humiliation. Since these were modern times, he was careful to do his humiliating in private. It was a shame too, because four of the five other counselors at this high school were excellent at what they did. The remaining one at least tried. Not good old Bud.

"I assume you have Daniel under control, and he won't be running away again." Bud's thick glasses magnified his eyes.

"He wasn't running away as much as he was running toward something," Cale explained. Technically, Danny had hitchhiked, which still made Cale shudder every time he thought about what could have happened.

Bud's upper lip thinned. "He's back now. Ready to buckle down and get to work and stop wasting precious time."

"Daniel took his mother's death very hard," Cale said.

Bud dismissed the excuse with a wave of his hand. "Coddling boys makes them effeminate."

Cale counted to ten. Bud had leaned back, his fingers

steepled beneath his chin, the epitome of the king staring malevolently at his lowly subject.

"As I was saying," Cale said. "Ellie's death was hard on him. It still is, but Daniel is extremely bright, and he's—"

"I know how bright he is, Cal. I understand you adopted him when he was very young."

The implication hit a nerve, just as Bud had intended. It was getting harder for Cale to ignore the purposeful mispronunciation of his name. "I'm sure you agree that Daniel is more than a brain with legs. He's extremely adept in the wilderness. He nursed a sick raccoon back to health and just four days ago released him into the wild in the care of an injured mother."

Bud picked up a pencil and began tapping it on the desk. "That would be very admirable if Danny were a normal boy."

Cale looked Bud in the eye and said, "But he is normal."

"You know what I mean."

Cale leaned back too, as if completely relaxed and at ease. "Why don't you spell it out for me, just in case all the exhaust fumes I've inhaled over the years in my auto mechanics class has affected my ability to comprehend."

"There was a time when you would have known what I meant. You used to be a real—" Bud stopped, as if he realized what he'd almost said.

"A real what, Bud? A real teacher?"

"You said it, not me."

Cale didn't lean forward, but if Bud could have seen beneath his desk, he would have known that Cale's leg muscles had bunched and his hands had squeezed into fists. "What constitutes a real teacher?"

Bud looked bored. "The languages, math and science. Now, those are real subjects."

"And history and social studies. Don't forget them."

Bud beamed. "My, yes, the core curriculum. I admire anyone who teaches those classes, especially under the conditions in today's public schools."

Cale leaned ahead slightly. "I admire anyone who teaches children."

Bud snorted so loudly, he failed to hear the door connecting his office with the principal's office open. "I'm sure the delinquents in your classes appreciate everything you show them."

Delinquents. *Delinquents.* DELINQUENTS! Cale forced a sense of calm he didn't feel. "I'll bet," he said, "you'd like it if only the smartest and brightest students, like Daniel, would be admitted into schools such as this one."

"Again, you said it, not me."

Bud Delvecchio had always been very good at getting others to say what he meant. "Danny's showing an interest in medicine," Cale said in an effort to lure Bud into a false sense of security as well as to buy time.

The little man snorted. "The boy has so much potential, and he's wasting all of it. That's why I was so disappointed when he failed to turn in the proper forms, which would have enabled him to participate in the young scholar competition taking place at Harvard this week. It would have looked very good for this school if he won."

It would have looked very good for Bud.

Cale decided to try a different tack. "I understand you're working on your doctorate."

The other man nodded. "If my doctoral dissertation gains the attention it deserves, one day soon I'll be pursuing a position as the administrator of an academy for the gifted."

"Then you could concentrate on only the brightest students."

Bud was nodding in earnest now. Cale almost had him.

"And you wouldn't have to waste your time with kids who aren't going to amount to anything anyway."

"I'll be able to leave the future grease monkeys, janitors, and French-fry makers to public schools and administrators who've bought into the whole everyone-is-created-equal baloney."

Bingo.

A sound across the room drew Bud's and Cale's gazes.

Daniel and the principal stepped into the open. Bud blanched. Recovering slightly, he dropped the pencil he'd been tapping on the desk and squared his shoulders. "Mr. Kennedy." And then, "Daniel. Your father and I were just talking about you. Welcome back. Why aren't you in class?"

Cale straightened in his chair. "Daniel and I are in town for only a few days."

"But . . . why . . . to what purpose?" Bud's eyes narrowed on the other side of his Coke-bottle glasses.

"It's called going to bat for my kid. *My* kid, Mr. Delvecchio. I'll tell you what we're going to do. Since it's in Daniel's best interest, and as his guidance counselor you have only his best interest at heart, we're going to open his file and make sure nothing has been entered in his permanent record that would hinder his chances of getting accepted into any college of his choice. Since you feel it's necessary to document his absences, we'll word it this way. Daniel Wilder and his father, a teacher certified by the state of Ohio, have taken a sabbatical to a fascinating place that had been special to Daniel's dearly departed mother. During their stay there, Daniel's education has been left in his father's capable hands."

Bud glanced up at Sam Kennedy, his expression clearly indicating that he would sooner have each of his fingers broken than write that. "Yes, yes, of course," he said quietly.

"Cale, Daniel," Sam said, his voice stern, his eyes boring into Bud Delvecchio. "Wait for me in my office. I'll have some papers for you to sign regarding this episode. We're going to do this by the book, just so there's no confusion."

Leave it to Sam to borrow Cale's favorite line.

Cale and Daniel left the counselor's office, closing the door behind them. "Something tells me," Daniel said, still in awe, "that Delvecchio's record is about to have a permanent stain."

Father and son shared a broad grin.

"We're bad," Daniel said.

"No," Cale countered. "We're good. We're a team." And then, on a more serious note, "I should have done that a long time ago. I never should have left so much up to your mother."

"She was good at it."

Yes, Cale thought, she was. When he'd first met Ellie, he'd been in awe of the bond she'd shared with her son and the devotion she had to the child. As the stepfather, and later the adoptive father, he'd tried to tread lightly, not overstepping his boundaries. Add to that his tendency to have difficulty voicing his innermost feelings, and, well, suffice it to say, he shouldn't have hidden behind that excuse. Ellie had known how much he loved Danny. And now, for the first time since they'd buried her, Cale felt as if he and Danny were a family—changed, yes, but strong and intact.

Sam Kennedy opened his door and stood in the doorway. His was a formidable presence. Shirt and tie notwithstanding, his stance, the breadth of his shoulders, and the glimmer in his eye still hinted of the streetwise juvenile offender he'd been a long time ago. Closing the door, he rotated a kink from the back of his neck. "If it was after hours, I'd uncork a bottle of Chianti and a can of root beer and propose a toast."

Cale took a seat on the edge of Sam's desk. "I wouldn't celebrate yet. Delvecchio's not going to take this sitting down. He's probably already put a call in to union headquarters. At the very least, he'll say you're biased, due to our longtime friendship."

Sam held up a list, a very long list, of students and their parents who were less than satisfied with Virgil "Bud" Delvecchio's counseling methods. "There's plenty here to nail him."

Cale had first met Sam twenty years earlier, when they'd attended the same high school. Even if Sam hadn't been three grades ahead, they wouldn't have hung with the same crowd. They met up again years later, both teachers at a school downstate. Back then Sam had taught science to kids who didn't know they liked it until after they'd spent a week in his class. The two men were the same height, but Sam outweighed Cale by a good twenty-five pounds. He had massive shoulders, tree trunks for legs, and a laugh, if you were lucky enough to hear it, that was contagious. Aside from a love of teaching and a passion for flying, they'd had little in common. Which just went to show that some of the strongest friendships were based on something that went deeper than background and upbringing.

With a nod at Daniel, Sam said, "Have you told him yet?"

Cale glanced from Sam to Danny. The boy looked nervous, Sam, a trifle knowing. "Have you told me what?" Cale asked.

Danny's Adam's apple bobbled slightly. "I've decided that I've kind of, that is, I'd sort of, I mean, I think it would be a good idea if I participated in that competition up at Harvard."

"I thought you'd had it with standardized tests and fill-in-the-box means of measuring intelligence."

Danny grimaced. "I have, but I don't want to pull weeds or hoe a row for the rest of my life."

Cale hid a smile.

"Not that it isn't honest work," Danny explained. "It's just that—"

"It's not for you," Cale finished for him. "The registration deadline is today. If I had my airplane, we could still make it, but I don't see . . ."

"There's always my plane."

Cale and Danny both turned to gape at the man who'd spoken. "Yours is only a two-seater, Sam. And you never let anyone fly your airplane but you."

Sam rubbed at another kink at the back of his neck. "I don't have any appointments this week that can't be rescheduled. And I meant it. I could really use a coupla days away from here. I'll take Danny to the competition at Harvard. It never hurts to rub elbows with the Ivy Leagues every now and then."

As usual, Cale's chest swelled with gratitude. Arrangements were made, a call was placed to Harvard, forms were faxed. Cale and Danny went home and threw the proper clothes into a suitcase. From there, they drove to the small airstrip where Sam kept his plane. Sam was already there, bag in the back, the engine checked. Danny waved to Cale just before the wheels lifted off the pavement and the plane took to the air. Cale watched until it disappeared from view.

On his own, he went back to the school, wandered down to his classroom, spoke to the substitute teacher and the students in fourth hour. From there, he picked up the cat Sam had been keeping for them at his place, then returned to the house he'd shared with Ellie and Danny for more than ten years. It smelled musty. Had he really been gone only two weeks? He mowed the lawn, paid bills, went to the bank, listened to the messages on his answering machine, turned on the TV, only to aim the remote and switch it off again. Without Danny there, he didn't know what to do with himself in his own house.

Danny called at six to say he'd arrived safely. Cale talked to his son for a few minutes, then he talked to Sam, who said that Danny wanted to show him the mountain. Therefore, the two of them would fly to Georgia sometime Friday evening. Cale gave Sam directions to the little airstrip closest to Dawsons Hollow, then broke the connection. With nothing better to do, he showered and changed, then went to a local steak house that doubled as a bar frequented by some of his fellow teachers.

Emily Johnson, the woman he'd taken to dinner a few months back, was there. She fed quarters into the jukebox and took a seat next to him. She wasn't pushy exactly, but she was forward enough to let him know she was interested and extremely willing. For some reason, Cale couldn't work up enough enthusiasm to return the sentiment. He nursed half a beer before it got warm. Leaving some money on the table, he left, alone.

He crawled into bed early, the pillow-top mattress curling under him like an old friend. In his mind, he could almost hear Ellie's voice telling him about the mountain where she'd spent summers with her great-aunt Vernice. He'd always known she'd loved it up in the Georgia hill country.

Why hadn't he insisted they go there so he could have seen it through her eyes? Instead, he'd followed their son there, and he'd seen it through Miranda's eyes.

Even though he still wished things could have been different, his heart didn't feel as heavy tonight. He would always miss Ellie, but he fell asleep thinking about mountain laurel and honeysuckle and a woman with amber-colored eyes and golden-brown hair.

He awoke refreshed, eager to be on his way. He got his breakfast at a drive-thru window. Back at his place, he gathered towels and sheets, a frying pan, and a stack of his and Danny's clothes to take back to the mountain with him. He retrieved an electric fan from the attic, along with two boxes containing Ellie's journals and mementos. Satisfied that he had everything, he placed Curly, Ellie's cat, in the cat carrier in the front and loaded everything else into the back of the '67 Ford.

The last time he set off for Dawsons Hollow, finding Danny had been the only thought in his head. Today, he had a woman on his mind.

CHAPTER
SEVENTEEN

Miranda placed a Beethoven disc in the CD player, careful to keep her eyes trained on the road. As the perfect notes of her favorite symphony, the sixth, wafted from the speakers, she merged into the heavy traffic streaming toward Atlanta on Interstate 85. She was going home. Although she'd decided only a few short hours before that today was the day she would confide in her parents about that awful day, the conversation itself had been fifteen years in the making. She still didn't know what she was going to say.

She hadn't heard from Cale since Sunday. She hadn't really expected to. But she missed him. She'd taken a risk when she'd become emotionally involved with a man who'd made no promises or commitments. She had as much to do to occupy her time and her mind as she had a month ago. And yet it had been years since she'd felt so listless, even longer since she'd felt truly lonely. The reason had brought her up short in the wee hours of the morning. She hadn't had the nightmare in three days; therefore, it wasn't fear that had kept her awake the remainder of the night. It was the realization that she was falling in love with a man she had no business falling in love with. Facing her feelings hadn't changed the facts. It had, however, forced her to take a close look at her past, her present, and her future. In the process, she'd examined her actions, her motivations, her accomplishments, and the loose ends she'd left to dangle in the wind.

She'd had good reasons to keep her secret from her parents all those years ago. That reason no longer existed.

She exited the highway automatically, turning onto a street leading to a section of Atlanta where the houses were large and antebellum in style, the lawns beautifully kept, shaded by hundred-year-old oaks draped with moss. She turned two more times before pulling into the driveway on the property that had been in her family for generations. The original house had been burned during Sherman's infamous march to the sea. Miranda used to love to listen to her great-grandfather tell the story of how the present structure had been built. Her younger sister, Gwen, had put the tale on paper. Her professor at Brown University had cited what he perceived to be holes in its authenticity. Gwen had been indignant, declaring that only a Northerner would question her great-granddaddy's word. The instructor had changed the grade to an A-. Letting herself in the side door, Miranda smiled at the memory. Never mind that their great-grandfather *had* embellished a few facts and Gwen a few more.

Miranda listened in the back hallway, wondering where everyone was. The kitchen was meticulous, supper dishes put away, Gertrude gone home for another day. Miranda hadn't called, but her father's Mercedes was in the garage beside her mother's Lexus. Even Gwen's little red sports car was present and accounted for. The operators, however, were yet to be found.

"Mother? Daddy? Gwen?"

After checking several more rooms, she found her father on the phone in his study, her mother on another line in the den. A notebook was open, a pencil poised over the name of a volunteer who wouldn't realize she was being railroaded into chairing some committee or other until after she hung up the phone. Smiling, Miranda mouthed, "Where's Gwen?"

Charlotte motioned toward the ceiling, and then her watch, her subsequent hand signal indicating that she would be with Miranda in five minutes or less. Nodding, Miranda did a little hand signaling of her own, then headed for the staircase where she and Alex used to get reprimanded on a weekly basis for sliding down the banister.

She found her younger sister in the room Gwen still used whenever she spent the night. "Hi," she said, leaning in the doorway of the room decorated entirely in shades of lavender.

"Oh," Gwen said, "I thought you were Mother."

Miranda sashayed closer. "What are you doing?"

"Thinking," Gwen said, looking at Miranda in the mirror. "Hair is supposed to be our crowning glory. Show me one woman who isn't terrified of her hair."

"Having a bad hair day, Gwen?"

"Oh, I don't know. We women spend small fortunes on styling products and haircuts and perms and colors. Eventually, we all must accept the fact that our hair is a living energy force that can occasionally be persuaded but never coerced."

Miranda studied her younger sister. They shared a passing family resemblance, but Miranda had always believed that Gwen was the true family beauty. "What's bothering you, sis? And don't tell me it's your hair. It's beautiful, and you know it."

"Mother's not speaking to me. Hasn't in nearly a week."

Miranda had spoken to her mother twice in as many days, and yet this was still news to her. Charlotte Sinclair was very good at hiding her emotions. Miranda had learned from a pro. "Does she have good reason, Gwen?"

Gwen lowered her hairbrush and swiveled to face her older sister. "I'm not going to marry Peter."

"I see."

"Yes, I think you do. You're probably the only one in this family who can. I don't love him."

Miranda sauntered closer. She and Gwen used to have talks like this all the time when they were growing up. Sometimes, it seemed like yesterday. Other times, it seemed as if it had been someone else's life. "If you truly don't love him, Mother will get over it."

"I don't know. She won't admit it, but I think she's getting a little desperate to have grandchildren. She seems to have accepted the fact that your patients are your life. Alex isn't showing a lot of promise in that department either."

For the flash of one instant, Miranda felt empty, bereft.

"I'm only twenty-nine," Gwen said, oblivious to her sister's faraway expression. "It isn't that I don't want children. I just want them with the right man. Peter's bright and ambitious and attractive. He knows which fork to use, and he almost never drinks out of the finger bowl."

The sisters shared a small smile at Gwen's stab at wry humor.

"He's politically correct," Gwen continued. "He's been groomed to take over his father's business. He's even Southern, just like every other man I've ever dated. I don't want a man who's stepped off the assembly line."

"You want someone unusual? Someone from up north?" Miranda strode to the window overlooking the side lawn where David Braxton had kissed her for the first time when they'd both been fourteen.

Gwen joined Miranda at the window. "I don't care where he was born and raised. But he has to have balls."

"Gwendolyn, please!"

Miranda and Gwen both turned at the sound of their mother's voice coming from the hall. With a wink at Miranda, Gwen added, "Not just ordinary balls. I want a man who has to put them in his pants with a shoehorn."

"Really, Gwen!" Charlotte Sinclair's hair was perfectly coiffed, her chin raised just enough to give her a regal, slightly haughty look.

"Hello, Mother," Miranda said, rushing toward the doorway. Charlotte kissed the air near Miranda's cheeks. "This isn't your usual monthly visit. Is everything all right? What are you doing here? Are you ill?''

Miranda had expected the smooth hand Charlotte pressed to her forehead. As usual, it made her feel eight years old. "Do I need a reason to visit my own family?''

"You usually have one,'' Gwen said.

"Your sister's right.''

How nice that her mother and Gwen had found something to agree upon. Miranda heard footsteps on the stairs. Within moments, a distinguished-looking man with gray in his hair and a smile on his face appeared in the doorway. "Is this girl talk, or can a man participate?''

Miranda stepped into her father's warm embrace. Charlotte cast Gwen a look that was part warning, part entreaty. Rising to the occasion, Gwen took the hint and refrained from saying something crass. Leading the way out of her old room, she said, "Of course you're welcome, Daddy. What do all y'all say we go downstairs and have a glass of lemonade out on the veranda? Up here, I feel as if I'm about to get grounded.''

Nestled in the comfy cushions on the veranda, Miranda sipped her lemonade and tried to begin. She ended up asking about Alex, and the neighbors, and her father's latest research. By the time they'd filled her in on all the inconsequential things, her father, mother, and Gwen were all looking at her strangely.

"You look tired, dear,'' Charlotte insisted.

"She looks lovely, as always,'' Maxwell said levelly.

Gwen leaned closer. "She looks well loved. Holy shit, you've met someone, haven't you?''

"Gwendolyn, please.''

"Have you?'' their father asked.

"Well, that is, yes, you could say that.''

"I knew it. You have all the luck. I'll bet he uses a shoehorn too.''

Maxwell looked to his wife for an explanation. Charlotte fanned the air as if at a bothersome insect. And Miranda said, "We're getting off the subject.''

"What subject, dear?" her father asked.

She hesitated. Stood. Turned.

Charlotte rushed forward. "You are ill, aren't you?"

"Mom, I'm fine. Really."

Charlotte drew herself up to her full height. Even in her pumps, she had to look up slightly to meet her daughter's gaze. "You called me Mom. Something's wrong."

"Mother, Dad. I have something to tell you. Something happened. A long time ago."

"Oh, boy," Gwen said, leading her mother and sister to the settee. "You'd better do this sitting down. If you don't spill it in the next second or two, we're all going to have a coronary."

Taking a moment to look into each of their eyes, Miranda said, "First, I want to assure you that I've never felt better. What I'm going to tell you happened a long time ago."

"What is it?" Charlotte asked. "What happened?"

"When I was eighteen years old, I was attacked. Raped."

Charlotte gasped. Gwen and their father held perfectly still.

"It happened when the three of you were in England." Miranda's voice shook as she told them about the night she'd been ambushed, brutalized, and left for dead.

It had been years since Miranda had seen her mother cry. Charlotte Sinclair cried now, one hand at her throat, the other clutching Miranda's. In an effort to protect them, Miranda didn't go into detail, but they were bright and read between the lines. Sniffling most unbecomingly, Gwen marched into the house, only to return with a box of tissues, which she passed around to each of them.

They asked questions, seeking answers, shaking their heads, and voicing their outrage at what had been done to her. Traffic on the street was light, the air heavy with humidity. Just as Miranda instinctively associated thunderstorms with violence, she would always associate the scent of wisteria hanging on the air with acceptance and unconditional love.

She told them about the police report, the hospital, and

how she'd finally healed in Verdie's and Nora's gentle care. She mentioned the counselor she'd seen the following years at college, and how afraid she'd been, of everything and everyone, until she'd finally returned to the mountain and faced her fear.

Night had fallen, the ice in their drinks long since melted when the four of them finally rose and made their way inside. Her parents insisted she stay the night. It didn't matter that she was thirty-three years old. She was still her parents' child, and they needed time to reassure themselves that she was truly all right.

Miranda called Ruby, who was taking phone calls from patients in Miranda's absence. "It's a quiet night on the mountain," Ruby said. "No word from Lavender, so evidently the baby hasn't decided to be born yet. Cale's back."

"Already?"

"He stopped by, asking about you."

"He did?" Miranda's family must have heard the excitement in her voice, because they all looked across the room at her. Forcing a more natural tone, she talked to Ruby for a few minutes, but when she hung up the phone, she was quiet, deep in thought.

She and Gwen played cribbage, more for their parents' sakes than for their own. Sometime after midnight, Miranda bid her parents good night. They hugged her tight, and she them, then she and Gwen crawled into the twin beds that had once seemed so big in Gwen's old room.

"So," Gwen said, moonlight spilling onto her pillow, an arm bent beneath her head. "Tell me about this new man in your life. Oh, and just so you know, I'm not jealous of you anymore."

"When were you ever jealous of me?"

Waving the question aside, she motioned toward the hall and winked. "About this gorgeous man. Caleb Wilder. You said he landed his airplane in a rock-strewn meadow during a thunderstorm. You've obviously found a man with balls."

Miranda laughed in spite of herself. "Gwen?"

"Uh-oh. I know that tone."

"I think I'm in love with him."

"That's wonderful." She paused. "Isn't it?"

"I'm not sure. It's complicated."

"Isn't it always?" Gwen asked, turning onto her side. "Have you told him?" Miranda shook her head, and Gwen said, "Why not?"

"I'm afraid to." Miranda really did not like how small her voice sounded.

Gwen rose up on one elbow and sputtered, "You're the bravest person I know. Surely you know that. If you can tell Mother and Daddy about what happened to you all those years ago, you can tell this man how you feel."

"Maybe you're right."

"What do y'all mean, maybe?" The sisters shared a smile in the moonlit room. "So," Gwen asked, a twinkle in her eye, "how is he in bed? That's one thing I'm going to miss about Peter. I mean, even mediocre sex is better than no sex, right?"

Out in the hall, Charlotte and Max shuddered as they made their way toward their room. "She could have been killed."

"But she wasn't, Charlotte. Thank God."

"She should have told us. It's so like her to shoulder the burden alone."

"She takes after her mother. Always has."

Charlotte raised her chin indignantly. "And whom does Gwen take after?"

"If she didn't look so much like me, I would have questioned the mailman, the gardener, the pool boy, and our accountant years ago."

"Maxwell, really."

Max kissed his wife's soft, slightly lined cheek. She closed her eyes, but he noticed her face had lost its pinched expression, and she very nearly smiled.

Cale stared at the darkness outside the front screen door. After a while, he repeated the process at the back door. He'd arrived back on the mountain around six. He'd been eager to share the events of his stay in Columbus with Miranda. Finding her gone, he'd paid Ruby a visit, then had stopped by the store for groceries and the diner for supper. After that, he'd tried to coax Curly the cat from his hiding place under the bed. Once the cat had made his wishes to remain in hiding perfectly clear, Cale hauled the cane-backed chair out to the porch and waited for the sky to gear up for its nightly production. He tried peering at the ridges in the gathering darkness. He fidgeted. He tipped his chair back in an effort to get comfortable. It was no use. His discomfort didn't stem from the seat of the chair.

He'd gone more than eighteen numbing months without sex. He wasn't numb anymore. In all honesty, there was more to the discomfort than a desire for sex. If that's all it had been, there were other ways to relieve it. He didn't want a quick and simple remedy. He didn't even want another woman. He wanted Miranda.

The boxes he'd brought with him from home were stacked on the old table. The sadness that had been dogging his every step since Ellie's death had eased. Eventually, he would have to open those boxes and touch the things Ellie had touched. He'd planned to do it tomorrow. Hands on his hips, he eyed the boxes. With a loud sigh, he lifted the flap on the first one, pulled out a chair, and sat down.

He touched a finger to an eagle's feather, fanned through a stack of birthday cards, smiling to himself. Ellie used to throw away important items like license plate tabs and receipts on a regular basis, and yet she'd never been able to part with anything sentimental in nature. Surely, she would have saved some tiny clue or memento of a man she'd once loved and who had been the father of her child. When they'd married, agreeing that their pasts weren't important had been fine. But Danny's search sure would have been easier if Cale had more to go on.

He stacked the items carefully, examining souvenirs collected by the girl who had become the woman he'd married. Very carefully, he read over the information on a copy of

Danny's birth certificate. There was nothing new there. Daniel James Stanoway had been born on June 7 nearly fifteen years ago at two thirty-five A.M. Verita Cook had signed the document. The mother's name was Eleanora Stanoway. The box for the father's name was blank. Next, Cale looked through an envelope containing photographs of Ellie as a child. She'd been plain as a young girl, growing more beautiful with every passing year. Danny had been an adorable baby, a striking child who was well on his way to becoming a ruggedly attractive man. Once, Cale remembered telling Ellie that Danny must take after his other father. She'd placed a gentle hand on Cale's cheek and said, "I would rather he took after you."

Had she been purposefully evasive?

Ellie had saved a tarnished friendship ring, notes from friends, hair ribbons, and the usual ticket stubs, but there wasn't a single photo of someone who might have been Danny's biological father. Cale continued looking. He discovered a journal tucked inside the second box. Ellie had been fifteen when she'd written the first entry, her handwriting loopy, her *i*'s dotted with hearts. When she'd been sixteen, she'd evidently been dreaming of the family she would one day have, because she'd compiled a list of baby names, mostly girls'. Her writing sometimes told of happy times and sometimes of sadness. Much of what he read, he already knew. For instance, her mother had died when Ellie had been little older than Danny was now. She hadn't wanted to move to North Carolina to live with her father's family. For a time after that, the entries depicted a lonely high school girl living with an uninvolved father and a difficult-to-please grandmother. Ellie seemed to find solace in her new friendships. Her grandmother died shortly after Ellie's high school graduation. The grandmother must have cared about Ellie, because she left what little money she had to her granddaughter. Ellie wrote a brief note on her first day of college, and in a later entry, she mentioned a boyfriend at school.

In the very last entry, she wrote of feeling ill. Cale stared at the date, at first wondering if she'd been experiencing morning sickness. But it was dated seventeen months before Danny's birth.

It was after midnight. Outside, the wind had died down. Even the insects had quieted. He scraped the chair out and stood, stretching stiff muscles. Going through the remaining mementos, he found clues of the girl Ellie had been but none concerning the child she'd borne or the man who'd fathered him. Disappointed, Cale began putting the items back into the boxes.

A packet of papers fell out of what he'd thought was an empty notebook. He unfolded them, the paper thin and slightly musty. He scanned the first few lines. It was late, and the writing blurred before his eyes. Although he'd never seen the forms, Ellie had told him about the surgery she'd had after her appendix had burst. There it all was, in black and white. The infection, the complications that left her unable to have more children. Cale was about to fold the paper and return it to the notebook, when his gaze went to the date. He looked closer. It couldn't be right. According to the date on the transcript, Ellie's appendix had ruptured seventeen months before Danny had been born. That was impossible. If the date was correct, she couldn't have conceived Danny.

Cale went very still.

He dug the journal out of the box and flipped it open to the page where she'd written of sickness and nausea and pain so severe, it had been nearly unbearable. The date on that entry was five days prior to the date on the medical transcript.

Cale sat down to keep from stumbling.

What the hell was going on?

He read the medical transcript so many times, he memorized it, along with the date written on the top of the form. How could Ellie have had the surgery on that day?

He scrubbed a hand across his face. This was absurd. Days after they met, Ellie had told him about her surgery. Cale tried to recall the exact words she'd used. She'd always wanted a house full of children, she'd said, but due to a

horrible twist of fate, that was impossible. It didn't matter,
she'd insisted, because she had Danny. Cale tried to remember if she'd ever actually told him she'd given birth to a
child, any child.

He pushed to his feet with so much force, his chair toppled
over, crashing to the floor. There had to have been a mistake.
Surely, there was a simple explanation. Someone had simply
typed in the wrong date. Surely, that was it. He would contact
the hospital first thing in the morning. The date couldn't
possibly be right.

What if it wasn't a mistake? The question left a bad taste
in his mouth and a sick feeling in the pit of his stomach.

If Ellie hadn't given birth to Danny, who in the hell had?

Cale raised the ax over his head and brought it down with
so much force, the log cracked wide open the first try.
Tossing it onto the growing pile, he set up another log. He
was splitting wood, working off his frustration. He'd been
at it since the crack of dawn. Another eight or ten hours
might do it.

"Are y'all expecting a blizzard?"

He turned slowly. Miranda was standing a dozen feet
away. She was wearing one of her sunny yellow dresses
and one of her sunny smiles. Cale wanted to throw down
the ax and haul her against him, rolling her beneath him,
and bury himself inside her. The fierceness of his desire
rendered him immobile.

He was agitated, sweaty, and had hardly slept last night.
In comparison, she looked rested and carefree and as pretty
as a summer day.

"A blizzard?" he asked, eyeing the clear blue sky. "It
would have to cool off a little to snow."

"A little, Cale?"

Cale hadn't expected to find anything to smile about today,
and yet Miranda's lazy drawl lured out his first grudging
grin of the day. "Ruby said you went to Atlanta." At her
nod, he said, "Did you tell them?"

Again, she nodded.

"How does it feel?"

She tipped her head slightly, eyeing him up and down as if she liked what she saw. "I'm glad it's over. I'm especially glad to be back in my own house with my own garden and my patients."

She didn't include him in the things she was glad she'd come back to, but it was there in her eyes. Cale had spent the better part of the night pacing, while questions that had no answers screamed inside his head. He was angry, but not at Miranda. The date on Ellie's medical transcript didn't make sense, but the desire coursing through him did. In fact, his desire for Miranda was the only thing that made sense. Here. Today. This moment.

"Cale? Is everything all right?"

"I missed you."

Miranda studied Cale unhurriedly. He seemed as surprised by his declaration as she was. He was naked to the waist, his upper body slick with sweat, his muscles well defined. "Is that why you're cutting wood as if there were no tomorrow?"

He ran a hand through his hair, shrugged one tanned shoulder. "I went through some of Ellie's things last night."

Miranda had a difficult time reading between those lines. Oh, he wanted her. That was blatantly clear. Gwen was right. She needed to talk to him, to clarify their relationship before it went any further or spun out of control.

"How did your meeting with Daniel's counselor go?" She glanced around. "Where is Daniel anyway?"

"It went well. Sam flew him up to Harvard to participate in a math and science competition."

"When will he be back?"

"Sometime tomorrow evening. Now that he's returned the raccoon to the wild, he's going to spend most nights here, where there are amenities. We have the place to ourselves until he returns."

Miranda knew exactly what Cale was suggesting. She was tempted to give in to the attraction arcing between them, to throw caution to the wind, if only for a little while. Instinct and pride held her back. "I have to be in Athens in forty-five minutes."

"You're going to Athens?"

They were inches apart now, her voice barely more than a whisper. "I have an important meeting with a group of medical professionals at the university. I can't be late."

"That's too bad."

The yearning in his dark blue eyes caught her in the chest. "I'll be back later this afternoon. I've cleared the remainder of my day and evening. We can touch base then." She shifted away from him slightly so that she could bring her hand up to his face.

He drew her face up as he lowered his, and in that instant before his lips covered hers, he said, "Then I guess this kiss is going to have to do."

That kiss very nearly did her in. It was intense, passionate, at odds with the anger she'd glimpsed when she'd first called his name. She backed out of his embrace, thinking that if the man had intended to confuse her, he'd succeeded very well.

A revving engine and the crunch of tires drew their attention to Cale's driveway. Emory Sturgis threw his car door open and shouted, "Thank God I found you. It's Lavender. The baby's comin' and Lavender's bleedin' bad."

CHAPTER EIGHTEEN

Miranda could hear Lavender's screams as soon as Emory turned into the drive. Joshua and Jeremiah were standing near the gate, their eyes round with fear. She knew the boys needed reassuring. Normally, she would have spoken to them, cajoling a grin out of Josh and a giggle out of Jeremiah. But today, she kept her eyes straight ahead, rushing into the house the moment Emory pulled the car to a stop.

The little girls were crying uncontrollably. Lavender was lying on the floor in a pool of blood, sobbing and writhing, her mother clutching her hand and calling her name.

"Oh, thank God," Lucille cried. "Miranda's here, Lavender. You're going to be okay. Miranda's here. Miranda's here." She said it over and over and over, chanting it like an invocation or a prayer.

Miranda glided to her knees. "There, there, Lavender, try to relax. It hurts, I know. Lucille, bring me more towels." Miranda glanced at Cale next. "Call the hospital in Toccoa. Tell them to send an ambulance. Emory, you give them directions. Oh, and you'd better call Randy at work."

Everyone jumped, relieved to have something constructive to do. Miranda made a quick assessment of Lavender's condition. She'd delivered babies at home, but she wished this one could be born in a hospital where there was state-of-the-art medical equipment and surgeons and specialists standing by. Emory had explained that there had been no time to drive to a hospital. Lavender's water had broken, and she'd doubled over right there on the living room floor. She'd given birth six times, but this one was different, the pain excruciating, the bleeding too heavy to be normal.

"It's gonna be all right, honey," Lucille said, bustling back with a stack of threadbare towels. "Miranda's here this time. This time, everything's gonna be all right."

Lucille continued to babble, and Miranda let her. If saying it out loud made her believe it, so be it. Miranda wasn't so sure. It didn't look good. Even if Lavender were in the hospital, her labor was too advanced to perform an emergency C-section. The girl was young, weak, thin, and bleeding. The baby was coming breech. Miranda prayed she could save them.

She didn't have time to put on gloves or cover her clothes. As gently as possible, she reached up, feeling for the baby. Lavender whimpered in pain. Miranda thought she felt the infant move. It was a good sign. The baby was small, which would give her a chance to deliver it quickly, without further damage to the young mother or the child.

She placed a steady hand on Lavender's swollen abdomen. Clearing her mind, she began chanting, inside her head at first, and then in a whisper, out loud. Once Lavender had relaxed, Miranda stopped chanting and started murmuring what she wanted the young mother to do.

"Push now." And moments later, "Easy. That's it. Another deep breath. Okay. Can you push again?"

Lucille held her daughter's head, wiped her brow. When Lavender started to writhe again, Miranda started to chant all over again.

Cale stood across the room, in awe. Moments ago, the house had been filled with weeping and chaos and noise. The little girls, barely more than babies themselves, had stopped whimpering, Lucille had stopped repeating herself, and Lavender had stopped crying. Even Emory had grown silent. Only the calming murmur of Miranda's voice and Lavender's shuddering breaths remained. Cale found it difficult to look away. But a child was being brought into the world. It was a personal time, a spiritual moment, one that warranted privacy.

"Emory," he said. "It's past lunchtime. The kids are probably hungry. Let's find something to hold them over and take them outside."

Emory came out of his stupor and reached for the toddler. "Come 'ere, Grace. You too, Jewel. Let's us go see what the boys are doin' outside."

The toddler dragged a bottle and a blanket with her. The three-year-old had to make do with her thumb. Cale wished to God the ambulance would get there. He grabbed the first two items he saw on the counter: a loaf of bread and a bag of store-bought cookies. By the time he reached the porch, Emory had already lowered himself into a rusted metal chair, its legs nearly hidden in the tall grass. Settling both girls on his lap, Emory looked nervously toward the house. All was quiet. Cale hoped that was a good sign.

The boys, Joshua and Jeremiah, slunk closer. "Is Mama dead?" the older of the two asked.

Emory was too choked up to answer, so Cale said, "No. She's having the baby right now."

For lack of anything better to do, he doled out the bread and cookies, showing the kids how to make cookie sandwiches. Even the three-year-old thought that was funny.

"You're good with young-un's," Emory said. "How come you only had one?"

Yesterday, Cale would have known how to answer. He would have simply said that his wife couldn't have more children after Danny. Today, Cale was at a loss for words. Naturally, Emory had no such problem.

"The wife and I had seven. Lost one when she was just a baby. It woulda been a lot quieter if we woulda stopped with two or three, but I wouldn't trade any of 'em. Still, it only takes one to make a family."

It was Cale's turn to get choked up. Beneath Emory's gift for gab was a lot of goodness. "Remember when you asked me if the name Stanoway rings a bell?"

Cale nodded.

"Took us a while, but the wife and I finally figured out why it sounded familiar. Before Miranda took over the practice, an old granny-woman treated the people of Dawsons Hollow and the surrounding area all by herself. The last coupla years before she died, Miranda helped her."

"Was her name Stanoway?"

Emory shook his head. "Her name was Cook. Verdie Cook. But it seems to me and Lucille that Verdie had kin off the mountain by that name."

Cale didn't know how that was going to help. Danny's birth certificate listed this county as his place of birth, not someplace off the mountain. If that information was incorrect, it was possible that other information was as well. A dozen questions raced through his mind. Cale felt ill equipped to deal with any of them.

"Verdie had a niece," Emory said. "Folks up here called the girl Nora, Nora Cook. Far as I'm concerned, I have two gifts. One is talkin', the other is a memory that cain't be beat. I remember seein' a letter addressed to Nora once. The name on the envelope wasn't Nora Cook. It was Nora Stanoway."

Cale was getting a bad feeling in the pit of his stomach, a suspicion that sat like a rock in his gut. Just then, a tiny mewling cry carried through the open window.

"See there?" Emory told his grandchildren. "There's your new brother or sister now."

Cale was still trying to make sense of this latest information. It wasn't easy to think about the past when a twenty-four-year-old girl might be dying on the other side of the porch wall that very second.

Poor Emory had to be thinking the same thing. "Thank God Miranda's here," he said just a little too emphatically. "I don't know how she does it, but patients do things for her they wouldn't do for anybody else. Not doctors, not nurses, husbands or mothers. If she asks them to lie still, they do. If she asks them to take their medicine, they do even if they know dang well it's just gonna come back up again. Ain't that right, kids? And when no one's looking, she does things for them no one else does. You saw the way my girl calmed down when Miranda laid her hand on her belly. She does that, smoothes a hand along a brow, covers a sick-un's eyes. Always wonder what's goin' through her head. Guess it's enough to know she's here.''

The door opened. All eyes turned as Lucille walked onto the porch. "It's a girl."

"A girl!" Joshua exclaimed. "Me'n Jer thought it was gonna be a boy."

"Well, it's a girl," Lucille said tiredly. "Your mama's got her. You can meet her in a little while. What are you eatin'?"

All four of the children inched closer to their grandma, Jeremiah offering her a bite of his sandwich.

"And Lavender?" Emory asked.

Lucille met her husband's gaze. "Miranda's still workin' on her." Her lips quivered. When she could speak again, she said, "Somebody's gonna have to tell Randy the baby's come."

"Not me," Emory stated emphatically enough to draw the oldest boy's attention. "I'd say more'n he wants to hear." There was a cold thread of anger in Emory's voice.

Cale wondered what had gone on in this house, and he wondered why Randy wasn't there. Even if it had been his place to ask, he wouldn't do it in front of the children.

The toddler climbed onto Lucille's lap. In the process, she dropped her bottle. Lucille leaned over tiredly to retrieve it. Seeing that the nipple was covered with dirt, she moved to get up. "Here," Cale said, "let me."

He took the bottle and let himself into the house, quietly closing the door behind him. Treading lightly, he strode toward the kitchen. He could see into the living room from there. Lavender was resting, her chest rising and falling evenly, a pillow beneath her knees, a blanket tucked under her arms. Miranda sat in an old rocker a few feet away, holding the baby in the little crook between her neck and shoulder. The child was wrapped in a faded pink blanket. She was unbelievably tiny, but her eyes were open. Miranda's were closed, tears coursing down her face, her expression unlike any Cale had ever seen.

There were moments in Cale's life permanently etched into his memory, moments that could be called up as clearly as pictures in a photo album. The expression in Ellie's eyes when she'd said I do. The look of wonder on Danny's face the first time he flew a kite. The sound of Danny's voice and the tear that had trailed down Ellie's cheek the first time Danny had called Cale Daddy. Today, another memory had been added. If he lived to be a hundred, he would never forget the look of rapture and longing on Miranda's face, the tenderness in the hand holding a tiny baby close to her heart.

Quietly, Cale went to the sink, rinsed the baby's bottle, then went back outside. Within minutes, a siren could be heard in the distance. Everyone waited in silence for it to come closer. Paramedics jumped out as soon as it pulled to a stop out front. A bustle of activity followed. The kids got their first glimpse of the baby while Miranda filled the medical personnel in on Lavender's condition. Questions were asked, vitals taken, orders given.

Lucille called Ruby, and she arrived to stay with the children while the paramedics were lifting Lavender and the baby onto a stretcher and gently carrying mother and child to the waiting ambulance. Randy Sprague arrived just before the paramedics closed the ambulance doors. Casting a glance at the group of people watching him, he climbed in the back with his wife. Everyone waved as the ambulance pulled away from the little white cottage, Lucille and Emory following in their big white car. Miranda took a step, stumbled. If Cale hadn't slid an arm around her waist, she would have fallen.

"Your job's done here," Ruby declared. "You did good, girl." Turning to Cale, she said, "Now she needs to rest. Take her home. You'll have to drive my car. Lavender's brother and sister-in-law are stopping by in a while to get the kids. I'll have them give me a ride home.''

Miranda allowed Cale and Ruby to help her to the car. Once seated, she closed her eyes. They started down the mountain. The windows were down, warm air streaming in, ruffling her hair and bringing relief from the heat of midday.

''Lavender thinks Randy is cheating on her.''

Cale glanced at Miranda. Her eyes were closed, her head resting on the back of her seat. ''I thought you were sleeping.''

''She told me in the middle of giving birth to that beautiful child. Maybe the fact that he came when she needed him was a good sign.''

She opened her eyes, and he saw the spark of some indefinable emotion, as if an unspoken pain had come alive inside her. He remembered how weary she'd looked after she'd treated the acid burns around little Benjie Winters's eyes weeks ago. This was different.

''Ruby said what you do for your patients takes a lot out of you.''

She made no reply.

''You really are a healer.''

This time, she nodded.

Why had he doubted it? He believed in God and intuition and prayer and love and other things that couldn't be seen or proven. Why had he doubted this?

''Have you always had the ability to heal?'' he asked.

She'd closed her eyes again, but she answered, her voice slow and quiet. ''Not before the rape. Only after. It's like the tiny sprig of green growing out of a charred forest. That night, after the man raped me, hatred roiled up in me, and I wanted to hurt him the way he'd hurt me. I kneed him with everything I had. His fist shot out, connecting with my jaw with so much force, I fell backward. The last thing I heard before darkness claimed me was the crack of my head on a large rock. Blackness engulfed me, surrounding me. But then the blackness seeped away, the man, the darkness, and the pain dissolving like a morning mist. I didn't feel alive, but I didn't feel dead. I think I'd gone to a place in between, a place where there was no measure of hours, no questions, no pain, and no sound. I might have remained there if Nora hadn't called my name. Hers was the first voice I heard, her tears warm on my face. I believe she saved my life that night. Dear, kind Eleanora.''

Cale jerked, staring at Miranda. She'd fallen asleep and didn't see. His thoughts careened, short-circuited. Ellie's full name was Eleanora. Miranda's best and dearest friend, Nora. And his beloved wife, Ellie. One and the same?

Impossible.

Ellie had befriended so many people over the years. Each and every one of them had been welcome in their home. Cale and Daniel had received Christmas cards from dozens of them last year. And yet until a few weeks ago, he'd never even heard of Miranda Sinclair. If Ellie and Miranda had been soul sisters, why had they had no communication with each other all these years?

If his Ellie was Miranda's friend, why had she waited until she was dying to try to tell him so many details about Dawsons Hollow? What had happened on this mountain to cause her never to return? What secret had she taken with her to her grave?

If her appendix had ruptured, rendering her sterile, seventeen months before Danny's birth, how had he come to be her child? The question screamed inside Cale's head, planting doubt and, above all else, dread.

Miranda woke up when Cale pulled into her driveway. Although she told him she didn't need help, he assisted her out of the car. He unlocked her door and ushered her inside. When she noticed the light blinking on her answering machine, it was Cale who pushed the button. There were three messages. One from her brother, one from her parents, and another from the head of the nursing program at the university in Athens. She'd missed the meeting.

"You can call them tomorrow," Cale said quietly. "Now you need to rest."

He helped her out of her shoes, then unzipped her dress so she could step out of her bloodstained clothes. He pulled back the spread so she could lie on her bed. She watched him all the while. She was too tired for a shower, too weary to ask him what was wrong.

"You don't have to stay," she whispered.

"Are you kicking me out?"

"No."

"Then I'm staying."

It wasn't the nightmare that haunted her in those moments before she fell asleep. It was the expression deep in Cale's eyes.

CHAPTER NINETEEN

Cale opened his eyes to the first tentative twitter of bird-song and faint morning light. Neither was strong enough to have awakened him. A movement on the other side of the bed brought him more fully awake. Miranda was beginning to stir.

It had been late afternoon when she'd fallen asleep after their return from Lavender Sprague's house. Cale had checked on her several times throughout the evening. She hadn't so much as moved. He'd spent the majority of the previous night rereading Ellie's medical transcripts and asking himself if and how and why. Yesterday had brought even more questions. By late last night, his mind had been groggy from lack of sleep and unanswered questions. He'd considered going back to his place, but he'd told Miranda he would stay. Being careful not to disturb her, he'd crawled into bed next to her.

He'd spent the night with her before, but this was the first time he'd watched her wake up. She was on her back, her face turned toward him, the sheet baring one shoulder. Her skin looked smooth in the early morning light, her face relaxed, everything about her serene. She moved an inch at a time, gliding her foot across his leg. Cale responded in the most elemental way.

She opened her eyes eventually, as if the joy were as much in the waking as it was in the sleeping. "Cale. Hello."

"Were you expecting someone else?"

He wondered how many people in the world woke up with a smile. "Of course not," she said. "I'm just surprised you're still here."

"I said I'd stay."

He hadn't meant to answer so abruptly. She touched a finger to his face, trailed it across his cheekbone and along his jaw. "Something's wrong."

Cale went up on one elbow. "If something's wrong, it isn't this." He kissed her without warning but not without tenderness and care. He skimmed his hand over her warm body covered only with the bra and panties she'd slept in.

Miranda's eyes fluttered closed, and she kissed Cale in return, her mouth opening beneath his, her hand automatically gliding to his shoulder. As if it were all the invitation he needed, he put his arms around her. And she let him. She knew she shouldn't, not if she wanted to keep the tenacious hold she had on her emotions, but she let him anyway, for the plain and simple reason that she wanted the heat he was offering, if only one more time.

It was a sobering thought. She tried to push it away.

He pressed a thigh between hers, letting her know just how much he wanted her. She could feel his desire in more places than one. It was in the bunch of his muscles, in the urgency of his touch. Some semblance of rationality kept her from giving in to the answering emotions his touch evoked. Before this went any further, she needed to talk to him about their relationship and the problems he was having but refused to talk about.

He must have felt her reluctance, because he straightened, breaking the kiss. He rolled to his back, swung his legs over the side of her bed, and sat up, his back to her.

"You're angry," she said.

Cale scrubbed a hand across his face, over his eyes. "Not with you." It was true. He wasn't angry with Miranda.

"With who, then?"

He didn't reply. He couldn't. Not yet. He could count on one hand the times he'd been angry with Ellie. He was royally ticked off at her now. It made him feel guilty. If the date on the medical transcript was wrong, his anger was unwarranted. He needed proof. "I discovered something when I went through some of Ellie's things the other night."

"Something about Daniel's biological father?"

"No. Something else." He made a decision then and there. "I have to go to North Carolina."

"Now?"

"Yes." Without further explanation, he rose to his feet and began dressing.

Miranda rose too and quietly slipped into her robe. She was stirring orange juice when he came out of the bathroom. "The coffee will be done soon, Cale."

"I'll get a cup before I hit the interstate."

"All right." She didn't understand the expression deep in his eyes any more than she understood the tension in the air between them.

He started to leave, only to turn suddenly and kiss her. It was a passionate good-bye kiss, ending as suddenly as it had begun. It left her reeling long after he'd gone.

Alone, she wandered around her house, lost in thought. She didn't know what Cale had discovered in his late wife's things. Whatever it was, it had upset him. Ellie Wilder still had a hold on him. Miranda wondered if she always would.

Cale waved to Sam and Danny before the plane came to a complete stop along the grassy runway. Yearning rose up inside him. He wanted to fly, to take the single-engine beauty for a spin above the clouds. Sam Kennedy would give Cale the shirt off his back, his last dollar, a kidney if he needed one. But nobody else flew his plane.

Cale rushed toward the tall, barrel-chested man and the tall, wiry teenager. "How was the flight?"

"Perfect," Sam declared.

"Awful," Danny said at the same time.

Sam ruffled Danny's hair. "The boy here was a little green around the gills at first, but he did okay."

Danny, who had never liked to fly, shrugged sheepishly. Cale was nearly overcome with the desire to turn his son around and herd him back onto the plane, to fly away from this mountain with all its problems and unanswered questions and to never return. But Danny would only come back again, so Cale settled for saying, "It's good to see you."

Danny eyed Cale strangely. "You too."

"How was the competition?"

Danny pulled a face only a teenage boy could manage. Reaching for the bags he'd dropped, Sam said, "Don't let his modesty fool you. He burned the place down with his intelligence, but what really impressed them was his common sense."

Cale and Danny shared a look before Danny said, "It's possible Uncle Sam is mildly biased."

Cale smiled for the first time in two days. He'd spent the night in North Carolina. After supplying the hospital with the proper forms and identification, he'd been allowed to view the copies of Ellie's hospital records. The date on the transcript wasn't a typo. It coincided with the dates on the insurance forms and admitting papers. The infection that had nearly killed her had left her barren. The damage had been extensive; she couldn't have conceived a child after that. Cale felt as if a hole had been blown through his chest.

He'd arrived back at the cabin near Dawsons Hollow hours ago. The cat still ventured out from under the bed only to eat and use the litter box. Cale thought that was where cats had it over people. He couldn't hide under the bed. Now it was a quarter to seven on Friday evening, and Cale didn't know what the hell he was going to do. Danny had run away to this mountain searching for answers regarding his natural father's identity. Uncovering this new information was more than either of them could have prepared for.

Sam and Danny tossed their bags in the back of Cale's truck, then climbed in after them. "Okay with you if Danny and I ride shotgun, Wilder?"

A quick glance at Sam turned into a much longer exchange of silent communication. Sam knew something was wrong. He was going to wait until he and Cale were alone to bring it up.

"Suit yourself," Cale said.

"I usually do."

Sam and Danny sat all the way at the front of the bed of the truck, their backs leaning on the cab, forearms resting on their bent knees. Cale drove carefully, and Danny pointed out ridges, passes, and creeks. Once, the boy pointed to the sky, where an eagle glided on an invisible current of air.

Back at the cabin, Danny and Sam hauled their bags inside. Danny made a beeline for the old-fashioned refrigerator, which Cale had stocked a few days earlier. Feeling his father's eyes on him, he closed the door and faced Cale, an apple in one hand. "What's going on?" he asked.

Cale rubbed at a knot in the back of his neck. "I'm thinking about going back to Columbus. For good."

"When?"

"As soon as possible."

"I just got back."

"I think it would be best, Daniel."

"Give me one good reason."

Be careful what you ask for, Cale thought. "Our home is there. Our life is there."

"We don't have our answers yet."

Cale didn't want any more answers.

Danny eyed his dad and then the mountain ridge in the distance. Cale knew that look. Danny gazed at the hills the way Cale had gazed at Sam's airplane.

"There are still a couple of hours of daylight left," Cale said. "You might as well go see if anything's happening on your mountain."

Danny bounded out the door. In the ensuing silence, Sam strolled around the small cabin. "So this is your new place. Interesting wiring system."

"It's a steal for only three hundred and fifty dollars a month."

"You're renting this for three hundred and fifty dollars a month?"

"It's a long story."

"Think you can tell it before darkness falls and Danny returns?"

Cale heaved a sigh loud enough to be heard across the room. "I could give an abridged version in less time than that."

From the couch, Sam studied Cale through narrowed eyes. "I think we'd better save the bottle of Chianti I brought for another time."

Cale retrieved the last beer from the refrigerator. Handing it to Sam, he took a seat on the worn chair and began to speak. "Ellie's name is on Danny's birth certificate, but she didn't give birth to him."

The only things that moved were Sam's eyebrows. "You know that for a fact?"

"She couldn't have," Cale continued. "Because her appendix ruptured seventeen months prior to Danny's birth."

"But I thought . . ."

"That's what I thought too," Cale said. "Looking back, I don't think she ever actually told me, in so many words, that he'd been born of her body. I'd assumed . . ."

Sam lowered the untouched beer to the table in front of him. "I take it you have proof."

"I read the medical transcripts. The infection almost killed her. The surgeon had to remove part of her uterus, her fallopian tubes, and one ovary. There was other internal damage as well. She couldn't have gotten pregnant, Sam."

"Any idea who put her name on the birth certificate?"

"It's written in the same handwriting as the midwife's signature."

"Have you talked to the midwife?"

Cale shook his head. "She's dead."

"There must be someone else you can ask."

Cale ran a hand through his hair and stood. "There is one woman."

"Is she here on the mountain?"

"She lives a mile away."

Sam stood too. "Looks as though you're going to be tied up for a while."

Cale would have preferred to put it off. A hundred years might do it. "What will you do while I'm gone?"

"Think I'll check out the night life in Dawsons Hollow."

"The only place open at night around here is the Bootleg-ger. Some of the old-timers play poker. If Jed Hershey's there, keep your eye on him. He cheats."

Sam slapped Cale on the back. "So do I."

Ten minutes later, Cale dropped Sam off in front of the Bootlegger. Making a U-turn, he drove to Miranda's place on the outskirts of town. He didn't recognize the car in the driveway and would have backed out to the road again if the front door hadn't opened before he had the chance.

Miranda strode onto her porch, watching as Cale got out of the truck. His gait was slower than usual, his shoulders hunched forward slightly, as if he carried a heavy burden. "Hello, Miranda."

There were dark circles beneath his eyes, worry lines between them. He looked like something the cat dragged in, so there was no reason for her heart to flutter before taking a nosedive into her stomach. "When did you get back?"

"This afternoon."

And he'd waited until now to stop by. There was a heavy stretch of silence. Trying to fill it, she said, "Nice evening."

He glanced away sharply, as if surprised to see that the sun was shining.

"Did you find the information you were looking for, Cale?"

"Yes and no." Cale knew he was being vague. He just didn't know how to proceed. It was becoming more and more apparent that Miranda's friend, Nora, and his wife, Ellie, were the same person. What little family Ellie had had died years ago. Therefore, Miranda was probably the only person he could ask about her. Just how did a man ask the woman he was sleeping with about his dead wife?

Cale was still trying to find the right words when the door opened behind Miranda and a woman wearing a cream-colored pantsuit that fit her like a glove sashayed outside. "Well, well, well. What do y'all have here?"

"Gwen," Miranda said, "this is Caleb Wilder. Cale, my sister, Gwen."

Gwen came closer and held out her hand as if she expected him to kiss it. He enfolded it in his own and shook it firmly. Eyes a shade or two darker than Miranda's widened, pouty lips slowly spreading into a smile. "Things are getting interesting around here. Too bad I'm on my way out."

"Where are you going?" Miranda asked.

"Thought I'd check out the night life."

"It'll be dark soon."

"Don't worry. I have my Mace and my stun gun with me."

Her expression changed before Cale's eyes, her tartness turning into remorse. "That isn't funny anymore, is it? Guess it never was. Don't worry. I'll lock my doors, and I won't be late."

"It was nice meeting you," Cale said.

"Why, aren't you just the sweetest thing?" With a wink at Miranda, Gwen said, "You're right. He does have balls."

She glided down the steps while Miranda was still gasping. "Her words. Not mine."

Cale surprised the hell out of himself and possibly out of Miranda, too, when he smiled. Three or four years younger than her sister, Gwen Sinclair was just as Southern and a lot more brash. Whether it had been intentional or not, she'd broken the ice. Miranda was still shaking her head after Gwen drove away.

Cale said, "How are you?"

She turned her head slowly. "I'm well, Cale."

She looked it. She was wearing blue slacks, flats, and a sleeveless blouse. Her hair was secured at her nape, wispy tendrils brushing her ears and forehead.

"The nightmare?" he asked.

"I haven't had it in days."

That explained the color on her cheeks and the serenity in her eyes. He supposed his behavior was responsible for the question he read in their depths. Out of the blue, she said, "Your friend and my sister have both gone to the Bootlegger. Should I be worried?"

"No offense, Miranda, but now that I've met your sister, I'm more worried about Sam." On a more serious note, he said, "I don't know what I would have done without him these past nineteen months."

"Since your Ellen died?"

He didn't correct her. "He's like a rock. I'm closer to him than I am to my only brother. Friends like Sam Kennedy don't come along every day."

"Nora was like that."

Cale stared at Miranda's profile. When his voice was steady, he asked, "Was?"

She'd strolled to the porch railing and was looking straight ahead, squinting into the sun. "Nora left the mountain nearly fifteen years ago. I've always wondered ... wanted ... dreamed." She sighed. "But what is is."

"You've never heard from her, not once in all these years?"

"No," she said quietly. "But then, I never expected to."

Why the hell not? Cale wanted to shout. Instead, he said, "What was she like?"

Even all these years later, thoughts of Nora brought a smile to Miranda's face. "She had curly red hair and beautiful skin. It wouldn't have mattered if she'd been homely as sin. She was one of those people who grew more beautiful every time you saw her. Even when I first met her, and she'd been filled with sorrow, she'd had a smile soft and warm enough to draw even the grouchiest person out of a bad mood."

That sounded like Ellie all right. Her warmth and kindness were the first things he'd fallen in love with.

"Nora was already a nurse when I met her," Miranda said. "But she'd been sick and was taking some time off to recover from a serious illness and subsequent surgeries. The granny-woman who lived on this mountain was Nora's great-aunt. According to Nora, Aunt Verdie was the only person on earth who exasperated her enough to make her argue."

Cale had a sudden flashback of Ellie glaring at him, hands on her hips, her chin raised defiantly. Aunt Verdie wasn't the only person who'd exasperated Ellie. God, he missed her. So much, in fact, that for a moment he forgot to be mad at her.

"Cale, would you like to come in?"

Yearning deep enough to drown in washed over Cale. He wanted to follow her inside, to close the door on his problems, his disappointments, and the gaping hole Ellie's secret had left in his chest. Running a hand through his hair, he shook his head. "Daniel will be back soon. I wanted to see you, if only for a few minutes. Would you mind if I stopped by tomorrow?"

"After Gwen leaves tomorrow, I'm driving up to Hickory Gap Road to check on Lavender and the baby. Would you like to come along?"

"I'd like that, Miranda."

He left without kissing her good-bye.

Daniel was rounding a bend in the trail when he noticed movement up ahead. Being extra careful not to make a sound, he crept closer. Willow was crouched low, peering at something beyond the ridge below.

Daniel moved toward her. The wind had picked up a while ago. It helped cover the sound of his footsteps and the leaves he couldn't help rustling as he made his way through the brush. Getting as close as he could, he said, "Do you have a license to spy?"

She yelped, spun around, and sputtered, her blue eyes

flashing with indignation. "Daniel Wilder, y'all ought to be ashamed. Scaring the living daylights out of me that way."

He placed his finger over his mouth in a shushing gesture. It raised her hackles all the more. Daniel grinned. It felt good to be the one doing the surprising for a change. It felt good to be back.

"You're watching the Spragues again?" he asked.

She patted the camera hanging around her neck, then took a yellow ribbon from her hair. Tying it to a nearby tree, she said, "I'm trying to take pictures, but we might as well go. Lavender's been inside ever since she got home from the hospital."

"Lavender went to the hospital?"

Willow nodded, the wind blowing the hair she'd just freed into her eyes. "She had her baby a few days ago. Almost didn't make it, but Miranda saved them both."

"Wow," Daniel said, falling into step beside Willow. "I leave for five days and all hell breaks loose." When she started to protest, he said, *"Hell* isn't swearing. It's a place, or, on a different level, a state of being."

With a heartfelt sigh, she began to fill him in on everything that had happened on the mountain while he'd been gone. They were nearing the meadow where Cale had landed his airplane when she said, "And Miranda asked me to take pictures of the houses and people in and around Dawsons Hollow. Told me I could choose who and what and how to portray them. And get this. She's going to pay me. Can you believe it?"

"Maybe you could take a picture of the eagle," Daniel said.

She nodded. "Miranda wants people, mostly." Without warning, she snapped a picture of him.

They weren't even trying to be quiet when they broke into the clearing, so it was no wonder the group of high school kids who were in various positions in and on the airplane noticed their presence. "Uh-oh," Willow said, stopping abruptly. "That's Bubba Gillespie. He skips school more than I do, only he's flunking out because of it."

"Look," a boy wearing faded jeans and a sleeveless T-shirt yelled. "It's that freaky Willow Pratt and her freaky boyfriend."

Daniel made a quick assessment of the situation. Bubba appeared to be the group's leader. There were three other boys and two girls. One by one, they dropped to the ground. If it came to it, it wouldn't be a fair fight.

"What do you think of my dad's plane?" Daniel called.

"What's it to ya?" the leader sneered.

"She's a beauty, isn't she? It's a single-engine Cessna Cardinal. Ever flown one?"

Bubba shook his head, and Daniel said, "Think you might want to someday?"

For a second, Bubba forgot to hide his interest. "I might. Have you?"

Hell, no, he hadn't. But a situation like this called for a little improvising. "My dad won't teach me until I'm fifteen. My birthday's coming up." He cast a look at the trees and rocks on either end of the meadow. "You probably heard how he landed during that thunderstorm a couple of weeks ago. It's a wonder he didn't crash and burn. He's going to need some help getting it out of here."

"How's he gonna do that?" one of Bubba's friends called.

"I don't know." Daniel looked some of the kids in the eye. "Any of you guys mechanically inclined?"

Bubba said, "I can take an engine apart and put it back together with one hand tied behind my back."

Daniel nodded sagely. "My dad's going to be looking for people like you. What are your names?"

They answered, one at a time, some proclaiming their names loudly, others mumbling them under their breath. "If you can't remember," one of the girls said, "just ask Willow. She has a photographic memory. Ain't that right, Willow?"

"And a really sharp knee," one of the others mumbled.

When the area kids left, Willow and Daniel headed back toward town. Willow said good-bye to Daniel, then ducked into the gravel lane behind the grocery store. Feeling good about himself, Daniel took the road that led to his dad's cabin.

his chest. Sam was right. Danny was exactly like him when

CHAPTER TWENTY

Cale was sitting stock-still on the porch when Danny returned. The boy didn't notice his dad until he was almost upon him. "Did you find Willow?" Cale asked.

"Yeah." His smile slowly disappeared. The grim line of his dad's mouth and the faraway look in his eyes put Daniel on edge. "Where's Uncle Sam?"

"He went to the Bootlegger a few hours ago. Can you picture that?" His smile didn't quite make it all the way to his eyes.

It wasn't like Danny to be the one to have to make conversation. His dad had always done that. He remained quiet a while longer, then finally said, "Willow and I came across some local kids over by your airplane."

"What were they doing?"

"So far, I think they were just curious. I told them you might be looking for some kids who were good with their hands to help you fix it and get it airborne again."

"Were they interested in helping?"

Daniel nodded. "I've got their names."

Cale knew he should be accustomed to the pride filling

his chest. Sam was right. Danny was extremely bright, but what most impressed him was the boy's common sense.

It was the quiet time of the day when the world hovered between daylight's bustle and nighttime's surreptitious scuttle. Cale had been sitting out on the porch for the better part of an hour, trying to decide what he should do. He'd come to the mountain to find Danny. In the process, he'd uncovered some painful truths, and he'd come damn close to falling in love. This was the worst possible time in his life to find love again. He'd never had so little to offer a woman. The one thing he had was the truth. And the truth was, he found Miranda beautiful and desirable, a ray of sunshine in an oftentimes dreary world. Tomorrow, he was going to tell her. Tonight, he stared at his son's profile. Danny deserved the truth too.

"I have something to tell you. It's going to take a while. You might as well sit down."

Danny lowered himself into a chair and cautiously asked, "Is this about my other, that is, my biological father?"

"No, son. It's about your mom."

For one millisecond, Daniel thought his father was going to tell him that it had all been a mistake. His mom hadn't really died. She'd been gravely ill and had been recuperating all this time. He'd imagined the scenario countless times. He'd been a boy then. He was older now and wise enough to know the difference between fantasy and reality. They'd buried her. She was gone forever.

"What about Mom?"

"We know how much she loved us, right?" Cale asked. "I mean, there's no question in either of our minds about that."

Danny shook his head, and Cale knew it was true. Ellie had loved them both with all her heart. Reaching beneath the chair, he unfolded the medical transcripts and handed them to Danny. "Four years before I met your mother, she almost died."

"Her appendix burst," Danny said, his voice edged with impatience. "There was an infection, complications. That's why she couldn't have any more kids after me. She loved kids too. She said that was why she liked working in the neonatal unit at the hospital. That way she could hold babies all day. She used to say that between us and those babies, her life was complete.''

"I believe that was true, Daniel. But look at the date on the top of those papers.''

Danny glanced at it. ''So?''

Cale's chest ached with what he had to say. ''That date was nearly a year and a half before you were born.''

Cale waited for the implications to sink in. He wasn't surprised it didn't take long. ''But she said the infection damaged her insides so she couldn't have babies.''

"It did.''

Danny jumped to his feet, the papers fluttering to the porch floor. ''The date on the form has to be wrong.''

Cale stood too. ''Yesterday, I drove to the hospital in North Carolina where her surgery was performed. The date is correct.''

Danny tore off the porch, only to turn abruptly. ''Then where did she get me? And why is her name on my birth certificate?''

Cale heard the anguish in his own voice as he said, ''That I don't know.''

Danny's hands squeezed into fists at his sides. ''Then she wasn't my real mother?''

"She loved you.''

"This sucks.''

He wasn't going to get any argument from Cale.

Daniel spun away. His first impulse was to run. But darkness had fallen while they'd been talking. It closed in on the ridges, the trees, him. He might have been able to find his way to the cabin in the dark, but what then? He remembered the night he'd lain awake, sick as a dog after eating wild berries. He paced to the edge of the driveway, peered into the shadows, scowled. The only thing worse than living through an unending night was living through it in a remote cabin without screens or lights or indoor plumbing.

"Have you eaten?" Cale called.

Danny shook his head, and Cale said, "Might as well come inside."

A lot of people couldn't eat a bite in stressful situations. He and Cale polished off a frozen pizza and a pint of ice cream. Lying in the bed upstairs, Danny heard Sam come back at midnight. There was a low murmur of voices, and then all was quiet.

Daniel was up before daybreak. He dressed hurriedly. After scribbling a note, he set off for the hills at first light.

He went to the old cabin first. Everything was pretty much the way he'd left it. The corner where the raccoon had slept was empty, the bed unbelievably narrow, the remains of the last loaf of bread he'd bought, green.

He wandered to the creek where he'd washed his clothes and to the pool where he'd taken more than one frigid bath. From there he hiked over to the ridge the Indians used to call Night Shadow, where the eagle so often soared. There was a feather lying near a huge outcropping of rocks. Daniel picked it up and thought about the feathers his mom had shown him when he'd been small.

His mom. She wasn't his mom. Then, who was she? She'd raised him. Did that make her his mother? He didn't know. He just didn't know. He fell asleep waiting for the eagle to make his majestic appearance and dreamed they were back in Columbus, the three of them, his mom, his dad, and him.

He woke up itching to get moving again. Setting off in no particular direction, he ended up near the trail where Willow had discovered the trapped raccoon. He waited, holding perfectly still until he thought he would come out of his skin. This time, his patience paid off. A raccoon with a noticeable limp ambled little more than a dozen feet away.

Daniel followed her until she climbed into a hole in the side of a tree. It seemed like forever before she came out again. When she'd disappeared into the underbrush, Daniel crept to the tree and peered inside. There lay a fat baby raccoon, sound asleep.

He touched the creature gently. The raccoon stirred, cowering. Obviously afraid, his memory short, he made a sound that brought the adult charging toward her den.

Daniel backed away quickly. He was satisfied to know the raccoons were doing well; he didn't want to disturb them anymore. He looked up at the sky, surprised to discover the tears running down his face. Taking a deep breath, Daniel started down the mountain toward the cabin of the man who had always been there, helping him stand on his own, catching him when he fell, remaining steadfast, and honest. His dad.

Miranda was ready when Cale arrived to pick her up for the trip up to Lavender's house. She and Gwen had talked long into the night. It had led to some intense soul searching. She'd taken Cale into her bed and into her heart. She believed he cared about her, but there was a part of him, a huge part, that he kept hidden. She could live without romance, but she had too much pride to settle for scraps.

"Hello, Cale." There was a slight chance she'd said it a trifle too sweetly, because Cale's smile slipped a little.

He glanced around, undoubtedly searching for the reason behind her nearly concealed displeasure. "Did Gwen leave?"

Of course. Gwen. It couldn't have been anything he'd done or hadn't done. Miranda locked her door behind her. "She left hours ago. I'm sure she's already arrived in Atlanta and is reporting back to our parents that I'm just fine and dandy as we speak."

"Are you fine and dandy?"

It was possible that she waited a smidgen too long to say, "Why do y'all ask?" She retrieved her medical bag from her Explorer, then climbed into Cale's truck as he held the door for her. Smoothing her skirt around her, she smiled sweetly. It felt good to use her feminine wiles. If it made him squirm just a little, so be it. She'd tried telling herself she had no right to complain. The heck she didn't. She'd shared her bed with him. She'd shared the horrors of her past. It was about time he fessed up and did a little sharing of his own.

"Is something wrong, Miranda?"

She batted her eyelashes at him. "Why, Cale, that's usually my line."

Cale's eyebrows lifted.

"I don't know why you would think such a thing. I mean, I haven't once clamped my mouth shut and retreated to my dark and gloomy cave. That is what you men do, isn't it, especially those who are all shoulders and sulk to begin with."

Miranda could see Cale looking at her and knew he was confused. He'd put the engine in gear and started up the mountain. "Please keep your eyes on the road."

He brought the truck to a crawl and reached a hand to her face. "I'm sorry, Miranda."

"Whatever for? No, let me think. Are you sorry for sharing your body but not your mind or your heart or a thousand other things that make you whole? Or are you sorry for landing in this meadow in the first place?"

"I'd like to explain."

He took his eyes off the road again. There was so much open longing in those blue depths, she didn't care if they hit a tree. "Are you sorry you crash-landed in the meadow in the first place, Cale?"

"I'm not sorry for that, because then I wouldn't have met you."

His declaration stole over her like sunshine, taking the wind out of her sails and putting hope back in her heart. She'd thought she was falling in love with him. Now she was sure. Oh, she'd thought she'd been in love before, once, but that had been a long time ago. And it had never felt like this. Every day she was with Cale felt brand new.

"I know I can be an insensitive clod. I sure as hell don't deserve you. But you're the best thing that's happened to me in a long time. I'd planned to tell you this later, in private, not while we're pulling into Lavender's driveway."

She turned her head. Joshua and Jeremiah were playing on the gate. "M'randa! Come see Mama and the new baby."

Miranda allowed them to take her hands and draw her toward the house. Cale followed with her medical bag. She glanced over her shoulder and smiled at the sight of him with the young boys dogging his steps. Miranda went ahead. By the time he entered the house, Lavender was halfway through the explanation about how the little girls were staying with her brother and sister-in-law until she got her strength back and how Lucille and Emory had wanted her and the baby to stay with them for a while. Lavender had decided it was best for her marriage for her and her young husband to stay in their own house.

"Wanna hold the baby?" Joshua asked Cale.

"If it's all right with you and your mama, I think I'll wait until she puts on a few pounds. The baby, that is."

Lavender smiled tiredly. There were still circles underneath her eyes, but she was already starting to look better.

"Come on, boys," she said, moving slowly toward the kitchen. "Let's us get Mr. Wilder somethin' to drink while Miranda rocks your sister."

Miranda had already picked up the baby and was getting settled in the rocker. "She always holds 'em," Lavender said to Cale. "She rocks the newborns, croons out-of-tune lullabies to the toddlers, whispers words of comfort and encouragement to those that are old enough to talk. She's got a way with 'em, no doubt about that."

Lavender reached into the refrigerator for a pitcher of apple juice. Pouring a portion into three plastic cups, she said, "I was gonna name the new baby Miranda and call her Randy after her daddy. But I figured having two Mirandas on the mountain might get confusing. Plus, there's already one Randy in this family."

Lavender Sprague was no dummy. "What did you decide on, then?" Cale asked.

"I named her Glorianna. The doctor said there aren't going to be any more babies. I figure we might as well go out with glory."

Cale and Miranda left soon after Lucille and Emory returned. Church bells were ringing in the distance as Cale pulled the truck off the road near Needy Creek. "Where are we going?" Miranda asked.

He reached for her hand, drawing her across the seat and out the door on his side. "To the creek."

Cale knew there was work awaiting Miranda and problems awaiting him. He didn't want to return to them, at least not yet. For a few minutes, he wanted to simply be a man walking with a beautiful woman along a shady creek bank on a balmy Sunday morning. And that was what they did. Miranda picked wildflowers and pointed out an unusual stone. When he tossed it into the creek, she gasped. "Do you have any idea how long it took that little rock to get out of that creek?"

"How long?"

"Perhaps millions of years." When he bent at the waist, she said, "What are you doing?"

"Rescuing that stone."

Miranda kicked off her sandals and rolled up her pant legs, following Cale to the creek's edge. The water was cool and invigorating. Finding that stone proved to be like searching for a needle in a haystack. They ended up splashing like children. Cale reached a finger to her chin. Tipping her face up, he kissed her. The water made a soothing sound as it meandered over the rocky creek bed and swirled around their ankles. The breeze feathered through her hair, lifting the lightest tendrils. When the kiss ended, she turned her face into the breeze and said, "Smell that air? It was the first thing I noticed when I came back here."

They climbed out of the water and sat on the grassy bank while their feet dried in the sun. Cale noted the subtle change in Miranda's mood, but still he was surprised when she started to talk about the rape.

"After it happened, the world lost its beauty, its color. Every sound hurt my ears, every surface was so rough, it left my skin feeling raw. I thought I was going crazy. I was bleeding—figuratively, emotionally. It wasn't until I faced my fear and returned here that I truly began to heal. It didn't happen overnight, but here the breezes felt soft, the wind in the trees, the call of birds and the scuttle of animals, lulled me. My days took on a new rhythm. I found purpose here."

"And you grew strong again."

He felt her hand tighten around his. Something warm and soothing inched through his veins, climbing up his arm, seeping toward his chest. He was glad she could open up to him and hoped she felt as soothed by his touch.

They drove back to her place in companionable silence. Cale thought about some of the ways life had of making people strong. Him, Miranda, Ruby, Daniel, even Lavender Sprague.

"Wasn't that baby the most beautiful, perfect child?" Miranda asked when they reached her front porch.

Cale tended to prefer kids after they'd grown into their skin and had gained control of their muscles. "You'd make a wonderful mother, Miranda."

Her silence drew his scrutiny. He'd noticed that she'd skirted the issue of motherhood before. "I know a lot of women choose to establish their careers before having a family," he said, "but I'm surprised some man, either from Atlanta or Timbuktu or from right here on the mountain hasn't slapped a ring on your finger and given you a baby or two by now."

A wave of sorrow passed through her eyes. In a voice that quavered, so deep and emotion filled that he barely recognized it, she said, "I had a child once. A baby boy."

Everything inside Cale went perfectly still. Miranda's words sent a dull ache of foreboding crawling down his spine. He wanted to cover his ears. He held perfectly still and waited for her to continue.

past, "I know I could have terminated the pregn...
...very... I couldn't bear to destroy... innocent human...
...of the man who raped me, but... a child, defenseless...
and dependent on me, like...

CHAPTER
TWENTY-ONE

Miranda looked out across her lush garden. She hadn't intended to talk about this. It never left her completely, but delivering a baby always brought it back to the surface—the pain, the love, the sadness of letting go. "In my mind," she said to Cale, "I can still see him, his downy hair, his serious gray eyes, his perfectly shaped fingers and toes."

"Was he a . . ." Cale's voice trailed away.

"A product of the rape?" she finished for him. "Yes." Her hand shook as she reached for her keys. She must have decided against going inside, because she slipped her shaking hand, keys and all, into her pocket. "There are only three other people in the world who have ever known about this, Cale. Ruby, Aunt Verdie, and Nora."

Cale closed his eyes. Ellie had known. The evidence was mounting, growing more staggering with every passing day. He could no longer chalk these things up to coincidence. "Where is the child now?" He feared he already knew the answer.

"I pray he's out there somewhere in this great big world, happy, and bright, and oblivious to the way he was conceived." She looked past him, into the distance or into the past. "I know I could have terminated the pregnancy. By the time I realized I was pregnant, I'd already felt the first tiny flutter of life. I thought I was going crazy. You'd think that would have driven me over the edge if anything would have, and yet it was that tiny life that made me hold on to mine."

Cale made certain she didn't hear his shuddering breath. For a long time, he'd felt as if Ellie's death had scattered the pieces of his life into the wind. One by one, the pieces were falling into place, forming a reality he felt ill equipped to deal with. He tried to picture Miranda as she'd been then, eighteen, clinging to her sanity by a thread, and pregnant with a child that had resulted from a savage act. "I don't know how you lived through it, Miranda."

"There were times I thought I wouldn't. But Nora was there, holding me when I shook, crying with me at the injustices of the world, encouraging me when I faltered, loving me always."

Tears blurred Cale's vision. The love Miranda spoke of, he'd felt too.

Miranda sniffled. "I became a hermit, living in one of Aunt Verdie's remote cabins high in the hills. Nora stayed with me through the morning sickness and the nightly terror and finally my labor. I'd carried my child inside me for eight and a half months. And then I held him in my arms for one night. I tried not to love him, but I did. He was precious, Cale, perfect in every way, and yet I found myself searching his face for a likeness to any of the men up here. What could an eighteen-year-old girl who was afraid of her own shadow offer a helpless, innocent child?"

"So you placed him in the empty arms of the dear, gentle young woman who had, in many ways, saved your life."

"Aunt Verdie wrote Nora's name on the birth certificate. Legally, it might have been wrong, but morally, it was the most right thing I've ever done. I couldn't have cared for him, Cale. And yet I cried for months after they'd gone."

There was one last thing Cale didn't understand. "Why have you never heard from them?"

A tear trailed down Miranda's cheek. "I made Nora promise not to tell anyone and not to contact me unless something happened to the baby. If I hadn't severed all ties, I couldn't have gone forward, and neither could she."

Ellie had said that this mountain was the place she'd loved the most. And yet she'd never come back here. It was the price she'd paid for getting Danny. Because in the end she'd loved Danny more than anything else. She'd loved Cale too. Not enough to tell him the truth. Or maybe one had nothing to do with the other. Maybe it was enough to know that she'd loved him with her whole heart. And she'd loved Danny no matter how he'd been conceived. She'd loved Miranda too, so much that she'd taken their secret with her to her grave.

Cale had been prepared to tell Miranda that he was falling in love with her. Uncertainty kept him silent. He had to consider what was best for Danny. He had to consider what was best for Miranda too. He couldn't tell her the truth, and he couldn't open his arms to her.

Miranda didn't understand the barely controlled tension in Cale. His fingers were flexed, his expression unreadable. She'd bared her soul. And Cale had withdrawn emotionally and physically. A slap would have hurt her less.

She was the first to notice the boy standing near the sourwood tree. "Daniel's here," she whispered.

Cale turned his head. Realizing he'd made fists out of both hands, he slid them into his pockets and took another quick step back. Danny started toward them. He'd spent the night in the remote cabin in the hills. From the looks of the dark circles under his eyes, it had been a long night. When he was small, Ellie had always known when he was coming down with something, be it a cold, the flu, or strep throat, by the shade of the smudges beneath his eyes. Today, they were the color of bruises. Cale doubted they had a physical cause.

Miranda's eyes were hooded too. As Danny neared, Cale couldn't ignore the enormity of what he knew. Danny wanted the truth. Miranda had taken life-altering steps hours after his birth to protect him from the truth. What in the hell was Cale going to do?

"Hello, Daniel."

Danny strolled closer, drawn to Miranda's soft voice as to cool shade on a sweltering day. Before he could return the greeting, his dad said, "What are you doing here?"

Miranda must have noticed the sharp edge in Cale's voice too, because she looked at him strangely. Danny said, "I came to ask Miranda if she wanted me to work tomorrow."

"You aren't going to have much time to work for Miranda. I'm going to need your help."

Now both Danny and Miranda looked at him strangely. "Doing what?" Danny asked.

Cale said the first thing he could think of. "I would appreciate your help fixing the airplane. You said you had a list of names of kids who might be willing to help. The damage to the plane itself was minimal. We're going to have to clear the meadow, lengthen the runway. I need your help, Danny. I don't want any argument."

Miranda didn't understand Cale. She felt drained, empty. Her emotions were a shambles, her mind reeling from her memories of the past. She and Cale had reached the point where their relationship needed to be resolved. Once again, she'd been open with him, and he'd turned gruff, shutting her out. She wasn't sure she could do this anymore. "It sounds as if you're going to be busy," she said to Danny. Her voice sounded as hollow as she felt. "I haven't paid you for the last day you worked."

"You don't have to—"

She cut him off, saying, "You earned it. I'll be back in a moment."

She turned then, unlocking the door with a shaky hand. When she returned, Cale and Danny had squared off opposite each other much the way they had the first time she'd seen them together when Danny had returned the thermos of milk. Her mind burned with other memories, her eyes clouding with tears. Keeping them in check, she held the money out for Danny. His reluctance was evident, but he took it, murmuring a thank-you before turning away.

She had to meet Cale's gaze next. She didn't know what demons he was fighting. Was he afraid to love her? Would he ever be free to love her? "What is it?" she asked. "Does it have something to do with your Ellen?"

For a moment, he looked as bereft as she felt, but he nodded gruffly and simply said, "Yes."

He'd retreated emotionally. She couldn't help him from behind the invisible barriers he'd erected.

Cale glanced over his shoulder. Danny had stomped off and had already reached the gate. Cale had spent weeks trying to reach his son, and now he'd angered him. Even worse, he'd hurt Miranda.

For a moment, when Miranda had first returned to the porch, he'd nearly blurted out his feelings, but then he'd seen the way she'd stared at Danny's outstretched hand. The more Cale tried to ignore the truth, the more it persisted. The nightmares that had returned, the fear and panic she relived, the hands that had mauled her, groped her, the man who had violated her. It had all come back to haunt her since Danny had returned.

The thought froze in Cale's brain. He was going to be sick.

Miranda was looking at him, waiting, as if giving him one last chance. After interminable seconds, she turned her back on him and went inside.

Cale swiped the sweat from his brow before taking the wrench Clyde Sturgis handed him. They'd been working on the plane for four days. The flat tire had been fixed, the metal bumped out, the bent propeller replaced. In the distance, three teenage boys wrestled a large rock onto a trailer. Danny worked side by side with Bubba Gillespie and a kid named Isaac, but he spoke only when spoken to. He wasn't talking to Cale at all.

Miranda wasn't speaking to him either. He'd run into her

twice in town. She'd averted her gaze, but not before he'd seen the disappointment and sadness on her face. Anger would have been easier to accept. Cale didn't see what choice he had.

Tensions seemed to be high throughout Dawsons Hollow. Everywhere he went, folks were talking about the way Randy Sprague had deserted his family. Everyone seemed sympathetic except Ruthie Pratt, who seemed more pleased than sorry that things weren't working out for the younger woman. Although more difficult to read, J.R. wasn't exactly friendly either. Cale didn't have time to worry about what bur the eldest Pratt had up his nose. Cale had problems of his own. He wanted to get the airplane fixed, a makeshift runway cleared, so that he and Danny could leave, and he could put an end to all this restless tossing and turning and yearning.

A car pulled up. As she had the past three days, Ruby parked in the area they'd cleared of rocks and trees, then took a picnic basket and a gallon jug of lemonade from the backseat. Everyone except Cale stopped working and gathered around her.

When they were finished today, she hefted the basket and carried it to the airplane. As if thoroughly exasperated with him, she said, "It's like taking the mountain to Mohammed." She waited until he'd polished off a tall glass of lemonade to say any more. "No sense asking how you are. You're as miserable as Miranda. Guess that's some consolation."

The sound Ruby made came from the back of her throat. Cale remembered the first time he'd heard her make it. It had been the morning after he'd crash-landed his plane, the morning after he'd met Miranda.

"Oh, she's doing everything she can to try to hide it, but she's miserable all right. You hurt her."

"I'm sorry."

"That's it? That's all you have to say?"

Cale didn't know what to tell her. "I understand Miranda's

need to lay her ghosts to rest. I know why she came back here initially. But why did she stay?''

Ruby ran a hand down the front of her faded housedress, her eyes on Clyde Sturgis in the distance. ''She says the mountain spoke to her.''

Cale made a derogatory sound.

''What's the matter?'' Ruby sputtered. ''Haven't you ever heard a stream babble? The wind sigh? A meadow whisper?''

''Those are metaphors.''

''Meta-whats?''

''Mountains, brooks, and breezes aren't alive. They can't talk.''

''I didn't say they talk. I said spoke. Speakin' and talkin's two different things. Like healing and doctoring, lustin' and lovin'.''

Cale was staring at the partially eaten sandwich in his hand, but it wasn't the bread that was hard to swallow. ''What I feel for Miranda is a helluva lot more than lust.''

''You have strange ways of showing it.'' Ruby studied Cale. ''Miranda said she told you about the baby.''

Cale nodded.

''Knowing that, can't you understand why Miranda's stayed here all these years? If there was a chance, no matter how small, that the baby I bore and never stopped lovin' wanted to find me someday, I'd stick close to the place he was born so he wouldn't have to look far, wouldn't you?''

Cale stared into Ruby's eyes, wondering if she knew. She looked across the makeshift airstrip where Clyde was working with the boys. ''Miranda thinks the reason you've turned your back on her is because you're afraid to love again. I think there's more to it than that.'' She met Cale's gaze. ''I ain't got all the answers, but I think that boy of yours is a big part of the puzzle. I've heard you talk about your Ellie. Miranda thinks her name was Ellen. Was it?''

Cale shook his head. And Ruby closed her eyes. She didn't say any more. She just gathered up her picnic basket and left. Cale went back to work on his airplane, but his heart wasn't in it. If Ruby was figuring out the truth, it was just a matter of time before Miranda did.

Had Miranda stayed here all these years hoping her child would return? If so, the truth wouldn't hurt her. Hope surged, only to be dashed all over again, because even if it wouldn't hurt Miranda, what about Danny?

"Ellie," he whispered, only to stop. He didn't know what to wish for. He needed divine intervention. Hell, he needed a miracle.

"That man's aching for you, and yet he won't come to you." Ruby straightened year-old magazines and picked up the toys scattered throughout the waiting area in the Morningstar clinic.

Miranda flipped the appointment book closed and sighed. She'd been having a difficult time concentrating all week. Ruby's incessant chatter wasn't helping.

"He's keeping secrets," Ruby declared, fitting the pieces of a wood puzzle into their proper places. "Why do you suppose that is?"

Miranda stood, strode to the window, only to return to the desk and the appointment book. If she knew the answer to that, she might be able to understand what drove Cale and what held him back. If he loved her, truly loved her, what possible reason could he have for keeping it from her? "He hasn't been honest with me, Ruby. Lies of omission are lies just the same. If he isn't ready to fall in love, to have a relationship, he should have told me."

"Maybe he isn't the one who isn't ready."

Miranda turned to stare at her friend. "What do you mean?"

Ruby said, "Folks have to be ready for the truth before they can face it. The airplane's fixed, the meadow is nearly cleared. Pretty soon he's gonna fly outta here. Then it'll be too late."

Miranda was afraid it was already too late.

Ruby left, and Miranda meandered into the back room, where her state-of-the-art medical equipment was stored.

She felt certain Ruby had been trying to tell her something. What in the world did she mean, a person had to be ready for the truth? Who wasn't ready? Cale or her?

If Cale wasn't holding back because of his feelings for Ellie, what was holding him back? The truth, Ruby had said. What truth? Did Cale know something that could hurt her?

It was almost as if he were trying to protect her. Protect her from what?

Questions. They were driving her to distraction. She couldn't eat or sleep or concentrate. Even working in the garden brought little relief or pleasure. Drawing herself up, she forced herself to tackle her filing system. Three files into the task, she found herself staring at her hand.

Hands, she thought, turning hers over. They had the power to touch, heal, nurture, console, and, sometimes, hurt. The psychologist once told her that she might never get over her preoccupation with hands. She always noticed the shape, texture, and size of a person's hands before she noticed anything else. Ruby's hands were chapped. Aunt Verdie's had been crippled with arthritis. Cale's were work roughened, strong. He was no healer, but those hands had the power to ignite her passion. Lavender's were long and narrow. Daniel's grip was strong for someone so young, his fingers blunt tipped, his—

Her own hand blurred before her eyes, then slowly came up to cover her mouth. Oh, my God. Another man on this mountain had had hands like those. Her mind reeled, short-circuited, then stopped altogether, only to rush forward all over again.

It was ludicrous. Impossible. And yet it wasn't. That was what Cale had been trying to protect her from. The evidence he'd discovered about his dear Ellie, the biological father Daniel was seeking. Ellie's name couldn't have been Ellen. It must have been Eleanora.

Nora.

Oh, Nora. A tear rolled down Miranda's face, for Nora had died.

Cale was protecting her from the truth. More important, he was protecting his son. Her son.

It wasn't until she heard the outer door open that she remembered she'd forgotten to lock it after Ruby left. "That you, Ruby?"

There was no answer.

"Cale?"

She saw a shadow on the other side of the doorway. Miranda rose to her feet moments before the shadow materialized into the shape of a person. The eyes staring into hers were blue, but they weren't the vivid blue of Cale's. These eyes glittered, as if crazed.

Daniel picked up a broom handle and poked it into the washing machine. Stupid machine. Stupid aching muscles and stupid blisters on his hands. He yanked the plug out of the wall, and the horrendous chugging stopped. In the aftermath of so much racket, he heard a sniffle and a shuddering sob.

Cale was out front, puttering on that stupid truck. Daniel glanced behind him into the underbrush and trees. Someone was in the shadows, a yellow ribbon in her hair. "Willow?" he called softly.

The sniffling and sobbing grew louder. "I don't want you to see me like this, b-b-but I didn't know where else to go."

"Willow, it's all right." He ventured closer. She stayed where she was, rocking back and forth, her arms and legs drawn up close to her body. Daniel ducked beneath some low-hanging branches, then went down on his knees before her. "Ah, Willow, what happened?" Her lip was cracked, one eye swollen shut. "Who did this to you?"

She sobbed uncontrollably, unable to talk. Daniel didn't know what to do. Relying on instinct, he wrapped his arms around her and hugged her gently. She cried as if her heart were breaking. "I'm ugly, and I'm awful." Her voice broke. "I'm a disappointment. There's something wrong with me, something that makes me impossible to love."

"Oh, Willow. There's nothing wrong with you. Who did this?''

Instead of answering, she sobbed. "Your family is supposed to love you no matter what, right? Why can't mine?''

Daniel was starting to breathe easier. At first he'd been afraid that some man had forced himself on Willow. But it seemed only her face had been injured. The poor thing. He wondered if this was the first time one of her brothers had hit her. Anger roiled up inside him. He wanted to demand to know which one had done it, but Willow was already upset. He drew away from her slightly. Reaching out his hand, he placed it ever so gently over her swollen eye.

A sense of calm came over Willow. She closed her eyes. Warmth shimmered, radiating from the tips of Daniel's fingers, soaking into her skin one layer at a time. She'd felt as if shards of glass were poking her cheekbone and the socket of her eye. The pain became less cutting, gradually easing into a dull ache. She opened her good eye as Daniel touched her cracked lip with his finger. The pain eased there as well.

"You have the touch. Just like Miranda." She started to cry again. "I'm the seventh child of the seventh child, and yet you're the one with the power. I didn't mean to be a disappointment, honest. I can't help it. I don't know how to do the things you and Miranda do."

He and Miranda. He and Miranda. He and Miranda.

Scenes flashed through Daniel's mind. Miranda, locking her doors when no one else on the mountain did. The warmth in her touch, the tenderness in her eyes, the way he felt so drawn to her, as if he'd known her in another life. The date on the top of his mom's medical transcripts, the way Cale had clammed up and closed himself off. The way he tossed and turned at night and barked orders during the day.

Daniel removed his hands and drew back. "What do you mean, I'm like Miranda?''

Willow sniffled. "You've got the power. Remember how that wild dog that had me cornered ran away when he looked at you? And that baby raccoon? You saved his life. And the trapped raccoon's too. Are you sure you're not a seventh child of a seventh child?''

Daniel found it difficult to swallow. The seventh child of the seventh child. Willow had once told him that her father had been the seventh child in his family. And Miranda locked her doors. And Cale knew something he wasn't saying.

Daniel hated what he was thinking. ''Willow, when were you born? What day?''

''What day of the week?''

''No. What date?''

''July ninth, why?''

Daniel couldn't explain everything swirling through his brain. But he'd been born on June seventh. A month earlier than Willow. Daniel had wanted to know who his biological father was. His mom had been trying to tell him something in his dreams. The truth, she'd said, was close at hand. He stared at his hands and remembered the way Miranda had stared at them a few days before.

Oh, my God!

''Daniel, what is it?''

Willow's voice brought him back to the present. She looked pathetic, her face swollen, bruised, streaked with tears. ''Come inside,'' he said. ''We'll wash your face and get you something to drink.''

He jumped to his feet, pulling Willow up with him.

Willow took a shuddering breath and followed Daniel inside. She felt shaky, emotional, weepy. Daniel was handing her a warm washcloth when Cale came in. He took one look at her face and rushed toward her. ''You've been beaten.''

She started to cry again. ''It's my fault. J.R. told me to stay away from Daniel. He warned me.''

Anger roiled inside Cale. He stormed toward the door. ''There are laws to protect children. He won't get away with this.''

''He? But, Cale . . .''

''You don't have to be ashamed, Willow. It isn't your fault. J.R. did this to you, didn't he?''

''J.R.?''

She rushed out to the porch, stopping him before he'd opened his truck's door. "J.R. didn't hit me." Her voice broke; fresh tears coursed down her face. "My mother did."

Daniel came up behind Willow, and Cale returned to the porch. Words began tumbling out of Willow's mouth. "I had just gotten home from the store when I heard a terrible racket. I hurried toward my room. She was there. She'd overturned my nightstand, broken my lamp. She was tearing up all the pictures I'd taken for Miranda. She clutched the photos of Daniel, and she started screaming that it wasn't fair. She said no wonder he'd looked familiar. She was supposed to have the seventh child. And now he'd come here, and everyone would know. All those years she put up with my dad climbing on top of her and sweating like a pig. All those times she put up with him calling her fat and lazy. She said she did it all so she could have the seventh child. I was supposed to be that child. She said it the first time she hit me. My lip cracked open, and I fell. She hit me again and again. By the time she was finished, she was crying, sobbing that she didn't mean to. It was that woman, she said. It was all that woman's fault."

"What woman, Willow?" Cale asked.

Willow was crying, making it difficult to speak. "Miranda."

Cale clenched his mouth tight and tried to force the sickening feeling of impending doom away. Ruthie sounded crazy to him. "You two stay here."

He rushed back to his truck. He had to reach Miranda before it was too late.

CHAPTER
TWENTY-TWO

Miranda's house was locked up tight when Cale got there. Damn. Where was she? He jumped back into his truck and sped toward town. Ignoring all the people who stopped to stare as he passed, he slammed to a stop in front of Pratt's Grocery Store and raced inside.

"Where's Ruthie!"

Tommy Lee Pratt sneered. "She ain't here."

Cale could see that. "I said, where is she?"

"What's it to ya?"

He grabbed the boy by the front of the shirt. Tommy Lee had just turned twenty. Suddenly, he didn't feel so brave. "She went to the clinic. What a hypocrite. Would never let any of us set foot in the place."

J.R. was walking in the back door as Cale rushed out the front. He'd just come from delivering groceries. He glanced at his younger brother, who was smoothing the wrinkles from his shirt. "What was Wilder doing here?" he asked.

Tommy Lee sneered. "The jerk came bustin' in here like he owns the place, demanding to know where Ma is."

J.R. peered around. "Where is she?"

"Went storming out of here ten minutes ago, sputterin' something about Miranda doing her wrong."

"Oh, no." J.R. threw down the empty carton and followed the path Cale had taken.

Cale ducked low when he passed the windows in Miranda's clinic. As quietly as possible, he let himself in the back door. Ruthie Pratt's voice carried to his ears, shrill, loud, nasty. He had no idea what she was capable of. She'd beaten Willow. Had she snapped?

"I wish I'd never laid eyes on you," Ruthie practically hissed. "You just had to come to this mountain, didn't you? I thought I was rid of you, but you had to come back."

Miranda thought she heard a sound in the back hall, but she didn't take her eyes off Ruthie. The woman had been ranting and raving for the past fifteen minutes, saying the same thing over and over. So far, all Miranda's efforts to calm her only incensed her more.

"It's all your fault. You came here, pretending to be sweet and innocent, wearing your expensive little clothes, laughing, carrying on. I'd see Jonas up at our house, watchin' you. A pretty little thing like you, barely older than his own kids, always flitting around, laughing with that little redhead. At first, I thought that's who he was lookin' at. But she was sickly, and you weren't. And you knew it."

Perspiration trailed below the V neckline of Miranda's dress. Most of what Ruthie said didn't make sense. Pieced together, it sent chills down Miranda's spine. Ruthie had taken a letter opener from her pocket and was running her fingers along its edge.

All these years, Miranda had sensed Ruthie's dislike, but she'd never imagined the reason. Jonas, Ruthie's husband, had watched her? Miranda hadn't known. But Ruthie had. Somehow, she'd known about the rape too. She'd twisted it in her mind, blaming Miranda.

"You lured Jonas away from me."

"I didn't, Ruthie. I never even looked at him." Miranda

could barely remember what Jonas Pratt had looked like. But she remembered the sound of his voice, the feel of his breath on her face, the texture of his horrible, horrible hands, the pain he'd inflicted when he'd raped her. Her stomach pitched; she was going to be sick. "I didn't, Ruthie. I swear to God I didn't."

"That's a lie," Ruthie said, spittle running down the side of her chin. "And now the child with the power, the seventh child of the seventh child, is here. He bears only a slight resemblance to Jonas." Ruthie took a step closer. "But he's built like him, tall and handsome, and he has his hands."

Oh, Daniel, Miranda thought. After all these years, he was here in Dawsons Hollow.

"I thought I fixed you when I got pregnant." Ruthie clutched the letter opener, pressing the tip into the palm of her hand with so much force, blood dripped onto the floor. "I thought you'd gone by then. Good riddance. But one night I followed Jonas in the dark, and I caught him lookin' in Verdie Cook's windows. I was eight months pregnant with Willow. I was going to be the mother of the seventh child of the seventh child. Know what he said to me? He told me I was fat and lazy, and you beat me to it. And he laughed. He laughed so hard, he stumbled and started to fall. And I let him."

"And so did I."

Ruthie and Miranda both turned as J. R. Pratt stepped into view, Cale close behind him.

"You were there?" Ruthie asked her oldest son, her voice so shrill, it hurt Cale's ears.

Nodding, J.R. crept steadily closer. "I followed him that night too. I saw him peeking in Miranda's windows. He was drunk, and I could hear him mumbling about how good he was, what a good time he'd shown her, and how he couldn't wait to have her again. I heard what he said to you, Ma. I was too far away to do anything when he stumbled toward the edge of the cliff. I didn't even try."

"But you were just a boy," Ruthie cried.

"I was sixteen. Old enough to know what he'd done.

Miranda didn't do anything. You know that. He raped her."
He looked at Miranda next. "He was dead. And then you
left the mountain. What good would it have done to tell
people?"

J.R.'s face was etched with grief and sorrow. All these
years, he'd known. Miranda wondered if it would have
helped ease her fears if she'd known the rapist was dead.
Probably. But J.R. had been a boy, no more than a year or
two older than Daniel was right now. He'd been busy step-
ping into the role of man of the family. He'd done his best
by his younger brothers and sisters.

"Put the knife down, Ma," he said. "It's over."

"Yes, Mama, it's over." It was Willow's voice, thick
with tears. Daniel was with her. Miranda's heart lurched
with longing.

"You don't wanna hurt anybody," Willow said, starting
to cry again.

Ruthie stared at Willow's swollen eye and cracked lip.
Then, as if seeing her hands for the first time, she stared at
the blood dripping to the floor. "I was the prom queen, the
prettiest girl on the mountain. Everyone said so. My people
were poor, but your daddy's family owned three stores. If
I married him, I knew I would never be poor again. He was
always a braggart, but after we got married, he turned mean
too. I threatened to leave him. He told me I was nothin'
without him. And he was right."

Ruthie was crying now too, still staring at her bloody
hands. "My only chance to be anything at all was to be the
mother of the seventh child of a seventh child. And now
I've beaten my own girl."

Cale and J.R. both moved closer to Ruthie. "I'm okay,
Mama," Willow said. "It looks worse than it is. It barely
hurts at all. See?"

Cale gripped Ruthie's wrist. The letter opener clattered
to the floor. She slumped into a chair J.R. slid under her
and sobbed, cradling her cut hand, quietly rocking back and
forth.

Miranda's gaze went around the room, but it settled on

Daniel. He stared at her, his Adam's apple bobbing slightly. Love welled up in her heart, along with pride and yearning and awe.

He glanced around the room too, lighting on Cale. "You knew, didn't you? You figured it out."

Cale's voice was thick with emotion as he said, "I put most of the pieces together, but I didn't know about Jonas Pratt until now."

Miranda reached one hand to Cale and one to Daniel. Ruthie continued to cry to herself. J.R. put an arm around Willow's shoulders. "Are you all right?" he asked his sister.

Willow sniffled, but she nodded. And with a dawning look of realization, she exclaimed to Daniel, "Great. Another brother is all I need."

Daniel, Cale, and Miranda all blinked through their tears and smiled.

Miranda hung up the telephone.

"How did they take it?" Cale asked, reaching for her hand.

She'd been talking to her family back in Atlanta for the past forty minutes, explaining everything four separate times to four separate people. Alex, the attorney in the family, had asked the most questions. Gwen, the family journalist, came in at a close second. Threading her fingers through Cale's, Miranda said, "They're all coming first thing in the morning. Mother and Daddy are eager to meet their grandson."

"And don't forget me." Cale's voice shimmered close to her ear.

"Never," she whispered.

They eyed the kids who had grown quiet on opposite ends of the sofa. Both Willow and Daniel appeared to be fast asleep. The knowledge that that boy was her child brought fresh tears to Miranda's eyes.

J.R., Earl, and LeRoy Pratt had taken their mother to a psychiatric hospital downstate. Miranda had offered to keep

Willow for the night. The girl had indicated that she would like to make it a permanent arrangement. Miranda wouldn't mind, but she and Cale hadn't worked out the details yet.

"Miranda?" Cale and Miranda both looked across the room at Danny, who wasn't sleeping after all.

"Yes?" she whispered.

"What am I supposed to call you?"

Cale stepped forward, but it was Miranda who answered. "For now, Miranda works for me." And then, in a voice so emotion filled it was difficult to speak, she said, "Would you like to hear about what your mother was like when I knew her?"

She showed Cale and Daniel the photograph she kept on her bureau in her bedroom. And Daniel retrieved his most recent photo from his wallet. She'd been young and beautiful in the early picture, her eyes bearing a deep sadness. Life had etched composure and dignity in her face in the later picture. Both portrayed a beautiful woman with a smile so warm, it made a person smile in return.

There was wonder in Miranda's voice as she spoke of her friend's humor and tears and joy and a stubborn streak a mile wide. When Miranda stopped talking, Daniel turned his back on them, embarrassed by his tears. A month ago, Cale wouldn't have known how to reach his son. Today, he took the few steps separating them, put an arm around Danny's shoulders and drew him to his chest the way he had when Danny had been small.

Danny took a shuddering breath, and so did Cale. Opening his eyes, Cale slowly extended his arm to Miranda. Tears ran down her cheeks when she stepped into Cale's embrace.

"I'm too old for this," Danny said.

"It'll be our little secret," Miranda whispered.

"Please," Danny implored. "No more secrets."

All three of them raised their heads and looked at one another. They hadn't expected to laugh, but laugh they did.

Sometime later, after Danny had crawled into bed in the spare room and Miranda had covered Willow with a light blanket where she slept on the couch, Curly the cat snuggled up next to her, Cale and Miranda strode out to her porch. Cale recalled the first time he'd seen this cottage. It had been raining, and he'd been delirious. A candle had burned in the window like a beacon. He'd come in search of Danny. He'd found him, and so much more.

"Listen," he whispered, an arm around Miranda's shoulder. "Hear that?"

"The wind in the trees?" she asked.

"Not just the wind, but all of it. It's harmony, Miranda. Nature's harmony. A mighty God's harmony. A soothing harmony. Do you hear it?"

She closed her eyes. "I hear it, Cale."

"Will you marry me, Miranda? And live with me, and Danny, and maybe Willow and our future children, right here on your mountain?"

She rested her head on his shoulder and peered up at the sky that was bright with a million stars. They couldn't hold a candle to the glow in her eyes as she lifted her face toward his. Their kiss was more than a joining of lips. It was a joining of hearts and of lives.

"I like the way you say yes," he said, his voice deep, husky.

He slipped behind her, wrapping his arms around her waist. He felt solid at her back, strong as only a man could be. She thought about the first time she'd seen him, the first time she'd laid her hands on his skin. She'd healed him that night. But he'd healed her too.

Her heart ached with the knowledge that Nora was lost to her forever. And yet it seemed fitting that the people who had loved Eleanora Cook Stanoway Wilder the most loved each other too. High in the north, a star arced across the sky. The Indians used to call shooting stars Spirit Hoppers. Miranda wondered if Nora was saying hello, or, perhaps, good-bye.

Cale drew Miranda tighter to his body, letting her absorb his heat and telling her without words how much he wanted her. "About our future children," she whispered.

"What about them?" he asked close to her ear.

''How many were you thinking?''

''How many would you like?''

Her knees were starting to turn to jelly. ''Oh,'' she said with a smile. ''One or two. Or maybe three.''

He turned her into his arms. ''We can have as many as you want.'' And just before his mouth covered hers again, he said, ''I love you, Miranda. Just so there's no confusion.''

Please turn the page
for an exciting sneak peek
of Sandra Steffen's next
contemporary romance, *Day by Day*,
coming in July 2002
from Zebra Books

CHAPTER ONE

Spencer McKenzie parked on a side street around the corner from Harbor Avenue. Reaching for the dark suit jacket he'd folded over the seat an hour ago, he closed his door and hurried toward Gaylord and Yvonne Wilson's summer home a block away. The breeze was uncommonly warm for an evening in late April. It was the first truly warm weather they'd had in this part of Michigan this year. Shirtsleeve weather, he and his brothers used to call it. He would have preferred to roll up his sleeves and remove his tie. Instead, he slipped into his jacket, smoothed a hand along the length of his lapel, and started up the steps leading to the estate situated at the top of a steep hill overlooking Lake Michigan.

Party balloons bobbed atop the gold-colored strings mooring them to the polished brass railing that meandered upward through well-lit, immaculately tended grounds. Three fourths of the way to the top, Spence paused, taking a moment to appreciate the view behind him. Trilliums were just starting to bloom on the sand dunes. Earlier that day, colorful sailboats had tacked back and forth near the shore. Farther out, yachts and tugs and tankers had skimmed across the horizon.

Tonight, darkness was fast obliterating the line where water met sky. Already, lights dotted the shoreline. In the distance, the beacon of the Grand Haven Lighthouse flashed at the end of the pier. The tourist season was nearly upon them. Local businesses thrived on it. Spence tolerated it, preferring the slower pace of the off-season when Grand Haven belonged to its local residents.

Several of those local residents were standing in small groups when Spence reached the patio on the first level of the Wilson estate. The breeze billowed through imported suits, designer dresses, and some pretty impressive stuffed shirts. It ruffled a toupee or two, but it didn't hinder the guests who had gathered for Gaylord's seventieth birthday celebration. Just as Spence had expected, anybody who was anybody was here. A rising star in the field of architecture, he was considered one of those anybodies, but he was here because his wife, Maggie, was here. Somewhere.

"There you are!" Gaylord's wife, Yvonne, placed an elegantly manicured and garishly bejeweled hand on his arm. "You're late."

Spence leaned down to brush his lips across the perfectly made-up, lined cheek. Yvonne made a clicking sound with her tongue. "All right, all right. I forgive you. The question is, will Maggie?"

He glanced around the courtyard for his wife. "Maggie knew I was going to be late. If she's upset, I'll have to think of some way to make it up to her."

Yvonne's eyes, slightly watery and faded, held warmth and humor. "If I were ten years younger." Looking him up and down, her expression became wry. "Better make that twenty."

"It's a good thing you're not," Spence said, indulging the older woman with one of his rare smiles. "Because that, Maggie wouldn't forgive."

"I'm pleased Maggie doesn't have to worry about that," Yvonne insisted.

For all her social graces, Yvonne Wilson had a voice like a foghorn. Even her whispers could penetrate steel.

Therefore, it wasn't surprising that several of her guests turned to look at them. Abigail Porter, whose husband was a known philanderer, strolled closer. Abigail and Yvonne had been friends for years, but not even Yvonne knew exactly how old her friend was. There wasn't a telling line on Abigail's face. In fact, her latest facelift had raised her eyebrows so far she wore a constant look of dismay.

"Every woman has to worry, darling," she said sadly. "It's the nature of the beast."

Not this beast, Spencer thought, casting another practiced eye around the courtyard for a glimpse of his wife. Since he didn't see Maggie on this level, he excused himself, accepted a glass of wine from a passing waiter, then made his way toward the steps leading to the patio on the next level.

Fifteen years ago, a noted architect from Chicago had designed the Wilson house and the surrounding tiered gardens and patios. Personally, Spence would have used less glass, chrome, and cement and more stone, iron, and other products that lent themselves to warmth and dimension, and blended with the rocky hills, sandy beaches, and jagged shoreline of Lake Michigan.

He wasn't there to critique the architecture. He was here because Maggie had asked him to attend. Although he didn't find her on the second level, either, he knew she was here because nearly everyone he came into contact with spoke of her. He shook hands with Gaylord's attorney, said hello to an accountant, spoke to a real estate tycoon who made it a point to attend all the right parties. Many of these men and women had been born to families who had made their fortunes in the shipping, mining, or railroad industries. Spence's association with the architectural firm of Hastings and Wiley might have been the reason the McKenzies had initially been invited to parties such as this one, but it was Maggie's warmth, charm, and poise that had won their hearts. She was their Cinderella, Grand Haven's princess. It wasn't only the elite who sought her out. Maggie McKenzie was a joiner, a doer, a woman with a dozen causes and a hundred friends. Everyone loved her. And she loved everyone. But she loved Spence most of all. And he loved her. She was the reason he got up every morning and came home every night. She and their two young daughters made his life about as perfect as a man's life could be. It wasn't that other men didn't have what he had. It was just that few men appreciated it the way he did.

It took Spence half an hour to reach the other end of the wide patio. He said hello to the men and women he met along the way, discussing everything from politics and global warming to local building trends. Placing his empty wineglass on another passing waiter's tray, he finally reached the stairs leading to the highest courtyard surrounding the house. This patio, with all its curving walkways, black and white tables and chairs and a host of abstract garden ornaments was the most ornate, and the most crowded.

He spotted Maggie immediately, just as he always did. It was more than her blond hair that made her stand out in a crowd. She was talking to four of her friends from the Ladies Historic Society, who, along with Yvonne's help, had planned tonight's surprise birthday party for Gaylord. It required effort to suppress Spence's grimace at the sight of one of those so-called friends. Jessica Michaels had been married to a friend of Spence's. She'd latched onto Maggie and then had proceeded to make a play for him behind Maggie's back. He'd turned her down cold, of course.

Spence wouldn't have had to tell Maggie. She'd already known. It was no use wondering how she'd guessed. Months later he'd asked her why she continued to be civil to the backstabber. She'd said, "Jessica isn't best friend material, but she can't hurt me, Spence. Only someone you truly love can do that."

He thought about that as he watched Maggie from a distance. The flicker of candlelight and the glow of dozens of Chinese lanterns threaded her hair with gold. Her only jewelry was a narrow watch and the tiny diamond earrings he'd given her for their second wedding anniversary when they'd been struggling beneath the weight of student loans and their first mortgage. She hadn't spoken to him for three days, but she'd worn the earrings every day ever since.

Her dress was a pale shade of blue and loose enough to allow for plenty of movement. It had a rounded neckline in the front and a row of pewter colored buttons down the back. Spence liked that dress, liked the fit and the feel. She claimed it hid the ten pounds she'd battled since Allison had been born six years ago. Spence happened to like where she'd put those ten pounds.

There wasn't a man at the party who could take his eyes off her for an extended period of time. She appeared oblivious to everyone except the people she was talking to at that moment. It wasn't an act. Maggie McKenzie was the most genuine woman he'd ever known.

He was so intent upon watching his wife on the other side of the courtyard that he didn't notice Edgar Millerton's advance until the old codger had stopped directly in front of him, planted his feet, and said, "Spencer, my boy."

And then it was too late. Spence was cornered.

Chewing morosely on a dead cigar, Edgar launched into his favorite topic, his fascination with ground water, sediment, pollutants, microorganisms, and their effect on all of mankind.

It promised to be a long night.

Maggie McKenzie hugged her arms close against a sudden chill. She'd been having a relatively innocent, innocuous conversation with Melissa Bradley and Hannah Lewis before Jessica Hendricks and MaryAnn Petigrue had joined them. Within seconds, the conversation had turned into a he-said, she-said gossip session, interspersed with a large dose of male bashing.

"Come on, Maggie!" Jessica declared. "Give us something lowdown and dirty on Spence."

Maggie pulled a face. "I hate to disappoint you, but I'm drawing a blank."

"Are you telling me Spence doesn't do anything that annoys the hell out of you?"

Maggie ran a quick check through her mind. The truth was, she didn't have many issues with men. Spence wasn't perfect, but she didn't expect him to be. He'd grown up with three brothers, and the toilet seat had been a problem at first. She'd taken a few midnight splashes early in their marriage, but these days they both knew how to work the lid. He had a serious connection with the remote control, and he loved a clean garage but never seemed to notice when the house was a mess.

For lack of anything more serious, she shrugged and said, "Well, he's late for a lot of things."

"Not Peter," Hannah exclaimed. "He's on time for everything, and when I'm running late, he has this look, not to be confused with *a* look or *that* look. I'm talking about *the* look."

"Uh," Melissa Bradley exclaimed. "I know exactly what you're talking about. Aaron does that, too. Ever notice that when you and your husband are getting along, you like most everything about him?"

"And when you're not," MaryAnn Petigrue interrupted, "you don't even like the way he breathes."

Even Maggie smiled at that one.

The surprise party had been a success in every sense of the word. She, Yvonne, and several members of the Ladies Historic Society had planned it down to the tiniest detail, and yet Gaylord had surprised *them* with his announcement that he was making a six-digit donation to the society. It would be all over the papers tomorrow. Tonight, Maggie just wanted the party to wind down so she could go home, kick her shoes off, slip out of her dress, and unwind with Spence.

She'd been feeling strange all day. She wasn't prone to bad moods, and although she'd read about people who had premonitions, she rarely experienced them herself. Her parents, who were doing missionary work in Africa, would have blamed it on atmospheric pressure and a change in the weather pattern. Neither Joseph nor Adelle Fletcher believed in premonitions. Perhaps premonition was too strong a word. It was more like trepidation. Maggie felt antsy, uneasy. For the life of her, she couldn't say why.

She wondered where Spence was. He said he'd be here tonight, and Spencer McKenzie kept his word. She didn't know many women who'd been married nearly thirteen years and still missed their husbands simply because they hadn't seen each other all day. Sometimes, she worried that she loved him too much. How could she love him too much, when he loved her just as fiercely? She was thirty-four years old and incredibly, undeniably happy. No one could ever accuse her of being weak. She didn't cling, and she certainly didn't define herself by her husband's success. It was just that she felt more alive when they were together.

The goose bumps that had been skittering up and down her arms trailed away. More relaxed now, she glanced at the guests scattered throughout the courtyard. Her gaze flitted over dozens of people, but it settled on one man.

Spence.

Their eyes met, held. Something unspoken and powerful passed between them. Just over six feet tall, he stood in the shadows with Edgar Millerton, looking more like a shipbuilder of bygone days than a modern-day architect.

No wonder she was no longer cold. He'd been watching her. All these years of marriage hadn't dulled or diminished the passion that had taken on a life all its own the first time they'd met, but time had honed their response to it.

She cast him a small smile and watched the affect it had on his features. His lips parted, as if he'd suddenly taken a quick, sharp breath. The breeze lifted his dark hair off his forehead and ruffled his tie. She couldn't see the color of his eyes from here, but she knew they were a deep shade of blue, as vivid and changeable as the great lake they'd both come to love.

Spence could have lived anywhere from Alaska to Timbuktu, but Maggie, the daughter of a career army man, had know this was where she'd wanted to grow old the first time she'd visited the area some fifteen years ago. She'd lived in twenty-two towns before graduating from high school, but she'd lived right here in this one small city for the past thirteen years. She and Spence belonged here, the way she'd always longed to belong as a child.

Spence nodded his head at the staunch old codger he'd been talking to, but Maggie noticed he didn't take his eyes off her. Almost of its own volition, her hand went to her hair. She twirled a lock around one finger. Nobody watching could have known that the simple mannerism was her way of telling Spence that her thoughts had taken a slow, luxurious stroll to the bedroom. But he knew.

He had an angular face, and, when he chose to use it, a devastatingly attractive smile. Bidding Edgar farewell, he proved it, smiling as he strode closer. He kissed her on the cheek, and old-fashioned, gentlemanly gesture few men bothered with anymore, then said hello to Melissa, Jessica, Hannah, and MaryAnn.

The other four women moved, en masse, to the buffet table. Maggie shifted slightly closer to Spence, so that her shoulder rested lightly against his arm. "How was the meeting?"

"All things considered, I'd say it went well. I'll tell you about it later. It looks like your party was a success, too, although everyone's more interested in talking about the surprise Gaylord had for all of you."

Maggie nodded. "Even Edgar Millerton?"

Spence ran the tips of three fingers up her arm, as if he'd waited as long as he could to touch her. Goose bumps of a different nature followed the path his fingertips took.

"You know Edgar," he said quietly.

Oh, dear. Maggie knew Edgar, all right. The man moved slowly, and spoke the same way. He took twenty minutes to order a sandwich. For excitement, he watched paint dry. Maggie herself had been known to go on and on about history, but even she had a difficult time staying focused when Edgar launched into conversation about sediment and water seepage. As tightfisted as Gaylord was generous,

Edgar's idol was Jay someone or other, the United States' first Ph.D. to study groundwater. Once, Edgar had invited all the members of the historic society to his home where he'd shown slides of how water drained through sand, gravel, and rock.

"Fascinating stuff, groundwater," Spence said close to Maggie's ear.

"You don't say."

"Did you know that it travels through pores in rocks one-seventieth of the speed of snails?"

Oh, dear. Maggie loved these social functions. She was perhaps the only person present who knew that they bored Spence silly. He made the best of them for her sake. It was one of the things she loved about him. There were plenty of other things.

"Biological reclamation is going well."

"Spence?"

"Evidently, it works by activating natural bacteria. It seems this natural bacteria eats most of the pollutants like degreasers and solvents and septic tank cleaners we humans have been dumping into the ground since they were invented."

She leaned slightly into him. "He must have had you cornered for a long time."

"It's hard to gage minutes when time is standing still."

She shook her head. "You were bored to death."

"I'm a big boy."

He was a big man.

"I'm surprised to see Jessica Michaels here," he said tersely. "Last I knew, she was living in the Caribbean."

Maggie shrugged. "It's Jessica Hendricks again. She took back her maiden name."

Spence gave a derisive snort. "She took John for everything he had. I'm surprised she didn't want to keep his name, too."

Maggie whispered, "I don't think I could ever do that."

"What? Keep my name?"

"No. Waste so much energy hurting someone I loved."

Sometimes, when Spence looked at her the way he was looking at her right now, she got lost in his eyes.

"I'd be a fool to give you a reason."

She smiled, because Spence was no fool.

With the barest movement of his head, he gestured toward the back steps. That was all it took, one look, and she knew he was asking how much longer she wanted to stay.

Earlier, the courtyards had been bursting at the seams. There were still some forty guests milling about on this level, but the party was winding down. "We should be able to make our escape in half an hour or so. What did you have in mind?"

The sound Spence made deep in his throat was half moan, all male. Taking her hand, he led the way to a small dance floor nearby where two other couples were dancing to music provided by a three-piece orchestra. Fitting her body close to his, he proceeded to give her a detailed outline of what he had in mind.

His words conjured up dreamy images that worked over Maggie like moonlight. Despite the heat emanating from him, she shivered again.

"Cold?" he whispered, close to her hair.

"Hmm. I don't know why, but I've been shivering all night." She closed her eyes, and for a moment, she felt as if she were looking at her life from outside herself, and something precious was about to slip away. A sense of dread washed over her. She kept her eyes wide open after that.

It didn't make sense. Her sister, Jackie, was home with the girls. Jackie loved Grace and Allison almost as much as she and Spence did. Jackie knew their favorite games, favorite foods, their latest secrets, and oldest fears. She also knew the Wilsons' phone number by heart. Grace and Alison both knew how to dial 911. There had been no sirens, no weather rumblings or threats of disasters. Even the sky was clear. Why, then, did Maggie have to force herself not to hold on to Spence too tight?

"About that getaway," she whispered.

"I'm listening.'

"Think anybody would notice if we crept away right now?" she asked.

Several guests turned at the sound of the little yelp she made when he followed his smooth turn in one direction with a surprise dip.

"Nice going," she chided once she was back on her feet. "Now everybody will notice."

"I aim to please."

Yes, she thought, he did. She was overtired, that was all. Everything was fine. Perfect. Feeling more like her old self, she finished the dance in Spence's arms. Then, hand in hand, they mingled with the other guests, enjoying being together, anticipating being alone.

They did manage to slip away half an hour later. Since they'd driven to the party separately, he walked her to the family van, then held her door. "I'm parked just off Harbor Avenue," he whispered. "I'll meet you at home."

Maggie smiled. Home, with Spence and their girls, was exactly where she wanted to be right now. And then, because it suddenly seemed of life and death importance, she called, "Drive safely."

He glanced over his shoulder and cast her another of his devastating male smiles. "You, too."

Maggie was shivering again as she started the van.